# PRAISE FOR KENDRA ELLIOT

"In Elliot's latest gripping novel the mystery and suspense are top-notch, and the romance embedded within will quench love story junkies' thirst, too. The author's eye for detail makes this one play out more like a movie rather than a book. It can easily be read as a standalone but is obviously much better if the prior three are digested first."

—*Romantic Times Book Reviews* on *Targeted* (4 stars)

"Elliot's latest addition to her thrilling, edge-of-your-seat series, Bone Secrets, will scare the crap out of you, yet allow you to swoon over the building romantic setting, which provides quite the picturesque backdrop. Her novel contains thrills, chills, snow and . . . hey, you never know! The surprises and cliffhangers are satisfying, yet edgy enough to keep you feverishly flipping the pages."

—*Romantic Times Book Reviews* on *Known* (4 stars)

"Elliot's best work to date. The author's talent is evident in the characters' wit and smart dialogue . . . One wouldn't necessarily think a psychological thriller and romance would mesh together well, but Elliot knows what she's doing when she turns readers' minds inside out and then softens the blow with an unforgettable love story."

—*Romantic Times Book Reviews* on *Vanished* (4½ stars, Top Pick)

"Kendra Elliot does it again! Filled with twists, turns, and spine-tingling details, *Alone* is an impressive addition to the Bone Secrets series."

—Laura Griffin, *New York Times* bestselling author

# A
# MERCIFUL
# SECRET

# ALSO BY KENDRA ELLIOT

### MERCY KILPATRICK NOVELS
*A Merciful Death*
*A Merciful Truth*

### BONE SECRETS NOVELS
*Hidden*
*Chilled*
*Buried*
*Alone*
*Known*

### BONE SECRETS NOVELLAS
*Veiled*

### CALLAHAN & MCLANE NOVELS
### PART OF THE BONE SECRETS WORLD
*Vanished*
*Bridged*
*Spiraled*
*Targeted*

## ROGUE RIVER NOVELLAS

*On Her Father's Grave* (Rogue River)
*Her Grave Secrets* (Rogue River)
*Dead in Her Tracks* (Rogue Winter)
*Death and Her Devotion* (Rogue Vows)
*Truth Be Told* (Rogue Justice)

# A
# MERCIFUL
# SECRET

## KENDRA
## ELLIOT

Montlake
Romance

Published by Montlake Romance, Seattle

www.apub.com

Amazon, the Amazon logo, and Montlake Romance are trademarks of Amazon.com, Inc., or its affiliates.

ISBN-13: 9781542047869
ISBN-10: 1542047862

Cover design by Eileen Carey

Printed in the United States of America

*To Megan and new beginnings*

# ONE

Mercy thought it was a deer.

But it was a girl who burst out of the brush along the dark road and into the headlight beams of her SUV. She stomped on the brakes and jerked the steering wheel to the right. Spinning sideways, her vehicle shuddered as her tires bounced along the snow-packed ruts of the road's shoulder. It rocked to a stop, and she clung to the wheel, gulping for breath.

*I didn't hit her.*

Hands slammed against her driver's window. "You've got to help me! Please!"

Red smeared the glass, and terror shone in the girl's wide eyes.

*Someone hit her and left.*

Mercy threw open her door, and the shivering girl lunged into her arms. "Please help her! She's dying!" Her hands were red with blood, and streaks of it covered her cheeks. She couldn't have been older than ten, and her short-sleeved T-shirt was deadly wrong for the freezing night air. She grabbed the front of Mercy's coat and yanked her toward the road. "She's this way!"

"Wait! Are you hurt?" Mercy snagged the child's wrist and examined her bloody hand, and then turned the girl's face toward her, searching for a source of the blood. The child fought to get out of her grip.

"It's not my blood! I'm not hurt, it's my grandmother! She's dying!" Her feet scrambled as she tried to pull Mercy away from her vehicle. "You've got to help us!"

"Where is she?"

"This way!" Her gaze pleaded with Mercy to follow.

Her heart racing, Mercy firmly led the girl to the rear of her Tahoe and grabbed a duffel bag from the back. "Won't it be quicker to drive to your grandmother?"

"The shortcut through the woods is fastest." The child froze and eyed her bag with hope. "Are you a doctor?"

"No." Mercy pulled out her cell phone. No service. *Dammit.* "Did you call 911?"

"We don't have a phone."

*Who doesn't have a phone these days?* She took a closer look at the girl. She needed a haircut, and her jeans were two inches too short. Her face was thin, with delicate features, giving her an elfin cast. "My mom has one, but she's not home. Can you hurry, please?"

Her terrified eyes nearly broke Mercy's heart. "I need one more thing." She glanced around at the towering pines on both sides of the road. Ten minutes earlier she'd left her cabin, but she was still in some of the densest woods on the east side of the Cascade mountains. The road rarely had traffic, and since it was nearly three in the morning, she knew no one else would be coming. She returned to the driver's side and grabbed her purse with its hidden weapon pocket and gun, wishing she'd worn her shoulder holster.

She slid the purse inside the duffel and looped the heavy-duty strap over her shoulder. She adjusted her balance for its heavy weight. "Let's go." The girl spun and dashed through the snow toward the brush where she'd first appeared. Mercy remotely locked her truck and fished a flashlight out of the duffel's end pocket.

*I'll do what I can and then go for help.*

The first aid kit in the duffel wasn't the type bought in a Walmart. She had scalpels, surgical thread, needles, epinephrine, and lidocaine in addition to the usual assortment of bandages and tape. She mentally took inventory of her duffel as she darted into the forest after the girl. Emergency blanket, fire starter, headlamp, hatchet, tarp, protein bars, water-purifying tablets. Mercy knew better than to blindly plunge into the woods without supplies.

She pointed her flashlight after the girl. She'd vanished. Mercy's beam scanned the brush where she thought the child had gone. "Hey! Wait up! Where'd you go?" *I don't even know her name.*

The elfin face suddenly appeared in the light. "Hurry!"

Mercy jogged after her, her boots sinking into the six inches of snow. "What's your name?"

"Morrigan." She dashed ahead of the flashlight's beam, nimbly avoiding fallen branches and big rocks.

Mercy tried to light both their paths, but Morrigan appeared to have the night vision of a cat. Mercy gave up and focused on not spraining an ankle. *No one knows where I am.* Her gut twisted at the thought, but she set it aside. Her boyfriend, Truman, and her niece Kaylie knew she'd gone to her cabin for the day, and her vehicle was parked on the side of the road. If someone looked for her, they'd find her.

*Hopefully in one piece.*

"Morrigan, what happened to your grandmother?" She pushed to keep up with the child.

"I don't know! She had blood everywhere."

"How far away is it?"

"We're almost to the house."

"We should have driven," she muttered.

"No, the road to the house twists way up to the north. This way is quicker. There it is!"

Mercy raised the beam of her flashlight. Far ahead she could make out the outline of a small ranch-style home. A dim light shone in one window. No outside lights. She'd never known there was a home in the area. For years she'd driven the old rural road and never seen a hint that someone lived in this particular section of the woods. *And I thought I valued my privacy.*

The girl dashed up a few crooked concrete steps and pushed open the door. "Grandma!" she shouted.

Mercy paused at the bottom of the steps and checked her cell phone for service. Nothing. *How am I going to get her grandmother to the Tahoe? I should have insisted on driving.*

She carefully entered the dark home, following the sounds of Morrigan's soft sobbing. She turned on a light switch, but nothing happened. Her flashlight lit up each corner of the room, as she was unwilling to enter the unknown. It smelled of old dust, as if it'd been abandoned for years, but it was fully furnished and there were clear signs of habitation. A book on the end table. A mug next to a stack of magazines. To her right was a minuscule kitchen, its limited counter space crowded with a dish rack and slow cooker.

"She's in here!" Morrigan called. "Hurry! Please!" The fright in her voice pushed aside Mercy's common sense, and she plunged down a dark hallway. Following the child's sounds, she found Morrigan in a bedroom that was poorly lit by a hurricane lamp. Her grandmother sat in an ancient easy chair, its back reclined forty-five degrees. She was a very thin woman, her body barely taking up a fraction of the big chair. A quilt covered her from the neck down. Even in the dim light, Mercy saw it was soaked with blood.

The woman's head had turned ever so slightly as Mercy entered, and she made a pleading sound. Mercy's fingers found another useless light switch, so she dropped her bag next to the overstuffed recliner and went down on a knee. *Stop the bleeding.* "Where are you hurt?" she asked as she gently took the woman's wrist to check her pulse. It felt like the weak fluttering of a baby bird. The woman made more pleading sounds and tried to sit up. "Hold still," Mercy told her. "Bring that lamp closer," she ordered Morrigan. "And hold my flashlight so I can see better." The girl obeyed, and Mercy caught her breath as she met the woman's desperate gaze. She pawed Mercy's arm, her fingers fumbling to grip the fabric of Mercy's coat as their gazes locked. Her eyes were wet, her lids wrinkled with age, and her sounds grew more urgent.

*Can she speak?*

Mercy gasped as she slowly pulled back the wet quilt, and Morrigan's grandmother let out a small cry.

The woman had been slashed across the chest, abdomen, and upper arms. The weapon had cut right through her thin nightgown. The dark stains made obscene patterns across the fabric, the wounds continuously seeping.

"Who did this to you?" Mercy couldn't move. Her brain wouldn't accept the brutal punishment that had been inflicted on the woman. The woman started to chant in a soft singsong voice, and Mercy couldn't make out the words.

"What happened to her, Morrigan?" she asked as she dug in her duffel for bandages.

"I don't know. I got up to use the bathroom and found her like this. That's when I ran to the road for help."

Mercy pressed thick bandages against the wounds. They quickly grew wet with blood. *There's too much blood.* She moved faster, using tape to bind the cotton in place. Her worry grew; she knew her small medical supply wouldn't be sufficient. She quickly used up the last of her bandages. "Get me some clean towels or sheets," she told Morrigan. The girl darted out of the room.

Mercy took the woman's hand, noticing it had more bleeding cuts. *Defensive wounds?* She forced a smile and looked into the worried dark

5

eyes. "You're going to be fine," she said with a sinking feeling in her stomach. The woman continued to chant, and Mercy wondered if she was American Indian. *She looks more Italian.* "What's she saying?" she asked Morrigan as the girl reappeared and dumped a stack of towels next to the chair. Mercy grabbed one and pressed it against the heaviest-flowing slash on the woman's neck.

The girl was silent for a moment. "I don't know. I haven't learned the spells."

*Spells?*

"I don't think it's a bad one. Her tone isn't angry."

*I guess that's good.* "What's her name?"

"Grandma."

"Her real name."

The girl thought hard. "Olivia."

"Olivia," Mercy said. "What happened to you? Who did this?" Olivia continued to stare, her lips still forming the foreign words. *It doesn't sound like Italian. Or any language I've ever heard before.* The chanting stopped, and the woman's breathing grew hoarse. She coughed, a deep hacking sound, and blood flew from her lips. Mercy pressed harder and directed Morrigan to apply pressure with another towel on the bleeding abdomen.

She obeyed. "Is she going to die?" she whispered through tears.

Mercy couldn't lie. "I don't know. It's bad."

Olivia coughed, and more blood flew. She shakily raised her blood-covered hand to touch Mercy's cheek. "Thank you." The first words Mercy recognized.

Her hand was warm and wet, and her fingers slid down the side of Mercy's face as she held eye contact. The terror in Olivia's gaze had evaporated, replaced with contentment.

*She's leaving.*

"No! I won't let you go, Olivia!" Mercy shook the woman's shoulder. "Talk to her, Morrigan. Make her listen to you." The girl started to plead with her grandmother, who turned tired eyes in her direction.

Panic simmered under Mercy's skin. She couldn't call for an ambulance. Her only choices were to carry the woman to her Tahoe, stay here and continue trying to stop the bleeding, or get the vehicle and risk the long drive back to the house before taking her to the hospital. Mercy weighed each option. *I've got to get the Tahoe.* She got to her feet. "I'm going to get my truck."

Olivia's hand shot out, grabbing her wrist. "Stay."

Mercy froze. And then slowly sank back to her knees, taking the bleeding hand again and holding the dying woman's gaze. *She doesn't want to be alone.* An inner calm flowed from the woman's hand to Mercy's and quieted her nerves.

*I will do this for her.*

Olivia looked from Mercy to Morrigan and then closed her eyes. Mercy watched her chest rise four more times before it stopped.

Numb, she held the woman's hand and listened to Morrigan wail.

# TWO

"Sorry about taking your clothes, Special Agent Kilpatrick," a Deschutes County deputy muttered as Mercy dropped her coat, sweater, and jeans into his paper bag after changing in Morrigan's bedroom.

"No problem. I always have another set of clothing with me." Once she'd gotten a look at her bloody sweater, she'd known the investigators would want everything she wore, but before she'd changed, the crime scene tech had photographed her in the stained outfit.

Mercy had stood and stared straight ahead as the young man circled her, snapping photos. He'd moved closer to photograph her face, and she fought down the guilt that crawled up the back of her throat over her inability to save Olivia. Awkwardly he asked permission to cut a chunk of her hair. Mercy nodded and watched as strands of her long black hair, thick with congealed blood, fell into his waiting envelope. Then he'd taken out a swab, dampened it, and touched it to her face. Olivia's blood was crusted on her cheek. The drying blood had pulled Mercy's skin, and she'd briefly scratched it before comprehending what it was. It was still under her fingernails, even after the tech had scraped them.

*I did everything I could.*

A shiver shot through her muscles, making her entire body spasm as she watched the deputy seal the bag. He gave her a quick glance, sympathy in his eyes.

She'd seen death up close before. Even clung to her brother's hand as he'd passed.

But this was different. Olivia's need for human touch, her need for someone to stay and not let her slip into death alone, had ripped open Mercy's heart.

The moment would stay with her forever.

She had sat with Olivia for a few minutes after she'd passed, and then Mercy had pulled Morrigan onto her lap and simply held her until she stopped crying and drifted off to sleep. She put a thick coat on the girl, carried her through the snow back to her Tahoe, and then drove until she found a cell signal. Exhausted, Morrigan had dozed in the back seat, her head bobbing on her chest. Mercy reported the death and tried to drive back to the house. She'd had to wake up Morrigan for directions. Morrigan had been right. The twisting side road to the little house took forever.

Now Deschutes County detective Evan Bolton waited for Mercy in the living room of Olivia's home. The detective was young, probably younger than Mercy, but his eyes were old and cynical, as if they'd seen every horror in the world. When he'd arrived at the crack of dawn, he'd silently listened to Mercy's brief story and asked minimal questions, but she'd had a gut feeling that he missed very little. Sympathy flashed in his brown eyes as she approached.

No doubt twenty-four hours without sleep showed in her face.

"Where's Morrigan?" she asked him.

"Showing one of the deputies her chickens and goats."

Mercy relaxed a fraction. She'd kept Morrigan close to her for the last four hours as they waited for Deschutes County to respond. She glanced out the window and saw the tech taking pictures inside her brand-new FBI Tahoe. It was bloody too. In her exhaustion Mercy had transferred Olivia's blood to Morrigan's coat and to her vehicle.

Rustling noises behind Mercy told her the techs were still collecting evidence in the tiny house. More than anything she wanted to leave the scene behind and sleep for a week, but the detective's eyes indicated he had other plans. "You want to interview me now, don't you?" she asked.

"I know you've been up a long time, but I want to hear the details again while they're still fresh in your mind."

She understood. "No one has reached Morrigan's mother?"

"Not yet. The phone number she gave us goes straight to a full voice-mail box."

"Did Morrigan say where she is?"

"She told us she went to town. When I asked how long ago she left, she said she didn't know. It could be a week or a day."

Mercy frowned. "When is child services getting here?" she asked.

The detective scowled. "We're working on it."

"Then I have plenty of time to talk, because I'm not going anywhere until Morrigan is taken care of. How long until the ME arrives?"

He raised both brows. "Within the hour. I thought I would be the one asking questions."

"Where do you want to do this?" Mercy glanced around at the crowded living area. Now that some daylight was coming in the windows, she saw the room was very clean, but the furniture upholstery was patched and the scattered rugs were worn down to the backing in several areas. The cabinets in the kitchen were missing several doors, but the dishes were in perfect even stacks on the shelves.

"Let's step outside," he suggested.

The two of them moved out of the cramped house, and Mercy sucked in a deep breath of icy air. Looking up, she saw the snow-frosted pines against a clear blue sky. *It must be less than twenty degrees.* Three days earlier the area had been hit with a snowstorm that had rapidly dumped six inches of white fluff. Since then every day had been gloriously clear but bone-chillingly cold. Typical for a Central Oregon winter.

She loved it.

Pulling her gloves out of the pockets of her heavy jacket, she led the detective to a small wooden bench and brushed off the snow. She wore thermal pants, a long-sleeved shirt, and snow boots from her vehicle's ever-ready stash. She sat, thankful for her thick pants, and he followed suit, removing a small recorder from his pocket along with a tiny notebook. The detective's blue coat nearly matched the sky. An oddly cheery note in the somber morning. Mercy was in black from head to toe, her usual attire.

"You said you'd been driving back to town from your cabin," Detective Bolton began. "Where exactly is it?"

Mercy gave him her address. "I'd driven about ten minutes before I saw Morrigan. So not too far."

"Do you often drive around at three in the morning?"

"Actually yes."

He held his pencil over his pad, looking at her expectantly. "Why?"

"I don't sleep much. Coming out here relaxes me."

"You live in Bend," he stated. "It must take you a long time to get here."

"It can. Depends on the road conditions." She wasn't in the mood to volunteer additional information about her nighttime habits.

"How long have you been with the Bend FBI office?"

"I started last fall. Before that I was at the Portland office for several years."

"And you've never seen Morrigan or Olivia before today?"

"That's correct. It's easy to blend into the forest out here. A person could be fifty feet away and you'd never know."

"That must be why you own a place here."

Mercy tensed, watching him, but she saw only idle curiosity in his eyes. "I like my privacy. It's nice to get out of the city."

He nodded. "Can you tell me again what happened after Morrigan stopped your vehicle?"

She knew she would tell the exact same story multiple times. A woman had been murdered, and she was a key witness. Mercy briefly closed her eyes and recited what she remembered.

Detective Bolton listened and made notes. "You couldn't make out any words or names in her chanting?"

"I couldn't. I've thought back over it several times, and I can't even guess the language. Morrigan said they were spells, and that she couldn't understand them."

The detective looked up from his pad, surprise in his eyes. "That's a new one. I want to talk to Morrigan, but I don't want to question her without a relative or CPS present." He looked at his watch. "CPS couldn't tell me when someone would get here, and I hate to let much time pass. She's young. Her story might change." Frustration crossed the detective's face.

"I can sit in," said Mercy. "I believe she trusts me, and considering the gravity of the situation, I think I qualify as an acceptable advocate."

The detective gave her a measuring look, weighing his options.

"Detective?" A deputy stood in the open door to the house. "I think you should take a look at this."

Detective Bolton immediately stood, shoved his notepad and recorder in his pocket, and strode to the house.

Mercy followed.

As they moved down the narrow hallway, Detective Bolton glanced over his shoulder at Mercy. She met his gaze head-on.

*I know this is your investigation. But I'm coming anyway.*

The deputy led them to an open door near the back of the house and then stepped aside. "We didn't know this room was here until a minute ago. The door was made to blend in with the hallway's wood paneling. I noticed a slight gap at the bottom where the paneling didn't quite line up with the carpet and gave the wall a push. I've never found a secret room before." Excitement danced in his eyes.

"Nice job." Bolton slapped him on the shoulder.

"It's tight in there," the deputy warned them. Bolton stepped through the doorway and halted. Mercy looked over his shoulder, thankful for her above-average height, and caught her breath. The windowless room had a rough wood counter on one side, with open shelves filling the wall above. On the opposite wall were knives. Hundreds of them. Their blades stuck to a dozen magnetic strips that went the length of the room.

"Someone is a collector," muttered Bolton.

Mercy silently agreed, her gaze scanning knife after knife. "This is incredible." Knives the size of her pinkie, knives as long as her arm, military-grade knives, knives that looked forged by hand, elaborate carved handles of wood, metal, and ivory, etched blades and curved blades. She looked for blank spots in the collection, wondering if the murder weapon had been removed from the wall. As far as she could tell, all were present. *Would anyone know if one was missing?*

"No murder weapon has been found yet, right?" she asked.

"No," said the deputy.

There was barely enough room between the counter and knife wall for two people to stand, but she and Bolton crowded into the space.

"Check out the jars," suggested the deputy.

Dozens of glass jars of all sizes filled the open shelves in perfect rows. Looking closer, Mercy saw powders, dried leaves, and rather crispy-looking dried bugs. She wrinkled her nose and leaned closer, spying a jar full of tiny translucent scorpions. None of the mismatched bottles were labeled. Mercy could recognize most fresh herbs, but the dried ones were difficult to her unpracticed eye. She couldn't guess the names of the powders. Rough yellow grains, fine white dust, chunky brown crumbs, fine gray grit. Jar after jar after jar.

This was no ordinary spice cabinet.

The counter was spotless and extremely neat. A canister held a variety of kitchen utensils, and she noticed four different mortar-and-pestle sets along with two perfectly folded piles of clean rags. Precise stacks of glass bowls and small glasses. Mercy remembered the neatness of the open cabinets in the kitchen. Was Olivia the organizer or Morrigan's mom?

"What do you think?" asked the deputy.

Bolton and Mercy exchanged a glance. "I think someone enjoys their hobbies," stated Bolton. "Unusual hobbies in our eyes."

"It's definitely interesting," agreed Mercy, wondering if Olivia dabbled in old-fashioned healing arts. *Spells.* Or maybe something else. She eyed the dried beetles and assorted other bugs as fairy tales of witchcraft buzzed in her head. *Ridiculous.*

"I don't see blood on any of the blades, but I'll have the techs take a closer look," said Bolton. "I don't think our murder weapon is here . . . although it could have come from here." He pointed at a jar. "Are those *chicken feet?*"

Mercy smiled. Clearly Bolton wasn't a farm boy. "Yes."

He sighed. "I'll find out how the techs want to handle this room." He motioned for Mercy to leave ahead of him. In the hallway she spotted Natasha Lockhart, the medical examiner, with her black bag in hand. Her face lit up at the sight of Mercy. "Were you the FBI agent that I heard found the body?" she asked after a greeting.

"That was me. She was still alive when I got here."

"Oh, good. You'll make my job easier." The tiny ME gestured for Mercy to follow her into the room where Olivia's body waited. Detective Bolton stood silently in the doorway, his eyes missing nothing, and the deputy who'd found the knife room stayed solemnly behind him. Inside, the ME stopped and took a slow scan of the scene. The tech who had photographed Mercy waited in the room, his camera ready to shoot any photos requested by the ME.

Mercy swallowed and looked at Olivia. The crime scene team had rigged up a light, and its bright glare cast harsh shadows on the peaceful face of the dead woman. Mercy's multiple field dressings still lay on the woman's body, their edges turning brown as they dried. The woman had been slashed at least a dozen times. *Deliberate torture or just rage?* The quilt covering her legs had a wedding ring pattern, its lovely pale-blue and lavender pieces forever stained.

"What's her name?" Natasha asked as she slipped on her gloves.

"Olivia," Mercy said and then looked at Bolton. *I never knew her last name.*

"Olivia Sabin," he answered.

The last name was faintly familiar to Mercy, which didn't surprise her. She'd lived in the nearby tiny community of Eagle's Nest until she was eighteen and had personally known a large percentage of the surrounding population. Her world had been much smaller back then.

"Is that your work?" Natasha gestured to the bandages.

Mercy nodded, unable to speak.

Natasha lifted the bandages and towels from the woman's chest and stomach, softly clucking her tongue in sympathy. With gloved hands she probed at the deep slash in the abdomen. "Was she conscious?"

"For a few moments."

"I suspect I'll find a nicked artery. Just enough for her to slowly bleed out. Or possibly the trauma was too much for her heart." She looked over her shoulder at Mercy, her gaze direct and firm. "I don't think there was anything you could have done to change the outcome," she stated, continuing to hold Mercy's gaze.

*Message received.* The knot in her stomach loosened at the ME's statement but didn't fully unravel. She'd always have a sliver of doubt.

"Could she have cut herself?" asked the deputy.

"Only if the knife walked away on its own," replied Bolton.

"The girl could have hid it," suggested the deputy.

Mercy doubted it. Morrigan would have mentioned it.

*Wouldn't she?*

Natasha's hands moved deftly across the woman's body, pressing here and there and bending the woman's fingers, testing the range of movement.

"What time did she die?"

Mercy looked at the old, yellowing clock on the wall. "Just after three."

"I'll still take some readings to confirm." She lifted a large thermometer out of her bag.

*I'm out of here.*

Mercy pushed past Bolton, then strode down the hallway and out the door. Outside she spotted Morrigan talking animatedly to a deputy, waving her arms as she spoke, clearly excited as she gestured to the woods. Mercy watched. *Kids are resilient.* She took in the rest of the property. A small pen with a chicken coop was to her left and a good-size barn to her right. The barn looked newer than the house. Its wood was freshly painted and its door hardware gleamed in the growing sunlight. The clearing surrounding the home was covered with footprints. The snow had been well trampled by the occupants of the house. There was little hope of finding the tracks of a killer near the home. They'd have to search deeper into the woods. *Unless he came by car.*

"You good?" Bolton asked, stopping beside her.

"Yes." She didn't look at him, choosing to keep her gaze on Morrigan.

"I'd like to talk to the girl now if you're up to it."

"Her name is Morrigan," Mercy said sharply. "And yes, I'm up to it."

# THREE

Truman Daly checked his phone for the twentieth time as he strode toward the police station.

Mercy still hadn't replied to his good-morning text.

It was their routine. After the nights they didn't spend together, they texted each other in the morning. She should have been up by now. He knew she had planned to spend a few hours in the evening at her cabin, and that those visits often went past midnight, but she never overslept.

A subtle uneasiness stirred in his belly.

He kicked a clump of dirty packed snow off the sidewalk and pulled open his department's door, a small sense of pride shooting through him at the sight of his name below the Eagle's Nest Police Department logo. Police Chief Truman Daly. He loved his job and considered it an honor to help the people of his tiny town. He'd given big-city police departments a try; it wasn't for him. He enjoyed the closeness of the community and had learned nearly every resident's name over the last year.

"Morning, boss," Lucas said, his big bulk squeezed behind his desk. "Nothing urgent yet this morning."

"Thanks, Lucas." Truman eyed the bright-red reindeer on his office manager's sweater as he took off his cowboy hat. "You know Christmas has been over for a month, right?"

The nineteen-year-old man glanced down. "I like this sweater. It's fucking cold, so I wore it. Makes more people smile now than when I wore it in December."

"Good point. Who's here?"

"Royce went out to a car accident, and Ben should be in any minute."

The uneasiness in his belly grew. "Any injuries in the car accident?"

"Nah, a fender bender and then one slid into a ditch. Both men are fine."

His tension loosened. *Not her.* Mercy had been in a horrible car accident last November, and her silence this morning was deafening to him.

He headed down the hall to his office, texting Mercy's niece Kaylie as he walked.

Tell Mercy to check her phone.

The response was immediate.

She's not here.
Where is she?

His phone buzzed in his hand as Kaylie called.

"She wasn't here when I got up this morning," the teenager told him.

"What time did she leave last night?"

"Around seven. Right after we ate. She said she'd be back after midnight."

"Did she come home and then leave early this morning?" Truman's uneasiness blossomed.

"I don't think so. There's no coffee in the pot. She always makes coffee."

*She does.*

Kaylie didn't sound concerned. "She probably slept at the cabin. She does that sometimes. I assume you tried to call her?"

"I texted."

"Cell service out there is spotty. Drives me crazy," she said with teenage disgust.

"Tell her to call me if you hear from her."

"Will do."

Truman stared at his unanswered texts. *I have to go out there.*

Mercy's cabin was her lifeline. Her center. Her balance. An upbringing in a family of preppers had left her with a soul-deep need to always be prepared in case of TEOTWAWKI. The end of the world as we know it. Truman understood the logic behind having a supply of water and rations in case of an emergency, but Mercy took it to a whole other level. She could live at her cabin indefinitely if the world drastically changed. Truman admired her dedication and didn't say a word when she spent hours chopping wood in the middle of the night or combed antique stores searching for old tools to replace electric or gas-powered ones.

*She could have sliced an artery with her ax.*

"Shit." He turned around, crammed his hat back on, and marched out to the reception area. "Lucas? I'm heading out. Call me if you need me."

"Hey, wait. This just came in. Elsie Jenkins can't get off her property because the highway snowplow left a huge pile at the end of her drive."

Truman pictured her rural farmhouse. "We only got six inches."

"Yeah, she said somehow the plows left all the snow to kingdom come blocking her drive. Her words, not mine."

"She's been stuck there for three days?"

"She waited to see if it'd melt down. But now she's low on Scotch and Triscuits. Again, her words."

Her old farm was in the general direction of Mercy's cabin. "I'm on it. Tell her I'll be there in twenty minutes."

"Got a good snow shovel?" Lucas asked.

"Always."

On his drive to Elsie's, Truman called the highway department and informed them their plows had trapped a senior citizen on her property. He threw in that she was running low on prescriptions. A small exaggeration.

The young woman on the other end of the call promised to send a plow over as soon as possible. Truman knew that could be hours from now and mentally prepared to do some shoveling. At least the sun was shining.

Thirty minutes later he was cursing the sun, which had compacted the fluffy snow into a dense, heavy sludge pile. Over and over he thrust the snow shovel into the giant pile. He'd hoped the shoveling would get Mercy off his brain, but it did the opposite. His mind wandered, and he hoped she was all right.

And he remembered the assortment of flyers on her kitchen counter two nights earlier. She'd been changing in the bedroom as he casually picked one up. And his heart had stopped. They were flyers for homes for sale. He'd quickly scanned the half dozen different papers. *She hasn't said a word to me.* He'd known her apartment was temporary, but he'd always assumed that at some point she'd move in with him . . . or that they'd look for a place together. In his future plans, Mercy was living with him.

Apparently she didn't share that vision.

He gave his shovel an extra-hard thrust, pushing the snow and his thoughts aside. Elsie was right about the crazy amount of snow. Truman directed his cursing to the unknown highway department driver who hadn't noticed her long driveway. His back had started to twinge when he finally heard the rumble of the plow.

*Thank God.*

He backed out of the way and watched as the plow effortlessly cleared what would have taken him three hours. The driver gave him a thumbs-up and went on his way. Truman eyed the results and spent another two minutes clearing the small berm left behind.

He climbed in his SUV and called Lucas. "Call Elsie and tell her she's all clear."

"Wow. You shoveled that fast. Was it small?"

"It was huge, but I used a really good shovel."

"Clearly."

"Any other calls?" Truman asked hopefully. If Mercy couldn't reach him for some reason, he knew she'd leave a message with Lucas.

"None. All quiet. Ben went on a doughnut run."

"Save me the apple fritter." He ended the call, started his vehicle, and headed to Mercy's cabin.

Forty minutes later he spotted a Deschutes County SUV parked along the main road a few miles before the turn to Mercy's property.

"Oh shit." He scanned for Mercy's Tahoe, wondering if she'd run off the road.

Nothing.

He pulled alongside the county vehicle and lowered his window.

"Morning, Chief. You're a long way from home," said the deputy waiting in the vehicle.

The deputy looked faintly familiar. "Everything okay?" Truman's insides clenched in a knot.

"A suspicious death." The deputy jerked his head at the woods. "I'm on guard duty."

Nausea rose into Truman's throat as he spotted a narrow road that wound through the tall pines. He'd never noticed it before. No signs or markers indicated the turnoff.

"Who's the victim?" he asked through clenched teeth as sweat broke out under his arms.

"Senior citizen. Female. Scene is in her home back there."

Instant relief left a throbbing ache in Truman's head.

"Pretty crazy situation. No phone service or vehicles present," continued the deputy. "Her ten-year-old granddaughter flagged down a passing vehicle in the middle of the night."

"Let me guess. An FBI agent was driving that vehicle."

Surprise filled the deputy's face. "You already heard?"

"Lucky guess." Truman blew out a huge breath. "Is the agent still here?"

"Yeah, she is."

# FOUR

Mercy sat next to Morrigan on the bench, the child's tiny hand clench-ing hers.

In the morning light, Mercy saw the girl was much thinner than her first impression. She didn't look malnourished, she looked wiry. Childish energy radiated from her, and she frequently squirmed on the hard seat. Detective Bolton had suggested they conduct the interview indoors, but Mercy had argued for the fresh air. And distance from Morrigan's grandmother's body. Now they were outside, the detective sitting across from them on a low stool he'd found in the house. He introduced himself and explained who Mercy was.

Morrigan drew back slightly and studied Mercy from head to toe. "You're a government agent?"

There was a touch of scorn in her voice, and Mercy wondered what antigovernment stories Morrigan had grown up with. They weren't uncommon out here.

"I'm an investigator for the United States," she simplified. "Just as Detective Bolton works for the people who live in Deschutes County, I work for all the people who live in the United States. Including your grandmother and you." She smiled, hoping to set the girl's suspicious mind at ease.

A small crease appeared between her brows, and after a moment her shoulders sank in acceptance. "I guess it's okay if I talk to you. You tried to help my grandmother." She blinked rapidly.

"I did. I wish I could have saved her." *Who told her not to talk to government agents?*

"There was a lot of blood," Morrigan said slowly. "I don't think anyone could have helped her."

"Morrigan," said Bolton in a kind voice, "do you know what happened to your grandmother?"

"She got cut."

"But how did she get cut?"

The girl leaned into Mercy's side, turning her face away from the questioning detective.

"I don't know," she whispered into the sleeve of Mercy's coat.

"Was there anyone else in the house last night?" Bolton asked.

Morrigan shook her head, her hair rustling against Mercy's coat.

"Did you hear anything? Did your grandmother call out to you?"

The girl sniffed and ran her forearm under her nose, risking a glance at Bolton. "No. I used the bathroom and went in her room because I heard her chanting and it didn't sound right. It sounded like she couldn't breathe."

"Did you ask her what happened at that point?"

"I don't think so. I could see the cuts, but I didn't know what to do."

"Wasn't it dark? How could you see?"

"She sleeps with a tiny lamp on all night. She says it keeps away the bad spirits."

Mercy remembered the hurricane lamp and how she hadn't been able to turn on the lights. "How come the lights in the home don't work, Morrigan?"

"Some of them do. We just need to buy more bulbs. Mom keeps forgetting."

"You said your mother was out of town," said Bolton. "But you don't know when she's coming back, right?"

The girl nodded.

"Where do you go to school, Morrigan?" asked Mercy.

"I'm homeschooled. My grandmother teaches me . . . taught me." Her face crinkled up and fresh tears flowed.

"Do you have other relatives close by?" Bolton asked.

Morrigan shook her head. "There's just us."

"But you have cousins or aunts and uncles that live somewhere else, right?" suggested Mercy.

"No, it's just us."

Mercy met Bolton's gaze. *None?* She filed the question away to ask Morrigan's mother when she showed up. *If* she showed up. Mercy was having her doubts about a woman who left no way for her daughter to reach her. She knew Bolton had tried the cell number several more times and sent texts to the number. No response.

*Did something happen to her mother?*

"What about your father?" asked Bolton.

"I don't have a father," Morrigan answered simply.

She and Bolton exchanged another look. "Did you used to have one?" she asked.

"No. I never have. Mom said she and Grandma were all I needed. We make a complete family." She wiped her nose with her sleeve again, and both Mercy and Bolton checked their pockets for tissues. Mercy found a coffee shop napkin and held it out to Morrigan.

"I don't need that," Morrigan said with another sleeve wipe.

"Take it," she said firmly. Morrigan took the napkin and held it in her lap.

"Morrigan," said Bolton. "Something very sharp was used to make those cuts. Did you see a knife when you went in your grandma's room? Maybe on the floor or on the quilt?"

The girl thought for a second. "No."

"How do you think your grandmother got cut?" Mercy asked cautiously, waiting for her to mention the room full of knives.

"Someone cut her."

"Then that means someone was in your house last night. Do you have any ideas who that could be?" asked Bolton.

Morrigan's eyes widened. "Mom is always telling Grandma to keep the doors locked. She never does. And now she's dead!" she wailed, turning her face into Mercy's coat again.

Mercy hugged her tight and rested her cheek against the top of her head, trying to avoid her own tears. "It's okay, Morrigan. Everything is going to be okay," she said softly, knowing the girl's life would never be the same. Her world appeared to be very small, making the loss of her grandmother a greater tragedy. Mercy wished she could shield her from the pain. *Where is her mother?*

"She told me she'd be okay," she muttered into her coat.

"Who told you that?" Mercy asked.

"Grandma. When I didn't know what to do last night . . . she told me she'd be okay. But I knew she was *wrong*! Her spells don't always work."

*There's that word again.*

"She does spells?" Mercy asked carefully. "Last night you said that's what she was chanting when I couldn't understand her."

"I don't understand the words either. Mom says I have to wait until I'm thirteen to learn."

Bolton raised a brow, meeting Mercy's gaze. *I don't know what to think.*

"What made you decide to run out to the road?" Bolton asked. "It was awfully dark and cold."

"I didn't know what else to do. I couldn't help her, so I needed to find someone who could. I know the woods and can't get lost even in the dark. If a car didn't stop, I was going to walk to someone's house."

"Whose house?" Mercy asked, knowing there were few homes in the area.

"Any house. I don't know anyone's name, but they'd me help, right?" She looked up at Mercy. "But I heard your engine before I reached the road, so I ran faster. I didn't know if I'd make it to the road before you passed."

"I nearly hit you."

"Morrigan." Bolton drew the girl's attention back to him. "Has anyone visited your grandmother in the last few days?"

"Not for a week or two."

"What does your mother do?" asked Bolton.

"Do?"

"Her job," he clarified.

"She sells stuff on the Internet."

"What kind of stuff?"

The girl shrugged. "She makes stuff in the craft room."

"The room with all the knives?" asked Mercy.

"Sometimes. Most of it is in her barn room."

"I don't think I've ever seen so many knives in one place," Mercy prodded. "Some were very fancy."

"I'm not allowed to touch them. They're sharp. And some have stuff on the blades."

Alarm rose in Mercy. "What kind of stuff?"

"Poisons."

Bolton rose and dashed into the house.

*Jesus Christ. What if one of the techs accidentally cut themselves?*

She thought of how she'd touched Olivia's wounds without gloves. *What if there'd been poison on that blade?* Mercy stared at her hands, looking for inflammation or redness. She'd used her stash's baby wipes to clean off Olivia's blood instead of washing in the bathroom, not wanting to destroy any evidence that might be recovered from the home's sinks.

Her hands looked fine, but her heart raced erratically. *Did I absorb something into my skin?* She closed her eyes and took deep breaths, willing her heart to slow. Opening her eyes, she found Morrigan staring at her with concern.

"Are you okay?"

"Yes." She forced a smile.

"Who's going to watch me now?" Her eyes were large in her elfin face.

Mercy brushed her unruly hair off her forehead. "Until your mom comes back, a kind woman from the . . . agency that helps kids will take good care of you." *Please be a kind person.*

"Oh."

"Hopefully your mom won't be gone for very long."

"She only took the small suitcase, not the big one."

*That's reassuring.* "Good." Her heart rate felt nearly normal. Both she and Morrigan looked in the direction of the road at the sound of a vehicle. Mercy recognized the black Tahoe with a light bar.

Relief and a spark of happiness filled her.

Truman could find her in any crowd.

Mercy drew his attention as if she harbored a homing beacon and he were internally wired to the frequency. His nerve sensors locked on her as she sat in the yard and wouldn't let go. His brain instantly calmed. Being unable to reach her had left him feeling disjointed and empty. Not to mention very worried.

She stood, a tall, slim figure all in black, her long, dark hair only a shade lighter than her clothing.

He frowned. She wore the backup gear from her bug-out bag. *What happened to her clothes?*

Her hand was held by a small girl in a brown coat and jeans that were too short. Truman assumed she was the granddaughter the deputy had mentioned and was stunned that the child had made it all the way out to the main road to flag Mercy down.

He parked and strode across the snow, his boots crunching, his eyes never leaving Mercy's green gaze. She gave a wide smile as he walked directly into her arms and held her tight. "You're going to get a mass of text messages from me when you get your cell service back," he said into her hair. He inhaled, catching the faint lemon scent from her hair, and the bulk of his anxiety floated away. His arms tightened slightly and he relished the solid feel of her.

"I'm sorry. I knew you might be worried."

He pulled back, took her face with both hands, and kissed her, not caring about their rule against PDAs when on the job. Four months earlier she'd walked into his town, and he'd known his life would never be the same. In the best way possible. They argued. They made up. They butted heads. But damn, it was fun. Life before her had faded from his memory, and now it felt as if she'd always been with him.

"Yes, I worried."

"Who told you where to find me?"

"I just followed my nose."

She scowled.

"I was headed to your cabin to see if you were still there and spotted county waiting at the end of this drive. He told me you were here. What happened?"

The story she recited made him shift his attention to Morrigan. "You went all the way out to the road in the dark?" he asked, holding tightly to Mercy's hand.

The girl pointed. "There's a shortcut through there."

Truman turned around and eyed the dense woods. *I wouldn't walk through there at night.* "You're very brave."

"I know," she answered with a shrug.

The home's front door opened and a man in a bright-blue coat stepped out. Mercy dropped Truman's hand as the man's gaze went from Truman to Mercy. He joined their group, and Mercy introduced the detective. Truman noticed the small, wry twist of Bolton's lips as they shook hands.

*Thought she was single, did you?*

*Think again.*

"Have the crime scene techs gotten to the knives yet?" Mercy asked Bolton.

"Not yet. And I talked to the ME. Told her there was a chance some poison could have been on the blade that—" Bolton stopped, his gaze shooting to Morrigan, who stood just outside their group, listening intently.

Mercy laid a hand on Morrigan's shoulder and looked around. Spotting a deputy in the doorway, she waved him over. "Morrigan is giving tours of her animals. Have you seen them yet?" she asked the deputy, who quickly got the message.

"Nope. I'd love to see them," he told Morrigan. "Do you have any rabbits?" Truman heard him ask as the two of them walked away.

"Did Natasha say that poison would be visible on the wounds?" Mercy asked Bolton.

"I didn't ask."

"The answer is, 'It depends,'" said Natasha Lockhart as she stepped out of the home. Truman liked the small medical examiner. She was witty and generous with her smiles for a person who daily worked with death. She joined them in the snowy yard. "Hey, Truman," she greeted him. "Did the two of you try that Thai place I recommended?"

"We did," he answered. "We've been three times already. I don't know how it stays in business. No one is ever eating in the restaurant."

"I think most of their business is takeout. Did you try—"

"What were you going to tell us about the poison, Dr. Lockhart?" interrupted Bolton. Mild impatience shone in his eyes.

"Right," she said. "Some poisons can cause cauterization at the edge of a wound, but it depends on their strength and type. Her wounds bled heavily, so I can't see much on the tissues, but I'll look for it and run some tests when I get her on the table."

"It might be nothing."

"It's a start." Natasha paused and looked over at the barn as Morrigan and the deputy disappeared inside. "It appears someone also tried to smother the woman. Clearly they weren't successful, but she has petechiae present in her eyes."

"The tiny red spots in the eyes?" asked Truman. "You think it happened before the stabbings?"

"Right now I think the attempted asphyxiation happened first. There was a pillow close by on the floor, so I asked the techs to bag it and check it for saliva. It looked clean, and I think it would have blood on it if they'd tried to smother her *after* the wounds."

"Don't most pillows get saliva on them?" asked Truman, thinking of nighttime drooling.

"Yes, but this was a decorative pillow. Usually people don't sleep on them. A regular pillow was still under her head."

"Was the pillow on the floor dark green?" Mercy asked. "The sofa has a dark-green throw pillow."

"It was." Natasha nodded. "Possibly someone brought it in from the living room."

"With the intention to suffocate her," added Truman, looking at Bolton. "What are your ideas on motive? Any sign of theft?"

"No indication of a break-in," said Bolton. "And Morrigan's mom is probably the only one who can tell if something is missing."

"Who would want to murder an old woman?" asked Mercy. "I got the feeling from Morrigan that she rarely leaves the house."

"Perhaps she wasn't the target," suggested Truman.

"All those cuts weren't made by accident," said Natasha.

31

"It would take a lot of rage to do the damage I saw," Mercy said slowly. "Our suspect might have been angry that his intended victim wasn't here. Perhaps the mother was the intended victim."

"We plan to take a hard look at the mother," said Bolton. "And neither you nor Chief Daly have any role in this case." He pointed at Mercy. "You're a witness, nothing else."

Truman recognized the stubborn tilt of Mercy's head and pitied Detective Bolton.

# FIVE

Mercy held the detective's gaze. *Like hell I'm stepping away from this case.*

"Excuse me, Detective Bolton?" came a voice from behind them.

Mercy turned in unison with the detective.

It was the deputy who'd gone to look at Morrigan's animals. The girl was nowhere in sight.

"Where's Morrigan?" Mercy immediately asked.

"She's feeding the goats. Cute little things." The deputy gave a half smile. "I know the barn was initially searched for a suspect, but has anyone taken a close look at what's in there?"

"What do you mean?" asked Bolton.

"There's a room at the far end that I assumed was for supplies, but it's packed full of . . . stuff. It looks like a miniature village in there. There's another workbench like in the house with some knives and other sharp tools."

"Morrigan said her mom has a craft room in the barn," said Mercy.

The deputy nodded. "It's definitely a craft room. My wife would live in there if she had one like it."

"I'll take a look," said Bolton, moving toward the barn with the deputy.

"I need to leave," Natasha said to Mercy. "I'll get to your victim tomorrow morning. I have a full schedule today."

*See? Even Natasha thinks I should be involved.* Mercy said her good-bye to the medical examiner and then exchanged a look with Truman. They simultaneously headed to the barn.

"Not your case," Truman said under his breath.

"Tough beans. Until I know Morrigan is safe, I'm keeping my nose in. What is taking the CPS agent so long?"

"Other kids who need her, six inches of snow, the long drive."

She side-eyed him. "I didn't mean literally."

His grin warmed her to her cold toes. "Where do you think her mother is?" he asked.

"Good question." Her shoulders sagged. "Can you imagine coming home to learn your mother has been murdered?" The second the words left her mouth, she wanted to take them back. Truman had found his uncle's murdered body.

"In a way, I can."

"Oh, Truman. I wasn't thinking." She took his hand as they walked, squeezing tightly. Jefferson Biggs had been more than an uncle to Truman; he'd been a surrogate father. His death was part of the FBI's domestic terrorism case that had brought Mercy back to Eagle's Nest after fifteen years away.

"It's all right." He didn't look at her, his jaw tight. "I miss him sometimes. He would have loved this hidden property in the middle of the woods."

"Yes, he would." Jefferson had subscribed to Mercy's bone-deep philosophy about being prepared for disaster. Any disaster.

Mercy stepped through the open door of the barn and breathed deep. Hay, grain, dirt floors, warm animals. The scents triggered warm memories of her youth. Morrigan was in a pen with three pygmy goats, holding one on her lap, scratching its horn nubs as it rubbed its head on her coat. The goat was in ecstasy.

*Nothing heals a broken heart like an animal.*

"They're down there." Morrigan pointed at the far end of the barn. "I'm not allowed in that room."

"How come?" asked Truman.

"I might break something." She looked down and rubbed under the goat's chin. "But sometimes I go in and look. I'm very careful not to touch," she confessed in a softer voice. "Mom doesn't want me getting sick either."

"Why would you get sick?" Mercy asked.

The girl frowned as she considered the question. "Some of the stuff in there is bad. Like in the knife room. But I would never touch or taste anything. I know better."

Mercy turned to Truman. *What the hell?* she asked with her gaze.

He shrugged.

They approached the room, Mercy feeling curiosity along with a strong sense of caution. "Detective Bolton?"

"Yeah?" he said from around the corner.

Exasperation rang in his tone. No doubt he'd thought she'd leave after his directive.

"Don't touch anything," she said as she stepped through the entrance. "Morrigan said she's been warned she could get sick from . . ." She and Truman stopped and gaped.

Mercy hadn't believed anything could surprise her more than the knife room. If the knife room was from a horror movie, this room was from a hobbit fantasy world.

The small work space was wider than the tight knife closet in the house, but it had a similar workbench, and shelves lined all sides of the room. Most were packed with tiny houses and buildings. Bolton and the deputy stood in the center, hands on their hips, scanning the fairy world.

"Do elves live in here?" Truman asked as he stared.

"Haven't seen any yet," answered Bolton. "But what in here could make someone sick?"

"Maybe it's in those." Mercy pointed. A dozen large glass jars of powders and dried herbs sat on a shelf below a metal strip holding two dozen knives, awls, and other carving tools. A wooden box with small satin drawstring bags sat under the shelf on the workbench. Next to the box was a stack of tiny cards, each one covered with elaborate cursive handwriting. Mercy peered at one. "Burn one tablespoon of the physic at midnight for five nights in a row," she read aloud. "Any left over after five nights must be buried two feet deep." A satin ribbon was threaded through a small hole in the corner of the card. Easy to fasten to a small satin bag. *Spells?*

"What the hell?" Bolton said. "These might be poisonous, but she's giving them to people?"

"I suspect she's selling them," said Mercy. She stepped back and studied the shelves behind her, stunned and delighted by the sight. The wall was full of eight-inch-high houses made out of hollow logs, with decorative windows and doors, sitting on beds of dried moss. She spotted one tiny building that appeared to be a miniature greenhouse made of small glass panels. Carefully carved flowers blossomed inside. Some of the buildings had straw roofs; others had roofs carved to look like mushroom caps. A lower shelf held tiny homes covered in seashells sitting on beds of sand.

"These are amazing," she whispered. "Can you imagine the work that went into each one?"

"She must sell the homes online," Truman stated. "You think she sells spells there too?" he asked, pointing at the satin bags and hand-written cards.

Mercy nodded, but didn't take her gaze from the rows of fairy homes. Two had been made out of old china teapots. The child in her wanted to open their tiny wood doors and peek inside. Christmas-themed homes filled one corner of the room. Reds and greens and snow decorated the houses hollowed out of logs. She grinned at one log that stood upright, a grumpy face carved into the bark. Someone had seen the potential in the pattern of the bark and brought it to life. A cranky wood nymph.

Bolton moved one of the note cards with his pen to look at another. "For two weeks, rub salve into bottoms of feet and immediately put on socks," he read. "What kind of garbage is she selling?"

"Hopes and dreams," answered Mercy. "Desperate people will try anything. But these homes are incredibly detailed . . . and very well done. I'd pay money for one if I was into that sort of thing."

She noticed a face peek around the corner of the entrance. "It's okay, Morrigan. We're just looking."

The girl moved to stand in the doorway. "My mom isn't going to like this." Her worried glance bounced among the four of them as she nervously flexed her fingers.

"I think she'll understand that we're looking for any clues to who hurt your grandmother." Mercy set one hand on her shoulder. "And I think we're done in here." She raised a brow in question to Bolton, who nodded.

"I'll get a tech to check the blades," he said.

Morrigan still looked upset.

"Can you introduce me to your goats?" Mercy asked. "We had pygmy goats when I was a kid. They're the best."

She nodded and reluctantly turned away.

Mercy glanced over her shoulder at the three men. "We need to find her mother."

*Could she be our killer?*

For Morrigan's sake, she prayed it wasn't true.

As Mercy left with Morrigan, Truman turned to Bolton. "What's been done to find the mother?"

"I have someone filling out a request to her cellular provider to get her phone records and last location. No one answers at her number, and the voice mail is full. I also put out a BOLO on her vehicle."

"What is it?"

"A green Subaru Forester. Eight years old."

"Morrigan wasn't any help with location?"

Bolton grimaced. "Sounds like the mother travels quite a bit and leaves her home alone with the grandmother. She doesn't know where she goes or when she'll be back."

"Poor kid. What's her mother's name?"

"Salome Sabin."

The hair stood up on Truman's arms. "Salome?" he said softly.

Interest lit in Bolton's eyes. "Know her?"

"No. Well, maybe . . . It was two decades ago . . . if it's her. That's not a name you hear very often."

"I Googled it," Bolton said. "It's a Bible name. Salome demanded the head of John the Baptist and had a reputation for being dangerously seductive. Who names their kid after someone like that?"

"Good question," Truman muttered. Tiny pricks of pain sparked in the two-month-old burns on his neck and he rubbed them, careful not to scratch. Although the burns from an arsonist's barn explosion looked healed, he knew from experience they might bug him for a year.

*It can't be the same woman.*

But in his lifetime, how many women had he met with that name? One. And he'd met her in Deschutes County.

He'd never known her last name. He'd been nineteen, drunk, and high on adrenaline as he and his friends crashed a party at a farmhouse outside of town. He hadn't known whose house it was, but the rumor that the owners were out of town for the weekend and the son had a few kegs of beer was enough to bring in partiers from twenty miles away.

Salome had dark, sexy eyes and a voluptuous body that drew the attention of every person in the room—even the girls. But their looks were catty and dismissive, and they turned their backs as Salome walked—no, glided—by. She oozed sex and danger as she prowled the room. She was older, he would learn later. Twenty-one. To him she seemed untouchable and out of his league.

A challenge.

"Stay away from that one," Mike Bevins had said to Truman in a low voice, but his fierce gaze hung on her every move, claiming he wanted to do the opposite.

"Who is she?" Truman asked, keeping an air of disinterest in his voice, though his gaze was glued to her like Mike's. Along with every other guy's.

"Trouble."

"That doesn't tell me anything."

"The last guy who dated her got in a bad car wreck the night he dumped her."

"So?" Truman took a sip of beer from his red plastic cup.

"They say you shouldn't cross her."

Mike was talking in circles.

"She seeing anyone now?"

"Jesus, Truman. Aren't you listening?"

"You aren't making sense. Why should I stay away?"

Mike took a long draw on his beer, wiped his lips, and turned unsteady eyes on Truman. "It's not good for your health if you make her mad. Sooner or later everyone breaks it off. You want to stay on her good side."

*He's still talking bullshit.*

"You just don't want me to try," Truman said. "Afraid I'll succeed?" He took another drink and searched for her. Heavily lined brown eyes met his. She smiled and heat raced through his veins.

"Keep it in your pants," ordered Mike. "Really, dude. She's bad news." He glanced from side to side and then leaned closer to Truman.

"They say she's a witch. Her mother was a witch and her grandmother was a witch."

"That's a bunch of bullshit." Promises and pleasure filled her eyes. Truman couldn't look away.

He took a gulp of liquid courage. "I gotta give it shot." He left Mike protesting in his wake as he crossed the room.

"Truman. *Truman.*" Bolton stared at him.

Truman focused on the detective. "Sorry. Was trying to remember . . . where I might have met her. I was just a kid," he hastily added.

"Remember anything useful that could help us find her today?" Bolton looked skeptical.

"No. Sorry."

Truman noticed the Deschutes deputy bent over with his face close to one of the Christmas houses, his finger an inch away from a dangling wreath on the tiny door.

"Don't touch anything," ordered Bolton.

The deputy jerked upright. "I wasn't going to." Guilt flushed his face. "Anyone else feel light-headed in here? There's a smell of dried moss or something weird that's getting to me. It's like I took a hit off a joint. Or maybe it's the tight quarters."

Truman suddenly felt the same. He scanned the childlike homes. *What else are they made of?*

"I feel it," said Bolton. "Everyone out."

Outside the room Truman welcomed the healthy animal scents, and Bolton rubbed his eyes. "Think there's something hallucinogenic in there?" Bolton asked. "Did you feel that?"

"I felt something. Could just be stale air or maybe an allergy," suggested Truman.

"Something all of us are allergic to?" Bolton was unconvinced. "Something is in there. I'll warn the crime scene techs." He glanced at Truman. "Probably time for you to get back to work. Tell Mercy to head home too. She's been up all night."

"She won't leave until CPS gets here." Truman spotted her in a pen with Morrigan, who was tying a pink bow around a black goat's ear. Three tiny goats pushed and shoved one another to reach the handful of feed on Mercy's palm, delighting her. Her laughter bounced off the dusty rafters.

The sound stripped his soul bare, warming him. He'd burn bridges and trudge across a desert for her. He was blessed to have her in his life. Was it love? *Hell yes.*

Truman turned back to the detective, who eyed him with a touch of envy.

Outside, the crackle of tires on packed snow announced the arrival of another vehicle.

"Maybe we got lucky and that'll be the CPS agent," Bolton stated. *I've been lucky for the last four months.*

# SIX

The arriving car had belonged to the CPS agent. Mercy had grilled the pleasant woman before allowing her to take Morrigan. Truman had given props to the agent, who'd smiled all through Mercy's interrogation. Morrigan liked the woman and was interested in meeting a ten-year-old girl who lived in the home where she'd wait until her mother turned up. After they left, Mercy drove home to shower and nap. Truman went back to work.

"Augustus McGee wants you to meet him at the diner," Lucas announced as Truman entered the Eagle's Nest police station.

Truman stopped, his cowboy hat in hand, halfway to its hook. Augustus was a town busybody. "Why doesn't he come here?"

"You know why."

"Really? He won't step foot in the office?"

"It's a government building. That's enough reason for the old coot."

"Sheesh. What's he want?"

"He was all secretive and wouldn't say, but he claims it's related to your case from this morning."

Olivia Sabin's death was the only case. It wasn't his case, but he couldn't imagine what else Augustus could be referring to.

"I'll be back in half an hour." Truman put his hat back on and zipped his coat. He'd planned to research Olivia and Salome Sabin at his desk, but it'd have to wait. At least he could grab a late lunch.

"Half hour. Right. If you're fortunate." Lucas's grin nearly split his face. "Have fun, boss."

The bright sun in the intense blue sky lied to him about the temperature as Truman strode toward the diner, two blocks down the street. The sun promised eighty degrees, not the actual frigid twenty-one. Summer wouldn't be here for another five months.

Through the diner's window he spotted a balding head with crazy gray tufts of hair above its ears. Augustus was waiting. Truman sighed and decided to tell Augustus up front that he had only a half hour for lunch. When Augustus had parked in a fire zone, their conversation had lasted nearly two hours. Augustus claimed he was a freeman. Several times the sovereign citizen had told Truman the police department didn't have jurisdiction over his person. Truman had an image of Augustus walking around in a huge bubble where no government agency had any authority, but apparently if Augustus had information to share, he'd deign to speak with a cop.

Inside, Truman shook Augustus's hand and slid into the booth across from him. Augustus McGee looked like a retired clown. All he needed was the red nose and white paint on his round face. He was a big man with pale-green eyes that viewed the world with deep suspicion. He believed in silent black helicopters, mind-reading radar from the cellular towers, and that the government's primary purpose was population control. Truman's officers claimed the man got crazier by the year.

"I've only got half an hour, Augustus, and I hope you don't mind if I eat lunch while we talk."

The waitress appeared. "Coffee, Chief?"

"Just water. And whatever your burger of the day is."

"It's Hawaiian. Ham and a ring of pineapple on the burger patty."

"Perfect for a snowy day," answered Truman. She poured his water and left. "What can I do for you, Augustus?"

Augustus leaned forward, clenching his coffee cup in both hands, his eyes intense. "Is it true that Olivia Sabin has been murdered?"

The Eagle's Nest rumor mill was faster than the speed of light.

"You knew her?" Truman asked.

"At one time. Is it true?" he repeated. His bushy eyebrows quivered at each word.

Truman tried not to stare. "Her death is viewed as suspicious," he said with caution. "We won't know until the medical examiner has results tomorrow."

Augustus sat back in the vinyl booth and exhaled, and his shoulders sagged. "We're all going to die at some point."

The round face had deflated. Sad clown. "How well did you know her?" A very small sense of pity touched Truman.

The man looked out the window and scratched at one of his gray tufts. "Well, I didn't know her that well. We haven't spoken in probably twenty-five years."

*There goes my hope of useful information.*

"You seem upset that she died," Truman prodded. "But you didn't keep in touch?"

"Well, you know how it goes. You always remember the good ones, you know what I mean?" Augustus made a lewd gesture with his hands, his gaze lecherous.

*That was more than I need to know.*

"So . . . the two of you were involved at one time?" Truman asked tactfully.

"Oh yeah. Involved. The best two weeks of my life." He leaned forward again, conspiratorially whispering, "You know she was a witch, right?" Truman's mother would have described Augustus as mad as a hatter.

Truman preferred the term *crazy*.

"I've heard something like that. You believe in that sort of thing?"

Augustus nodded emphatically. "Absolutely. I've seen it with my own eyes. How do you think she pulled me in for two weeks?"

Truman knew better than to ask for details. "Know any reason someone would kill Olivia Sabin?"

"It's not easy to kill a witch, you know. Takes someone with a lot of power. But I'll wager she angered somebody with one of her spells. Ruined their finances or gave them cancer." His eyes narrowed. "Sounds a lot like what the government does. But I don't think she worked for them, did she?" Conspiracy theories had bubbled to the surface in the man's brain.

"No, not that I know of."

"You know the world government is trying to reduce the population down to five hundred million, right? More manageable. It's easy for them to do. All those vaccinations and bottled water."

"World government?" The question slipped out. *Crap. Now he'll never shut up.*

"That's right. They're hiding behind the facade of the United Nations. That's just a front. The real power is like an octopus, all its arms causing havoc in different countries. They want a world where they rule implicitly. The best way to achieve that is division and unrest in the populations."

*Sounds like Hydra from Captain America.* "Seen any movies lately, Augustus?"

The man waved Truman's question away. "I know you want to hear about Olivia Sabin. She would chew men up and spit them out. You need to look at the daughter, the other witch. Her power is ten times stronger than her mother's."

"Salome?"

The old man crossed himself, surprising Truman. "That's the one. An unholy birth, you know."

*Now I'm totally lost.* "What?"

Impatience lowered the man's brows. "No father. No one fathered that child. Olivia had told me she wanted a child, but no one was good enough to contribute the genes." He snorted. "Made every man wear protection. Don't know why. There's pills for that."

*I'm not giving him a lecture on safe sex.*

"Who fathered Salome?"

Augustus glanced around the diner and, deeming no one within hearing distance, he whispered, "A demon."

Truman was speechless. Thankfully his burger arrived and he took two big bites as he searched for an appropriate reply to shut down Augustus's crazy tangent. "A demon. Huh." *Brilliant comeback.*

"No one knew she was pregnant. One day she just showed up with a baby." He nodded solemnly.

"Interesting." Truman took another bite, not knowing what to say.

"That girl was evil. You could see it in her eyes."

"You met her?"

"Well, no. But I heard about her."

Truman sighed.

"Everyone said the mother and daughter fought like cats and dogs. Is it true the daughter is missing? That's your killer."

"Because they fought doesn't mean Salome would kill her mother." The quiet little home in the woods hadn't appeared to be a place of fighting. It was neat and clean and had a barn full of animals. "And why would she leave her daughter behind?"

Augustus's bushy brows shot up. "You seen the child?"

"Yes. Pleasant kid."

"Another unholy birth. They say it was the fae this time, not a demon."

Truman's fury boiled over. "You know, Augustus, your information is a bunch of malicious gossip. I've met that girl. She's kind and caring and devastated that her grandmother is gone." He slid out of the booth and fished a twenty out of his wallet, then tucked it under his water glass. "If I hear that you're perpetuating this bunch of crap, I'll haul you in and give you a dozen vaccinations myself. And make you drink some bottled water at the same time."

Truman nodded at the wide-eyed waitress, grabbed his burger with a napkin, and strode out of the diner. His icy march back to the station did little to cool him down, and he munched as he walked. *Damned old gossip. Spreading bullshit about a child.* He recalled Morrigan's face, the elfin features and slight build. *Fae?*

He put the thought firmly out of his mind. *Has that poor family been ostracized due to rumors? Decades of rumors?*

And where was Salome Sabin?

◆  ◆  ◆

Mercy couldn't sleep.

She'd gone home after the eventful morning and had every intention of napping for the rest of the afternoon, but during her shower her brain had shifted into high gear and wouldn't turn off. She'd lain in bed for a full hour, trying to get the image of Olivia's abused body and Morrigan's teary face out of her mind.

She couldn't do it. Instead she drove to work, planning to find information about Olivia Sabin.

Even if it wasn't her case.

As she walked through her office's parking lot, a tall man slid out of a black Range Rover. "Agent Kilpatrick?"

Mercy stopped and wrapped her fingers around the pepper spray in the pocket of her coat. Every coat had one. The stranger had dirty-blond hair that needed a cut and sported a healthy tan even though it was January. His coat looked fresh from an expensive sporting goods store, but his heavy boots were beat up. He held up his hands in a calming gesture and flashed a charming smile. "My name's Michael Brody. I'm an investigative reporter for *The Oregonian*."

Mercy relaxed a fraction. "What can I do for you?" She kept the pepper spray in her hand.

"We have a mutual friend. Ava McLane."

She'd worked with Ava at the Portland FBI office. "So?" Reporters had never approached Mercy before, but she knew some agents had worked on high-profile cases and complained of their pestering.

"I'd like to talk to you about the murder of Malcolm Lake." Brody's intense green stare reminded her of a hawk's.

"Who?"

Brody frowned. "He's a judge for the United States District Court of Oregon."

She was clueless. "I don't know anything about it. He was murdered?"

"The night before last."

She'd been out of the office the day before, working from home with the TV and Internet off. "What does this have to do with me?"

Brody glanced at his watch. "Really? No one's contacted your office yet? I can't be the first."

"I wasn't in the office yesterday and haven't gone in yet today." She gestured at the door. "You're keeping me from doing so."

"You were at the murder scene of Olivia Sabin this morning, correct?"

Mercy said nothing.

He nodded as if that were confirmation. "Her body was deeply slashed several times?"

She kept her face blank, but alarm started to churn in her stomach. *How did the press find out I was there? Who leaked that detail?*

"Judge Lake was found in the same condition in his home. The extent of his injuries haven't been released to the public."

Stunned, she blurted, "Then how did you find out?"

He smiled. "I have my sources."

*Asshole. There's no way Ava is his friend.*

"What I'm trying to figure out is why an important judge like Lake was murdered in the same manner as an old woman living in the woods. The only connection I can see is that the judge lived in this area at one time."

"I can't help you. Contact Deschutes County. It's their case."

"Ah. Not any longer. With its similarity to the murder of a judge, which of course is being investigated by the FBI—our mutual friend, Ava, has the judge's case—the murder of Olivia Sabin now will be included in the FBI's investigation."

Mercy was speechless. *The FBI now has Olivia's case?*

"I had assumed the local case was given to you since you were present at the scene this morning. I guess I'm wrong about that."

"How the *fuck* did you know I was there?" Anger had replaced her shock.

"It doesn't matter. People talk; I listen."

"Well, your source left out some important details." She clamped her mouth shut, nearly having spilled that she'd found the dying woman. She wasn't going to be Michael Brody's next "source."

"Like what?"

"Why don't you go talk to Ava? And there's no way you're a friend of hers."

He gave a lazy grin. "I am. To both her and her fiancé, Mason Callahan. *Very* good friends. Their dog Bingo adores me, I've drunk wine in their newly remodeled kitchen, *and* I'm on the guest list for their wedding this summer."

So was Mercy.

"You're a cocky son of a bitch, aren't you?"

"It's one of my best qualities." Another guileless smile.

A small part of her softened. A *very* small part. The man was charming, but not in a smarmy way. He had an honest air about him. "I don't have any information for you."

He glanced at the building. "Maybe you should go see if Ava has arrived yet."

"She's coming? Here?" Despite the horrible circumstances, the thought of seeing her friend cheered her immensely.

"I might have beat her to town. Once I heard the investigation was shifting to Bend, I left."

"Are we done, then?" Mercy asked.

"You didn't say why you were at the scene this morning. If you weren't there as investigator, then why were you there?"

She gave her own lazy grin.

*"Hmph,"* said Brody with a twist of his lips. "I'm not scared of a challenge."

Neither was Mercy.

# SEVEN

Mercy stopped at Special Agent Eddie Peterson's office. "Is Ava here?"

Eddie jumped. He'd been deep in thought, frowning at his computer screen. "Hello, Eddie," he said in a high-pitched voice. "Nice to see you today, Eddie."

"Sorry. Good morn—afternoon, and I don't sound like that *at all*. Is Ava here?" she repeated, moving to stand in front of his desk.

He leaned back in his chair, his gaze studying her through his thick-framed glasses. The young agent hadn't changed one bit since he'd transferred to Bend from Portland at the same time as Mercy. He stuck out in the suburban office with his slim-cut slacks and skinny tie. During the weekends he wore plaid shirts, cuffed jeans, and a brown knit hat that looked identical to one Mercy had had when she was ten. It was a hipster-lumberjack look that suited him.

"McLane? Why would Ava be here?" he asked.

"I heard she was coming to investigate . . . the death I was at this morning." Abruptly the crime scene flashed in her mind, and her tongue stumbled through the words.

"Why? That has nothing—"

"You didn't have to come in this afternoon," Mercy's supervisor, Jeff Garrison, said from the doorway. "I know you were up all night."

"Thank you, but I couldn't sleep."

"Understandable. I'm sorry you were there during her death," said Jeff, his brown eyes sympathetic. Her boss was a good guy and a pro at making people relax, but he was married to his job. Mercy suspected he'd be snatched up by a bigger office soon. He was moving steadily up the government's ladder.

"I'm glad I was there, otherwise she would have died alone. And Morrigan could have gotten lost trying to find help." Mercy doubted her last statement. Morrigan was completely at home in the woods.

Jeff slapped the file in his hand. "I've got news." His tone shifted from sympathy to business. "We've been notified that the murder of Judge Malcolm Lake in Portland yesterday strongly resembles Olivia Sabin's death."

*One point for Brody's sources.* Mercy kept her face carefully blank. "Who made the connection?"

"The medical examiner. This morning Dr. Lockhart heard a few details from Judge Lake's autopsy and she immediately contacted the state's head examiner, stating she'd seen a similar case just this morning. Comparison of the injuries shows they are nearly identical."

"Where was the judge killed?" Mercy asked. "I didn't hear about it since I was out of the office yesterday."

"In his Portland home, right in his own bed. His housekeeper found him yesterday morning."

"We're over three hours away from Portland. Maybe even over four because of the crappy roads," Eddie pointed out. "Why cross the Cascade mountain range to murder an old woman in the woods?"

"Dr. Lockhart cleared her schedule and did the autopsy late this morning. According to her, the similarities can't be ignored. The Portland special agent working Judge Lake's murder is coming sometime today."

*Two points for Brody.*

Eddie shot a narrow glance at Mercy. "Ava McLane?" he asked Jeff. Jeff glanced at the file. "Yes." He scowled. "How did you know?"

"Ask Mercy. Somehow she knew before both of us."

The two men stared at her.

"Five minutes ago I ran into a reporter outside. He told me."

Jeff pursed his lips. "That's not good. But with Judge Lake's death, I'm not surprised it's getting media coverage. Was he local?"

"Portland. *The Oregonian.*"

"Refer any media to me," Jeff said. "Eddie, you're to work with the Portland agent . . ." He looked at his file again. "McLane."

"I'd like to be kept in the loop," Mercy said; she knew Jeff would never assign her a case in which she was a witness, but she *had* to keep her finger in this pot. Olivia's face was imprinted on her memory.

"Unofficially," said Jeff. "I don't need the complication of a witness involved in the investigation." He placed the file on Eddie's desk.

"Understood." Mercy would follow his rules, but finding Olivia's killer had shifted to priority level in her brain.

Her boss disappeared, and she raised a brow at Eddie.

"This is *my* case," Eddie stated. "Go away."

"I think you need to interview your primary witness: me," she pointed out. She wasn't going anywhere.

"True—hey, there's Ava." He gestured out his window at the parking lot. Mercy took two steps to get a view. Her friend had just been stopped in the lot by the same tall reporter.

"That's the reporter," she told Eddie. "He claimed to be a friend of Ava's." Mercy laughed as the dark-haired woman waved her finger in the man's face, clearly upset at something he'd said. "It looks like she doesn't appreciate his nosiness. I knew he was full of crap when he said she was—oh!"

Ava was hugging the tall man. She pulled back, smiled, and patted his cheek.

"They look like friends to me." Eddie poked her in the shoulder. Mercy stared as the two parted, clearly on good terms. "Huh."

A minute later Ava was shown into Eddie's office. The Portland FBI agent gave Mercy a quick hug and shook Eddie's hand. "Country living looks good on both of you." Her low voice always reminded Mercy of melted caramel. Rich, smooth, and sweet.

"It's not the boonies," Eddie said defensively. "We've got nearly eighty thousand people in Bend."

Ava's dark eyes danced at his tone. "I understood why Mercy took this post, but I was surprised to hear that you threw your hat in the ring. Your hip, two-hundred-dollar hat."

"I like it out here." Eddie scowled. "The air's cleaner and the beer is just as good. Maybe better. And you can't beat the scenery."

"Touché. I'm always stunned by all the beautiful mountain peaks. Especially after a fresh snow. But your roads really suck right now."

"Nothing's melting," agreed Mercy. "And supposedly we've got another big storm rolling in." She glanced at Eddie. "Five minutes ago we were told the reason you are here. What happened to the judge?"

Ava sank into one of the two chairs in Eddie's office and indicated for Mercy to take the other. Her eyes were tired, but she jumped right into her information about Judge Lake.

"The judge was discovered yesterday morning by his housekeeper. She cleans two days a week, starting at ten a.m. His office had tried to contact him when he didn't show up for work, but no one had considered anything suspicious. When his housekeeper realized he was dead, she backed out of the room and called 911."

"She didn't compromise the scene at all?" Eddie asked.

"No. She saw the blood on the bed right away and proceeded into the room with caution. She didn't touch a thing . . . not even the body, because he was clearly dead. The medical examiner estimates that he was murdered between six p.m. and midnight."

"Cause of death?" Mercy asked, knowing the answer.

"He bled out," Ava said grimly. "He had multiple deep lacerations on his abdomen, chest, and neck. The medical examiner said three of the cuts damaged vital arteries and each alone could have killed him."

"Overkill," Mercy said.

"An apt description," said Ava.

"Any evidence?" asked Mercy.

"The front door to his home was left unlocked, and there's no sign of a break-in. The housekeeper didn't see anything missing in a cursory look. His wallet with several hundred dollars was on his nightstand, so robbery is low on our list of motivations," said Ava.

"It sounds personal," pointed out Mercy. "What about cameras?"

"No cameras. A security system, but not with cameras."

"You checked to see if any of the neighbors have cameras that might give a view of his property or the street?" asked Eddie.

"Yes. Two had street views and showed eleven vehicles passing by between eight and twelve that night, but none of their plates were caught on camera. We identified which vehicles belong in the neighborhood, but that left four others." Ava took a breath and went on. "No weapon has been found, and we're running prints, but so far they've all been his or the housekeeper's."

"Any family?" Eddie scribbled on his notepad.

"An ex-wife who lives in Bend and two adult sons. Neither are married." Ava paused. "Gabriel Lake is his son who lives in Portland and Christian Lake lives in Bend."

Mercy straightened. "Wait a minute. I know Christian."

Ava's eyes lit up. "You do?"

"Yes. I worked at the same restaurant as him when I was eighteen . . . he was older, probably twenty-five. Nice guy, totally geeky, and we hit it off. I read he went on to start Lake Ski and Sports sporting goods stores." She combed her brain for other facts. "I remember he came from a really rich family. The other employees used to tease him about working in a crappy steak house when his father was some big-time lawyer and drove nice cars. I never met or saw the father, Christian was living in his own place by then."

"He owns Lake Ski and Sports?" Eddie blurted. "That's the most exclusive sporting goods store in Oregon and Washington. Carries all top-of-the-line gear. The Bend store is fantastic. It has a great rock-climbing wall inside."

"Did you interview Christian already?" Mercy asked Ava.

"Briefly. I told him I was heading to Bend and wanted to meet with him. Understandably he's very upset about his father's death."

"I've been in a few of his stores," said Mercy. "They're gigantic." She frowned. "I thought Christian moved to Portland. I've seen pictures of him at Portland-area fund-raisers and read about his support of various causes. He's been touted as one of Oregon's most eligible bachelors or some crap like that. But I was always pleased that someone from Eagle's Nest went on to do something awesome."

"Yes, he's single and owns a condo in Portland's South Waterfront area," said Ava. "I gathered that he doesn't use it much. He spends most of his time at his home outside of Bend. It appears to be quite the showpiece."

"What about the other son?" asked Eddie.

"He heads up a law firm in Lake Oswego outside of Portland. He's in California right now, but is trying to get back as soon as possible. I'll meet with him when he gets to town."

"What do you have so far?" asked Eddie.

"We're investigating Judge Lake's court cases, starting with the most recent, looking for anyone who might be out for some revenge. As you can imagine, it's a giant task. He's been a district judge for over twenty years."

"Age?" asked Mercy.

"Sixty-two. Single since the divorce decades ago. His secretary says he hasn't dated anyone in a few months, but he's had several relationships in the past few years. We're also looking at those." A wry smile crossed her face. "An assistant DA has been identified as one of his past relationships."

"Ouch," said Mercy. "Did she try any cases in his court?"

"Luckily, no. But she wasn't happy to talk to me and begged me to keep her name out of it. She didn't want the press or her boss getting wind of it."

"Speaking of press." Mercy tipped her head toward the window. "I saw you with a reporter in the parking lot."

Ava's face brightened. "That's Michael. He's a good guy."

"He approached me when I came in. He's lucky he didn't get a face full of pepper spray." Mercy wasn't convinced.

"He's a bit intense, but he's extremely smart and his intentions are always in the right place. He and Mason go back a few years. There's a bit of a reluctant bromance there that I don't understand." Ava grinned. "I trust Michael implicitly, but I did chew him out for racing to Bend and lying in wait for me."

"I thought he was waiting for me," said Mercy. "He questioned me about my morning. I don't know how he heard I was at the Sabin murder scene."

"He seems to get information from thin air," said Ava. "But trust me, you want him on your side."

Mercy didn't trust anyone without her own proof. "I'll consider your recommendation," she said sourly.

Ava went on. "We've pulled the judge's phone records, his office visitors log, and gone through his social media. No red flags yet, but it's early. Now tell me about Olivia Sabin. I don't know how her death is related to the judge's. So far the only connection is that the judge lived in this area long ago and it appears Olivia was here at the same time. The patterning of the gashes in both deaths is definitely similar. I'm glad your medical examiner had her ears open, otherwise we never would have made the connection."

Eddie pointed at Mercy. "It's my case as of five minutes ago; I know nothing. But your primary witness is right here. I was just about to interview her."

"Start from the beginning," Ava told Mercy.

For the fourth time that day, Mercy gave her version of events.

It wasn't any easier after multiple recountings, and her voice cracked at times.

"I'm sorry," Ava said, her blue eyes sympathetic. "That must have been horrible for you."

"I won't forget for a while," agreed Mercy. *I'll never forget.*

Eddie's cell phone rang. He did a double take at the screen. "It's Truman. Is he looking for you?" he asked Mercy as he answered the call.

Mercy checked her own phone. No missed calls or texts.

"You're still seeing the police chief?" Ava whispered loudly, a wide grin on her face.

Mercy rolled her eyes at her nosy friend. "Yes."

"Nice!" Ava sat back in her chair and nodded in approval.

"You don't even know him," Mercy pointed out.

"Oh, you can be certain I looked him up when I heard." She winked.

Mercy's face warmed; she was unused to discussing her love life.

"What'd he have to say?" Eddie asked into the phone. He made some more notes on his pad. "Uh-huh. Uh-huh. Seriously? He sounds like a fruitcake." He listened silently for a minute and then ended the call.

Mercy frowned. "Why did Truman call?"

"Well, he believes you're at home sound asleep, and Jeff told him I caught the Sabin case. Truman met with a local resident today who claims that Olivia Sabin is a witch."

Both women sighed. "And?" asked Ava.

"The local said to look at the daughter for the murder. He claims their relationship was extremely volatile, but of course he didn't witness this for himself; it's all hearsay." One side of his mouth turned up. "And he swears that everyone knows the daughter was fathered by a demon and her young child by a fairy."

"Oh, for Pete's sake!" Ava threw up her hands. "Why did Truman talk to this guy?"

"There's often some truth buried in rumor," said Mercy. "I can see why the witch story is out there. Some of the things in the home and barn were definitely odd. Who was the source?" she asked Eddie.

He glanced at his pad. "Augustus McGee."

"Wow. He lowered himself to talk to Truman?" Mercy was pleased that the sovereign citizen had enough trust in Truman to share the information, no matter how crazy it sounded. The relatively new police chief was winning over more people than he realized in his little town. As an outsider, Truman had struggled for acceptance from the locals even though he'd spent several summers in Eagle's Nest while growing up.

"Augustus claims he had a fling with Olivia decades ago."

"Well, that makes him a star witness," muttered Ava. "Who is this daughter of a demon?"

"Salome Sabin," said Mercy. "I told you her daughter, Morrigan, said she'd been gone for a few days."

"Right." Ava wrote something on her notepad. "Interesting name. What have you done to try to find her?"

Mercy looked to Eddie, who said, "I'll check with Detective Evan Bolton at county and see what his investigation has turned up. And let him know he now has us as a federal partner on the case."

"If she's missing, is it possible Salome could have been in Portland when the judge was murdered?" Ava asked.

Mercy sucked in her breath as she followed her friend's train of thought. "She could be in Cancún for all we know. All we can say is that she wasn't at the house when I was there."

"Well, let's find out," stated Ava. "Introduce me to the county detective so we can get this case rolling."

# EIGHT

Two hours later Mercy dragged herself up the stairs to her apartment. It was seven o'clock and her body achingly nagged about every single hour of sleep she had missed. She'd lowered her vehicle's window on the drive home, using the icy breeze to keep her awake. The shock of the freezing air had cleared the cobwebs out of her brain for the drive, but they were quickly returning.

Sliding her key into the lock, she heard laughter inside. The sound of Rose's voice warmed her heart, and she thrust the door open, ready to see her sister who'd been blind since birth. She was greeted by heavenly scents of toasted coconut, chocolate, and vanilla. And a messy kitchen. Her niece Kaylie had every baking appliance, measuring cup, and mixing bowl out on the counter, and the room was warm and welcoming from the heat of a busy oven.

"Mercy!" Rose had been facing the door as she entered, no doubt having recognized Mercy's steps on the stairs. Mercy hugged her sister and planted a kiss on her soft cheek, her lips feeling the faint groove of a fading scar from when Rose had been kidnapped and a killer had viciously sliced up her face.

A Merciful Secret

"What are the two of you doing?" Mercy asked, aware the obvious answer was, "Baking."

"Kaylie asked me for Mom's coconut cake recipe. She said Mom refused to share it."

"She's protected that recipe as long as I can remember," said Mercy. "She claims we'll find it in a safe-deposit box when she dies."

"Well, I've watched her enough to know what was in it," said Rose, with a grin at her word choice. "I'm a little fuzzy on the measurements, but Kaylie is guesstimating. So far the first two haven't been quite right."

"Mmmm." Mercy spotted two rejected cakes on the counter, multiple bites missing from each. She found a fork and tasted one. "You're right. This isn't quite right." She tried the second. "This tastes nearly right. Did you add the vanilla pudding mix?"

"Ohhh!" exclaimed Rose, clapping her hands together. "I forgot about that!"

"The mix is the one ingredient I remember," admitted Mercy. "That and how she insisted on toasting her own fresh coconut."

"Instant pudding mix?" asked Kaylie skeptically. "The dry stuff in a box?"

"Yes, I don't have any, but I can buy some tomorrow."

Kaylie turned up her nose, and its tiny blue piercing sparkled. "I don't use that sort of thing." Mercy's niece was picky about her baking ingredients.

"Then it will never be quite right," said Rose with an understanding smile. "Do you want to replicate the recipe or come up with your own?"

The teen's shoulders drooped. "I associate that cake with every special occasion in my life. You bet I want to master it. If I can get it right, I'll add it to the bakery case at the coffee shop." She gave Mercy a curious glance. "Do you think Grandma will mind?"

"I won't tell if you won't," said Mercy. "But Pearl will notice. You'll have to tell her." Mercy's oldest sister ran the Coffee Café, which Kaylie

61

had inherited when her father, Levi, was murdered by the same man who'd attacked Rose.

Kaylie eyed the giant mess on the counters and in the sink. "I guess I'm done for the night if we don't have the pudding mix. Thanks for your help, Aunt Rose. Do you want me to drive you home now?"

"I'll take her," said Mercy, ignoring her exhaustion. "You clean up. Is your homework done?"

"Yes, *Mom*."

It was said in jest, but Mercy liked the title. In the four months since she'd met her niece, Kaylie had become the closest thing to a daughter she'd ever had. Levi's dying plea had been for Mercy to raise his daughter, who'd been abandoned by her mother when she was an infant.

It had been a steep learning curve to raise a teenager, but Mercy believed she'd done pretty darn well so far. Kaylie wasn't missing any limbs, nothing new had been pierced, and her last report card had been all As. Mercy approved of her boyfriend, Cade, although Kaylie recently admitted some of the shiny excitement of the relationship had faded. Cade's new construction job was at a housing development nearly an hour away. Making time to see each other had become work.

*Welcome to real life. It's not like the movies.*

Mercy placed Rose's hand on her arm and guided her to the door, noticing that Rose's pregnancy had finally started to show. The bump was small, but for four months her beautiful face had been enhanced with a pregnancy glow. Their sister, Pearl, complained that her pregnancies had given her acne, not a glow.

"I'll be back in about forty minutes," she told Kaylie. Rose tapped the door frame with her cane and they moved to the top of the familiar outdoor stairs, which she took as confidently as Mercy.

"Thanks for the ride," said Rose as Mercy led her to her vehicle.

"Thanks for entertaining Kaylie."

"I adore her," said her sister. "She reminds me a lot of you at that age."

Mercy took that as a compliment. "She looks like me too."

"I heard you've had a long day," Rose said.

Mercy gave her a brief account of her day as they drove toward the farm where Rose lived with their parents.

"Olivia Sabin," Rose murmured to herself. "I can't quite place the name. It sounds familiar."

"She has a daughter named Salome who we haven't found yet."

*"Salome?"*

"Know her?"

"I know of her . . . by reputation only."

Mercy sighed. "Don't tell me you heard she's a witch fathered by a demon."

Rose turned in Mercy's direction. "Yes, I have heard that. Now I remember the stories I've heard about Olivia and her daughter." She shook her head in disgust. "And you can believe I told the gossiper what I thought of her spreading such bullshit about women."

Rose rarely swore.

"What else did you hear?"

"Mostly a lot of suspicious muttering. I know people in town used to go to Olivia and now to Salome for help with their love lives or health. People may whisper that they're witches, but they visit them first when they want help."

"What kind of help do they give?"

"Well, Melissa Johnson showed me a sachet she'd bought from Salome with instructions to put it under her pillow for two weeks. I smelled mint, rosemary, and basil in it. The sachet was to catch the attention of a certain young man."

"Did it work?"

"Yes and no. The guy Melissa had her eye on never came around, but she started dating his best friend during those two weeks. They're still together, so in a way it worked."

"Hmmm." Mercy wasn't sure what to think of that. "A confidence builder?"

"Probably."

"Anything else?"

"Someone went to her for help with an infection in their foot that wouldn't clear up. I can't remember who it was . . . An older man. Salome wouldn't take his money and ordered him to go to the emergency room. I heard he was pretty ticked, but he finally went. They removed two toes."

"Wow. At least she knows her limitations. Did you know about her daughter, Morrigan?"

"Not until you told me. I've heard men brag about sleeping with Salome. They viewed it as an accomplishment—almost like a dare—but I never heard that she was pregnant."

"Did you hear that she fought with Olivia?"

"No. People always grouped them together when gossiping, though. Said Salome was exactly like her mother."

"Not a compliment?"

"No. Is she really a suspect in her mother's death?"

Mercy took a deep breath. "We need to know where she was when Olivia died. I wouldn't call her a suspect, but we—I mean Eddie needs to talk to her. According to Morrigan, Salome appears to be the only person Olivia interacted with for the last few years."

"That's sad," said her tenderhearted sister. "Now I wish I'd gotten to know Olivia."

"You're a good person, Rose." Her sister had always been the voice of love and affection while they were growing up. She'd known how to skillfully soothe each of Mercy's other three siblings and their parents. Now she embraced the idea of having a baby—one fathered by the man who'd raped her and murdered their brother.

He'd died when he fired at Mercy and Truman. Mercy was mostly at peace with the fact that she'd helped kill the man who had grievously wounded her family.

"Would you be able to drive me to the lumberyard tomorrow on your lunch?" Rose asked, interrupting Mercy's thoughts.

"I don't see why not. What are you doing there?"

"Nick Walker has something for me to pick up."

"Nick, the owner? What is it?"

"I'm not sure. He says it's a surprise."

Mercy didn't miss the note of curious excitement in Rose's voice. *Is that about the surprise or Nick?* They'd both known Nick all their lives. He'd been friends with their brother Levi—or was it with Owen? Mercy remembered him as a quiet man. He hadn't gotten the best grades in school, but had been known for his woodworking skills. Understandable, since his father had owned the local lumberyard. Mercy had learned Nick was now the owner when she and Truman went in to pick up boards for one of her cabin's sheds. He was still a quiet person but had a sadness in his eyes that Mercy hadn't recalled in their past. Truman later told her Nick's wife had died from breast cancer five years before.

*Hmmmm.* "I'd be happy to take you."

*I want to satisfy my own curiosity.*

# NINE

The next morning the ping of Truman's cell phone relaxed the knot of stress between his shoulder blades.

Mercy's reply to his good-morning text had arrived two seconds after he sent it. He didn't need a repeat of the anxiety of yesterday morning. His worry and subsequent search for her had disturbed his mind-set for the entire day. *Not a good thing.*

Or was it? His concern showed he cared deeply about her. Something he hadn't experienced for a woman in a long time. If ever.

*A good thing.*

Now that he'd heard from Mercy this morning, he could focus on his day's work and then do a little Internet digging about the judge whose death had been linked to Olivia Sabin. Truman scanned Ben Cooley's incident report from a 3:00 a.m. call. A car wreck on Old Foster Road. One of two drag-racing teens had hit a slick patch and rolled his car. An ambulance had taken the teen to the hospital, where he had been diagnosed with a concussion and a broken arm. He was lucky.

*Who races on snow-packed roads?*

Truman had never been that stupid as a teen. Correction: Truman had been extremely lucky in his stupid moments as a teen. No one had died or broken any bones. A few trips to the local jail had been the worst he'd experienced.

The memory of Salome's dark eyes and lush curves flashed in his brain.

*Yes, that was one of my stupider moments.*

Luckily he'd escaped unscathed.

The woman had frequently popped into his thoughts since yesterday. He hadn't thought of her in two decades, but for the last twenty-four hours he'd struggled to get her out of his mind. The memories of her were like a serpent, slithering about his brain, refusing to be ignored.

*Did she kill her mother?*

He'd walked away from his long-ago encounter with Salome knowing she was dangerous. A woman to avoid. He'd dipped a foot in her murky waters and was thankful he'd broken off the encounter when he did. She'd unnerved him and rattled him to his soul.

*Doesn't mean she'd commit murder.*

Morrigan's charming smile pushed her mother out of Truman's thoughts. He saw nothing of the mother in the daughter, but for her daughter's sake he hoped Salome turned up soon. The girl shouldn't be with living with strangers after watching her grandmother die.

*A mother would never kill someone and leave her ten-year-old daughter to discover the body.*

*Right?*

Ben Cooley rapped his knuckles on the frame of Truman's office door. "Mornin', Chief."

"Did you get that wrecked car towed?" Truman asked, thankful for the interruption by the gray-haired officer.

"Yep. Took the tow truck long enough to get out there. Nearly froze my ass off."

"The boy was lucky. He could have been killed or hurt someone."

"You shoulda heard his father cuss him out. He won't be driving again anytime soon, and once that broken arm heals, his dad said he'd be shoveling manure for the next six months."

"Good."

Ben hovered in the doorway, mangling a pair of gloves, his forehead wrinkled in concern.

"Something else on your mind, Ben?"

"I've been thinking about that Sabin murder. It's all anyone in town can talk about."

Truman gave him his full attention. "What about it?"

Ben glanced over his shoulder and then lowered his voice as he held Truman's gaze. "They're saying she was a witch."

*This rumor is getting old.*

"Don't tell me you believe in witches."

"They say all three of them practiced magic . . . mother, daughter, and granddaughter. They make up their own coven, handing down secrets from generation to generation," he whispered.

*Enough malicious rumors.* Truman exploded. "Fuck me, Ben! Are you seriously giving credence to that bullshit? I met that little girl. She's an innocent child who doesn't deserve to be gossiped about."

Ben had the decency to duck his head, looking abashed. "It's crazy talk. But I think some of the tales about Olivia might be true."

Truman noted the familiar use of her first name. "Did you know her, Ben?" Augustus's claim that Olivia had "known" many men ricocheted in Truman's head, and acid filled his stomach.

*Ben Cooley? The man who just celebrated fifty years of marriage? Tell me it isn't so.*

"I didn't know her, but my older brother did."

Truman exhaled. "Explain."

Ben relayed a story that echoed Augustus McGee's.

*How many similar stories will the investigation uncover?*

Truman was ready to hear something positive about the women who lived in the woods. "Why are you telling me this, Ben? That doesn't shine any light on who might have killed her."

Ben squirmed and twisted his gloves. "I know. But if the daughter is anything like the mother, there might be a lot of men with an ax to grind. I'm just theorizing."

"Sounds more like vicious gossip." *Curves, soft flesh, welcoming eyes.* "Let's keep a lid on the chatter in town. Let people know it's wrong to spread rumors and stories. It's no help to the investigators. If someone can come forward with some *facts*, that'd be helpful."

"Hard to keep tongues from waggin'."

"Do your best," Truman ordered. "Refer anyone with *facts* to Detective Bolton at county or to the FBI."

Ben's head jerked up. "The FBI? Why the FBI?"

Truman bit his tongue, silently cursing at himself. The similarity between the judge and Olivia Sabin's deaths was not public knowledge. Yet.

The older officer raised his brows as he spotted Truman's discomfort. "Ah. Can't say?"

"Said too much already."

"Mum's the word."

"Thank you, Ben."

Lucas's face appeared above Ben. The six-foot-four former high school football star dwarfed the older officer. "You've got a visitor, boss." Lucas scowled. "He's a reporter from *The Oregonian*. Won't tell me what he wants to talk to you about, so I told him you could only spare a minute."

"We done, Ben?" Truman asked.

"Yep." The officer squeezed past Lucas's bulk in the narrow hallway.

"You willing to see him?" his office manager asked.

"Why not?" Truman was ready for a distraction from witches and rumors.

"Hey!" Lucas hollered down the hall. "Reporter guy. Come on back."

Truman winced.

A tall man about Truman's age appeared and did an awkward passing hallway dance with Lucas. Truman knew Lucas was being difficult on purpose. The visitor was nearly as tall as Lucas and also moved with the confidence of an athlete, but he resembled a nimble quarterback rather than an offensive lineman. Truman stood and held out his hand, and they exchanged names. Michael Brody's grip was strong, his gaze direct, and the watch on his wrist the same as that of Truman's brother-in-law, the Microsoft executive. Translation: way out of Truman's price range.

*He can afford that on a reporter's salary?*

"What can I do for you?" Truman asked as he took a seat and gestured for the reporter to do the same.

Brody perched on the end of his seat, his torso leaning toward Truman. "I'm investigating the story of Judge Malcolm Lake's death."

Truman kept his expression even.

Brody studied Truman's face. "I see you've already heard of the connection between Lake and Olivia Sabin."

Again Truman showed no response. "I'm not sure what that has to do with me. I didn't know either one of them."

"*But* you were at Olivia Sabin's home yesterday morning. Why would you respond to a death that was out of your jurisdiction? And you were there pretty early . . . too early for news of her murder to have gotten out."

"Who told you that?"

"Does it matter? And the FBI was there even earlier. How did they know her death would be connected to a federal investigation?"

"They didn't—" Truman clamped his lips shut.

The intensity of the reporter's stare lightened a degree. "So they *didn't* suspect the deaths were connected. Then why was Agent Kilpatrick on the scene so soon?"

"I don't think I'm the person to answer your questions." Truman started to rise to dismiss the nosy asshole.

Brody held up his hands. "I'll back off. When I get on the scent of something big, I pry wherever I can."

Truman settled back in his seat, never taking his gaze from the reporter. "I don't like your career choice."

The reporter laughed, flashing perfect teeth. "I hear that a lot. But I give a voice to people who might never be heard. I think of it as helping out the little guy . . . sorta like what you do in your position."

Truman's annoyance multiplied. "Now—"

"My story last year on prescription drug abuse led to the arrest of more than twenty dealers. And two drug recovery programs stepped up to offer free help to the three mothers I featured whose lives had been turned inside out by their addiction. Results like that is why I do my job."

Truman was silent.

"I already approached Agent Kilpatrick. She shut me down."

*Good.*

"But as I looked at who else was at the scene and I dug deeper, I found you to be another anomaly." Brody tilted his head, and his green stare seemed to penetrate Truman's brain, probing and assessing. "The more I dug into you, the more I wanted to meet you face-to-face. The officer who nearly died trying to rescue a woman from a car explosion two years ago."

Instant nausea triggered sweat at Truman's temples.

"And had every reason to never return to the big-city police force, and then he turns up in this remote town. Possibly licking his wounds? Looking for a slower pace?" The gaze softened slightly. "Couldn't leave the job completely, could you?"

Truman couldn't speak. The asshole was baiting him.

"I don't know if Agent Kilpatrick has ever mentioned Ava McLane to you, but I've heard Ava talk about Mercy and a police chief who caught her eye. And then she packed up and moved."

*He knows about Mercy and me?* Confusion swamped him. The reporter had nimbly danced, faked, and jabbed Truman in the chest when he wasn't looking—multiple times. As much as it pissed him off, a small part of Truman reluctantly admired the reporter's interview skills.

"What do you want, Brody?"

The reporter was silent for a moment. "I never know when I'll need to rely on good people. You're staring daggers at me right now, but you've kept your cool. No name-calling, no blaming others, no slime. I might be able to help you one day. And vice versa."

*Is he trying to convince me to make a deal with the devil?*

"My soul isn't for sale," Truman drawled.

Brody's smile filled his face. "I expected no less." He rubbed his hands together. "Now. Someone needs to follow up on the anonymous visitor to Judge Lake's office. This person came in one of the days before his death. I know there's video—"

"*Wait.* Why are you telling me this? And how the fuck do you know that?"

"You'll soon learn that asking for my source is a question I never answer. And I'm telling you because I try to spread myself around. I can't push every leak through the same person."

*Leak?*

"Look," started Truman. "This case has nothing to do with me and—"

"I know. Go tell it to someone who matters. But I think coming from you instead of me, it might get a little more notice. Interview the judge's executive assistant. She's turned over the visitor logs, but they're not complete. Video should back up her story." Brody frowned. "If it hasn't been tampered with."

"Why doesn't the assistant just tell the investigators?"

"Because she believes she's following the judge's wishes. Total dedication and all that bullshit."

"Doesn't she understand this is a murder investigation?"

"She does. But I think she's afraid of making the judge look bad."

"An affair?"

Brody shrugged. "He was single. I don't see the problem."

*Maybe she's protecting someone else.*

"I'll mention it to Mercy. She'll figure out who to tell. Why are you covering your ass?"

"I always cover my ass," said Brody, lifted one shoulder. "I think of it as being smart."

"All I have to do is say I got the lead from you."

"Very true. But every law enforcement agency I've ever worked with hates to admit they got information from a reporter. They don't like attributing leads to us. Makes them look lazy. And possibly gullible if it goes nowhere."

*True.*

"If you're done manipulating me, you can get out of my office now."

"Can you recommend a place to get a good cup of coffee? Not the watered-down diner brew."

"Coffee Café," Truman said reluctantly. "Two blocks up on the left."

The tall man touched two fingers to his brow in a casual salute and silently left.

Truman stared after Brody, feeling as if he'd been professionally dissected and glued back together.

*What the fuck just happened?*

Mercy knocked on the door of the small Craftsman home and waited.

The three snowmen in the front yard had lifted her spirits as she parked at the curb. The silent trio testified that good people lived here. People who believed in getting their kids outside to experience the elements. She hoped Morrigan had helped build them.

Mercy had been driving to work when she'd abruptly pulled over and made calls until she received permission to visit Morrigan's temporary foster home. She'd awoken with the child's face front and center in her brain, and knew she'd never focus at work if she didn't see that the girl was in good hands.

A sense of responsibility for Morrigan poked at her consciousness. For her own sanity, Mercy knew that she'd keep tabs on the child until her mother returned. Maybe even after Salome returned.

*What if Salome isn't fit to care for her? Or is arrested?*

She'd cross that bridge when she came to it.

The woman who opened the door had a toddler on her hip. "Good morning," said Mercy. "You must be Hannah?"

Hannah was around Mercy's age, very slim, and wore her blonde hair pulled back in a messy but stylish bun that Mercy immediately wanted to duplicate. Her smile was kind, but the lines around her eyes indicated she'd been up half the night. Somehow Mercy suspected the woman didn't mind. She'd immediately picked up a sense that Hannah was happy to dedicate her time to caring for children.

"Yes, and you're the agent that Morrigan has been talking about nonstop."

Mercy couldn't hold back her smile. "How's she doing?"

"I'll show you." Hannah flashed a deep dimple and gestured for Mercy to follow. The toddler's round blue eyes stared over Hannah's shoulder as Mercy trailed behind through the home. *She must be Hannah's child. They have the same hair and eyes.*

The home was neat and clean and smelled like pancakes. Peals of girlish laughter reached Mercy's ears. *All good signs.*

They entered a family room where Morrigan sat cross-legged on the floor next to another girl of the same age. Both gripped video game controllers and were focused on the television, where they'd dressed an animated model in denim shorts, green hair, and spike heels. Giggles ensued as one of them changed the hair to bright pink.

"She'd never held a game controller before," Hannah whispered to Mercy. "I almost hated to let her do it. I loved the idea that she'd never been plugged into electronics, but Jenny insisted they both play. Morrigan mastered it within minutes."

Mercy nodded, understanding Hannah's reluctance. This generation of children would never know what life had been like before the Internet, video games, and social media. Morrigan had been innocent and pure. A rarity.

Survival without electricity and modern amenities was bred into Mercy's bones. But every day it grew harder to stay on her toes, ready to respond if the electrical grid failed or a catastrophic natural disaster occurred. Some days she *needed* to vegetate in a jetted tub and watch movies on Netflix and forget that these luxuries could vanish in the blink of an eye. The relaxation never lasted long; awareness of an alternate harsh reality always simmered just below her skin.

"She's a good kid," Hannah continued. "Polite and kind. She wept over her grandmother, but has a strong faith that she's moved on to a better place. She said her grandmother had a lot of pain."

"Has she mentioned her mother?"

"She says she'll be back soon. It doesn't disturb her at all that she hasn't called. She does wish her mother could have said good-bye to her grandmother . . . and sent her off with 'words of guidance.'" Hannah paused. "That's exactly how she said it. It was such an odd phrase for a child her age."

"Hello, Morrigan," Mercy said.

Both girls spun around, and Morrigan's eyes lit up as she spotted Mercy. "Hi, Mercy. Did you see what I did to her hair?" The girl pointed at the screen, delight on her face. She wore flannel pajamas patterned with cat faces, similar to the pajamas Jenny wore. Both sported matching braids, and Mercy wondered if they'd done each other's hair.

Mercy had done that with Rose.

"Does she have to leave now?" Jenny asked, her eyes pleading for Mercy not to take away her playmate. Morrigan's expression mirrored her new friend's.

"No. I'm just here to visit and see how you're doing." *Clearly she's in a good spot.* A weight lifted from her shoulders; she hadn't realized she carried stress about Morrigan's safety.

"Have you heard from my mom?" Morrigan asked.

"Not yet."

"Okay." Morrigan turned to Jenny. "Let's find her a ball gown."

Mercy exchanged a look with Hannah. *No anxiety in that child.*

The two of them headed back toward the front door. "She's amazingly well adjusted," said Hannah. "I've had a number of temporary fosters and usually they're emotional and scared. It's almost eerie that she's doing so well."

"Do you think she's avoiding the feelings?"

Hannah thought. "I don't think so," she said slowly. "She was very open with her sorrow about her grandmother, and she exudes confidence about her mother's return. I think she's simply a resilient, well-grounded kid."

"Knows how to roll with the punches." Mercy approved. Morrigan had held it together quite well during their emotional hours together. Mercy's admiration for the child grew.

Along with her determination to find the mother.

She thanked the kind woman, who emphasized that Mercy was welcome to return at any time, but Hannah's gaze faltered as the sentence left her mouth.

Unspoken words hung between them; if Mercy had to return, it meant there was a major issue with Morrigan's mother.

# TEN

Mercy drove to the medical examiner's office, pleased that Morrigan was in a good place.

Eddie had texted her as she left Hannah's home, asking her to meet him and Ava at the examiner's office. The ME wanted to discuss her findings and had specifically asked if Mercy could be present since she'd been at the death.

Her cell phone rang through the speakers in her Tahoe as she drove. Mercy glanced at the screen on her dashboard. Truman.

Happy butterflies fluttered in her stomach. *At what point in a relationship does that feeling go away?*

Truman filled up the lonely and vulnerable parts of her brain. The subtle scent of his aftershave, the shadow on his jaw every evening, the heaviness of his hand at her waist. It wasn't all physical. Truman understood her; he got her. He'd seen her deepest fears and accepted them. She didn't scare him.

She accepted the call. "Hey," she said. "How's your morning?"

"Interesting. Yours?"

She gave him a positive update on Morrigan.

"Did you meet the reporter from *The Oregonian* yesterday?" he asked in a restrained voice.

Mercy looked at her dashboard as if she could read Truman's face. "I did. Ava later vouched for him. Why?"

"He paid me a visit and suggested that the investigators look into a mystery visitor at Judge Lake's office. He claims someone was there one of the days before he died and it was kept off the visitor log. He said the judge's assistant knows more than she's told investigators."

"Why did he tell you? That makes no sense. And how on earth would he know that?"

"Trust me, I asked the exact same questions and got convoluted answers. Let's just say it makes sense in Brody's head. Can you pass the tip on to Eddie?"

"I'm on my way to meet with him and Ava now."

"Good. Gotta go. I love you," he said in a low, warm voice infused with innuendo.

Her face flushed with heat and her smile broadened. "I love you too."

It was easier to say those three little words to Truman now than it had been two months earlier. Mercy had struggled with the simple oral contract of commitment. In her head she'd believed it meant she was reliant on him. A tough situation, as she'd promised to never allow herself to rely on anyone. This independent philosophy was the core of everything she'd learned as a child of preppers. To her surprise she'd discovered that loving Truman made her more confident, fearless. After she ended his call, a piece of her longed for him with an urgency that still unnerved her. That need for another person.

The instant love she'd felt for Kaylie had emboldened her to take that plunge with Truman. Her heart had easily expanded to make room for her niece and then expanded again as she repaired fences with her formerly estranged family. Being deliberately cut off from her family had left her with an empty heart for years, but since she'd returned to Eagle's Nest, she suddenly had a small crowd to care about.

It hadn't weakened her foundation. She was stronger.

Her oldest brother, Owen, had finally accepted her return, and Mercy had quickly added his wife and children to her "my people" list.

The only holdout was her father. She suspected it was pride that kept him from speaking to her.

*One day.*

She parked and strode into the ME's building, where she spotted Eddie and Ava in the waiting area. She greeted them and recounted her visit with Morrigan. "Anything new on Salome?"

Ava looked grim as she shook her head. "There's been no activity on her cell phone for three days. She has one credit card, and it hasn't been used in months."

Suspicion weighed heavy in Mercy's gut. "Do you think something has happened to her?"

"We were just talking about that," said Eddie. "We can't rule it out."

"I don't want to discover that she's the third victim," Ava stated. "But damn, it's not looking good. People don't just vanish."

"People vanish all the time," argued Eddie. "Especially out here. If they don't want to be found, we won't find them."

"I can't believe she'd leave her daughter behind," countered Ava.

"Maybe she feels her disappearance is protecting the girl . . . leading a killer away," suggested Eddie.

Mercy's brain spun with the possibilities, but in her mind only one thing mattered right now. "That poor child. She needs her mother." *What will happen to Morrigan if Salome doesn't come back?*

"Let's hope we're wrong. We'll handle it if it comes to that," Ava stated briskly, shutting down the topic.

Eddie cleared his throat. "We did find out that so far none of the knives tested positive for poison or blood. The lab was surprised to find how clean they were. Usually there's something left on even the cleanest knives."

"Maybe they're never used," suggested Mercy, remembering the rows and rows of blades. "Perhaps they're truly a collector's hoard."

"I saw the pictures," Ava said. "I've never encountered anything like that. It was creepy."

Mercy silently agreed. "Say, Truman called me and said your reporter friend claims that Judge Lake had a mystery visitor at his office one of the days before he died. Brody claims this person was deliberately left off the logs and that the judge's assistant might be covering it up."

"Why didn't Michael just tell *me*?" Ava sighed. "Never mind. I know he likes to do things his own way. I've learned not to question his actions." She rubbed her neck, her gaze unfocused, as she considered Mercy's statement. "The assistant, huh? Marcia Mallory. I talked to her. I thought she was very forthcoming. I guess I need to pay her another visit."

"Are there video cameras in the judge's office?"

"In the waiting area. Not in his chambers. We pulled the recordings, but they haven't been reviewed yet. We went through the logs first. We were going to check the video if we found something odd in the logs." She sighed. "I guess I better get someone on the recordings to compare them to the logs. Although I don't understand why Marcia would hold back information that might help us find the judge's killer. She seemed very devoted."

"Maybe she worried this visitor would tarnish his reputation," Mercy suggested.

"He's dead," Eddie pointed out.

"It can be important to some people."

Dr. Lockhart appeared, looking more like a college student in scrubs than a medical examiner. The slick, perky ponytail added to the facade. "Come on back," she said, directing the three of them through a door and down a hall to a large office. Mercy had expected the office to be extremely neat and organized. It wasn't. There were stacks of files and journals on every available surface. A life-size skeleton hung from a stand in the corner. The lower half of its arm was missing and Mercy spotted it on a nearby stack of files, its bony structure looking lost and lonely. Boxes and thick textbooks were crammed into three crowded, ceiling-high bookshelves. Natasha's framed degrees and numerous awards hung on the wall, and Mercy fought the urge to straighten the lowest one.

Mercy exchanged a look with Eddie, who also looked surprised. The mess wasn't what they'd expected from the tiny ME.

Small knickknacks cluttered Natasha's desk, leaving her little space to write. Stepping closer, Mercy saw they were all cats. Glass, plastic, ceramic.

"You're a cat lady?" asked Eddie with a grin.

"I like cats," Natasha answered. "But I only have two real ones."

Natasha took the chair behind the desk and gestured for them to sit. Mercy removed a stack of files from a folding chair, and Eddie picked up an open box from another chair and searched for a place to put it. "Just set them on the floor," ordered Natasha. They did.

"Everyone has read the preliminary report I sent yesterday, correct?" asked the doctor.

"Not me," stated Mercy. "But I've heard some facts secondhand. You said at the scene that you believed someone tried to smother Olivia first. Did that turn out to be true?"

"Yes. She may have passed out for a few moments, leading her killer to believe she was dead."

"And that's when they cut her?" asked Eddie.

"I believe so," answered Natasha. "The throw pillow came back positive for saliva, as I expected." She paused. "Olivia was awake for part of the attack. She has defensive wounds on both hands."

Mercy pictured Olivia's bloody hands, remembering the wet warmth against her palm as the woman took her last breath.

"And I was right that she slowly bled out from minor damage to several arteries. Even though some of the slashes were quite long, the artery nicks were small, prolonging her death."

"That's horrible," murmured Ava. "Judge Lake had several arteries with major damage. They say he died quite rapidly."

Dr. Lockhart nodded emphatically. "The patterning of the cuts is very similar."

"I didn't see any pattern on Olivia," said Mercy. "All I saw was blood. And sliced flesh." She shut down her mental images of Olivia's suffering.

"Once I heard about Judge Lake's injuries, I immediately got Olivia on the table." Dr. Lockhart's face softened. "I know this isn't important, but Olivia wouldn't have lived more than another few months. She had advanced pancreatic cancer. It moves very fast."

"Morrigan said her grandmother had been in pain," added Mercy. *Did Olivia know she was so ill? That poor woman.*

"Definitely," agreed Natasha. "And surprisingly the blood labs I ran here show no presence of painkillers. I sent samples out for more extensive testing, but my gut tells me they won't find anything."

"Were prescription medications found in the home?" Mercy asked Eddie.

"None. Not even over-the-counter stuff like Advil or Tylenol."

"That's crazy," stated Ava. "I'm healthy, but I always carry a small pharmacy in my purse. What if Morrigan had a fever? Nothing for her either?"

Mercy thought of the glass jars of powders and herbs. "I suspect they used natural ingredients to treat that sort of thing."

Ava sniffed. "Along with spells? Ridiculous. God made drugs for good reasons."

"Is it possible Olivia hurt herself?" Eddie asked. "If she knew she was terminally ill . . ."

"No," stated Natasha and Mercy in unison.

"One of the officers asked that at the scene," said Mercy. "There was no weapon nearby and she wouldn't have tried to smother herself with a throw pillow."

"Inefficient," Natasha wryly added.

"If she wanted to kill herself," said Mercy slowly, "I suspect she could have made a concoction from those workroom jars that would peacefully do the job. But I don't think she would do it if she knew her granddaughter would be the one to find her body."

"Agreed," said Ava. "They immediately ruled out suicide with the judge for a number of reasons too. The first being no weapon left behind."

Natasha had turned to her keyboard, and Mercy was amused to see she typed with only her pointer fingers, but her keystrokes were rapid and confident.

"Take a look at these." Dr. Lockhart turned a large monitor for the three of them to view. "On the right is Olivia Sabin. On the left is Judge Lake."

Mercy sucked in a breath. The photos were from the autopsies, the stainless steel of the tables looking sterile and stark in contrast to the abused torsos. The two photos showed the bodies from the neck to the groin area. The victims were both old, their wrinkles and folds stating they had lived full lives. Olivia didn't match the memory in Mercy's head. Here she was a faceless body, almost a mannequin's torso in her anonymity. But her flesh gaped where the killer had made his marks.

*Or is the correct phrase "her marks"?*

Mercy's gaze jumped from one image to the other; the bodies couldn't have been more different. The judge was clearly male and had tanned skin, indicating a recent sunny vacation. Olivia was extremely thin, her breasts deflated with age, and Mercy wondered if her low weight was due to the cancer.

But the pattern of the slashes was similar. Too similar. Nearly identical.

"Son of a mother trucker," said Eddie under his breath.

Dr. Lockhart raised a brow as she looked his way.

"I'm trying to swear less," admitted Eddie.

Mercy's brain had instantly translated Eddie's statement. "That's not an effective technique."

"Either way, Eddie's words are accurate," stated Ava. "I've never seen anything like this, and I've seen a lot of nightmares."

"What is the image?" asked Mercy, trying to make a pattern out of the cuts. "Clearly it means something."

"I've sent pictures to the Portland gang unit and reached out to a tattoo association," said Natasha. "I feel like I'm grasping at straws, but I'd hoped it'd be familiar to someone."

"The FBI must have someone in a random department who specializes in something like this," said Ava. "Send me the photos and I'll get them to the right person. I know we've searched our databases for other similar murders, but nothing has turned up. Yet."

Mercy pulled a pen and notebook out of her bag and tried to sketch the shapes. She shook her head at her finished product. "I can't see what it is. But it definitely is *something*."

"I'm pointing out the obvious question again," said Eddie. "But why is it on these two seemingly unrelated people?"

"I think the key word there is *seemingly*," stated Mercy. "Our job— your job is to find the connection."

Truman stepped through the doors of the church without knocking, feeling like a trespasser. It wasn't a Sunday, so simply being in the building felt off-kilter to him. He took a left and headed down a long hall that he knew would lead to David Aguirre's office. He assumed the minister was in the building because his ancient Ford pickup was parked in back of the church.

Truman had spent his lunch break at his desk, using Google to do a bit of research, and had a fresh appreciation for the rule about not believing everything on the Internet. Unable to get some of the rumors about Olivia and Salome Sabin out of his brain, he'd decided to educate himself on current-day witchcraft.

He was now more confused than when he'd started. He should have stuck with his previous education from Disney villains.

From what he'd read, there appeared to be no rhyme or reason to witchcraft. He saw it in his mind as a giant tree. The trunk was the catch-all witchcraft label and the hundreds of branches were the possibilities for how to practice. There was no consistency. Black magic, white magic, evil and good. Solitary practitioners and covens that ranged from a few to hundreds. He'd decided to pick David Aguirre's brain. The minister had lived in Eagle's Nest all his life, and Truman hoped he had a bit of insight into the rumors that surrounded the Sabin women.

The faint sounds of a TV show came down the hallway, and Truman stopped outside David's office door. It was ajar. He knocked and then pushed it open. David sat at an ancient wooden desk, tapping away at a keyboard. The back of a giant monitor faced Truman, the Apple logo prominently displayed. Behind the minister a small television was tuned to a cooking competition show that Truman often watched with Mercy.

David stood and held his hand out over the monitor. "Hey, Chief. What brings you to church on a weekday?" David had been close friends with Mercy's oldest brother, Owen, all his life. She'd shared stories about when the two men were in their teens that had made even Truman—who'd thought he'd heard and seen everything—shake his head. Mercy still harbored a bit of dislike for the man who'd set aside his fast-track-to-hell ways and now stood behind a pulpit. Truman understood. Something about the minister had bothered him during his first few months in town, but Truman had put his dislike aside after David's actions a few weeks earlier at the funeral of Joziah Bevins, a longtime Eagle's Nest resident.

David's words over Joziah's casket had been heartfelt and sincere. Truman had watched as David took charge of Joziah's grieving son,

Mike, one of Truman's closest friends. Truman's respect for the minister had grown substantially that day. David cared about the people of his town, just as Truman did. They offered their support in different but similar ways.

"I assume you've heard about the murder of Olivia Sabin," Truman began.

"Yes." David nodded and gestured for Truman to take a seat in an old wood chair to the side of his desk. "It's all I've heard about for the last twenty-four hours."

"Gossip train full speed ahead."

"Exactly." David did up the buttons of his thick sweater, and Truman realized the office was quite cold. Glancing around, he realized the monitor was the only item in the office that was less than a decade or two old. No doubt David kept the heat low, saving money so he could afford to properly heat the building on Sundays.

"Did you know Olivia or Salome?" Truman asked.

David leaned back in his chair, a reluctant look on his face. "Why are you asking?"

"I was there yesterday morning," Truman told him. "I saw the home and Mercy happened to be there for her death. I can't get some of the things in the house out of my mind. And like you, I've been inundated with gossip since it happened. I'm trying to sort out what's real from the bull." He paused. "You know they haven't been able to locate Salome, right?"

"I'd heard. I hope she hasn't been hurt." David sat forward and rested his arms on his desk, his gaze holding Truman's. "You want to know if I think the two of them could be witches."

Stated like that, it sounded ridiculous. "Something to that effect. I've been reading up on witchcraft, trying to get a sense of what could be going on in their home."

David pressed his lips together and appeared to be weighing his words, debating what to share. "I met Olivia once," he started. "This was years ago . . . way before Morrigan was born. She came to see me."

"She did?" Shock shot through Truman. "I thought—"

"You thought she'd have nothing to do with a church, right? Well, she was seeking counsel, just like any other person in town might do. She had no one else to talk to. Her daughter, Salome, seemed to be the only person in her life, and Olivia was worried about her . . . like any mother who worries about her daughter."

Truman was fascinated. "What did she say?"

David frowned. "I feel most of that conversation is private, but I can tell you she was concerned for Salome's future. She didn't want her daughter to be ostracized from society the way she had been."

"Didn't Olivia choose to live removed from others?"

"She did. But she knew what people in town said about her. Locals crossed the road to avoid meeting her on the sidewalk and never made eye contact in the grocery store."

"That's horrible," admitted Truman.

"That day I saw a lonely woman who simply wanted her daughter to be accepted."

"How old was Salome at that time?"

"Somewhere in her twenties."

"Old enough to do as she wished."

"That was part of Olivia's heartache. Salome embraced the witchcraft rumors and may have even perpetuated some of them. Olivia said her daughter enjoyed the suspicion and fear."

*Dark, challenging eyes. Dangerous curves.*

"I can see that."

"I told Olivia she couldn't change her daughter's behavior. Salome was an adult. Olivia could only sit back and love her."

"What about the witchcraft?" pressed Truman.

David shifted in his seat, discomfort crossing his face. "Olivia assured me she only practiced white magic."

"You don't seem pleased at that."

"I can't condone anything of that nature."

"What I've read about white magic sounds like it's based in nature. Almost a reverence for the elements."

"Yes, we had a discussion about how she celebrated the world that my God had made. She didn't see any harm in that."

"But she lauded the results, not the maker."

Relief crossed David's face. "Exactly. Our discussion was polite and interesting, but I don't think I convinced her of the error of her ways. She wasn't a bad woman . . . just misguided."

"Some ministers would have ordered her out of their office."

"She was a human being with feelings and a family. Just like you and me. She came to me in desperation, and I helped her as I would have done for anyone. I'm not here to pass judgment. That's not my job."

Truman's respect for David rose another notch. The minister might occasionally lapse into a piousness that annoyed him, but his heart was in the right place.

"Did you ever meet Salome?" asked Truman.

The minister took a deep breath. "I did."

Truman waited ten seconds, but David didn't speak. "I met her," Truman stated. "She rattled me pretty good."

"Yes." A skeptical light shone in David's eyes. "That was it exactly. I only met her in passing, but I swear she saw every fault in my soul. I didn't like it."

"I experienced the same."

"Danger and thrills radiated from her," David said. "It was disturbing, but it helped me understand why so many men fell prey to her looks. Her words and actions implied that she offered escape from the humdrum life."

"Only a momentary escape," clarified Truman.

"Right. But sometimes men don't look beyond what is right in front of them."

The existence of Truman's job backed up this statement. Most of his arrests were of people who hadn't considered the consequences of their immediate actions. Or else simply didn't care.

David got out of his seat and went over to the giant bookcases. He ran a finger along some spines, searching for something. "I know people have gone out to the Sabin home, looking for assistance with their problems."

"Problems?" Truman asked.

"Hoping to get help with their health, or financial situation, or love life."

"That's not the first time I've heard that."

David pulled out a book, glanced at the cover, and put it back, continuing his search. "Everyone wants a shortcut. If they hear that someone offers a magic pill, they try it." He removed two more books and nodded in satisfaction at the covers. He handed them to Truman. "Maybe these will help you understand what happened in the woods."

Truman reluctantly accepted the books, ill at ease with the titles. "You have books on witchcraft?"

"I have books on everything. You can't answer questions about something unless you study it."

"Do you think Olivia could have been killed for her beliefs?"

David held Truman's gaze. "Absolutely."

# ELEVEN

Mercy steered over a large chunk of ice in the center of the road.

"Dad got called out on a birthing cow," Rose stated, sitting next to her in the Tahoe.

Their father was known for his knowledge and talent with livestock. For as long as Mercy could remember, Karl Kilpatrick had gotten calls in the middle of the night, neighbors stating that the vet was busy, but their cow or goat needed someone *now*. He never turned anyone down. He wasn't a vet—and he always reminded the owners of that fact—but he knew his way around the inside of a cow and easily recognized nutritional deficiencies in horses, goats, and pigs. Some neighbors would call Karl before they contacted the vet, but he always knew when a situation was beyond his ability and urged them to get professional help.

Animal medicine was a valuable survival skill that made him an asset to other preppers in his community. If Karl Kilpatrick was around, they could rely on him in a livestock emergency. Livestock were worth their weight in gold if healthy, but if sick or injured, they could threaten a family's bottom line. If modern conveniences vanished, the loss of a cow could mean the difference between life and death for a family.

"Three nights ago Dad pulled twin calves," Rose went on. "The Rickmanns couldn't get anyone out to their place, and the poor cow had been trying to deliver for hours."

"Both calves lived?"

"They did," Rose said with pride. "I would have loved to touch them."

Mercy had watched her father deliver dozens of reluctant calves. Some lived, some died. When possible he had brought his kids along, sometimes hauling them out of bed in the dead of night in the belief that they should learn how to handle an emergency situation. Mercy hadn't watched her father slide his arm inside the hind end of a cow in years. As a child she'd never been bothered by the sight; that was how it was done, and immediate action was vital to save the life of the cow and calf. But right now the memories were slightly disturbing. If the calf was dead inside its mother, he'd send young Mercy and her siblings out of the barn. Except for Owen, the oldest of the group. He'd use Owen to help him remove the calf. Sometimes in pieces.

But when a healthy calf was born, her father beamed. Many times she'd watched him run his hands over a newborn cow as it nursed, pride filling his face. He'd kindly slap the mother's hide, telling her she'd done a good job. Back then, when a slimy, live calf landed in the hay, Mercy envied the praise the mama cow got from her father. He wasn't an easy man to impress.

"I haven't touched a newborn calf in years," said Mercy. *Big eyes, wet nose, awkward legs.*

"I'll let you know when we have one at the farm," Rose offered.

Mercy pulled into Walker's Lumberyard on the outskirts of Eagle's Nest. It'd been a town institution all her life, but its previous owner had had a reputation for crotchetiness. "What happened to old man Walker?" she asked.

"He died about ten years ago. Nick has been running it ever since then."

"He would have been rather young to take over," observed Mercy.

"People took right to him," said Rose. "Dad has never complained about Nick like he constantly did about his father. I think Nick worked hard to be the exact opposite of his predecessor."

"I always liked Nick," said Mercy. "He was in Levi's circle of friends, right?"

"Yes. I always thought of him as the one in that group with a bit of common sense."

"It didn't take much to gain that title. Most of those guys acted like idiots." She parked while watching Rose out of the corner of her eye. An aura of excitement surrounded her sister. Her hands wouldn't hold still, and she sat straighter in her seat than usual.

The building was a huge yellow metal structure with three sets of giant sliding doors. A wooden sign over one of the doors announced that they'd arrived at Walker's Lumberyard. Neatly stacked piles of boards filled one end of the parking lot. Someone had taken the time to dig them out of the snow.

After crossing the plowed lot, Mercy opened the only human-size door and was greeted by the scent of fresh-cut wood. On Mercy's arm Rose paused and inhaled deeply. "I love that smell," she admitted.

"One of the best," agreed Mercy. They entered a small salesroom that was closed off from the warehouse portion of the lumberyard. A space heater whirred, and a few metal chairs lined the far wall. The sales counter was unmanned and an ancient ornate cash register took up a third of the counter's work space. Mercy remembered the gold-colored metal register from her childhood lumberyard visits; the relic had to weigh several hundred pounds.

A door between the warehouse and salesroom opened. A large German shepherd and Nick Walker entered, and Nick's eyes lit up as he spotted the two women. "Good afternoon, ladies."

"Nice to see you, Nick," Mercy replied as Rose told him, "Good afternoon." Her grip tightened on Mercy's arm, and the black-and-brown dog nosed Rose's other hand.

"Hi, Belle," Rose said to the dog, and Belle turned her attention to Mercy, begging for a head rub.

As in high school, Nick gave the impression of being all gangly arms and legs, even while wearing his winter coat and heavy pants. He was tall and slightly stooped, with a long, angular face, but his brown eyes were warm and kind.

And focused on Rose.

"I'm glad you could come down today, Rose," Nick said. "I thought about delivering it to your home, but I first wanted to be certain it was something that interested you."

"I'm dying of curiosity," admitted Rose.

He stepped forward and offered his arm. Mercy transferred Rose's hand and felt oddly alone as Nick led them through the door into the warehouse. A small forklift zipped back and forth near one of the huge doors, swiftly picking up and transferring stacks of lumber as if they were weightless. The driver raised a hand at them, never missing a beat, and Mercy waved back, impressed by his rapid pace.

"It's over here," Nick said.

Mercy stayed five steps behind, watching as Nick kept glancing at her sister, his smile growing wider each time. Belle trotted on Rose's other side as Nick led them into a corner filled with workbenches, electric saws, and woodworking tools. Mercy stopped to admire a thick slab of wood that featured a cross section of a gigantic knot and couldn't stop herself from running her hand across the polished surface. Instead of being rejected for its deformity, the unique wood was stunning and highly desirable for a one-of-a-kind table.

Reluctantly pulling her gaze from the wood, Mercy looked over at her sister and caught her breath. Nick had just placed Rose's hand on an intricately carved cradle. It was tall, with widespread legs that rested on gently curved rockers. The ends arced like the headboard of a sleigh bed, and the sides had elegant flat spindles.

It was beautiful.

Rose's mouth dropped open as she realized what was under her fingertips. Her face lit up and her hands flew over every aspect of the cradle, pausing over the complicated design carved into the arched ends. "Oh, Nick." She gave the cradle a push, feeling it smoothly rock. "It's lovely."

Mercy blinked hard as the cradle blurred. "Did you make that, Nick?" She already knew the answer.

"I did. Do you like it, Rose? I didn't know if you already had one." He was entranced by her reaction; his gaze locked on her face.

"It's amazing, and no, I don't have one." Her fingers returned to the pattern on the ends. "Are these flowers? I feel leaves too."

"They're roses." He said the name of the flower in the same tone with which he'd said her name. With deliberate respect. "I debated that it might be too girly if you have a boy, but then I decided that a baby wouldn't care."

Rose laughed, a sound that filled Mercy's heart. "It's for me to enjoy, and I *love* it." She turned her shining face to Nick. "Thank you so much. You've created an heirloom." She lifted both arms in his direction, and Nick stepped into the hug. "I can't believe you made it for me."

His eyes closed as he returned the hug, and the expression on his face made Mercy catch her breath again. Rose pulled away, turning her excited face to Mercy. "Describe it for me."

"He stained the oak a lovely golden shade," said Mercy. "It reminds me of rich honey. It's both elegant and homey at the same time. The grain of the wood is very elegant. You're right; it will be an heirloom."

Rose's right hand explored the cradle again as her left gently touched her coat over her growing belly. Nick rubbed Belle's ears, never taking his gaze from Rose's movements. The dog watched her too.

"I can deliver it this afternoon if you'd like," he told Rose.

"That'd be wonderful. I don't know how to thank you. This is the most wonderful gift I've had in a long time."

The elated look in Nick's eyes stuck with Mercy as she drove Rose home.

# TWELVE

A snowplow driver had called in the vehicle, claiming it'd sat on the side of the remote road for two days. Truman had responded to the call and was now parked behind the SUV.

Truman studied the screen on his police vehicle's computer. The new Lexus SUV hadn't been reported stolen.

No snow covered the black SUV's hood, so it hadn't been present during the last snowstorm. Truman got out of his truck and approached the vehicle. Several footprints surrounded it in the deep snow, but the driver who'd called it in had said he'd peeked inside to see if someone was hurt. From the look of it, a few other people had also stopped. Truman counted three different sets of tire tracks where vehicles had stopped. People who'd probably checked to see if anyone was inside and then gone on their way, seeing it as none of their business. A typical attitude in this area. Truman was slightly surprised that the abandoned SUV had been reported after only two days, but he suspected the value of the vehicle had shortened the time period.

He checked the interior. It was empty and nothing appeared damaged, but he couldn't see into the rear section, which was covered by the interior cargo cover.

He studied the surrounding area. Fenced snowy pastures. A few trees. Nowhere for anyone to go. Whoever had been driving the car had either been picked up or walked the three miles back to town. No footprints led away on the shoulder, but the driver could have walked on the plowed road. Truman started back to his vehicle, but he paused. After a second he turned around and pounded on the rear hatch of the Lexus. And listened.

Silence.

He leaned closer to the rear hatch and sniffed. All he smelled was icy cold air.

Relieved, he got back in his vehicle and took another look at the name and address of the registered owner.

Christian Lake.

Bells rang in his head. *There was a victim named Lake who might be tied to Olivia Sabin's murder.* But the victim was a judge who lived in Portland. It was the similarity of the two murders that had sparked the interest of the FBI.

*This vehicle can't be related.*

Truman started his SUV, plugged the owner's address into his GPS, and pulled back onto the plowed road, his curiosity growing. He'd see if the owner was related to the victim before calling the FBI.

Christian Lake's home was stunning. Truman wouldn't call it a mansion, but it was pretty damned close. The huge mountain-cabin-on-steroids-style house sat on a high ridge, overlooking a lake. A location Truman found mildly amusing considering the owner's last name.

He parked, noting the six-car garage connected to the giant home by a long covered walkway. An old Hummer was parked in front of the closest garage door, an early model Truman recognized as being desirable among collectors, and he wondered what other types of classic vehicles were hidden behind the doors. He called in his location and got out of his SUV.

"Can I help you?" A stocky man had emerged from the home's end of the walkway. He looked about Truman's age and wore a Mount Bachelor cap and thick black jacket. His breath hung in the cold air.

"Are you Christian Lake?"

"No. Mr. Lake is a bit busy. Can I give him a message, Officer?"

Truman pulled off his gloves and dug a business card out of his pocket. He held it out to the man, noting he could be actor Jason Stratham's twin. He even had the beard stubble and scowl. "Is he missing a black Lexus SUV?"

The man frowned at the card. "Why are you asking?"

"Because it's been sitting on a road's shoulder for a few days."

"*What?* Hang on a minute." He strode to the garage, punched a code into a keypad, and vanished through the door that opened.

Truman waited. *He has to take inventory?*

The man reappeared five seconds later. "Where is it?"

"I'd like to talk to Christian Lake. He's the registered owner." Truman wasn't budging until he talked to Lake.

The man glanced at Truman's department SUV and back to the card. "Okay, Chief. I'm trying to keep people out of his hair today, but I think he'll talk to you." He gestured for Truman to follow him into the home.

Truman gaped as he entered.

Golden wood gleamed. Everywhere Truman looked, he saw polished wood and glass. Tall wainscoting, custom cabinets, end tables, and elaborate baseboards. The ceilings were sky high and decorated with rustic beams, amplifying the multimillion-dollar-cabin feeling. In the middle of the open common area, a three-sided fireplace made of river rock immediately drew his gaze. It was the centerpiece of the room, stretching up to the grand ceiling. Floor-to-ceiling windows looked out to the lake and showed off a giant deck that appeared to surround the entire home. Truman felt as if he were indoors and outdoors at the same time.

"Nice home." *An understatement.*

The other man glanced back at him. "It is. Wait here and I'll get Christian." He pointed at a sitting area and then jogged up a curving wood staircase.

*Mercy would love this.*

*Actually, she'd say it was too big to maintain in an emergency. Although she'd like the remote location.*

Truman suddenly looked at the home with new eyes, wondering about power and heat for the home if society collapsed. He didn't know whether to appreciate or be annoyed that he viewed the world a bit differently since Mercy had come into his life.

But he could still acknowledge an incredible home.

The interior was ornate but welcoming and casual. The overstuffed furniture had been arranged to create several different seating areas that begged for conversation and friends and wine. Scents of coffee and cinnamon created a homey ambiance, softening the fact that the room was devoid of people. Except Truman.

Instead of sitting, he walked over to the tall windows and looked out at the lake. Standing closer, he realized they weren't just windows . . . they were glass panels that slid to the sides when the owner wished to open the entire back wall to the outdoors. *I'd love to see this during the summer.*

Footsteps sounded, and two men came down the stairs. Christian Lake was around forty and tall and clearly spent time in a gym, the muscle definition in his arms showing through his long-sleeved shirt. Truman wasn't one to judge another man's looks, but he suspected Mercy would do a double take if Christian Lake walked by. If the first guy looked like Jason Stratham, Lake resembled Ryan Reynolds.

Truman felt as if he were on a movie set.

Christian Lake's brown eyes were bloodshot, and he looked exhausted. He held out his hand to Truman. "I'm Christian, Chief Daly. I understand you found one of my vehicles?"

His handshake was solid and his gaze direct. The man Truman had met outside hovered several feet behind Christian, his arms loose at his sides, his gaze watchful and assessing. *Bodyguard?* He could easily hide a weapon under his heavy coat. Truman studied Christian Lake. *Why does this man need protection?*

"I found a black Lexus SUV registered to you out on Goose Hollow Road. It's been sitting there for a few days."

Christian briefly closed his eyes. "Oh crap. I loaned it to Rob Murray a while back. I'd forgotten with all the—" He turned to the man behind him. "Rollins, can you give Rob a call?" Christian looked back at Truman. "Was it wrecked?"

"No. It looked fine." *If I owned an SUV like that, I wouldn't loan it to anyone.*

Relief crossed Christian's face.

"I didn't call for a tow yet," Truman said. "I'll leave that to you since you seem to know what happened."

"I'll get to the bottom of this, but I'm surprised he'd just abandon it. That's not like him. I hope he's okay."

"He's a friend?" Truman asked.

"He works for me."

"No answer," Rollins said, sliding his phone into his pocket.

Frustration crossed Christian's face. "Do you mind taking care of the car?" he asked Rollins. "I've got an appointment in a few minutes." Rollins nodded, took a hard look at Truman, and then disappeared down a hallway on the other side of the stairs.

"Rollins works for you too?" Truman hadn't cared for Rollins's parting look. It'd warned him to toe the line.

"He does. Thanks for driving out here, Chief Daly. I know I'm out of your way."

"Do I need to look for your friend?"

Christian frowned. "I'll call him again later. I'm sure it's nothing. His car was having issues, so I loaned him mine for a few days. I've been distracted since—" The man looked away, swallowing hard.

Truman studied the bloodshot eyes and decided to ask the question that'd been ricocheting through his brain. "Are you related to Malcolm Lake?"

As Christian's face fell, Truman instantly wished he hadn't asked. "I'm sorry for your loss. I'd heard about his death, but I wasn't sure you were related."

"He was my father . . . and thank you."

Truman paused, wanting to ask if Christian was aware of the similarity between his father's death and Olivia Sabin's. *None of my business.* His gaze fell on a series of award plaques behind Christian on the wall. Even at this distance, he could see LAKE SKI AND SPORTS engraved in the metal.

"You're Lake Ski and Sports?" he blurted before thinking.

"Yes."

The protective actions of Rollins made a little more sense now. Christian Lake was a very, *very* wealthy man . . . although Truman had been clued into that fact as he drove up to the house. Truman had heard the owner of Lake Ski and Sports was developing a new type of ski that might rock the entire industry, along with several other new sports equipment–related improvements. He'd been hailed as an innovator by the media and condemned as a disrupter by manufacturers because his inventions threatened to make their products obsolete.

Lake was sort of a smaller-scale Bill Gates or Elon Musk of sporting goods.

Truman held out his hand, feeling he'd overstayed his welcome. "I'm sorry about your father."

"Thank you. I'll show you out." He led the way to the front door, giving Truman new mind-boggling views of the home's elaborate interior. Out front a huge covered porch overlooked the grounds. Even though it was covered in snow, Truman suspected the extensive property was perfectly landscaped. As he went down the steps, a small SUV came up the long drive and parked.

He blinked as Mercy stepped out of the back door on the driver's side. A dark-haired woman emerged from the passenger's side, and Eddie slammed the driver's door, instantly spotting Truman. "Hey, Truman!"

Christian Lake's appointment was with the FBI.

Truman glanced back at Christian, who now curiously eyed him.

*How can I convince them to let me sit in on their interview?*

Hiding her pleasure at unexpectedly running into Truman, Mercy introduced him to Ava as they stood in the snow in front of the giant cabin.

"I've heard a lot about you," the Portland FBI agent told him with a wink and warm grin.

Mercy elbowed her. "Stop it."

Truman's smile indicated he found Ava amusing.

"What are you doing here?" Mercy asked Truman.

He jerked his head toward a man who waited several yards away on the front porch. Christian Lake. He looked good. Long gone was the geek she'd worked with at the steak house. Now he was movie-star handsome. And rich.

*Will he remember me?*

"I found an abandoned car," Truman said. "Turned out to be his, so I came out to let him know about it."

Eddie eyed the big vehicle in front of the garage. "That old Hummer?"

"No. A Lexus SUV. It's still on the side of the road."

"Where is it?"

"Goose Hollow Road."

The three agents exchanged a glance. "Did he leave it there?" asked Ava. "Was it damaged?"

It was Truman's turn to frown. "No and no. He said he loaned it to an employee. Why?"

Mercy bit her lip. "We need to know where Christian has been for the last few days. An abandoned vehicle is interesting."

"I put together that he's Malcolm Lake's son. I didn't ask any questions about his father's death, but he's clearly upset about it," stated Truman. "And besides, the SUV is registered to him. If he thought he was hiding it, he's not very sharp," Truman said dryly.

Ava grinned at his comment and a spark of jealousy flared in Mercy's chest, catching her by surprise. She instantly let it go and enjoyed the signs that two of her favorite people might share the same sense of humor.

Truman said, "I assume you're here to talk about his father's murder?"

Ava and Eddie nodded.

"But why are you here?" Truman asked Mercy. "This isn't your case."

"I knew Christian. He grew up in Eagle's Nest and was a few years older than me. Ava is hoping I can get him to open up a bit more." *And I want to find Olivia's killer.*

"Christian wasn't cooperative on the phone," said Ava. "And he didn't go to Portland after being told about his father's death. I find that very odd."

Mercy knew Truman wanted to stick around. And by the inquisitive look on his face, he wouldn't mind listening in on Christian's interview, but there were no grounds for it. He reluctantly told them good-bye and drove off in the snow.

Ava watched him leave. "Truman's even better in person."

"Tell me about it," muttered Mercy, keenly feeling his departure.

"Mercy goes around moony eyed all the time," added Eddie.

Mercy glared at him. "You're the same way about that female friend of Jeff's."

He stiffened, a guilty look in his eyes behind the thick frames. "I don't know what you're talking about."

"Children," lectured Ava. "Behave. We've got work to do." She marched up the stairs and introduced herself to Christian Lake. She turned and introduced Eddie and then Mercy.

Christian shook her hand and blinked as he held her gaze. "Kilpatrick . . . *Mercy?*" A grin filled his face.

"Good to see you too, Christian. I'm sorry it's not under better circumstances."

"You're an FBI agent?" he exclaimed. *"You?"* He hadn't let go of her hand yet.

"And *you're* rich and famous," she emphasized. "I've followed your career. I still think of you as the line cook who constantly burned my orders."

"I was the epitome of a nerd. You were always kind to me, and I appreciated that," he said sincerely. He noticed he was still shaking her hand and let go, looking to Ava and Eddie. "I had a huge crush on Mercy back then. She was a cute young thing."

Mercy spotted Ava's smug grin. *I'm her secret weapon.* But Christian was sharp. He wouldn't share anything he didn't want to. He hadn't become this successful without learning a trick or two.

Three minutes later the four of them were seated at a dining room table for sixteen. Mercy had counted the chairs while trying not to gawk at the chandelier of wrought iron and glass. It had to be five feet tall and just as wide. Ava sat at the head of the table, taking charge of the interview as Mercy sized up this new Christian Lake.

He looked exhausted and as if he'd been hating life for days.

Exactly what she'd expected of someone whose father had been murdered.

"Why didn't you go to Portland when you got the news of your father's death?" Ava pulled no punches with her first question. She sat straight in her chair, her gaze focused on the son, her attitude all business.

Christian glanced down, his hands gripped together on the table before him. "My father and I have been estranged for a while."

"What happened?" Ava asked.

The son looked out the window, and Mercy followed his gaze to the picturesque lake that reflected the perfect blue of the sky. "It's an old story."

"I'd love to hear it," said the Portland agent.

Christian shifted in his chair. "My parents divorced when I was eight. It was pretty brutal and my father essentially left my mother for another woman. Of course, the relationship didn't last." He gave a satisfied smile. "But he'd moved to Portland and decided to stay. I'd hear from him occasionally. A card on my birthday. Crap like that. Twice during my teen years, he acted like he wanted to be back in my life. He'd call and write persistently for a month or two, but I hated him. I'd sworn never to speak with him, and I ignored him until after I finished college. I'd finally started to think maybe it was time for me to have an adult relationship with him. The hatred seemed so juvenile, and so we tentatively began to talk, even met for a beer a time or two. I kept those visits short. I was always civil, not ready to embrace him as family.

"But ten years ago, I received a sizable inheritance from my aunt . . . my father's sister. She'd hated what he did to my mother. She didn't have kids and left me the bulk of her estate—she left my father and my mother each a good amount too, but I got three-quarters of a twenty-million-dollar settlement. It didn't help my relationship with my father."

"That's a lot of money for someone in their twenties," commented Eddie.

Christian gave a wry grin. "It was, but I knew exactly what I wanted to do with it."

"Your father didn't like the split of the money?" Mercy asked.

"My mother didn't either because my aunt barely left any to my older brother, Gabriel. My mother—and brother—found it very unfair."

"Why didn't your brother get the same amount?" Ava asked.

Christian shrugged. "She liked me best. She was the type to play favorites. I always thought it was a good thing she didn't have kids. My father was furious when he heard how I was planning to spend that inheritance. He considered it a slap in my aunt's face to invest all her money in something doomed to fail. So again, we were no longer on speaking terms."

"You bought the sporting goods stores," Eddie stated.

Christian's smile was strained. "I found the struggling store here in Bend and saw it as the stepping stone to my dream. My father said I would go bankrupt."

"And you remained estranged because your father didn't agree with your goals?" Mercy sympathized, her father's face prominent in her mind.

"He's rather stubborn," stated Christian. "I guess I am too."

*Touché.*

"It got to the point where we were both simply acting out of pride." A sheepish look crossed his face. "My determination to make the stores successful and prove him wrong was one of my biggest motivations. I wouldn't be where I am today if I hadn't been driven by his lack of confidence."

Mercy nodded, wondering if she would have gone into law enforcement if her father hadn't been so antigovernment.

*I didn't select my career to shove it in his face.*

She was proud of who she'd become. Part of her was also pleased to show him that she hadn't grown horns while working for the FBI.

"Where were you the night your father was murdered?" Ava asked.

Christian took a deep breath. "I fully expected you to ask that question, but I've got to say . . . even being prepared, it still hits me in the chest like a bullet." He looked straight at Ava. "I was here. I haven't left Bend in two weeks. Next you'll want an alibi?"

Ava nodded.

Christian winced. "All I have for an alibi is Brent Rollins. He lives on the grounds and manages the estate. I didn't see him that night, but he's usually aware of my comings and goings. Ask him."

"He lives in this house?" Eddie asked.

"No, he lives in one of the cabins about a hundred yards east of here. They're blocked by the trees, so he may have not seen that I was home that night."

Ava made a notation on her pad. "I know you said you're estranged, but do you have any idea who'd kill your father?"

The son shook his head. "I don't. When I heard about it, I assumed it was a random break-in or else related to one of his cases. I haven't talked to him about his cases in a long time, but I know he's put away some very angry people. I'm sorry, but I don't recall any specifics."

"We're looking into his cases," Eddie said.

"Do you know Olivia Sabin?" Ava asked.

"No, I don't think I know the name," Christian answered, his gaze holding Ava's.

*He hesitated.* Mercy swore a small flash of surprise had lit his eyes. *He knows who she is.*

"Why?" he asked. "Is she a suspect?"

"No," Ava stated. "She was murdered the night after your father. In a very similar manner."

*There's that flash again.*

"That's horrible." Christian looked nauseated. "Was she a neighbor or a friend of his?"

"Neither." Ava didn't expand.

Silence filled the room. Christian looked expectantly from Ava to Eddie and finally to Mercy. She bit her tongue, knowing Ava had a reason for her questions and explanations.

"But you think it's related to my father's death," Christian finally stated.

"We're considering that possibility." Ava's answer was vague.

"Is there evidence from her death that could help find my father's killer?" he asked.

"We're still collecting and examining the evidence." Another non-committal reply.

Frustration briefly filled his features. "I hope you can find who did this." The look in his eyes told Mercy he knew the FBI was deliberately not giving him clear answers. "It doesn't matter that we parted on bad terms. That was a horrible way to die. I don't wish that on anyone."

# THIRTEEN

Truman strode from his office to the pizza parlor, his stomach growling. He'd offered to pick up a pizza and meet for dinner at Mercy's apartment. It was just past five o'clock and he glared into the dark sky. He was ready for the sun to stick around longer each day. The early darkness made him crave his bed by 7:00 p.m., and then he *still* had to drive to work in the dark the next morning. But the idea of hot and melty pizza with Mercy and Kaylie cheered him up.

Eagle's Nest was quiet. A few cars cruised through the city, no doubt heading home, their drivers thinking about dinner just as he was. The only open shops were the pizza parlor and the diner. Just ahead of him a car turned into the pizza place's parking lot. He automatically looked at the rear of the vehicle, reading the plate and the make of the car.

Subaru. It was dark green.

Bolton had told him Salome Sabin drove a green Subaru Forester.

The car pulled into a space under a light in the lot and parked. The driver opened her door but stayed seated for a moment, focused on something in her lap.

His heart pounding, he crossed the lot, unable to look away from the car, worried that it would drive off before he got there. He walked around the rear of the vehicle and stopped several feet from the driver's open door, not wanting to spook the woman. "Excuse me?" he asked. "Do you need help with something?"

The startled woman glanced at him and grabbed her door to yank it shut, but then she spotted the cloth police badge on the front of his winter coat and froze. Her gaze went to his cowboy hat, back to the badge, and then to his face. Her expression cleared as she decided he wasn't a threat.

Salome Sabin stepped out of the green car. She was dressed in jeans, hiking boots, and a black jacket with a wide fur collar. Her long hair rested on her shoulders, nearly as dark as the fur. The sultry gaze from his memories blazed in front of him. She was older than he remembered and still as beautiful. A mesmerizing power radiated from her confidence and the angle of her chin. "I'm fine, Officer. I don't need anything." She tilted her head, her gaze traveling up his body, a small smile curving her lips.

"Are you Salome Sabin?" he asked, knowing the answer.

Caution shut down her confidence, and she drew back, dark eyes suspicious. "Why?"

"Have you been home today?"

"Why? Why would you ask me that?"

Truman searched for a gentle way to break the news to her. There wasn't one. "There was an incident at your home yesterday. Your mother was murdered."

Her hand went to her neck. "Morrigan?" she croaked, stepping back and bumping into her car.

"Your daughter wasn't hurt. She's absolutely fine." Truman cursed himself for not stating that immediately.

"What happened?" she whispered. Panic had replaced her assurance, and her breaths deepened. She swallowed multiple times, trying to keep her control.

"We're not sure." *I shouldn't be the one informing her.* He moved closer and placed a hand on her shoulder, his heart splitting at the devastation on her face. "I'm very sorry for your loss." *Useless words.*

"Where is she? Where's Morrigan?" Tears started down her cheeks. "Where's my mother?" She grabbed the front of his jacket, terror stiffening her posture.

"Morrigan is staying with a foster family—"

"No! I want her with me." Anger blazed in her eyes. *"Not strangers!"*

"It's a good place," Truman started. "One of the FBI agents went and—"

*"FBI? Why the FBI?"*

He paused, rattled and scrambling for the right words. "Your mother's death resembles the murder of a Portland judge—"

*"Who?"*

"Judge Malcolm Lake, he's—"

Salome whirled away and bent over. Her hands clutched her abdomen and she dry heaved, her long hair hiding her face. The retching sounds froze Truman in place. *I fucked this up.* He should have delivered the news in a softer way. And not blurted out the name of another victim.

*Stupid.*

He carefully placed a hand on her back, uncomfortable with touching the distraught woman, and his brain blank of words of comfort. "Let me try to get you in to see Morrigan tonight." It was the first option he could think of to calm her.

Turning back to him, Salome brushed her hair out of her face and wiped her dry mouth. Her eyes were wet and angry. Very angry. "She's *my* daughter. You damned well will let me see her! I want her out of there tonight! She should be home with me!" Her face paled. "My home . . ."

"You should find a hotel tonight." Truman glanced at her car. "The investigators have been trying to reach you. Where have you been?"

Salome briefly closed her eyes, regret speeding across her features. "I lost my Goddamned phone. *Fuck!* I thought I'd be okay without it for a few days." She turned a fierce gaze on him, her shoulders squared.

"Get me to my daughter. *Now.*"

A series of lengthy calls to Mercy, Ava, and the foster mom landed Truman the address of Morrigan's foster home.

"She has the right to see her daughter," he'd argued to Ava when she stated she wanted to interview Salome first. The protective heat in Salome's eyes had reminded him of Mercy's attitude about her niece. You don't get between a mother and her child.

"Fine," Ava finally said. "But we're going to meet you there. I want to talk to Salome *tonight.*"

Truman wondered how the FBI would interview Salome with her daughter present, but it wasn't his problem. Right now his goal was to reunite the mother with Morrigan. Salome was beside herself, agitated that her daughter was not in her sight. She couldn't hold still, pacing in the parking lot, monitoring his conversations, and alternating between tears and anger.

Between his phone calls, she had peppered him with questions about Olivia's death, unhappy with his lack of knowledge. He'd offered to drive her to the foster home, believing she shouldn't be behind the wheel at that emotional moment, but Salome had surprised him. She abruptly locked down her emotions and turned her energy to reuniting with her daughter. "What's done is done," she'd stated. "I'll get details about my mother later. Right now the only thing I can change is my daughter's location. And you can be damned sure that is happening *tonight.*"

The drive to the home took fifteen minutes. He parked in front of the foster home and checked his rearview mirror. Salome's car was right behind him.

She darted out of her vehicle and raced up the driveway before Truman could open his door. *Shit!*

She rang the doorbell and beat on the door several times. He caught up and grasped her upper arm, stopping the pounding. "Hang on. You're going to terrify the mother. Not to mention the kids."

"Don't put your hands on me!" She jerked her arm out of his grasp and he backed up, both hands in the air.

"Sorry! I'm just trying to slow you down."

Outrage flamed on her face. "Don't touch me again!"

"Yell at me all you want, but have some respect for the family watching your daughter," he snapped. "These are good people. They don't deserve your anger."

She froze, staring at him, and her expression cleared as she looked away. "I don't like people touching me," she said in a calmer voice.

"Understood."

The door opened two inches, stopped by a chain, and a woman's cautious eyes studied them. Truman pulled out his badge. "Hannah? I spoke to you on the phone. I'm Chief Daly. Sorry about the pounding."

She closed the door and released the chain. Opening it wider, she sized up Salome with one hard look. "You're lucky my toddler wasn't sleeping."

"I'm very sorry," Salome said, trying to look over the woman's shoulder. "I need to see Morrigan."

*"Mama?"*

Hannah was pushed aside as Morrigan darted out the door and flung herself at her mother, wrapping her arms around her waist. Salome exhaled as she held her daughter, closing her eyes and burying her face in her daughter's hair, murmuring words of comfort over and over. Hannah watched the pair with a small smile on her lips, but her eyes were sad.

Truman understood. He was relieved to reunite the pair, but there were a lot of questions to be answered and the murder of Olivia to face.

The next few days wouldn't be easy for the two of them. Maybe even months.

Three car doors slammed behind them. Salome was caught up in her daughter and didn't turn around.

But Truman did. His heart sped up at the sight of Mercy but faltered as he spotted the determined look on Agent McLane's face. Nothing would get in the way of her questioning the mother.

*Salome didn't answer when I asked where she'd been.*

*Will she tell the FBI?*

Two minutes later he had his answer. Salome refused an interview, stating she needed to be alone with her daughter and demanding to contact her lawyer first. The three FBI agents weren't happy.

"We're trying to find out who murdered your mother." Eddie tried to reason with her.

"*I know.* But nothing I tell you tonight is going to make any difference. *She's dead.*" Salome glanced down with a guilty look, seeing Morrigan, who was listening and watching. "Right now I want to find a hotel room. Tomorrow I'll tell you everything you want."

"Mama, that lady was with Grandma." Morrigan pointed at Mercy.

Salome gave Mercy a sharp look. "What do you mean?" she asked her daughter.

"I was there the night your mother died," Mercy said softly.

Truman shifted his feet. This wasn't a conversation to have on a front porch. With a child present.

"What do you mean you were there?" Salome's focus zoomed in on Mercy. "What were you doing in my home?"

"She helped me. And she helped Grandma." Morrigan's voice quivered as she shot anxious looks between her mother and Mercy.

"Let's do this somewhere else," stated Ava.

"*Tomorrow.*"

Truman knew nothing would change Salome's mind. Her chin was up, her voice full of steel.

Silence hung over the porch.

Hannah broke the tension. "I'll get Morrigan's things." She closed the door behind her, leaving the tense group outside in the cold.

Truman didn't blame her.

"All right," Ava agreed. "Let's get you into a hotel and then meet first thing in the morning."

Salome nodded. "Agreed."

Suspicion prickled at the base of Truman's skull. *I don't believe she'll be helpful.* He glanced at Mercy, who was studying the woman, her lips pressed together.

She didn't either.

# FOURTEEN

Eddie marched into Mercy's office the next morning. "They're gone."

She didn't need to ask who he meant. "Completely gone?"

"Her car's gone and the hotel room is empty. Ava is furious."

"I suspected Salome wouldn't answer any questions, but I didn't know she'd split," admitted Mercy. "I thought she'd lawyer up."

"We put out another BOLO on her car. We'll find her."

"I don't understand why she'd leave when we need her help to find out who killed her mother," began Mercy. "Does she suspect someone? Why not tell us? What are we missing?"

"We're missing everything because we haven't found any damned answers!" Eddie paced in front of her desk. "I don't know whether to be relieved or angry that she took Morrigan."

"She won't harm her daughter."

"She's making things worse for herself. No judge is going to appreciate her taking the child," Eddie muttered.

"It's her kid," Mercy pointed out. "And Salome wasn't under arrest."

"Still pisses me off. Two people are dead and Salome was the best lead we've had."

"I saw a desperate mother last night," Mercy told him. "Whatever is going on, she believes she's doing the right thing for Morrigan."

"The right thing is to help us solve her mother's murder. This doesn't put her in a good light."

Mercy agreed. By running, Salome made herself look guilty. "I can't believe she'd kill her mother."

"Make no assumptions."

He was right.

Eddie's phone rang. "How come Truman calls me more than you these days?" he asked before taking the call.

Mercy watched with interest as he answered.

"Mercy's here too," Eddie said into the phone. "Can I put you on speaker?" He touched the screen of his phone and moved closer to her desk, holding out the phone so she could hear.

"Hey, darling." Truman's voice was warm, sending good shivers up her spine. He'd stayed the night with her and left before the sun came up. She'd woken in an empty bed, the scent of him on the pillow next to her.

"I thought this was a business call," drawled Eddie, giving Mercy a meaningful look.

"It is." Truman switched to his all-business voice. "David Aguirre reported a break-in at the church last night."

"Was anything stolen?" asked Mercy.

"He doesn't think so. He's still looking. Frankly, I don't think there's much worth stealing in there."

"Then how did he know there was a break-in?"

"Broken window. Open door."

"Why are you telling us this, Truman?" Eddie asked.

"Because a neighbor reported that they saw a dark-green vehicle at the church around two a.m. And they swear it was driven by a woman with long, dark hair. The description reminded me of Salome Sabin."

Eddie and Mercy stared at each other. *Why would Salome break into a church?*

"Did you know Salome took off overnight?" Eddie asked.

Truman's curse was loud. "Did she take Morrigan?"

"Yes," Mercy said. "But why would she stop at the church? That sounds like a big risk to take. Did you tell David that the driver might be Salome?"

"No, I kept that to myself. I called Eddie so he could include it in her interview this morning, but I guess that won't be happening."

"This makes no sense," complained Eddie. "Why the church?"

"Oh . . ." Truman started to speak and then stopped.

"What is it?" Mercy asked.

"I talked with David Aguirre yesterday. I was looking for some information on . . . witchcraft." Embarrassment filled his tone. "David told me Olivia Sabin came to see him several years ago."

Amused by Truman's interest in an unusual element of the case, Mercy leaned across her desk, wanting to be closer to the phone. "And?"

"Olivia was worried about Salome. She didn't like the way her daughter was behaving."

Ava strode into Mercy's office. "What's this about Salome?" She'd adopted the Bend office's casual dress code, wearing jeans, a thick sweater, and boots.

Although Eddie had described Ava as furious, she projected a perfect image of calm control. Eddie brought Ava up to speed on Truman's phone call.

Her eyes turned thoughtful as she weighed the new information. "I think it's time I see the Sabins' home. I had Deschutes County go check on the house once I found out Salome had split, but no one was there. They've watched the home part of the time, but they couldn't keep someone there nonstop. She might have stopped in before she left." She studied Mercy. "I want you to come with us. Walk Eddie and me through what happened out there the night of the murder."

"No problem," Mercy replied as she swallowed hard, visions of Olivia's death rushing her thoughts.

*Am I ready to return to the place where I watched a woman die?*

Mercy drove her Tahoe with Ava in the seat next to her and Eddie in the back. The sun had risen in the southeast against a brilliant blue sky, and Ava couldn't pull her gaze from the landscape, raving several times about the snow-covered trees and pristine white fields. Unease sat low in Mercy's stomach, twisting and turning. As they drew closer to the turnoff to the Sabins' home, she felt as if she'd been called to the principal's office.

She abruptly realized her anxiety wasn't from returning to the crime scene. It was from the fact that they were close to her own cabin. Eddie and Ava both knew she owned a cabin, but they didn't know what she did there. They didn't know she could live there indefinitely if the nation's power, water, and food supplies vanished. They didn't know she spent all her free time stocking supplies and expanding her resources.

Only Kaylie and Truman knew her secret.

*Why am I still hiding it?*

It wasn't odd for people in Central Oregon to be prepared. It'd been a bigger deal when she lived in Portland and drove over nearly every weekend to work at her cabin. Back in Portland people rarely had enough groceries to get through a week. Power outages made them huddle in their cold homes, waiting out the temporary inconvenience, confident in the utilities to eventually restore life to normal. Portlanders wouldn't understand.

*If I talked about it, people out here would comprehend.*

But discussing her plans went against everything she'd been taught.

Telling people that she was prepared for the end of the world would send them scrambling to her place in case of an emergency. Growing up, she'd been taught to be tight-lipped with her friends, never to discuss her family's wealth of stores and equipment. Even though her family were known as preppers around Eagle's Nest, no one knew the extent of their preparations. This was where a hard-to-find location and a solid defense were important. The driveway to her parents' home was easy to miss; that was on purpose. Weapons skills were taught at an early age to protect their supplies. A plan was always in place.

Preparation.

"We're sitting in a palace," her father had said. "But few people know exactly where. You can be certain that when the world goes to hell, they'll come looking for us. We need to be ready to defend our home. We take care of our own."

*A selfish philosophy.*

But a little voice inside her head agreed. She couldn't feed and protect everyone.

Her father had a small circle of people who subscribed to his beliefs, ready to have one another's back in time of need. Each person brought a valuable skill to the exclusive community. Midwifery, livestock health, plumbing, electronics, medicine. He didn't have room or patience for useless people.

Mercy's knuckles grew white as she gripped the steering wheel. *We're just going to the Sabins'.* No one knew where her cabin was.

She spotted the area where she'd nearly hit Morrigan. Her tire tracks were still on the snowy shoulder. She stopped the SUV and pointed. "That's where Morrigan ran out in the road." She squinted, peering into the dense forest. "I see our footprints heading toward the home. Without following those, I couldn't find it on my own."

Ava and Eddie studied the road and forest. "How far is the house from here?" Ava asked.

"A few minutes straight through the forest or ten minutes by road."

"Take the road."

Mercy drove on. That night she'd been headed in the opposite direction, coming from her cabin. Discomfort weighed heavily on Mercy as she continued to drive in the direction of her secret. Even though she watched carefully, she almost missed the turnoff to the Sabin home.

"Wow. I thought you were accidentally driving off the road," said Ava. "I never would have spotted that turn."

They spent the next several minutes bouncing along the rutted tracks. She crossed her fingers she wouldn't meet any other vehicles on the narrow road, because there was little room to pass. The knot of anxiety in her stomach loosened as she drew closer to the Sabin home.

"That's it."

The little house. The barn and corrals. Mercy looked at the home with fresh eyes, acknowledging some of the smart decisions at the property. The area was well cleared of brush and trees, leaving a good margin between the home and forest in case of fire. She spotted a pump house she hadn't noticed before and a group of fruit trees close to the forest. Goats bleated from the barn. She knew the county sheriff had fed the animals but wondered how long that would continue. Farm animals took consistent maintenance.

There were no animals at Mercy's hideaway. She hadn't bought any because her job could keep her from visiting for several weeks. She had plans for pens and some animal sheds, and her long-term plans included goats and chickens. No pigs. She'd debated buying cows but couldn't see herself handling the slaughter. Goats made milk and chickens made protein and she could manage them on her own.

*Will I be alone?*

She knew Truman had spotted her home sale flyers a few nights earlier. He hadn't asked any questions, and she didn't know how she felt about that.

Common sense said she needed a bigger place. Emotions said she should include Truman in the decision making. *But it's my house. I have to make my own path. I can't make decisions based on hopes for our relationship.*

She put the dilemma out of her thoughts, refocusing on their visit.

"Peaceful out here," commented Ava. "I guess this works for people who want to be left alone."

*Exactly.*

"I don't think we'll be able to tell if Salome has been here," said Eddie. "Look at all these tire treads."

"I need to see the scene anyway," said Ava. "This is definitely different than the site of the judge's murder. He lived in a house that overlooked the city. Damn thing sits on stilts on the steep slopes along the west side of Portland. Stunning views, but I wouldn't be able to sleep, terrified the house would slide down the hill or collapse in an earthquake."

Mercy knew the exact area Ava described. She'd peered up as she drove along the city's freeways, wondering who dared to live in such precarious settings. The prices had to be in the millions of dollars.

A sharp contrast to the tired home before them.

They exited the vehicle and tramped through the packed snow to the house. Mercy remembered dashing after Morrigan across a yard of untouched snow. Now hundreds of footprints marred the scene.

"We're good to go in," Ava said, removing the crime tape crossing the door.

The smell of blood was still strong. Mercy touched her nose, wanting to cover it with her hand. Instead she focused on the details of the home that she'd been too rattled to notice that night. Photos of Morrigan hung in the living room. She stepped closer, a smile hovering at her lips at the sight of the happy child. Beside Morrigan's pictures was a woven wall hanging of three feminine figures, simple silhouettes showing three generations of females. Small, medium, and large. Scanning the home, Mercy noticed two similar sculptures of a trio of feminine shapes.

Ava noticed the same. "Cute. Three generations of women who live in the same house."

Eddie cleared his throat. "The feminine trio is a revered symbol in Wicca."

Mercy and Ava both looked at him. *Wicca?*

He shrugged his shoulders. "Am I the only one who did the reading? With the constant stories of these women being witches, I did some digging into the subject. Based on the interviews I've looked over and what I read in the evidence reports, I suspect they are into Wicca, not witchcraft."

Ava's gaze narrowed on him. "What's the difference?"

Olivia's death chants whispered in Mercy's ears.

"Depends who you ask. The lines between the two are blurry. I read a lot of different opinions, but what I primarily gathered is that Wicca is a spiritual practice and focuses on an individual relationship with the divine. There's a lot of emphasis on the feminine." He glanced around the house. "Wiccans are big fans of nature. They bring it into their homes and seek harmony with it." He pointed at several collections of greenery and candles that Mercy had written off as leftover Christmas decor. "Those are pretty fresh and there's no holiday theme to the candles. It looks like something with a permanent place in the home."

Mercy silently agreed. "The crafts in the barn also have strong nature elements."

"So what's it mean for us?" Ava asked, stepping closer to look at the candles. "There's a history of visitors seeking magical help, right? Could we be dealing with an angry customer who didn't get their desired results?"

"A lot of Wiccans don't cast spells. It's more about appreciating the gifts of nature."

"There are spells attached to bags of herbs out in the barn," Mercy pointed out.

"I suspect they were simply taking advantage of people's misconceptions. If someone asked if I could help them find love and offered me cash, I'd make something up." He indicated a worn spot in the rug. "Especially if I needed money."

"What exactly is the feminine trio thing?" Ava asked.

Eddie rubbed his chin. "I don't quite remember. Something about a moon goddess who is made up of a crone, a mother, and a maiden."

*Olivia, Salome, and Morrigan.* "How much reading did you do?" Mercy was duly impressed.

"Not much. Trust me, I'm no expert."

"How does it all tie to a judge in Portland?" muttered Ava. She wandered down the hall and halted as she looked through a doorway, her shoulders suddenly tense.

Mercy felt the knot in her gut tighten. *I know what's in there.* Ava looked over her shoulder at Mercy, her eyes gentle. "Can you talk me through this?"

Nodding, she joined Ava and tucked her emotions behind a brick wall and recited what she remembered. The blanket that had covered Olivia was gone. So were the pillows. A square of fabric had been cut out of the chair, and a large section of the rug was missing. Black fingerprint dust splotched every surface. Hanging on the wall was another feminine trio silhouette. Mercy looked at it with new understanding and then noticed that candles sat on several surfaces. She wondered if they were for worship, not light.

The three of them stood in silence as Mercy gazed at the blood-soaked chair. *I hope your pain is gone, Olivia.*

After a few respectful moments, Ava asked to see the room of knives. Mercy led the way.

"Are knives common in Wicca, Eddie?" Mercy asked as she watched Ava's eyes widen at the huge array of blades.

"I remember some mention of knives, but I don't think it is a huge element." He leaned close to study an elaborate handle. "This is an insane collection. The photos didn't do it justice."

Ava's sharp gaze traveled over the shelves of glass jars, her lips pressed in a tight line. "Nothing came back as poisonous so far, but they haven't checked all the samples. I understand Morrigan was the one who mentioned poison on the blades?"

"That's correct," Mercy said.

"I'd like to know where the murder weapon ended up," Ava said. "And determine if the same blade was used on the judge."

"Have the medical examiners given an opinion on that?" Mercy asked.

Regret crossed Ava's face. "All they can say is that it's inconclusive . . . but that doesn't rule it out." She exhaled. "Show me the barn."

Relief and light filled Mercy as she stepped out of the home. An overwhelming sense of sadness had permeated the air inside the house, and she wondered if Salome and Morrigan would ever live in the home again. *If it'd been my mother, I couldn't.* But perhaps Salome had no other options. Mercy slid open the barn door and welcomed its rush of scents; they were the smells of the living. Hay, animals, dirt, and even manure. The atmosphere of life soothed her after the deathly air of the house.

*If this is the reverence Wiccans feel for nature, I understand.*

The pygmy goats pressed their noses between the boards, begging for attention, and Mercy was pleased to see a pile of fresh alfalfa and some grain in a low trough. Ava leaned over the pen wall to scratch eager heads, delight on her face. "Gosh, they're cute."

Mercy moved closer to pet one and caught her breath, staring at the black goat. It had a pink bow tied around one ear. Two days earlier Mercy had watched another goat yank the bow off its ear, and Morrigan had rolled her eyes in exasperation because she'd just tied it on. When they'd left the barn, the ribbon had been draped over the rail, out of the reach of the goats.

"They were here," she announced, unable to pull her gaze off the cheerful black goat nuzzling Ava's hand.

"How do you know?" Eddie asked, and Mercy shared her story of sitting in the pen with Morrigan and the goats.

"I don't think any of the county deputies would bother to tie a bow on the goat's ear," she pointed out.

Ava agreed, turning to study the rest of the barn. "What did Salome and Morrigan do here in the middle of the night? No doubt they also went in the house. I couldn't tell anyone had entered since it was sealed up."

"I bet Salome sent Morrigan to the barn, keeping her out of the home," said Mercy. "Especially once she saw the crime scene tape."

"Where's the workroom with the little elf houses?" Eddie asked.

Mercy led the way, not surprised that Salome had been to the property. *No doubt she waited until she saw the deputies leave.*

She stepped back and gestured for Eddie and Ava to enter the workroom, enjoying their exclamations at the sights. Mercy was pleased the houses hadn't been disturbed by the evidence teams. The small row of knives had been removed, but no black powder covered the miniature works of art on the shelves.

"I heard the officers got light-headed in here," Ava said. "Anyone notice anything?"

They all inhaled deeply, looking from one to another.

Mercy felt nothing. And judging by the other faces, they didn't either.

"Huh," said Ava. "Something must have been stirred up in here at that time. Seems okay now."

"Morrigan said she sells these houses, right?" Eddie asked. "Where are her records of sales? How does she advertise them? Or does she take them somewhere to sell? It might be a good starting place to track her movements."

"Good points, Eddie," agreed Ava. "There wasn't a computer in the house, so I bet she keeps a laptop with her." She snapped her fingers. "What about Etsy? That online store where people sell their crafts? This stuff is perfect to sell on there. I bet she has a storefront on the website . . . or maybe on a similar site." Speculation gleamed in her eyes. "Would the Portland computer forensics lab be able to pinpoint a location she accessed her storefront from? You know . . . like see the IP address if she signed in on another Wi-Fi?"

Mercy and Eddie exchanged a look. "I have no idea," admitted Mercy. "That's a question for the computer guys. They intimidate the hell out of me. I never know if they're going to laugh at my question and tell me I watch too many movies, or roll their eyes because I have the computer knowledge of an eighth grader."

"I suspect you just insulted a lot of eighth graders," Eddie added.

Mercy didn't disagree.

The three of them left the craft room and stopped to scratch goat heads on their way out of the barn. Outside they paused and considered the property one last time. "Gorgeous," Ava said under her breath as she looked up at the snowy pines against the blue sky. "But too damned isolated for me . . . and that's saying a lot. I like my alone time."

"I'm with you," Eddie added. Mercy said nothing.

"Mercy, how far away is your cabin?" Ava asked. "You were headed back to town, right?" Ava smiled as she asked the question, but Mercy felt as if she were in an interrogation spotlight.

"It's about ten minutes in the other direction."

"I'd love to see it. Is it as quiet as this place?"

Her stomach churned. "I think we should head to the office. There's not much to see and yes, it's very quiet. As isolated as this home." She wasn't ready to share her secret.

"Why were you driving so late?" Ava asked.

"Because I arrived at the cabin late. That evening was the first chance I'd had to check the place since the last snowstorm. I did what I needed to do, made certain the snow hadn't caused any damage, and left. I didn't plan to stay overnight." She steadied her breathing.

"Morrigan was lucky that night," Eddie said.

"Definitely," agreed Ava.

They trudged across the snow toward her Tahoe, and Mercy stepped across the multiple ruts left by the law enforcement vehicles. A dozen different tire treads were imprinted in the snow. Wide ones and thin ones, mostly with large snow-eating treads to grip unplowed roads. She lifted a boot to step into the widest one and stopped, her foot in midair. "Wait a minute," she said. "Don't move."

Ava and Eddie obeyed and then looked at her expectantly.

Mercy looked at the tracks to her left and to her right, her confidence building. "Look at this track." She pointed to the one she'd nearly stepped in. "It's huge. And I crossed its mate several steps back."

"That's a wide vehicle," Eddie agreed. "Must be one of the evidence vans."

"No," Mercy disagreed. "Those vans are probably narrower than my Tahoe. This vehicle is *wide*."

"Christian Lake's Hummer," stated Ava.

"That's my first thought too," Mercy said.

Eddie looked from Mercy to Ava and back to the tracks. "Let's not jump to conclusions," he said slowly. "Those tracks could have been made by a lot of different vehicles." His tone lacked conviction.

"I knew Christian was lying when he said he didn't know the Sabins." Mercy's mind spun with possibilities. "This track overlaps nearly all the other ones. He's been here recently."

Ava had her phone in hand. "I'll get an evidence team out here to take a mold of the tracks. Then I'll ask Christian to let us print his tires."

"He won't agree to that. Get a warrant first," Mercy said. "And you can't make a call out here. You'll have to wait until we go down the road a few miles."

"Crap." Ava pocketed her phone. "Warrants take time. I've found asking the owner for permission works a lot faster." She batted her eyelashes. "People don't like saying no to me. We'll get a warrant if he refuses me."

Mercy studied the deep tracks again.

*Why was Christian Lake at the Sabins'?*

# FIFTEEN

I had to run.

I had no choice. All my life my mother warned me, and now it had started.

I will not let him harm Morrigan. She is my heart, my soul, my everything. My sole focus is to protect my daughter.

The fact that she physically exists outside my body is one of the miracles of motherhood. How can she run and play in my sight when she is part of me? When I feel every heartbeat, every scraped knee, every moment of her joy?

She is my daughter and I will protect her with my dying breath.

As my mother did for her.

I'll never know why Morrigan didn't wake as my mother was murdered. I suspect my mother muted the noises, both hers and the murderer's, and then blurred his vision to the sight of my daughter sleeping in her bed.

There is a hole in my heart from my mother's absence, but I've shut down everything and refuse to dwell on her death. Later I will mourn and say good-bye in the way I was taught. But not now. My emotions are numb, my thoughts shocked into a protective vault. I can't think about her murder if I am to function.

Instead I remember our past.

All my life we lived in the woods. I hated it.

*"One day you'll understand,"* my mother told me. *"One day you'll thank me for saving you."*

*"Saving me from what?"* I'd cry. *"You keep talking about this person who will ruin our lives, but you won't tell me who it is! You make us live in fear of a ghost!"*

*"Right now we are protected. In the future that might change, and we'll need to hide."*

*"We are hiding! Everyone thinks you're a witch and that I am your cursed spawn."*

That is when I'd start to cry. I hated our life, I hated her, and I dreamed of her death.

If she was dead, I'd be able to live as I pleased, see who I wanted, be normal.

But it wasn't that simple.

When I was young, she taught me to read and write at home while I longed to sit in a classroom with other children. We shopped in the bigger, more crowded towns and stores, blending in with the crowds. I stared at the children who ran through the stores, laughter ringing in their voices. I wanted to be like them, play with them, talk to them. I grew up believing our seclusion was normal, but as I became a teenager, I demanded freedom and she relaxed some rules. She allowed me to get my driver's license and enroll in high school.

I went to school with enthusiasm, convinced my life would change. I would have friends and confidants and be normal. Instead high school was a foreign land. The students stared, pointed at my clothes, and snickered at my shoes. The girls hated me, but the boys wouldn't stop looking. Their gazes were different from the girls'.

I liked the stares from the boys. I was noticed.

So I manipulated the attention, learned how to foster it, how to tease them, how to make them pant after me like dogs.

Outside the woods my eyes were opened to how money ruled society. Money bought you beauty, big houses, and cars. Our family's lack of money was a painful, glaring sun in my eyes.

My mother always managed to get by. We had food, a solid roof, a dependable car, and what she believed were enough clothes. She ran a small business out of our home, taking advantage of society's darkest desires.

Her clients were satisfied, and they always came back for more.

I watched through cracks from behind doors, ordered to keep out of sight. The female visitors spoke in high voices and laughed too often, their gazes darting to every corner of the room, rarely looking my mother in the eye. They joked that they didn't believe in my mother's arts, but in their eyes I saw their desperation. They wanted beauty, love, and eternal youth. They wanted to know their futures. Their greed compelled them to take risks and enter our strange house, speak to a so-called witch, and hand over their cash for my mother's concoctions.

I could smell and feel the air pressure change with their entrance, showing me their true intent. I thought everyone could smell emotions . . . It was like smelling a color. Blues smelled fresh and felt light. Reds spicy and heavy. Greens damp and mellow. People emoted colors and changes in the air; I read them. It was that simple. Later I learned this was my special gift.

Some tried not to pay for my mother's wares. Usually it was the men. Their discomfort showed in different ways, but men were just as easy to read. They were scornful and belittling, hating that they'd stooped to what they considered unnatural. But they had the same desperation in their eyes as the women. They wanted their cancer to go away, money to fall in their laps, and a woman to worship them.

My mother knew how to make her clients believe in her. Image was the first step, she told me. She dressed in brightly colored long flowing dresses and grew her wavy hair to her waist. It didn't gray until she was sixty, and then it happened rapidly. I swear in one month her hair changed from solid black to silver. She looked the part and spoke the part, her voice low and melodious, her words sometimes foreign. The buyers ate it up.

I watched, learning body and facial language from the visitors. I knew how to spot fear, distrust, desperation, sorrow, and wariness without a word from their lips. Physical cues. The twitch of fingers. The set of the lips. The hesitation in a step. The picking at skin. Humans told their stories without speaking.

Later I used these skills for my own benefit.

I recognized Truman in the pizza parlor's parking lot. I can't place him, but I know we've . . . been involved. It must be long ago since the memory is fuzzy. There have been too many men over the years, and their faces blur together. I feel unclean when I meet their gazes in a store. The recognition flashes and they quickly look away, a flush creeping up their necks. Often there is a woman at their side. Her gaze is usually dismissive or locks on me with hatred.

*I'm sorry you married such a weak man.*

Truman didn't look away. Compassion shone in his words and eyes. Perhaps he doesn't remember me.

I can't stop staring at my daughter as she sleeps. For the moment we are safe. Her bed is warm, the room is secure, and we have food.

But how long can we hide?

He killed the judge. That was how I knew it was him.

When Truman first told me of my mother's death, I denied the possibility that her warnings had come true, telling myself it couldn't be him. We knew her business had dangers. My mother risked her life every time she sold a spell or told someone's future. We both knew that if someone physically attacked, we could be hurt or killed. She wouldn't allow guns in the house for our protection. Another root of our fights.

But when Truman said the judge's name, I knew my mother's fears had become truth, and my body physically rejected his words. Everything she'd warned me of was in motion. No one could protect me from him. He was too powerful, too connected.

I had to run.

# SIXTEEN

Truman couldn't sit idly by. Curiosity about the two murders was driving him insane.

Feeling like a spy, he'd looked up Rob Murray, the employee who had borrowed the Lexus, and decided to pay him a visit. After all, the car had been found in Truman's jurisdiction . . . well, almost in his jurisdiction . . . and it was his responsibility to see that the man hadn't been injured.

*Right?*

Rob Murray lived close to Bend. He definitely didn't live in the Eagle's Nest city limits, but Truman was a thoughtful cop. He liked to know everyone was okay. Maybe Rob would say a good citizen of Eagle's Nest had helped him out when he abandoned the SUV, and Truman could go thank them. Community involvement should be recognized.

*I'm full of shit.*

Shoving away his guilt at sticking a finger in a case that wasn't his, he knocked on the door of the apartment. Rob Murray lived on the second floor of a building that had seen better days. Truman dared not touch the outdoor iron stair railing, fearing its one remaining support would give way. On the second level he'd walked by apartment windows with curtains made from sagging floral sheets and one covered with a Seattle Seahawks beach towel. Rob hadn't bothered with window coverings. Through his small apartment window, Truman could see Rob's chipped kitchen sink, piled with a half dozen milky bowls and plastic spoons. An open box of Lucky Charms sat to the right of the sink.

*Bachelor diet.*

The door opened, and a man dressed in splattered white painter's clothing glared at him. "What?"

His eyes were dark, and a cigarette dangled from his lips. He looked about thirty, and he had the pasty skin and the soft, round body of a man who lived on cold cereal and beer.

"Rob Murray?"

He squinted, and his suspicious gaze bounced from the business card Truman held out to the badge on his coat. He took the card and didn't look at it. "Yeah?"

"I'd like to ask you about the Lexus we found on Goose Hollow Road yesterday."

The suspicion cleared. "It's not mine. I borrowed it, and the owner got it back already."

"Why was it just left there?"

"Because it died. I don't know what happened. It needed a tow."

"How come it sat there for a few days? Why didn't you call for the tow right away?"

Rob shuffled his feet and looked away. "I forgot," he muttered.

"You *forgot* about a vehicle? An expensive SUV you'd borrowed?" *Bull.*

The man worked his cigarette for a moment and reluctantly moved his gaze back to Truman's. "My buddy who picked me up wanted to party. It slipped my mind."

"How long was this party?"

Rob winced. "A day or two. He had some great weed." Defense squared his shoulders. "It's legal here now. We can do that."

"Don't I know it." Truman tried a different approach. "Christian Lake told me you work for him."

"Yeah, I'm sort of a handyman for his place. It takes a lot of upkeep. Stuff's always breaking."

"I've seen the house and can I imagine it takes a lot of work. It's massive. I guess I assumed Brent Rollins took care of that sort of thing."

Rob gave a short laugh. "Rollins doesn't like to get his hands dirty. I've always said my job is to do the stuff Rollins thinks he's too good for." Resentment simmered in his gaze, and he sucked hard on his cigarette.

Truman prodded. "Not the best boss?"

He blew a cloud of smoke to the side. "Rollins is the pain in the butt, but Lake is great. That's why I asked Christian for the loaner when my truck wouldn't start. I knew he'd help me out."

"Nice loaner."

More puffing on the cigarette. "Yeah, I expected him to offer the Ford truck. It's a little beat up and used for hauling stuff on the property. I knew he kept every vehicle stocked with gas and emergency supplies in this type of weather. Surprised the crap out of me when he handed over the Lexus keys."

Truman gestured at the white clothing. "You doing some painting up there today?"

"Nah, I've got another job today. Rollins called and told me to stay home for a few days. I have a painter friend I help out when they don't need me."

"That makes it hard to count on a paycheck."

"Christian pays me a salary. Some weeks I have sixty hours of work to do; some weeks I have ten. It all balances out, and I get a regular paycheck in my account."

"What day did he loan you the Lexus?"

Rob screwed up his face, thinking hard. "Three days ago . . . No, four. It was the day I repaired the greenhouse. The snowstorm cracked some panels. I finished up and my truck wouldn't start."

Truman remembered how Rollins had to step into the garage to confirm the SUV was missing. "Is the greenhouse close to the main house?"

"Nah, it's back a ways through the woods. There's an open area that gets good light."

"Your own truck was parked out of sight of the home?"

"Yeah, until yesterday after Christian called me about the Lexus. The tow truck driver who returned the Lexus checked my battery and gave me a jump. I figured that's what it was."

"Why didn't you just ask Rollins for a jump that day?" *With a six-car garage, surely there was a vehicle to use for a jump.*

He smirked. "And risk the engine of one of Christian's precious vehicles? I knew what he'd say."

"You know, you're lucky you have a job after leaving the boss's precious vehicle on the side of the road for days." Truman would have fired his irresponsible ass.

Rob managed to look contrite. "Rollins chewed me out."

*But didn't fire him?*

"Christian didn't say anything?"

"No, he's cool."

*Cool enough not to care about a ninety-thousand-dollar Lexus?*

"Why were you on Goose Hollow Road? That isn't on your way home from the Lake house."

"I was headed to my buddy's house."

"Can you give me his name and address?"

"Why? We didn't do anything." Rob's scowl grew. "I don't have to give you that. You know there's privacy laws and shit, right?"

*I'm speaking to a lawyer.*

"Just asking," Truman said as he gave his best troubled look. "There were some disturbances out on that road a few days ago," he lied. "And I wondered if you or he saw anything. It's part of the reason I came to you about the Lexus. I didn't know if the car being abandoned was a result of one of them. You didn't see anything suspicious on that road, did you?"

Rob stroked his chin, his suspicion gone. "No. It's a quiet road." He rattled off his friend's address and phone number, and Truman wrote them down.

He thanked Rob for his help and excused himself, feeling like the world's biggest con man. He reviewed the discussion in his mind, making certain he hadn't asked anything that could affect the true investigation.

*Will the FBI question Rob too?*

They'd shown interest in the abandoned car, hoping to link it to Christian Lake's whereabouts on the nights of the two murders. But clearly Rob Murray had been the driver.

*A dead end?*

Truman climbed in his SUV, wanting to call Mercy and wondering if they'd tracked down Salome Sabin yet.

*Not my case.*

It wasn't her case either, but she was in it up to her neck.

Ava's charming phone call to ask Christian for permission to print the Hummer tires didn't work, and Mercy wasn't surprised when he told her to get a warrant. Back in the Bend offices, Ava asked Eddie to write up a request for the warrant and then started to review the next steps in the investigation.

Mercy inched away from the duo, toward the office door. Jeff had more work for her. She couldn't hover around Eddie and Ava, expecting to be informed about every little phone call on the murders of Olivia Sabin and Malcolm Lake.

"I think we need to go back to Portland," Ava abruptly stated.

Mercy halted her slow escape. "You just got here." If Ava and Eddie left, she'd be out of the loop.

"I've seen the scene and talked to Christian Lake. The warrant will take a little time, and the tire treads need to be taken by a crime scene tech, not us. I don't see what else there is for us to do right now. Any other evidence results can be emailed to me, and I don't want to sit around waiting for it. What I want to do is meet with the judge's assistant, check the video footage, and see if there is any truth to the mystery visitor. I also want to talk with the judge's ex-wife again. Christian painted a different picture of Brenda Lake compared to what I picked up during my first interview with her." She looked at Eddie. "You'll go with me."

Eddie glanced at Mercy, and she spotted the sympathy in his eyes. He knew she was personally invested in the case and wanted to be close to the investigation. "Just for a few days," he agreed.

"Then you need to go today," said Mercy reluctantly. "The next round of storms is supposed to start tonight, and the passes will get hammered with snow."

Ava checked the clock on the wall. "Good idea. Can you be ready in a half hour?" she asked Eddie, who blanched.

"Give me an hour."

"Seriously?" Ava asked. "Clothes, toothbrush, and toothpaste. What else do men pack?"

Mercy coughed. She'd seen Eddie spend twenty minutes on his hair and iron three different shirts before he was satisfied with how he looked. Packing with urgency wasn't something he knew how to do.

"I need an hour," he confirmed.

"Fine. Meet back here. One hour."

Mercy told them both good-bye and called to see if Truman could meet her for lunch. She got in her vehicle and decided to get a big dessert to soothe her disappointment about being left behind as the investigation moved to Portland. She walked into her favorite farm-to-table café and spotted that damned reporter at a window table, sinking a fork into the exact gooey chocolate bread pudding she'd planned to order. Michael Brody spotted her and waved her over.

*Not who I want to talk to.*

But she went anyway and even sat down when he stood and gestured at an empty seat directly across from him.

*What am I doing?*

"You're looking at me as if you suspect I stole your car." He took an enormous bite of the dessert and her stomach growled.

"Ava confirmed she knows you."

"I don't lie. Not too much, anyway." Another bite disappeared into his mouth.

The waitress stopped at the table, her hands full of dishes. "The usual, Mercy?"

"Please."

"Is Truman coming too?" she asked.

"He's trying to. Don't put his order in yet."

She nodded and took her load into the kitchen.

Michael raised a brow at her. "That confirms my impression that the food here is really good. My sandwich wasn't a fluke." He looked at his dessert. "And this makes me consider moving to Bend."

"When are you leaving?" Mercy asked. The reporter made her want to scratch her neck. She couldn't relax around him.

Amusement lit his green eyes. "Ready to get rid of me so soon?"

Mercy said nothing.

He took a sip of coffee and wiped his mouth with a napkin. "I still need to interview Christian Lake. I'm doing a big article on his father's legacy. I can't do it justice without talking to the sons, but he's not taking my phone calls." He held her gaze.

*There's no way he found out that I know Christian.*

"Maybe you should start with the other son," she suggested.

"I plan to talk to Gabriel after I talk to Christian. Brenda Lake too. She's already agreed to meet with me to talk about her ex." His big smile told her he'd charmed the judge's ex-wife into an interview. "I've done all my research about Malcolm Lake's role in the D'Angelo case. Of course, I remember a lot of it from when it happened. It was hard to miss."

Mercy agreed. The notorious movie star Beau D'Angelo had murdered his wife during a visit to Portland. Malcolm Lake had shot to fame as the trial judge who told D'Angelo to shut the fuck up when he complained during a witness's testimony. The national press had already blanketed the trial with coverage, and D'Angelo's marriage and career were daily news staples. But once the judge's curse caught the media's attention, their repetitious reporting created a new celebrity. Eventually D'Angelo walked on a technicality and the public uproar was deafening. For a brief time Judge Malcolm Lake was a household name. In Portland he became the most wanted guest for every elite dinner party and fund-raiser. He fed on the attention, and lawyers whispered that the coverage had inflated his ego.

Mercy faintly remembered reading about Christian in some articles during the trial, usually as one of the judge's successful sons. She wondered how he had felt about the publicity. Now it was back again, and she'd heard the judge's murder was the top news story every evening. National media had descended on Portland and filled its airtime with flashbacks of the famous Beau D'Angelo trial. Before the trial the movie star had backed out of a signed contract because he would be stuck in a courtroom for a month. His career tanked. A few years later he popped up on a reality TV show, stranded on an island with other minor celebrities. D'Angelo was the first one kicked off the island, hated by the other contestants on the show. Last night Mercy had watched an online interview clip in which D'Angelo had shared kind words about the judge, stating his thoughts and prayers were with the judge's family.

*Thoughts and prayers.*

Mercy tried not to snort.

Not a word had been said in the news about the death of Olivia Sabin. So far the reporter across the table appeared to be the only member of the media who had connected the two cases. Mercy crossed her fingers that time would stay on their side, keeping the media out of this aspect of the investigation.

The waitress set down a spinach salad topped with a few slices of medium-rare steak in front of Mercy. Michael eyed it. "I should have known you were a salad person."

Then her own serving of chocolate bread pudding appeared.

He grinned. "That's more like it." His gaze shot over her shoulder, and Mercy knew Truman had arrived.

Truman squeezed her shoulder and leaned down to kiss her before shaking Michael's hand. Mercy spotted the same caution in Truman's gaze that she felt around the reporter. He wouldn't let his guard down either. He took the chair next to her and raised a finger at their waitress across the restaurant, who nodded and winked at him.

*Truman always gets the female winks.*

Or the lingering stares and the second glances. Especially when he wore his coat and badge. He naturally exuded stability, integrity, and honor. He was crack for women. Single or married.

"Are you getting a salad too?" Michael asked.

"Not today. It's a BLT for me," answered Truman. He picked up a fork and took a bite of Mercy's dessert. "Sweet baby cheeses, that's as incredible as always."

Truman had not had a sweet tooth until he met her. Sugar was one of Mercy's primary vices. One she'd been unable to shake. That and caffeine. She'd laid in a huge store of the luxury items at her cabin.

Her father wouldn't have approved.

"Mercy didn't tell me we were meeting you for lunch," Truman said.

"You weren't. You got lucky."

Mercy suddenly wondered if the reporter had been lying in wait for her again. She ate lunch at the restaurant at least twice a week. *I shouldn't be so predictable.*

"Why are you here, Michael?" she asked. The subtle twitch of one eye implied her suspicion had been correct.

"I want you to get me an interview with Christian Lake."

She sighed.

"Why ask Mercy?" asked Truman.

"They know each other."

"Barely," added Mercy. "I haven't seen him in years."

"Except for yesterday," added Michael with the lift of one eyebrow.

"I can't tell him what to do." Mercy stabbed her spinach, aware there was no point in asking how the reporter had gotten his information.

"Did he tell you his brother Gabriel is in town?" Michael asked.

Her head jerked up and Truman tensed beside her. "He's back from California? Why didn't he go home to Portland?" she asked.

"That was my question too. He flew in this morning and headed straight to Christian's home."

"Did you tell Ava this? She needs to interview him."

"Not yet. I've called her twice and asked her to get back to me. It hasn't happened yet."

Mercy checked the time. "She and Eddie just left for Portland."

"I guess Gabriel's interview will have to wait until they get back."

She tamped down the urge to leap out of her seat and drive to Christian's home.

Truman's phone buzzed. He scowled at the screen and excused himself to take the call outside.

Mercy stared at Michael, her appetite gone. Even the bread pudding held no appeal. The reporter's minibomb about Gabriel clogged her thoughts. Silent tension floated between her and Michael.

"You know you want to go out there," Michael said quietly. "I'm a good excuse for you to go to his home. You'll simply be making an introduction. Your presence will smooth the way for Christian to open up to me."

He sounded like the devil sitting on her shoulder. "Do you always manipulate your conversations?"

Michael shrugged. "I like to be efficient with my time."

She grudgingly respected that. No doubt their two encounters had gone exactly as he'd planned. But she wasn't ready to lead him to Christian. She respected their old friendship too much. Michael would have to find another way. She opened her mouth, ready to tell him exactly that, when alarm crossed his face as he looked past her.

She spun around in her chair. Truman was striding toward their table, his face grim.

"What happened?" she asked.

"Rob Murray has been murdered. I need to go."

Her mind scrambled to place the name. "The guy who abandoned Christian's car?"

"Yep. That was Evan Bolton from the Deschutes County Sheriff's Office. Murray's neighbors reported that my vehicle was at his apartment building a few hours ago, so the detective called me."

"Were you at his apartment?" asked Michael.

"Yes." Truman was tight-lipped, his face pale. "But he was breathing when I left."

"I'm coming with you," stated Mercy.

# SEVENTEEN

When I was sixteen I sold my potions to the girls at school. Business was brisk. Word of mouth kept my sales flowing, although none of the girls would speak to me except when they wanted their fix. It was amazing what a little bit of vodka mixed with fruit juice would allow a girl to do when she stood in front of her crush. Inhibitions went down, and the teenage boy's interest was snagged.

Easy money.

But I was lonely. I started attending every party I heard about. Masses of teens would cram into someone's home while the parents were out of town. Beer flowed and pot was passed around. I would heavily line my eyes, wear my tightest, shortest skirt and a sheer top. I wanted them to see me and they did.

Worn pages from fashion magazines papered my bedroom walls. I would spend hours copying their makeup and attitudes. The pictures were a snapshot of a world I'd never known, and I did my best to bring it to my life. At first I shoplifted the makeup, but as my potion business grew, I paid for the items, taking pride in my ability to take care of myself and swearing that I'd never rely on someone for my needs.

The guys from my high school noticed.

At the parties they were the snakes and I was the piper. In low voices they told one another I was dangerous; I became a glorified conquest. They celebrated getting in my pants and surviving without a curse placed on their heads. Quick sex in the bathroom, bedroom, or garage. Even outdoors on pool furniture. My reputation spread. To the guys I was easy. To the girls I was a slut, bitch, and whore. Probably because I would target couples. I lived for the rush of power from drawing the gaze of a "committed" guy.

I preferred guys who claimed to be in a relationship. They would go running back to their girlfriends once I was done with them, their tails between their legs, terrified I would tell their partners. Like I cared. It was the predatory older men who made me cautious. Why would a man in his twenties pursue a teenager? It spoke of their mind-set and maturity—both lacking.

I researched everything I could about my infamous namesake. I danced in my bedroom, learning the movements that would capture and hold the gazes of men. Once I asked my mother why she'd named me after the woman who had reputedly called for the death of John the Baptist. She held my gaze for a long time before answering. "Because I believed it would make you strong."

I didn't reply, but my mind raced with questions. *Why me? Why do I need to be strong? Don't all the Kathys, Debbies, and Emilys of the world need strength?*

In my mind my name was synonymous with seduction. It was a legacy I strove to fulfill.

When I was a senior in high school, I attended a party where several older men were reliving the glory of their high school years. I disdained adults who needed to mingle with teenagers, but the other students felt important as they rubbed shoulders with men who could legally drink.

One man brought me a red cup, his gaze hot and intense, his goal apparent. My night had been slow, so I accepted and drank, turning up my allure to level ten. He was tall and attractive, wearing slacks and a dress shirt, unlike 95 percent of the other guys at the party. Success radiated from him and caught my interest. I explored. A subtle hint of red danger reached my nose, but I also scented a playfulness in his aura, an overriding need to pursue pleasure.

My kind of guy.

We talked and flirted and danced. I ignored the rest of the party, my focus on his brown eyes. Soon I saw nothing else. I was happy, a dizzy euphoria ripping through my veins. I didn't want the night to end.

Then I was in his car, the front seat reclined, and he was on top of me, fumbling to pull up my skirt. I didn't care what he did to me. My mind floated in a deep need to simply sleep and allow him to have his way.

Shouting. Noise. His hands ripped my blouse as he was pulled off me, my skin suddenly exposed to the cold night air. Through sleepy eyes I saw two men fighting. And my lover was losing. I watched as if from a great height, not caring what happened.

I closed my eyes and drifted away. At one point I was covered and lifted. A kind voice assured me I was safe. Had I been in danger?

I woke in a strange bed, a strange room. A man awkwardly slept in the easy chair near the door. Not a man. I recognized him as another senior from my school. I'd classified him as a geek, a skinny cross-country runner who got straight As and hung out with other nerds.

In other words, not worth my time or focus.

I sat up. It took great effort, and the room spun slightly as I sat on the edge of the bed. The nerd woke and was at my side before I could blink, steadying me in case I tipped off the mattress. I looked into familiar brown eyes, reminiscent of the man I'd danced with the night before. A fresh bruise was forming around one of his eyes, and I saw dried blood in his nose. The memory of a fight flitted through my brain.

"How do you feel?" he asked.

I considered his question, taking inventory of my body. "Exhausted."

He nodded. "You were drugged."

I jerked up straight, shaking his grip from my arm. "I was not."

"You were," he said grimly. "And he was about to rape you in his car."

"I chose to be there." I was always in control with my men. He couldn't tell me different.

"I don't think you were able to make any intelligent decisions at that point."

"You didn't need to interfere," I snapped. "I would have been fine."

"Do you remember me driving you here last night? Or leading you to this room?"

"No." I couldn't recall any of it, and a flicker of fear lit through me. I studied his bruised eye and noticed a recent cut on his lip.

"You should be more careful." His brown gaze was serious. "Why do you fuck around with so many guys? You're going to end up dead in a ditch and on the news one day when you leave with the wrong one."

Anger heated my face and I pushed to my feet, intent on getting out of the room. "Fuck off."

I took a step and my knee buckled. In a flash he was at my side again, gentle hands guiding me back to the bed. "You aren't in any condition to go anywhere."

I was vulnerable, not in control. I hated it and grabbed command of the situation. I held his gaze, tipped my head down, and gave the smile of an experienced seductress.

He drew back, disgust on his face. "Don't try that shit on me."

I was stung.

"Are you gay?" I tilted my head ever so slightly and licked my lips. "Scared to be with a *woman*?"

"You're not a woman; you're a senior just like me. And no, I'm not gay. I'm simply not an asshole who takes advantage of girls." He kept his distance, but his hands were ready to grab me again if I started to fall.

I tried again, lightly touching his hand. "You *are* gay. That's okay. I bet I can turn you. Wanna give it a try?"

He sighed. "Give it up," he ordered. "I'm not sleeping with you."

I was flummoxed. No one turned me down. He had to be gay. No other man had responded with such disdain.

"Now," he said. "Talk to me like a regular person. Not a person you're trying to fuck. I've seen you at school, but I don't know anything about you except that all the girls hate you and the guys drool over you. Do you have any siblings?" His brown eyes were sincere.

I stared.

"I know you came to our school in the middle of your sophomore year. Where did you attend before that?"

"I was homeschooled," I said in spite of myself.

His eyes lit up with interest. "Really? What was that like? I've often wished I didn't have to deal with the extra shit that comes with school and just study what I want to learn."

I told him. I told him about my crazy mother and our home in the woods. I told him how excited I'd been to attend high school and how it'd crushed me when I was rejected. We talked for the next hour and I slowly relaxed. He brought me juice and a bagel and sat with me until I felt nearly normal. He told me his mother wasn't home and that he'd only been at the party because a friend had dragged him to it.

"I guess I owe you for getting me out of there," I finally admitted. "You were right. Someone must have drugged me. I've never felt like this, and I'm lucky you were paying attention."

He was silent for a long moment. "My older brother drugged you. He was the asshole I pulled off you."

"You fought your brother?"

"It wasn't the first time," he said ruefully. "I doubt it will be the last. Luckily he was wasted last night. He outweighs me by about fifty pounds and usually kicks my butt."

He was incredibly thin, but it was the lean build of a runner. His brother's handsome face flashed in my memory and I saw the resemblance. I didn't know what to say. My pride was at war with my shock at his actions, and I was in the unusual position of being beholden to someone else. In other words, I wasn't in charge, and again I was thrust out of my comfort zone.

"Thank you." The words were difficult.

"I'm sorry he did that to you."

An honest aura surrounded him, and I scented fresh trees and grass. His brother might be an asshole, but this man was not.

"I don't know your name," I admitted in embarrassment.

"Christian."

It suited him. Just as my name suited me.

Eventually I felt strong enough to leave the room. His home was beautiful and reeked of money, and I tiptoed as we walked the polished wood floors, terrified to touch anything. He drove me in a Mercedes back to the party house to get my car. I was embarrassed as I stood by my clunker hatchback, but he was too polite to mention it. He waited to make certain my vehicle would start and then waved good-bye.

I figured that was the end.

To my surprise he found me at school the following Monday. Usually I ate lunch alone in a small, quiet alcove with a book in my hand. I jumped as he set his tray on my table. He sat down and drew me into conversation. Christian became my friend. We were two outcasts, the geek and the slut. But we each found something special in the other person.

I never tried to seduce him again; I wouldn't do that to my friend. He wasn't gay, but he was a virgin who believed no girl would give him a second glance. He put his energy into his studies and helped me with my math. I gave him tips on his clothing and pushed for him to gain some weight. Other students gave us odd looks. Together we were an unusual sight. Several guys asked Christian if he'd fucked me and refused to believe his denials, but regarded him with a small degree of admiration. We laughed over his jump in status. I curtailed my prowling at parties, but only by a little bit; I enjoyed it too much. I never accepted another drink and paid more attention to what my senses told me about a man. Together we made a difference in each other's lives.

It was a friendship I would treasure forever.

# EIGHTEEN

Truman's stomach churned.

*Who killed Rob Murray? Does the killer know I was there?*

He marched up the unreliable stairway to Rob's apartment, Mercy right behind him. The officer out front had signed them in, not questioning why an FBI agent was at the scene. Mercy was skilled at pretending she was where she needed to be, and few people questioned her.

His mind raced through his earlier conversation with Murray, searching for a clue that the man had been in fear for his life.

Nothing came to mind.

Deschutes County detective Evan Bolton met them in front of the apartment. Truman was relieved that he'd already met the man at the scene of Olivia Sabin's death. A familiar face. Bolton's expression narrowed as he shook Truman's and Mercy's hands.

"Why are you here?" Bolton bluntly asked Mercy.

Mercy exchanged a glance with Truman. "This murder might be related to Olivia Sabin's," she said.

Truman admired the way Bolton's countenance didn't flicker.

"Explain," the detective ordered.

"It's complicated," Mercy hedged.

*That's putting it mildly.*

"I'm not in a hurry." The detective's gaze darted from Truman to Mercy. "Will I also be handing this case off to the FBI?"

"It's very possible."

Bolton finally showed an emotion: resignation. "Spill it."

Mercy gave an abridged version, tracing the connections from Olivia Sabin to Malcolm Lake to Christian Lake and then to Rob Murray.

Realization dawned in the detective's eyes, and Truman jumped on it. "What? You're thinking of something."

The detective took a deep breath. "It's not quite the same, but Murray was killed with a blade of some sort. I don't see the deliberate pattern of cuts that I saw on Olivia Sabin, but I can't ignore the similarities." Bolton turned a pensive gaze on Truman. "You've turned up at two of the murder sites."

"So have I," Mercy interjected.

"Not before this guy was killed," Bolton pointed out.

Truman said nothing. He wouldn't let the detective get under his skin.

"Tell me again what brought you to see Rob Murray earlier this morning?" the detective asked.

Truman explained his curiosity about the abandoned vehicle after learning Murray worked for the murdered judge's son.

"How did Murray seem?" asked Bolton.

"Mellow. He was about to leave for a painting job and wasn't concerned that he'd left his boss's expensive vehicle on the side of the road. I would have been more contrite about an SUV that probably cost three times my salary." A thought struck him, and Truman turned to the parking lot. "I take it that's Rob's truck?" He pointed at a beat-up Chevy being photographed by a crime scene tech on the far side of the lot.

"You're sharp."

Truman ignored the dig. "It was parked right next to the stairs this morning. I had to walk around it. I remember because of the obnoxious hitch cover."

"What's the hitch cover have on it?" Mercy asked.

"A dangling pair of balls."

"What's obnox—oh. Never mind," she finished.

"My point is that he moved the truck at some point *after I left*," stated Truman, knowing he had no way to prove that the truck had been parked near the stairs. "Who reported the murder?"

"That doesn't mean Murray was the one to move the truck," said Bolton. "His painter friend called it in. The guy was pissed that Murray was a no-show and came over to chew him out. He said the door was slightly open when he arrived."

"And?" Mercy asked.

*She's itching to see inside.*

Bolton was silent, a struggle in his gaze, and Truman saw the moment he gave in. "Bootie up," he ordered. "This is against my better judgment, but since you saw the Sabin scene, I'd appreciate any insight."

Truman and Mercy accepted booties and gloves from an officer. Apprehension rolled off Mercy, and he wondered if she was second-guessing her desire to see the scene. He knew finding Olivia Sabin's killer was a personal goal of hers, but he doubted she wanted to see another murder scene.

Unsurprisingly, the inside of Murray's apartment reeked of cigarette smoke. An overflowing ashtray sat on the coffee table in front of a sofa that had bits of stuffing peeking out of its cushion holes. A flat-screen TV nearly twice the size of Truman's hung on the wall.

*Priorities.*

The two of them glanced into the minuscule kitchen, and Mercy's nose wrinkled at the mess. Bolton led them down a short hallway and past a small bathroom where Truman glimpsed black scum growing in the shower.

"Sheesh," muttered Mercy. "Men."

"Hey." Bolton looked over his shoulder. "I scrub my shower every week. With bleach. Don't lump us all together."

"Sorry."

Bolton stepped aside and gestured to the doorway of the sole bedroom. Truman swallowed and halted at the door, Mercy beside him. She caught her breath.

"There's never a way to prepare for this," she said softly.

Rob Murray lay on his back on the floor, and his sightless eyes stared directly at Truman. Bolton had been right about the use of a blade. Murray had multiple slashes across his face and torso, but the death stroke had to have come from the knife left in his neck. His white painter's uniform was soaked with darkening blood.

Mercy pressed the back of her hand against her nostrils; the odor in the room was reminiscent of sewage.

"He left the weapon," she stated.

"He or she," corrected Bolton.

"It has quite the ornate handle," Mercy pointed out.

"Possibly stolen from the Sabin house?" Truman suggested, looking back at Bolton.

Bolton nodded. "I'd wondered the same. Maybe even the same weapon used on Olivia Sabin."

Truman took a careful step forward and squatted, taking a closer look and breathing through his mouth. He didn't see the distinctive patterning Mercy had described to him from the bodies of Malcolm Lake and Olivia Sabin. The slashes in Rob's clothing looked random. Brutal. Angry. Multiple cuts covered his hands and arms. Rob Murray had tried to protect himself.

"I take it the ME hasn't been here yet?" Truman asked.

"Not yet."

Truman noticed Mercy examining the room and did the same. Grimy bare walls, a bed with no bottom sheet, dirty clothes left on the floor. The open closet was nearly empty, a few wire hangers dangling. It appeared Rob left most of his clothes on the floor or in the overflowing laundry basket. Mercy peered at a crime novel next to another full ashtray on the nightstand.

She turned in a circle, frowning. "I don't see anything that reminds me of the other murders except for the use of the knife. It looks like he put up a fight. No neighbors heard anything?"

"We're still checking. Anything else?"

Truman noted the hopeful tone in Bolton's voice. He needed a lead.

"I don't see anything," Mercy said. "Can we get out now?"

*I don't blame her.*

Truman was done too. Leaving, he noted a crime scene tech rooting under Rob's bathroom sink with a wrench, removing the trap to search for evidence the killer might have left behind. Outside he took a breath of clean icy air and removed his gloves and booties, dropping them in an evidence bag.

"I heard Morrigan's mother returned," said Bolton.

"She did," answered Mercy. "Morrigan only spent one night in temporary care."

"That's good. Hate to see kids kept away from their parents." His eyes were questioning, and Truman heard the unspoken question about Salome Sabin.

"Salome wasn't arrested," he stated.

"Good. I didn't want to think that Morrigan's mother would leave her behind after that murder. She must have been cleared?" Another leading question.

Truman looked to Mercy. *Do we tell him?*

She nodded, but she wasn't happy about it. No law enforcement wanted to admit a suspect had slipped away. "She hasn't been fully cleared." Mercy cleared her throat. "She disappeared with Morrigan last night."

"No shit?" Bolton's expression vacillated between amusement and concern.

"I know," said Mercy. "We're not happy about it. She'd agreed to an interview this morning and we trusted she'd show up. Her concern about her daughter made us all believe that she wouldn't have left Morrigan in such a horrible situation. We were suckered."

"That means she could have been here today," Bolton said softly.

His first instinct was to defend Salome, but Truman knew Bolton was right. "Three victims make a serial killer. Is this the third?"

"Actually the FBI recently defined it as two, but we aren't positive the same person killed Judge Lake and Olivia," Mercy pointed out. "Murray could be totally unrelated. Let's not get the media believing we've got a serial killer in the area."

"The first two similar death scenes can't be ignored," Truman argued. "I agree the method of murder used on Murray appears a bit different, but that fancy knife sticking out of his neck makes me think it's at least related to Olivia Sabin's."

Mercy watched a uniform going from door to door, asking if residents had heard or seen anything unusual. "You'd think in an apartment building where the walls are this thin, someone would have heard something. I can't believe Rob Murray died silently. I hear plenty of racket from my neighbors, and my building has pretty thick walls, but there are some things you can't tune out."

*Like the screams of death?*

"Another reason I want to move out of there," she added.

Truman froze, wondering if she'd bring up her new real estate hunt. Instead she said good-bye to Bolton, and Truman followed her down the stairs. *Why hasn't she talked to me about it?*

A heaviness weighed him down, and his steps slowed.

Maybe Mercy didn't see them living together in the future. Or she could be overprotective of Kaylie, not wanting to set an example by shacking up with her boyfriend. *But wouldn't she have told me?*

He shoved the paranoid thoughts out of his head. He liked what he had with Mercy. She made him smile and look forward to getting out of bed each day. He'd been focused on his job to the exclusion of everything else during the six months before she came to town. Now the world looked and felt different to him. He liked it.

She stopped at her vehicle as her phone rang. "It's my mother." Her forehead wrinkled. "We had coffee recently, I don't know why she'd be calling."

Her relationship with her mother wasn't as close as she wanted, and Truman knew Mercy kept trying. But she didn't want to come between her father and mother. Right now her mother's first loyalty was to her husband, and he didn't want Mercy in their lives.

"Mom?" she said into the phone. As she listened, her forehead wrinkled even more and her lips parted. "She did what? What did Dad say to her?"

Truman waited.

"Jesus H. Christ. Are you sure I should come?" Mercy met Truman's gaze and slowly shook her head, rolling her eyes.

*Not too serious.*

She hung up. "Dad is upsetting Rose. Something to do with the cradle that was delivered. Mom thinks I can calm her down."

"Rose upset? That doesn't sound right. She's the calm one in your family."

"Exactly. If something set her off, it must be pretty rough. I'm headed over there."

"I'll be right behind you," Truman stated.

# NINETEEN

Her father opened the door, and Mercy took a step back.

He had never been one to show emotion, but she immediately knew he was frustrated and possibly angry. "Your mother wants to see you," he stated.

*Your mother. Not me.*

His gaze shifted to Truman, and he gave the police chief a polite nod as he gestured for them to enter. In the living room Mercy spotted the beautiful cradle from Nick Walker.

"That's amazing," said Truman. "Walker made that?"

Mercy had given him a brief account of her visit to the lumberyard. "He did an incredible job."

Truman ran a hand along the polished wood. "This would cost a fortune in a store."

Mercy agreed, wondering where her mother and Rose were. A door closed upstairs and she recognized her mother's footsteps on the hardwood stairs. Deborah Kilpatrick's eyes were red and her lashes damp. She gave Mercy a brief hug and greeted Truman.

"What happened?" Mercy asked. "Where's Rose?"

"In her room," her mother said, with a glance at her husband, who stood stiffly out of the way. "I think we pushed too hard."

Mercy didn't buy that, knowing it was her father who had pushed too hard. "Is this about the baby again? You know you can't force Rose to settle down in a house with a white picket fence with a man she barely knows just because you think the baby needs a father. I thought we'd settled that."

"Nick Walker has intentions," her father stated.

*What an old-fashioned term.*

"We could see it when he dropped off the cradle," her mother clarified. "It was clear he's soft on Rose. Of course, she can't see it, and when we told her—"

"You told Rose that Nick is interested in her? You thought she didn't know that?"

"He'd make a good husband," Karl Kilpatrick intoned. "Solid. Stable. A good provider. She can't do any better."

*Does he think that little of Rose?* Mercy fought to find her voice. "Did you tell her she *can't* do any better?"

Her parents were silent.

*Poor Rose. Do they believe she's incapable of finding love?*

"Did you embarrass her before or after Nick left?" Mercy fumed.

Her mother put a hand on Mercy's arm. "She didn't get upset until Nick left," she clarified. "Karl and I received the exact same impression when he was here, and we believe he'd be a good man for her. The way he looks at Rose can't be denied . . . and the fact that he made her a cradle shows he's accepting of her child."

*Do they think her baby is undesirable?* "Any *decent* man will accept Rose's baby. Don't tell me you told her that too."

Her parents exchanged a look.

"Dammit! Could you have torn her down any more? I suppose you suggested a spring wedding?"

"They just need to go before a judge—" her father started.

"Stop talking!" Mercy held up a hand. "Rose decides who'll she marry and when she'll get married. *If she wants to get married.* No one else. Where is she?"

Deborah pointed up the stairs, and Mercy concentrated on not stomping as she went up the steps. She knocked on the door to the bedroom she'd once shared with Rose and Pearl. "It's Mercy."

After a few silent seconds the door opened, and Mercy saw her father's temper in Rose's expression. Her beautiful sister was livid.

"They're crazy," she told Mercy. "When is this going to end? At least Owen doesn't pester me about finding a father for my child anymore, but Dad hasn't given up. They think no one could ever want me!"

"What happened?"

Rose moved to sit on the bed and Mercy followed, sitting beside her. The bunk beds from her youth were gone, replaced by one double bed. A desk sat under the window, piled with several Braille books, and more filled a small bookshelf. Mercy knew Rose often listened to audiobooks, but she'd said she preferred to read on her own. The room was a pale, icy green. The walls were empty of paintings or pictures, but several stuffed animals looked at home on the bed.

"Nick dropped off the cradle. We were having a pleasant conversation, and Mom and Dad chatted with him a bit too. As soon as he was out the door, Dad jumped all over me about not being kind enough to Nick. I had no idea what he was talking about. I'd thanked Nick for the cradle a dozen times." Her eyebrows came together. "*Then* he told me that I needed to invite Nick to dinner and be more flirtatious."

"*Flirtatious?* Dad actually used that word?" *Are we in the 1950s?*

"Right? So I asked if he'd set Nick up to build the cradle and be nice to me. He denied it, saying I better not let Nick slip away because he's the best I could do, but I think Dad orchestrated the entire thing."

Rose slumped, looking crushed, and Mercy's heart broke into a million weeping pieces as she remembered the joy on her sister's face at the lumberyard. It'd been full of happiness and hope.

"I don't think Dad set Nick up."

"I can't be sure. Several times he's tried to maneuver me to meet with some man he thinks would be a good husband. It's infuriating. Now he's done the same thing with Nick. I honestly thought . . ."

"You know when we first saw the cradle at the lumberyard?" Mercy began. "I knew that day Nick was sincerely interested in you. It was written all over his face. I wish you could have seen the way he looked at you, Rose. It was as if you were a gleaming piece of jewelry; he was mesmerized."

Rose caught her breath. "What?" Cautious hope flowed into her expression.

"I'm serious, Rose. It's rare that I see a man look at a woman the way Nick looked at you. He didn't hide anything." Her face warmed as she remembered how Truman always looked at her. *Hungry, infatuated, hopeful.* "I wish you could see a man's face when he feels strongly about a woman. There's nothing like it."

"You think he's genuinely interested in me?" Rose's voice was hoarse.

"I know he is. I doubt even Dad could scare him off."

Rose's face fell. "It can't be possible." Her hand went to her belly. "Everyone knows how I got pregnant. No man will take on both of us."

Mercy caught her breath, torn by her sister's pain and doubt. Relationships weren't Mercy's strong suit. And advising her sister about love made her feel as if she were standing in front of a college physics class, expected to teach a subject she'd never taken.

But she'd taken the crash course.

She took Rose's hand and organized her thoughts. "How do you feel about Nick?"

Rose was silent.

Mercy took that as a positive sign. "The man made you a cradle. Something specifically for your baby. I think it's his way of telling you he's open. He could have made you . . . a chair . . . or a table . . . something normal. But he carved a *cradle*, Rose. He's a silent type of guy, but I think this speaks very loudly. No one is telling you to marry him. Well, except Dad, but he doesn't count, and I think Mom was just following his lead. You need to open your heart and explore what he's offering. That's all."

"Dad didn't set him up?" she whispered, still uncertain.

"Hell no. Nick was so excited to show you the cradle. Dad can't force a man to feel that way—no one can. I saw it, Rose, plain as day on his face, and I think you felt it too, right?" Mercy held her breath, watching her sister's face as emotions fluttered across.

"I'd hoped," she finally admitted. "I thought I'd imagined that feeling from him because it's so unlikely—"

"Stop right there," Mercy commanded. "Any man who loves you is going to be the luckiest man in the world. Don't you dare write yourself off."

"I'm part of a package deal." Rose's voice had a touch of amusement. "And no one knows what's in the tiny package. It's like choosing a curtain on a TV game show. Who knows what you'll get?"

"Some men are happy to take risks," Mercy said, remembering Truman's persistence. "It's a good thing some people are risk takers, otherwise our species would die off."

Rose flung her arms around Mercy, hugging her tight. "Thank you."

"I didn't do anything."

"Yes, you did. Dad had me thinking in circles."

Mercy remembered her father's stunned expression when she held up her hand and ordered him to stop talking. "I think Dad will hold back for a while."

"What should I do about Nick?"

"Well, how about stop by the lumberyard before lunch tomorrow to thank him for the cradle. And if he doesn't invite you to lunch, then you do it."

Rose nodded, determination on her face. "I can do that."

Mercy stood, partly pleased that she'd helped her sister and partly terrified that she might have steered her sister toward getting her heart broken. *It's not just Rose's life. It's the baby's too.*

But Mercy felt good about Nick. Rose had known him a long time and experienced his character. Her sister wasn't one to throw her heart on the line without a lot of careful thought, and Mercy knew Nick wouldn't deliberately hurt her sister.

*But what if Rose gets hurt anyway?*

Only her sister knew how much risk she was comfortable with. It wasn't Mercy's place to protect her.

*Unless I know the guy is a true jerk.*

"Your ultrasound is this week, right?" asked Mercy.

"Yes. I can't wait."

Rose was at the halfway point, where she could find out the sex of the baby.

"You'll call me, right?" Mercy asked as she turned the doorknob.

"Absolutely."

"Are you coming downstairs?"

"I'm not ready to deal with Dad yet," Rose said. "Tell them I'll be down later."

"Will do."

As Mercy reached the bottom of the stairs, she abruptly remembered she'd abandoned Truman with her parents. Feeling guilty, she followed the sound of their voices. The three of them had moved to the kitchen, where Truman and her father sat at the table eating apple pie. With ice cream. Her mother poured more coffee in Truman's cup and beamed. Mercy felt as if she'd walked into a stranger's house. Who were these amiable people sitting around enjoying pie?

Truman thanked her mother and then met Mercy's gaze over the rim of the coffee cup as he took a sip. His eyes sparkled with amusement.

"Would you like a slice of pie?" Mercy's mother asked her. "Rose made it." Her father focused on his plate, chasing the last few bites with his fork.

Mercy's stomach growled. And then she remembered the mutilated body of Rob Murray. "No, I'm good. Rose will be down in a while."

"Is she okay?" asked her mother.

"Yes. Just don't pressure her." She looked at her father, but he continued to eat, his gaze down. "Rose will do what's best for her and her baby."

He looked up at that and opened his mouth to speak, then thought better of it and went back to his nearly empty plate.

"I'm going home," Mercy told them, lifting a brow at Truman. "Don't let me take you away from your pie."

He finished the remaining half of his slice in two bites, wiped his mouth, and stood. "Tell Rose her pie was fantastic, Deborah."

Mercy's mother beamed again, looking up at Truman. He shook Karl's hand, and they said their good-byes.

Outside he stopped Mercy before she got in her SUV. "How is Rose?"

"She's okay. Just confused."

"Nick is a good man, and he must feel strongly about Rose."

"How do you know that?"

"I have eyes. That's no ordinary gift in your parents' living room. I hope she won't avoid him."

"No. She wants to explore the possibility."

"Good." Truman looked extremely satisfied. "Your mother likes me," he said with a grin. "She fed me pie."

"I saw."

He leaned against her vehicle and pulled her into his arms. Mercy exhaled, letting the long day roll off her shoulders as she sank into his embrace. No dead bodies, no angry father, no missing suspect.

Truman smelled male and solid and comforting. She pressed her lips against Truman's neck and his entire body tensed. Pleased with her power over him, she kissed a line up to his ear. "Kaylie is spending the night with a friend," she whispered. He closed his eyes and shuddered at the sensation at his ear.

"Say no more." He kissed her firmly and gave her a push toward the driver's door. "I'll be right behind you."

# TWENTY

I never met my father.

When I was old enough to notice that the children in my books had a mother *and* a father, I became curious. For a few years I accepted my mother's answer that I'd never had one. When I was thirteen I realized that was physically impossible and confronted her again.

We were outside, walking the forest path to her favorite spot, where she prayed in the sunny clearing between the tall pines. She was often gone for several hours. "Harmonizing with nature," she called it. She had taught me to look for the miracles in the outdoors. Every leaf, each bird, and even the dirt under my feet. I studied the amazing network of veins in the leaves and wondered at their colorful transformations and eventual deaths. I watched the birds fly and ached to join them, to be weightless, to soar. What had God drawn inspiration from to create the fragile creatures that flitted from tree to tree? When I magnified a handful of dirt, new galaxies were revealed, a cosmos of different grains, minerals, and pebbles.

There was much to learn if you took the time.

We reached her spot. Several old stumps stood in the center of the small grassy area. She set a thick candle on the biggest one and gestured for me to sit on one of the smaller. She lit the candle and closed her eyes, taking deep, even breaths, inhaling the scents of the forest's life. After a moment she took a seat beside me and met my gaze.

"Your father is in prison."

I don't know what I had expected, but that was not it. "Why?"

She was silent. "It is a long story."

"Isn't that why you brought me here?"

She looked to her candle. "It is."

I waited, knowing I couldn't rush her. She would explain when she was ready, but my blood rushed hot through my veins. My father was a criminal. Embarrassment flooded me as if a huge audience had heard the dirty secret. But no one had heard her words except the trees and dirt.

Or *did* other people know? Was my father one of the reasons my mother was avoided as she walked the aisles in stores? Why no one except her customers came to our home?

"I was young once, you know. I was beautiful, and male eyes followed me."

"They still do." I never thought of my mother as old, although I knew she'd been nearly thirty when I was born.

She scoffed. "They don't see me in the same way."

I waited.

"I met your father in a dance club—"

"*What?*" I couldn't imagine my cloistered mother in such a social environment.

"Hush and listen. I will only tell you this story one time."

I pressed my lips together; I believed her. I'd never seen her current expression before. Sad, pensive, and pondering. She didn't sit as straight as usual, and the lines across her forehead had deepened. I smelled an earthy beige aura around her; usually it was a calm, ocean-scented blue. I listened.

"He was handsome and charming. His eyes made my insides melt, and his words were crafted by a master of seduction."

I wrinkled my nose.

"At that time I lived in a small home on the outskirts of Bend. He lived in the city but soon spent all of his time at my home. We married three months after meeting." A slow smile filled her face as she stared at her candle. I hung on every word, trying to imagine my mother in love.

"He rarely spoke to me of his work. I knew he worked for an important man and was highly regarded in his job. He described his job as 'whatever my boss needs me to do.' Later I realized that frequently included a gun."

"A gun," I repeated in a whisper. The weapons were a mystery to me, something that pirates and soldiers carried in books.

"During our first year, our love crumbled. He was often out of town, never telling me where he went. 'It's work,' he'd say, and it was the only explanation I would get." Her fingertips lightly touched the edge of her jaw near her chin. "I learned to never push for more answers."

I swallowed as a presence of pain circled her, its sharp odor burning my nose.

"One morning I discovered blood spattered on his shirt and pants. He'd come home at three in the morning, changed his clothes, and wordlessly crawled into bed while I stayed silent and stiff beside him." She paused. "He smelled of death, and I knew not to ask questions. I soaked his clothes and washed away the spots, but I felt their presence every time he wore them. As if a soul had stayed connected to the blood.

"The demands of his job increased, and his temper grew short. At least once a month, death followed him home, and I secretly searched for a way out of the marriage. I'd learned his boss was a feared man, a man who took from people in the guise of helping them. If you needed money, he would help you, but the cost was your dedication and absolute faithfulness. When people are desperate, they will accept a deal from the devil."

Rapt, I listened. Her story sounded straight out of one of my novels. "Then he turned on me."

Her fear and sorrow overwhelmed me, and my vision tunneled as I grew light-headed.

"The details aren't important, but he was arrested. As he sat in jail, his boss showered the police with evidence of my husband's crimes. Everything implicated my husband; his boss had been meticulous in his preparations and distanced himself from the deadly crimes.

"When he went to trial, I testified against him. I refused to meet his eyes as I spoke through a wired jaw, and I felt the jury's sympathy surround me. He went to prison for three murders and my abuse. His sentence was long."

I waited for more of the story. When she was silent, I asked, "When will he get out?"

Sad eyes met mine. "That is unknown. I know the length assigned, but often that is not what they serve. Things happen. People are let out early. In the courtroom, he swore vengeance on me and my unborn baby."

"Me," I breathed.

"Although his boss had betrayed him, I knew his boss's network was far-reaching. Your father had friends who didn't agree with his punishment and always supported him. I would never be safe and neither would you."

"That is why we hide," I stated. Claustrophobia swallowed me as we sat in the sunshine. *Will we ever be safe?*

Her somber brown gaze met mine. "He's sworn to kill me and you. I will never let that happen."

"We need to leave," I begged. "We're too close. We can go to Africa or Canada." Faraway, exotic-sounding countries that I'd read about in books and dreamed of visiting.

"He believed I left. The story was spread that I moved far away."

"Why didn't we go?"

"I can't leave," my mother whispered. "My heart and soul belong to these trees and this soil. I won't leave them. In my time of need, they gave me strength. They are still my strength."

Her words were true. Once I'd seen the connection: nearly invisible, hair-width ribbons of blue and green that sparkled as they flowed between her and the forest. More often I heard the bond as she moved through the trees. A subtle twinkling sound . . . like faraway chimes.

"Never forget that he promised to wipe me and my children from the face of the earth. Your children will also be in danger."

Today my gaze rests on Morrigan, quietly reading the books I hastily packed. The same books that brought the outside world into my isolated home. My heart quietly crumbles at the knowledge of the danger we are in.

He is out.

My mother won't be his last victim. The threat has roared to the surface after decades of hibernation. I will protect my daughter if it kills me. So we hide. Deeper than ever before.

Should I tell Morrigan I know who killed her grandmother?

She's too young.

Guilt swamps me, and I silently beg my mother for forgiveness. So many times as a teen I ranted at her, angry at the rules she set upon me, furious at the bubble she'd raised me in. The threat she shared with me that day in the woods later felt nonexistent after the passage of a few years' time. Our calm lives had given me false security, and my teenage hormones had taken over my brain.

I shake my head at the stupid teen I was.

Shouldn't my mother have been notified if he was released from prison? I snorted. I doubt the prison knew how to find her.

Or did one of his associates do the murder for him?

It doesn't matter. We will keep running.

# TWENTY-ONE

Mercy sat at her desk the next morning. The predicted snowstorm had rolled through overnight and dumped eight inches of snow in Bend and two feet of white fluff in the Cascade mountain range. All the mountain passes had been closed, cutting Central Oregon off from the populous Willamette Valley. This sort of snowstorm was rare for the Bend area. It always got some snow each year, but not like this, and the city struggled to keep up with the plowing. Bend didn't have enough plows to clear all the main roads. It had to prioritize.

Mercy's 4WD had made her drive to work slightly less dangerous, and Kaylie was pleased that school had been canceled while she was stuck at her friend's house. She informed Mercy they planned to watch movies and bake cookies all day.

*I wish I were home baking cookies.*

Her morning had consisted of a long reluctant good-bye to Truman, a dicey drive to work, and several hours of computer tasks.

Snow continued to fall, and she spent several minutes with her chin resting on her hand, enjoying the sight from her window. The city was covered in a magical white blanket, and she tried not to think what her evening commute might entail. More snow was predicted over the next few days. Her mind went to her cabin and the new pump system she and Truman had installed. She'd rather be checking on the winterization of her place than tapping computer keys.

A small cloud of claustrophobia hovered over her head. An inability to immediately reach her cabin, her safety net, kept her from fully relaxing. She could probably drive to it. She had chains for her 4WD and a shovel. But there was no emergency on the horizon. Her usual morning scan of national and international news reports had raised no red flags.

It appeared the world would be stable until the snowstorm was over.

*I need to be mentally prepared to take the risk in weather like this.*

Maybe this storm would be a good time for a cabin practice run with Kaylie. She'd never done one in heavy snow. In fact, all her drills had been in sunny weather. Twice she'd called Kaylie out of the blue and told her it was time to leave town. The teen had responded beautifully, dropping what she was doing and meeting Mercy at their rendezvous point. No supplies were needed because both their vehicles were already stocked to last a week in rough conditions. The only things needed from the apartment were Mercy's two backup weapons in their locked cases. Not that there weren't sufficient weapons at the cabin.

Speed was the priority. Unplowed roads could be a problem.

Kaylie had a little front-wheel-drive sedan that was fantastic in a few inches of snow. Was it enough? Mercy debated trading in the teen's car for something with 4WD or even AWD. If Mercy couldn't get to the rendezvous point on time, Kaylie's instructions were to drive to the cabin in the mountains on her own.

*I definitely need to upgrade her vehicle.*

Suddenly the beautiful snow outside had shifted from a winter wonderland to a dangerous obstacle, and she looked away, directing her brain to focus on work. Specifically on the case that she had no part of.

Last night her boss had deemed the Rob Murray murder part of an overarching case that included the Lake and Sabin murder cases. Truman was at the county sheriff's office, giving a statement about his visit with the murder victim. Forensics was poring over the knife left in Murray's neck but had yet to officially connect it to the death of Olivia Sabin or Malcolm Lake. Mercy believed it had come from the knife collection at the Sabin home, but there was no supporting evidence.

Her phone rang, and Ava was on the other end.

She didn't waste time with pleasantries.

"I asked Jeff if you could go interview Gabriel Lake at Christian's home."

"Why?" asked Mercy. She tamped down the excitement in her stomach, impatient to grab any opportunity to sink her teeth into the ongoing murder case.

"The agent Jeff sent to conduct the interview was turned away and told to contact Gabriel's lawyer. Of course, no one went to work today because of the snow, so there is no reaching his lawyer until tomorrow at the earliest. I don't have time to wait around, and I think Christian will let you in."

A silent cheer erupted in Mercy's brain. "I can't guarantee his brother will talk to me. And the roads out here are a nightmare. I'm surprised the first agent made it to the house."

"He said he almost didn't. But I know you can. My efforts to reach their mother, Brenda Lake, have hit the same lawyer speed bump. She was happy to chat with me the other day, but my second interview request was shot down, and I was referred to her lawyer."

"Considering Malcolm and Gabriel are both lawyers, that doesn't surprise me one bit."

"It bothers me that the family is suddenly uncooperative."

Mercy understood. "I'm sure they're just protecting their rights, but it does make them look bad. Has Christian been informed of Rob Murray's death? Since Christian was willing to loan him that SUV, I assume they have a good working relationship."

"To my knowledge, neither we nor Deschutes County have been able to talk to the Lake brothers since our visit. If Christian knows, it wasn't from us. Has there been media coverage?"

"Not that I've noticed."

"I assume there've been no sightings of Salome or her daughter?" asked Ava.

"I've heard nothing. Jeff mentioned that local police are checking hotels, and they have a BOLO out for her vehicle, but they could be miles away by now."

"Dammit. I hope she's still close by," said Ava.

"I'll let you know if I hear something, and I'm happy to give you whatever help you need."

"Can you go to Christian's home this morning?" pressed Ava.

Mercy thought about the snow-covered roads. The chance that her route to Christian's had been cleared was extremely small. A challenge.

"I'm on it."

Mercy unclamped her hands from the steering wheel, turned off the ignition, and exhaled.

It'd been a bitch of a drive to Christian Lake's home. She'd had to shovel her way out of one snowdrift when an oncoming car hadn't stuck to its side of the road. Jerking the steering wheel to avoid him hadn't been a good move. And the asshole had kept driving, not caring that she was stuck.

*The things I do for justice. And my own curiosity.*

That damned reporter had wanted to use her to interview Gabriel. She had considered calling Michael Brody, simply to have someone with her for the treacherous drive, but she'd rejected that idea immediately. This was an official visit, not a press tour. After Ava's call she had changed her clothes and then checked the supplies in the back of her Tahoe. Now she looked dressed to go ice climbing instead of to an FBI interview. She'd grabbed a few bottles of water from the break room, not wanting to tap into the water jugs she always carried. A quick inventory of her duffel had assured her she could last a week if she got stranded.

Peace of mind.

But damn, the drive had sucked away her energy. She'd slacked on her exercise over the winter. Her treadmill had been silent for several nights in a row. Staying healthy and fit was an important part of her paranoid lifestyle. Who knew what medical services could be like after a disaster? She was getting lazy.

*Unacceptable.*

She looked up at Christian's grand house and sighed. It was as glorious as she'd remembered. Part of her had believed that she'd built it up in her mind since her last visit. Nope.

No vehicles were visible, and she wondered if Ava had ever gotten the warrant to take tire prints from the old Hummer. She assumed it was safely tucked away in the long garage today. Mercy had no idea how to take tire prints, but maybe a photo of the treads could be helpful. Now to come up with an excuse to get in the garage.

*Did Gabriel Lake drive out here? Or did Christian send a car to meet him at the airport?*

A search on Gabriel Lake had revealed a man who resembled Christian. Attractive and tall. Gabriel headed up a successful law firm, and she discovered many articles singing about his skill in the courtroom.

A man appeared on the front porch. Brent Rollins.

Mercy grumbled. She'd hoped to avoid the watchdog and get to Christian first.

He jogged down the freshly shoveled stairs and strode to her vehicle, a grim expression below his hat brim. Mercy slid out of her Tahoe and closed the door, indicating she wasn't about to leave.

"Christian and Gabriel aren't seeing anyone today," Rollins announced as he drew closer. Recognition flashed in his eyes as he reached her.

"I think Christian will see me."

"No. We already told the FBI to go through the lawyers."

Mercy gestured at the snow. "No lawyer is working today. In Bend or in Portland. We're losing time to find who killed their father."

"They're not available." His gaze was ice as he studied her from head to toe. "You don't look like an FBI agent."

"I wasn't aware there was a standard. And I wasn't about to tackle that drive without dressing appropriately. I'm lucky I only had to shovel my truck out of one drift."

Respect flitted across his face.

Mercy seized the momentary dropping of his defense. "Did you ever meet Malcolm Lake?" she asked. "I know he and Christian were estranged."

"That's none of your business." He continued his imitation of a statue.

"Why are you trying to stall this case? Their father was murdered. Some might even accuse you of obstructing justice." She was fuzzy on the legalities of her statement but didn't care.

He folded his arms across his chest. "Call the lawyer."

Mercy played a wild card. "Did you hear about Rob Murray?"

The stocky man showed no surprise. "What about him?"

She stayed silent but raised a brow and gave a half smile. *I know something you don't.*

"What about him?" Rollins repeated.

"I think I should tell his boss what happened to him."

Irritation shone in his eyes as he weighed his choices. The decision was snatched from him as Christian stepped out on the porch and waved. "Hey, Mercy!"

She gave Rollins a satisfied smirk. *I'm in.*

He deftly controlled his emotions and waved her toward the stairs.

Christian greeted her like a long-lost friend and hustled her into his kitchen, offering her coffee and something to eat. Mercy gawked at the luxury kitchen, which was the size of her apartment. A glassed-in wine room, two huge stainless-steel refrigerators, a cooktop with enough burners for a small restaurant, an island big enough for a king-size mattress, and a built-in espresso machine the size of her SUV's dashboard. "Jeez, Christian. Do you operate as a restaurant on the weekends?"

He slightly ducked his head. "The builder said it had to match the rest of the house."

"It definitely does." She eyed the espresso machine. "Can you make me an Americano?"

"No problem."

She leaned against the island and watched him push buttons and clank metal.

"Why are you here, Mercy?" He met her gaze as his hands automatically made the espresso. "I assume this isn't a visit between friends?"

She wished it was. "We need a statement from your brother."

He nodded and finished her drink. "Cream?"

"Heavy cream if you have it."

"I do." He added the luxurious white liquid and stirred with a slender spoon. He handed her the mug, holding her gaze. "Gabriel doesn't want to talk to the police without his lawyer present."

He sounded like a recording.

Mercy took a sip, weighing her next move. "I'm surprised he's in your home. At our last visit you implied that you don't get along."

Christian poured himself a cup of coffee from a ready pot. "We have our differences, but he's my brother."

"And this is about your father. He was murdered, Christian. Horribly. We need to move fast, and it's already been too many days."

A struggle filled his handsome face. Mercy stayed silent, letting him battle his own demons. He was dressed in cargo pants and a half-zip sweatshirt, looking ready to go for a hike except for the heavy slippers on his feet. He wore his wealth casually without a pretentious bone in his body, and she wondered how he was still single.

"What did Brent say to you outside?"

*Is he stalling?* "He told me to go home and call the lawyer."

"Who needs a lawyer?"

Mercy immediately identified Gabriel Lake as he stepped into the kitchen and refilled his coffee mug. He took a long drink and studied Mercy, curiosity on his face.

"This is Mercy Kilpatrick, Gabriel. We go back a long way."

*Why didn't he identify me as an agent?*

"Nice to meet you," Gabriel held out a hand and Mercy shook it, echoing his statement. "You drove out here in these conditions?"

"It wasn't too bad," she said. "How long are you visiting Christian?"

"I haven't decided. With the passes closed, there's no point in trying to get home to Portland."

Mercy fished a business card out of the pocket of her coat. Handing it to him, she said, "I'm with the Bend FBI office."

His fingers automatically took her card but he stiffened; surprise filled his face but was quickly replaced with irritation. "No comment."

"I'm not the press," Mercy pointed out. "I'm here because your father was murdered. It's standard operating procedure to interview family. You've been avoiding us."

"Call my lawyer." He shot an annoyed look at Christian and turned to leave.

"Gabriel," Christian snapped. "What the hell is keeping you from helping the police?"

His brother stopped under the glorious rugged rock arch that separated the kitchen from a back hallway. "I know how the standard operating procedure works. Every family member is regarded as a suspect until they're cleared. I don't need to be treated that way."

"Then clear yourself! You're prolonging the inevitable. What's the worst that can happen?"

"How about you answer only the questions you're comfortable with?" Mercy suggested, desperate not to let the older brother slip away. "We're trying to get a picture of your father's last days."

Gabriel stood silent, his gaze darting between her and Christian.

"She doesn't bite," Christian added.

"I'll give you twenty minutes," stated Gabriel, looking at his watch for emphasis.

"Are you going somewhere?" Mercy couldn't contain the retort.

"Make that fifteen minutes."

"Let's sit down," Christian suggested and pulled out a bar stool at the island for Mercy.

She sat and pulled out a small notebook. Gabriel slowly took a seat, giving her his attention.

*My, won't this be fun.*

# TWENTY-TWO

Truman opened the door to Eagle's Nest's tiny library, noting someone had already cleared snow from the steps and several yards of walkway and then spread salt. The smell of old books, dust, and a touch of mildew reached his nose. Fluorescent lighting, ancient tables with hard chairs, and shelves and shelves of books greeted him. He was definitely in a library.

"Ruth?" He spoke loudly. "It's Truman." No one answered.

He moved to the tall counter where the librarian processed checkouts. The counter was the sole piece of luxury in the bare-bones library. It had originally been a welcome desk in a fancy hotel that had been torn down in the 1950s. After being found in someone's garage four decades earlier, it'd been transferred to the library, where it'd stood like a silent sentry ever since. It was solid oak and elaborately decorated with hand-carved nature scenes that must have taken master craftsmen months to create. It easily weighed a thousand pounds.

Ruth Schultz appeared from a doorway behind the counter. "Truman! Good to see you. Ina gives me reports on you as if you were a favored grandson."

If Truman were to look up *librarian* in a dictionary, there would be a picture of Ruth Schultz. She looked as if a Hollywood studio had outfitted her to play a cranky librarian. Gray hair in a bun. Reading glasses on a chain around her neck. Cardigan, slacks, dull shoes. But she was one of the kindest women he'd ever met. Constantly in motion, full of chatty conversation, and a fountain of knowledge on any random subject.

"I'm surprised you're open today," Truman said after her hug. "Two-thirds of the businesses are closed on account of the snow."

Ruth dismissed the idea with a wave of her hand. "Of course I'm open. The city pays me to be available, so I'm going to be here. A little snow won't stop me."

"Did you clear the steps?"

"First thing when I got here. We get a lot of older patrons. I can't have someone slipping and breaking a hip." Her pale-blue eyes twinkled. "It'd be hard to get them to the hospital today."

"Next time call the station. I'll send Lucas or Royce to take care of your snow."

"Now aren't you polite." She nodded in approval and leaned forward to whisper, "How about sending Ben Cooley? I haven't chatted with him in forever."

Truman knew why she hadn't seen his senior officer. Ben was terrified of Ruth. Even though he'd been married over fifty years, Ruth still flirted with him as if they were teenagers. He froze and clammed up every time he saw her. A silent Ben Cooley was a wonder to behold.

"I hear you had a problem." Truman knew it was time to change the subject.

"Absolutely. After I did the steps this morning, I went to shovel off the concrete slab at the back door and discovered the lock was broken. The door was closed, but anyone could open it."

"Anything missing?"

"I immediately checked my little cash box. It doesn't hold much. Just enough to make change when someone pays their overdue fees. It hadn't been touched." She frowned. "There isn't much of value in here to steal. Why steal a book when you can just borrow it? Seems like a lot of work to break into a library when you could stroll right in."

"Any cameras?"

Ruth snorted.

"I know. Your budget," he admitted. "But I had to ask. Did this happen last night? Or at least sometime after you closed up yesterday?"

"I wasn't open yesterday. We're on a reduced schedule and only open three and a half days a week now. Tax cuts, you know," she said with disdain. "But I know the door was locked when I left the evening before last. It's part of my closing routine to check it."

Truman took a slow look around the library. Ruth was right. He didn't see anything to motivate someone to break open the door. His brain wouldn't let him ignore the fact that two nights earlier someone had broken into the church. Someone who possibly drove a car similar to Salome Sabin's. *Did she break in here too?*

He was jumping to conclusions.

"What about rare books?" he asked.

"I sent them to the county library. They have the facilities to take proper care of them."

"I wonder if someone was looking for a place to get out of the cold."

"That was my thought too once I didn't see anything missing." She paused. "But there was one unusual thing I noticed . . . but possibly I didn't take care of it before closing."

Truman waited.

"Two microfiche rolls left out near our machine." A frown flitted across her face. "I swear I checked that table before we closed."

"Microfiche? People still use that?" Truman remembered the old system from his high school library. A dated technique of preserving newspapers and magazines on film.

Ruth sniffed. "We don't have the money to transfer the film records to a digital system. I won't replace something that isn't broken."

"Where is it?"

She led him to the far end of the library, where a table holding what looked like an ancient computer monitor sat on top of a film feeder. Next to the table was a long wooden storage unit with dozens of small drawers. "Is that where the films are filed?" He noted the drawers didn't lock.

"Yes."

"What publications are on film?"

"Well, I have decades of *The Oregonian* going back into the eighteen hundreds, but once they started digitizing their records we no longer got new ones. I also have the *Bend Bulletin* up to about twenty years ago and our own local paper, which goes back to the middle of the century. It used to be published every day, you know. But about five years ago, it dropped to a weekly paper. Pretty soon that will probably be my library's schedule."

"I hope not," Truman told her. "I know you do an important service."

"No one researches in books anymore. It's all available online. Even our fiction circulation has dropped. People are switching to digital book subscription services."

"There will always be a place for libraries." Truman hated the sad look in her eyes.

"I still see some regulars every week, and moms bring in their toddlers for story time, but I never see teenagers."

"You said some rolls of film were left out. Do you remember which ones?"

Ruth grabbed a small box off the top of the storage unit. "I haven't refiled them yet."

Truman took the box and pushed the rolls around with his pen, reading their labels. "This one holds a few months of *The Oregonian* from about forty years ago, and the other is our local paper from the same time period." He smiled. "But they fit a whole year of our town's paper on one roll." He met her gaze. "You sure these weren't accidentally left out?"

Ruth's face was a study. He knew she was convinced nothing had been left out when she closed, but there was an infinitesimal chance she'd missed them. "I'm ninety-nine percent certain this table was clean."

"Do you mind if I take these for a bit?"

Her face said she minded very much. "I guess not."

He dumped them into a plastic bag from his pocket, wondering if there was any point in fingerprinting them. They would have forty years of prints. The content on the films was the key. But how would he know what the suspect had been looking up? And what good would that information do? As he sealed up the bag, he realized he needed the huge reader machine to look at the evidence.

"I'd prefer it if you didn't take my only machine," she stated, reading his mind.

"I don't want to take it," he admitted. "I'll come back and use it when I have time to look through these rolls."

"In that case, I need you to check out the rolls. This is highly irregular," she pointed out. "I only allow people to view the rolls here."

Truman signed his name on the cards she produced, amused at her thoroughness. There was a reason she'd been the librarian for the last thirty years. "Don't touch the back door or this machine anymore. I'm going to send someone to dust for prints."

"Just as long as they clean up after themselves. I've heard that powder makes a horrible mess."

He promised not to lose her rolls and headed back to his office.

Inside his vehicle he sat for a few moments, his brain connecting dots. No one in town had reported a break-in in months. Suddenly he had two—possibly on the same night. Logic told him it was the same person, which was why he would collect prints.

In a perfect world he'd find a print that matched one he'd lifted from the church, and a suspect would pop up on a search of his first fingerprint database.

Rarely did he work in a perfect world. But it was worth a shot.

*Is it Salome Sabin?*

He'd interviewed the witness who claimed he'd seen a dark-haired woman driving a green car at the church the night of its break-in. Fred lived kitty-corner from the church and had been getting a late snack when he spotted the car around 2:00 a.m. He hadn't seen the car stop or anyone get out, but he swore it'd slowly circled the block three times, immediately catching his attention.

Truman had tried not to stare at the Coke-bottle lenses on Fred's glasses. They were smeared and scratched, so he asked when Fred had had the prescription checked. Offended, the senior citizen said it'd been updated three months earlier. Truman had his doubts. Unless Fred used burlap to clean his lenses, they shouldn't be foggy with minuscule scratches in that short a time.

Fred's statement was shaky. But between the driver description and knowing that Salome and Morrigan had disappeared that night, it continued to sit on Truman's radar.

Truman focused on the bag of film rolls he'd set on the passenger seat. Someone had looked up articles from forty years earlier. He hadn't been born yet. He typed "Eagle's Nest" and the corresponding year into Google on his phone and scrolled through the hits. Most referred to graduating high school classes or population counts of the town.

*The two break-ins are my cases. My town. I need to investigate.*

It wasn't like the gray area of his involvement in the Rob Murray murder.

He started his vehicle, remembering Detective Bolton's frustration during Truman's morning interview about his visit to Rob Murray's apartment. Truman had had little to tell the detective. He'd visited the man and left. He hadn't seen anyone hanging around, and Rob hadn't appeared in fear for his life. Truman was still convinced someone—hopefully it was Rob—had moved his pickup truck before his death. He couldn't see a reason for the killer to move it afterward. The murderer could have rifled through it, looking for anything of value to steal, but why move it?

*Rob had to be the one.*

He knew none of the agencies were seriously looking at him for Rob Murray's murder, but it still bugged the hell out of him that he was even involved. It was as if he had a big black X on his perfectly clean record. He wanted it erased. And it was all because he'd nosed into a case where he had no business.

*That's what I get for satisfying my curiosity.*

# TWENTY-THREE

The summer after we graduated from high school, I stopped by Christian's home. I'd had an argument with my mother, and I needed someone to listen to me grumble. Christian and I had grown close over the last six months, and we leaned on each other when we were feeling blue.

He was my best friend. My only friend.

His parents had divorced ten years before, and he'd told me his mother still carried a lot of bitterness. I had yet to meet her. They lived in an impressive ranch home in the nicest neighborhood. I knew his father was some hotshot lawyer in Portland, and I assumed he still sent money to his ex. The elegance of the home struck a chord in me. This was what I dreamed of. A two-car garage, a manicured acre of green lawn, and neighbors whose homes were as dignified as mine. I wanted to fit in.

Instead we had our odd cabin deep in the woods. Hiding from the world.

I rang the doorbell and waited, admiring the terra-cotta planters overflowing with petunias. The door opened and I found myself face-to-face with his mother for the first time. Brenda Lake was petite, blonde, and rake-thin. Everything I was not. Wealth shone in her perfect hair, gold rings, and pedicured toes.

I identified myself and asked for Christian. Her stare burned into my eyes. I exhaled and subtly sniffed. Red-orange. Anger. Sorrow. Hatred.

Christian was right. She still carried a lot of bitterness.

I forced a smile and asked again for Christian.

"What do you want with my son?" Her tone was cool, but I felt the ripples of ire under the surface. Her face formed a hard mask, and she didn't step aside to welcome me in.

I was rattled. "He's expecting me. We're going out for lunch."

Her lips pressed into a hard line. "He doesn't need—"

"Salome?"

He grinned at me over his mother's shoulder, and I focused on that face as if I'd been thrown a lifeline.

"Where are you going?" his mother snapped.

"Lunch," Christian stated. His beautiful smile faded, and he placed a hand on his mother's upper arm to gently push by her. She guarded the door like a statue.

"I need you for two minutes first," she told him. Brenda glanced in my direction. "He'll be right out." She shut the door in my face.

I couldn't breathe. I stood there like an idiot, staring at the iron door knocker, as if I thought she'd swing the door back open, laughing and saying that it had been a joke. It didn't open. I walked backward off the small porch and nearly fell as I missed the single step.

*Why is she so rude?*

Then I knew. When the door first opened, recognition had flashed in her eyes. I'd attributed her angry aura to the constant bitterness Christian had told me about, but it'd erupted because she knew who I was.

She knew I was the witch. The slut. The whore.

I turned to go to my car, fury heating my limbs. Most times I embraced my notorious titles, but this woman's disdain struck me deep in my heart. I'd hoped the mother of my best friend would be different.

Their voices came through the window and I stopped, unable not to eavesdrop.

"You were rude!" I'd never heard Christian so angry.

"I *know* who she is," his mother hissed. "I know the type of life she leads, and my son will have none of it!"

"You don't know crap. It's all bitter gossip."

"Her mother was a whore and her daughter is just like her. Penniless, dirt-dwelling sluts."

"And you're a snob! You can't see past someone's clothes and car," Christian exclaimed. "Salome is awesome and I like spending time with her."

My heart warmed.

"She's going to drag you through her mud. We're better than their kind. I know they're witches." The last word sounded as if she was about to vomit.

A long moment of silence followed.

"You're a horrible person." Christian's anger was in control, but it vibrated through every word.

"Where are you going? Come back *here*." His mother sounded desperate. "See? She's cast some sort of spell on you."

"Give me a fucking break." His voice was suddenly closer to the door, and it opened an instant later. He smiled at me, but his eyes were furious.

"You don't have to go," I told him. "We can do this another day."

"Ignore her. She can't stand that I won't let her tell me what to do anymore." He strode past me toward the street and then spun around when he noticed I hadn't followed. "Are you coming?"

"I don't want to be a problem between you and your mother." My fights with my mother broke my heart. I didn't want that for him.

A sports car pulled into the driveway. I knew nothing about cars, a curse of living in the woods, but I instinctively knew this one was expensive. A gasp left my lungs as I recognized the driver. Christian's older brother.

Christian moved closer to me, his gaze on his brother as he got out of the car and came toward us, a grin on his face as he loosened his tie. "Hey, little bro." Gabriel's gaze went to me and I saw no recognition.

The man who'd drugged me and nearly raped me didn't even remember me.

"Who's this?" he asked with a kind smile.

"A friend. We're going to lunch." Christian grabbed my hand and dragged me away.

Numb, I let him open his car door for me, and I sat staring through the windshield. I shouldn't have come.

A moment later he climbed into the driver's seat. "Hey." He took my hand and tugged until I met his gaze. "My family sucks. I'm sorry both my mother and brother are horrible."

"It's okay," I answered automatically.

"No, it's not. No one deserves their crap. He didn't even recognize you, did he?"

I shook my head.

"Asshole."

"Your mother doesn't want you to have anything to do with me." Strength flowed back into my spine. "Does she *really* think I bewitched you?" The absurdity of her words finally amused me. I was used to people avoiding me and whispering behind their hands. I didn't give a fuck what others thought, but I'd hoped Christian's mother would be more like him. Instead she was more like her oldest son.

"Clearly she's heard the gossip," Christian admitted, "but I never thought she'd react like that."

"She knew instantly who I was. What have you told her about me?"

"We've never discussed you."

I snorted. "That doesn't make me feel any better." But I said it with a smile.

His mother had caught me off guard and stabbed her way through my shields. It wouldn't happen again.

"You're not a witch, right?" he joked as he started his vehicle.

"I only help others." We'd touched on this topic several times. I'd shown him the ointments and teas I sold and explained what was in them. He'd ordered me to stop selling the potions with booze, worried someone could get hurt. I saw his point and stopped. Ever since school was out, the demand had dried up anyway. I'd never told him about my sensory talents. It was too difficult to explain.

"I'm sorry she was a bitch," he told me.

Scents of regret and embarrassment filled the car. I touched his hand. "It doesn't matter."

"I can't wait to get out of here for college."

He was going to California. Briefly I'd considered following him, but the financial numbers simply didn't add up. I also didn't want to scare away any potential girlfriends. His friends were uncomfortable when I was around, so I knew no girlfriend would approve of our close friendship.

I would miss him dreadfully.

# TWENTY-FOUR

Eyes like Christian's looked at Mercy from Gabriel's face and unnerved her. The brothers also tipped their heads in the same curious manner, and had identical voices.

Gabriel carefully recited his answers to her questions. She frequently glanced at Christian, wondering if he knew how much they sounded alike.

"Why did you come here instead of go to your home in Portland?" Mercy asked.

"The media was all over the murder," said Gabriel. "My neighbors told me reporters had been camping out on my street. I knew Christian's home was secluded. Besides, family is important at a time like this."

Christian shifted his feet and looked out the window.

*There's not much affection in this room.*

"Have you talked with your mother?"

"Of course," said Gabriel. "Even though they've been divorced for decades, my mother still cared for my father."

The younger brother shifted his feet again.

The signals were obvious. Every time Gabriel said something that Christian didn't agree with, he couldn't hold still. He kept his mouth shut, but the energy of his objection came out through his movements. Mercy wondered if their differences were due to the divorce. It appeared they'd both been left behind with Brenda Lake, their bonds broken with their father. But Gabriel's commitment to his mother had continued, while Christian seemed to have slowly drawn away from both parents.

Gabriel was painting a picture of his family, but Mercy didn't know if it was an accurate picture or simply the one he thought the investigators should have.

"When did you last speak to your father?"

His shoulders slumped. "Two days before his death, I talked to him on the phone. If I'd known I'd never speak to him again, I would have said something more meaningful."

"What *did* you discuss with him?"

"Ummm . . . I can't quite remember. It was purely a check-in call. You know . . . 'What's going on? What are you up to?'"

"You don't remember what he said he'd been doing?"

"Nothing's sticking in my head, so it must have been the usual reports about his fund-raisers and golfing trips."

"Do you call him often?"

Gabriel lifted one shoulder. "I'm better than I used to be. I was angry with him for a long time after the divorce, but we've worked through it over the last five years or so." His face brightened. "Now I remember what we talked about!" Gabriel launched into details of a case that he'd shared with his father and some of the restaurants he'd mentioned eating at on his last trip to Palm Springs.

Her time was ticking away. He had looked at his watch a few times while they talked, clearly marking off the minutes until he could escape.

*How can I keep him talking?*

"Did you hear about Rob Murray?" she asked Christian. Out of the corner of her eye, she saw Gabriel perk up.

"Who's that?" he asked.

"A guy who does some work for me," said Christian. "What's up with Rob? I told him I wasn't upset about the Lexus."

"He was murdered yesterday." Mercy watched both men.

Christian stared at her, the blood draining out of his face. Gabriel tilted his head and frowned. He spoke first. "That's horrible. Did you know him well, Christian?"

Christian swallowed. "Wait a minute. I saw him yesterday." His voice was hoarse. "He came up to apologize about the SUV."

Mercy leaned toward him, Gabriel momentarily forgotten. "What time was that?"

He stared at the floor as he thought. "Right before lunch. I'd just finished in the gym and was starving when he came."

Truman had visited Rob in the morning. *So Rob did go somewhere after Truman's visit.* She knew the information would relieve some of Truman's anxiety.

"His body was discovered not long after lunch," said Mercy.

"What happened to him?" Gabriel asked, his gaze probing.

"He was killed in his apartment. I really can't discuss more than that."

"You're sure it's murder?" asked Christian.

"Positive."

"I can't think of anyone who'd want to hurt him," Christian said. "He was usually easygoing, but I guess I didn't know him all that well. I know he did some painting when he wasn't working here. That's about it. Does that make me a crappy boss?"

"Ease up on yourself," suggested Gabriel with sympathy. "You can't know everyone."

Christian turned a thoughtful gaze on his brother. "I try very hard to get to know the people who work for me. I think it's important. But

I've focused on my employees at the office. Not here at the house. Do they have a suspect?" Christian asked.

"I don't know yet. But I'll let the detective know you saw him yesterday, so you'll probably get another visit."

He sighed but nodded. "Did Rob have family?"

"I don't know. But he lived alone."

"That's good . . . I guess."

"The investigator will want to talk to your manager, Brent Rollins."

"That shouldn't be a problem," said Christian.

"I saw him this morning out by the garage," added Gabriel. "He was shoveling the walk."

Christian slumped a bit. "I'll tell Brent about the death. I wouldn't say he and Rob were friends, but he'll still be shocked."

"Are you done with me?" Gabriel spoke up.

Mercy mentally shifted back to her interview of Gabriel. "No. Did you father ever tell you he was worried for his life? Did he ever express worry for his safety during a case? Did he ever mention threatening letters, calls, or concern over a visitor?" Mercy rattled off the questions.

"No, yes, and yes." He didn't expand.

Mercy waited.

"Come on, Gabriel," Christian urged.

Gabriel shot a look at his brother. "He got a lot of publicity during the D'Angelo trial. People from all over the world sent him mail and tried to call. Some positive contact, but a lot of it wasn't. People liked that he mouthed off to D'Angelo, but they didn't like that he wasn't convicted. Dad got threats, but I don't think any of the senders got physically close to him. People are comfortable hiding behind a phone or computer screen to say crap. Standing in front of you face-to-face is different."

"And that was a dozen years ago, right?"

"Right."

"No more fallout from the case since then?" Mercy included Christian in the question.

He took a quick look at his brother and shook his head. "Not that we're aware of."

"That's the only case you recall where people bothered your father?

Gabriel threw up his hands. "We don't know. He didn't tell us anything. Neither of us have lived with him since I was twelve and Christian was eight."

"Your mother never remarried," Mercy stated, jumping to a different subject. "And you just said she still cares about your father. Thirty-two years is a long time to carry a torch for someone."

"She's not in love with him," Gabriel said. "Not after what he did to her and us. She simply acknowledges that he helped bring their children into the world."

"She can't stand to be in the same room with him," Christian clarified. "Or the same city."

"Leaving your wife and kids for another woman is a pretty low thing to do," Mercy said. "She must have been very angry."

Gabriel grinned. "I can see what you're doing. I'm a lawyer, you know."

"It's a fair statement," said Mercy. "You can't tell me it was rainbows and ponies during their divorce."

"More like hurricanes and alligators," said Gabriel. "Our mother wouldn't wait over thirty years to murder our dad. She would have done it back then. And made him suffer."

*He did suffer.*

"Is the FBI ready to start looking for the real murderer?" Gabriel asked. "Are you done hounding our family yet?"

Mercy smiled at him. "I can see what you're doing. I'm an investigator, you know."

Christian laughed. "She got you, Gabriel. This is the first step and you know it."

Gabriel took a deep breath and closed his eyes. "You're right." He opened his eyes and a contrite gaze met Mercy's. "I'm being a jerk. I haven't slept in three days and my patience is wire thin. I know you're just doing your job."

She agreed he looked exhausted. His eyes were bloodshot and his shirt limp and wrinkled. He didn't seem like the type of man who would let himself appear so disheveled.

"Can we start over? I'll cooperate."

She raised a brow at him, slightly skeptical.

"Truly. The FBI was involved in a case of mine a few months ago. You could say I got my ass handed to me. When you said you were with the FBI, every defense I had shot up."

Christian nodded. "I'm surprised Gabriel had any ass left after that trial."

"Don't fight us," Mercy said. "We're trying to find your father's murderer."

"I know." He straightened his back, his gaze clear. "Everything I've told you is accurate. And again, I apologize for the attitude."

"Do you know Olivia Sabin?"

Gabriel's gaze intensified. "Christian told me you think her murder might be related to our father's. Who is she? What's their connection?"

"That's what we're trying to figure out."

He was silent as he held her gaze, and she could almost see the wheels turning behind his eyes. Being a lawyer, he wouldn't jump to conclusions—which she appreciated. He'd want to know all the facts once the FBI had them.

"Do you have a service planned for your father?" Mercy asked.

The brothers exchanged a glance. "We're hoping to hold it three days from now in Portland. We haven't made a formal announcement because we're watching the weather."

Mercy felt an affinity flow between Malcolm Lake's sons. They grieved in different ways, but they were still sons of a murdered man. She suspected this was the first thing in a long time that had brought them together.

*Time lost.*

Her own strained relationship with her family popped into her mind.

*I'm glad I'm not wasting any more time.*

# TWENTY-FIVE

"Tell no one."

The detective's warning raced through Truman's head as he sped to the hospital in Bend. Last night Michael Brody had been shot in a Bend park. No one had known who he was until he woke up today. His wallet was missing and his vehicle gone. If some late-night snowstorm partiers hadn't stumbled across him in their drunken wanderings, he would be dead.

A Bend detective had called Truman because Michael requested it. He told Truman that Michael had first asked for his wife to be called and then ordered that his shooting stay out of the media. His third request was for the detective to call Truman.

"What happened? Is he okay?" Truman had asked the detective.

"He's gonna live. He'll have a scar to show off near his collarbone and he lost the top part of an ear and some of his scalp when the guy tried to shoot him in the head."

"Jesus Christ."

"The guy shot him while he was down in the snow and I suspect he believed he'd put one in his brain." The detective paused. "Brody wouldn't tell me why he wanted to see you, but he kept emphasizing for you to tell no one."

Truman didn't understand either. It would have been more logical for Michael to make a call to Ava or Jeff. But Truman believed Michael's message of silence was an order for him not to notify the Bend agents. Including Mercy. He'd respect Michael's wish until he heard the reason.

The reporter did things his own way.

"I don't have an answer for you," Truman told the detective. "But I plan to find out. I just met the guy this week."

"Hmmph. Did you know this guy is the son of Maxwell Brody?"

Truman searched his memory for the familiar name. "The former governor—No, he was the United States senator. That's news to me." Brody was full of surprises.

"His uncle was the governor. Now he's sitting in prison."

A jumble of old news reports flashed through Truman's brain. Something about the death of the senator's other son and the governor being behind it. The Brodys weren't your everyday family.

"I'll have to ask him about it," said Truman.

"I don't recommend it," said the detective. "He nearly bit my head off when I asked about his uncle. For a guy who was shot twice and nearly bled to death, he's still got a mouth on him."

"Noted." Truman wasn't surprised.

At the hospital, Truman showed ID twice to get to Michael Brody's floor. Then he showed it a third time to the Bend officer at Michael's door, who looked seriously disgruntled to be standing guard in a hospital hallway.

Inside, Michael's green gaze immediately locked on to Truman. His head was covered in bandages, as were half of his chest and left shoulder.

"Did you tell Mercy?"

"Nice to see you too, Brody."

Annoyance flashed in his eyes. "This is an opportunity, and I didn't want to risk any leaks reaching the media from the Bend FBI office."

"No one at the FBI office would leak something."

"I don't *know* everyone there. They have support staff that might talk," asserted Michael. "If the media doesn't get any information about my shooting, then the shooter will probably assume I'm dead."

Truman didn't understand the reporter's thinking. *Maybe it's the head injury?* "And?"

"I was making him nervous."

*"Who?"* He wondered how much medication the reporter was on.

"The only thing I'm working on is the Lake and Sabin shootings. Someone didn't like me nosing around."

"And so they shot you? You think whoever killed those two decided to shoot you too?"

"I find it logical."

"Knives were the murder weapons in both," Truman pointed out. "And did you know one of Christian Lake's employees, Rob Murray, was found murdered yesterday morning? Guess what the weapon was? It wasn't as orchestrated as the other two deaths, but there are enough similarities that it can't be ignored."

The reporter's eyes widened. "No one told me." His brows came together in deep concentration.

"Now he decides to change it up and shoot you? What other kind of trouble did you stir up around here?"

"I want him to think I'm dead. It'll make him comfortable, and perhaps he'll screw up or get cocky. The detective asked the hospital to notify them if anyone calls and asks about a shooting victim from the park. And the Bend Police Department is keeping it quiet. There's still an investigation at the scene, but the cops have been ordered to share no information with curious gawkers. Not even to say if someone died or survived."

Brody closed his eyes, suddenly looking pale. "Fucking room is spinning."

Truman cast around for . . . anything and grabbed an empty water pitcher. "I've got you covered if you're gonna puke."

Brody took a deep breath, opened his eyes, and attempted to focus on Truman. "I made a dozen phone calls in the hours before I was shot. I gave a list of the calls to the Bend detectives this morning. You can get the numbers from my phone—fuck. I keep forgetting that my phone was stolen."

"Along with your wallet and truck."

"Right . . . but they found those. Right before you came in I was told my truck turned up in the Walmart parking lot with the wallet on the seat. Of course, the cash and credit cards were missing. The police didn't know to look for my vehicle until I told them."

"One positive thing."

"I'm still breathing. I'd also call that a positive. Although by the way my wife reacted when I talked to her today, you'd think I'd be better off dead."

"A little upset?"

"Furious." He grinned. "Jaime's always claimed I'm going to piss off the wrong person and get shot one day."

"Smart lady. Now who did you call yesterday?"

He closed his eyes again and recited, "I called Ava, I called the Bend FBI office, the Portland Police Department, Detective Bolton at Deschutes County, the Bend state police office, and Judge Lake's assistant in Portland. I called Brenda Lake and tried to reach Gabriel Lake—"

"What did you get out of Brenda Lake?"

"She told me to stop calling or she'd call her lawyer."

"Who I assume is Gabriel Lake."

"Most likely."

"But nothing came out of those phone calls that you think would make someone want to shoot you?"

"Not that I know of."

"Then perhaps you were the victim of a robbery, since your cash and cards are gone. We can't rule that out."

"Too reasonable," muttered Michael. "I don't like it."

"It doesn't seem likely, but I can't disregard the possibility. Why were you at the park?"

"I have no idea."

*"What?"*

Michael grimaced and shifted his legs under the hospital blanket. "I don't remember going there. The last thing I remember is driving in town." He pointed at the wrap on his head. "I suspect this has something to do with my short-term memory loss. I'm stunned that I can remember every phone call from yesterday but can't remember anything I did past four o'clock."

"So the identity of your shooter might be buried in your brain."

"They say I was shot from the back, so maybe I didn't see him."

"Or her."

"Or her," Michael agreed. "Apparently I have a hard skull. Tough enough to deflect a bullet . . . a poorly aimed bullet."

"Something to brag to your wife about."

"I think she already knows. The doctor said even though the bullet didn't crack the bone, the deflected impact was enough to cause swelling inside my skull. Hopefully after the swelling goes down, I'll get that chunk of memory back."

"How much pain are you in?"

"A lot. And my ear is constantly ringing, and each time I turn my head, fireworks go off in my brain. You try getting shot in the head."

"I've had my share of near-death experiences."

"That's right. I remember reading your history."

"Try to remember who shot you."

An annoyed glare was his answer.

Questions ricocheted in Truman's brain. *Is Michael's shooting related? Did he rattle the Lake and Sabin killer?* The whole situation made him very uncomfortable, and he knew the FBI would want to know as soon as possible.

"Are you okay with me notifying Mercy, Ava, and Jeff now? I'll give them your reasons for keeping it quiet."

"Yes, let them know. I think it was our murderer trying to add one more victim to his list."

*Who would shoot the reporter?*

Mercy understood how Michael Brody could annoy a lot of people, but enough to kill him? As she drove back from Christian's home, her mind attempted to process why their killer would shoot Michael. According to the phone call she'd just had with Truman, Michael believed he pushed someone's buttons with his investigation of the deaths.

*He might have been very close to an answer.*

Entering her office, she pulled off her coat and scarf, and her cell phone rang.

Ava.

"Did you hear about Michael?" were the first words out of Ava's mouth. Elevated concern rang in her tone.

"I did. I talked to Truman a few minutes ago."

"Michael has a good point about keeping the shooting quiet," Ava admitted. "I like the thought of our murderer getting cocky, believing he's cleaned up behind himself. Maybe he'll make more mistakes. The fact that he shot Michael instead of taking his time with a knife could mean he's getting impatient."

"Was Rob Murray killed because he caused him a problem too?" asked Mercy.

"I think so. Either Rob saw or knew something about one of the first two deaths. I suspect it was Olivia Sabin's death, since hers was in his vicinity. I'm surprised he didn't say anything when Truman showed up on his doorstep."

"I think that indicates Rob wasn't aware he'd seen something important to the killer."

"Could Rob have been involved with the murders?" Ava wondered.

Both women were silent for a moment as they processed theories.

"The doctors say Michael will be okay." Relief filled Ava's tone. "He might never get that chunk of short-term memory back, but it appears to be a small time period that is missing. He can deal with that."

"He got too close," stated Mercy. "Just like Rob."

"I agree. I told the investigating detective that the FBI is interested in his shooting and he gave me a list of phone calls Michael made yesterday. I hope I can shake something loose. This investigation is taking too long."

Mercy remembered Olivia Sabin's hand in hers and shuddered. "I don't disagree with you. No one wants this killer found more than me."

"How was your talk with Gabriel Lake?"

She gave Ava an overview, summarizing that Gabriel had no information about his father's activities before his death.

"Did you talk to Judge Lake's assistant yet?" Mercy asked hopefully. She was tired of dead ends.

"We did this morning. She swore there were no off-the-book visits and that every visitor and meeting had been logged."

"Maybe Michael's information was wrong," said Mercy. "He didn't have anything to back up his claim about a mystery guest."

"True, but I'm going with my gut that there's something here. Eddie's finally been able to view the video from the hall outside the judge's office door and compare the people to the visitors list."

"Sounds dull."

"He's made that very clear." Amusement rang in Ava's voice. "He told me that it's not as simple as it sounds. Various office workers from all over the big building are in and out of the office nonstop, and of course they aren't logged in. He had to recruit an employee from one of the other offices to help identify them. Delivery people are causing issues too. Eddie was momentarily excited about a lunchtime visitor with long, dark hair who wasn't logged in until his helper identified the Thai delivery bag in the mystery woman's hand."

"Ugh. Do you think the judge's assistant is lying?"

Ava was silent for a moment. "I'm not sure. I'd like to give her the benefit of the doubt."

"Could she be in danger?" Mercy asked. "I know Michael's attack was quite different from the three murders, but if our killer is getting desperate and cleaning up his tracks, she could be a target."

"Dammit. I didn't think about that. I'll get the local police involved. At least it appears our killer is currently on your side of the mountain range. He won't be getting back to Portland anytime soon."

"I heard they should have at least one of the passes open tomorrow," Mercy told her.

"And I heard the week's weather forecast. They're wasting their efforts, because the range is going to get hit again."

"Looks like Eddie won't be back for a while."

"I might keep him. He's a sharp one. I'm trying to convince him to come back to the Portland office."

Possessiveness rolled through Mercy, surprising her. She'd miss his jokes and friendship. "Good luck with that. He's sold on the Bend branch."

"For now," stated Ava.

A few moments later Mercy ended the call, still rattled at the thought of losing Eddie back to the big city. *There's no way. He loves it here.*

A rap on her door frame caught her attention and her mood immediately lifted at the sight of the tall man holding a cowboy hat. She felt like the only woman in the world when Truman's intense gaze focused on her. His dark eyes were expressive, reflecting his immediate thoughts. And right now he appeared to be thinking about their time in her apartment last night.

Heat flooded her face, and he grinned. "You too, huh?" he asked, raising one eyebrow.

"I don't know what you're talking about."

He glanced over his shoulder and then took two quick strides, then sank his hands into her hair as he covered her mouth, indicating he'd seen no one watching. Trusting him, she melted into his touch.

*How does he do this to me?*

Whenever he appeared, she became whole. The moment they locked eyes, she'd feel the physical change. A piece she'd never realized was missing audibly snapped into place when he was close. Every. Single. Time.

Now that he'd been in her life, she would always be less of a person without him.

*How did I not know I was missing a vital part of myself?*

But she *had* known something was lacking. She'd chalked it up to the burden of being an introvert. The hours spent toiling through school by herself, developing her peace-of-mind cabin on her own, and completing assignment after assignment at work. She'd been driven, determined to fill that gaping hole with satisfaction from work and activity. All that time she'd been pursuing the wrong leads.

She pulled back and smiled, feeling the happiness in her chest grow as if he'd sprinkled Miracle-Gro, rain, and sunshine on her. Her breath caught at a shadow in his gaze. "What's wrong?"

The shadow vanished.

"Nothing. Except murders and gunshot victims."

*He's not telling the truth.*

"How long will Michael be in the hospital?" she asked, feeling off-kilter at the discord between his eyes and his answer.

"They don't know yet. A few days at least. I came here before I headed back to Eagle's Nest because I wanted to get your take on something. I'm thinking it could be related to your case."

"Not my case," she automatically stated, knowing she was up to her neck in it.

A twist of his lips acknowledged her weak assertion, and he told her about a visit with the Eagle's Nest librarian.

"You're not positive it happened on the same night as the church break-in?" she asked.

"There's a fifty-fifty chance it did."

"When did you last have a business report a break-in?"

"Months ago."

"Have you looked through the film?"

"I haven't had time, but when I do I'll start with the local paper film and focus on the months that correspond to the roll of *The Oregonian*."

"What months are on *The Oregonian* roll?"

He told her and she did some quick math. "That's forty-one years ago."

"Almost exactly."

"Isn't Salome around forty? She's still the main suspect for the first break-in, right? Could she have been looking up something around the time of her birth?" Mercy knew it was a giant leap of logic.

"I thought of that too and checked her birth date. She was born the year after the one on the rolls. I'm still not sold on the claim that it was a woman that night at the church. The witness doesn't have the best vision."

"Well, don't churches store records? Especially small-town churches? Births, baptisms, marriages. Maybe big-town events? Could someone have been looking up the same time period at the church?"

He stilled. "Why didn't I think of that?"

"Because you're a sinner who's never stepped foot in a church?"

"Not true. My parents dragged me to church until I moved out. But it was a huge city church." He gave her a smacking kiss on the lips. "Thank you for the idea. I'll stop by and talk to David Aguirre again, although I don't know what to look for during that time period."

"I would help you, but I can't get away this afternoon. Would your librarian let you use the microfiche after hours?"

His face stated he sincerely doubted it. "I'll check."

# TWENTY-SIX

Truman decided to walk to the church from the Eagle's Nest library. Ruth had grudgingly given him a spare key, promising to make his life hell if he forgot to lock up.

He told himself the walk was a chance to get a close look at how his town was handling the snowstorm. But the truth was that he needed to exorcise a memory he'd suppressed for days. He'd refused to let his mind explore the path that Salome Sabin had led him down nearly two decades earlier. When David Aguirre had admitted that he'd met Salome in the past, Truman had seen the same cautionary fear in David's gaze that Salome had triggered in Truman's gut.

His breath fogged in the cold air as he exhaled and thought back to that night.

It'd been a hot summer night when Salome had led him out of the party like a dog on a leash. Mike Bevins's warning was a fading voice in his mind as Truman followed her out the door, his gaze glued to her ass under her snug short skirt. They both carried cups of beer, their other hands clasped together, and she'd looked over her shoulder back at him, dark eyes dancing with promises of pleasure. Truman stumbled over his own feet as he panted after her.

Outside she led him past the pool to a lounge chair near the fire pit. Someone had lit a fire, but it'd burned low as the partiers stayed in the air-conditioned home, avoiding the stifling heat. The outdoor lights were off except for the underwater lights of the pool, and the low flames of the fire added to the arousing ambiance. Never letting go of his hand, Salome lay down on the lounger and pulled Truman on top of her. His beer cup hit the ground as his hand shot out to prevent him from crashing into her chest. She laughed, a low, sex-filled sound that made his muscles tighten down low.

Every cell of his body wanted her.

She set her beer on a small table, sank her hands into his hair, and pulled him close. Fake nails ran along his scalp and shot his desire into overdrive. The low flames cast dancing shadows across her face, making her eyes liquid chocolate in the dim light. She licked her lips, and his mouth was immediately on hers.

He couldn't think.

A rapid burn rushed through his veins as he kissed her. She was skilled, with experience and confidence in every touch of her tongue and lips. Truman was no virgin, but the headiness that overtook his brain made him feel as if he was on the cusp of something brand new. Pressure mounted and he pressed his hips against her thigh, triggering another low laugh that vibrated against his lips. Pleasure blazed a path to his head, better than any alcohol-induced buzz.

He slid his hand under her tank top and she arced, pressing her full breast into his hand.

No bra.

Her skin was as silken as her tongue. *I need to see.*

He pulled away from her mouth and pulled down her top, exposing one breast. He caught his breath at the sight of a tattoo near her nipple. "Did that hurt?"

"Hurt like the devil himself carved it." She stared up at him, her dark eyes challenging.

"What does it mean?" It was three flower petal shapes with their points meeting in the center, overlapped by a circle.

"It's my protection."

"Protection from what?"

Her sultry gaze ran from his eyes down to his waist, her meaning clear. *Like she needs protection from me.*

He lowered his head and slowly ran his tongue over the tattoo, and she gasped. She tasted lightly of salt and smelled of an earthy perfume gently blended with hops and wheat. Her hips pressed up and her head tilted back, her mouth open, her lips glistening in the firelight. He moved back to that mouth and she touched his belt.

*Yes!*

"Wait a second."

He pulled back at her words. She moved her top into place and reached for the tiny purse she'd set by her beer. She dug inside. "Let me up for a minute."

He unlaced his legs from hers and sat back on the lounger, his gaze locked on her bag, expecting a condom. Instead she pulled out a small vial and moved to the fire pit. She glanced back at him, her eyes invisible in the dark. "Come stand beside me."

He obeyed, his excitement still racing full speed ahead.

She opened the vial, closed her eyes, and softly chanted, her words indistinguishable. With a flick of her wrist she flung a powder from the vial into the fire. The flames flared up in the dark with sharp cracks and slowly died back down as an exotic scent filled Truman's nose and turned his legs into rubber.

A trickle of fear shot down his spine.

"What was that?" he asked.

The air around them grew thick with the rich odor as she turned, eyes flashing in anticipation.

"What were you reciting?" Dread crept into his hormone-driven brain.

She didn't answer either of his questions, and his arousal started to fade.

"Have you ever tasted the blood of another person?" she asked, a challenge in her low tone.

He swallowed hard as his arousal evaporated completely. "No."

The night air grew oppressive as the heat of the day continued to radiate up from the concrete deck. More heat drifted from the fire and from her skin, and sweat trickled down his back.

Then he saw the blade in her hand. It was small and delicate, perfect for her feminine grip, and the firelight glinted off the sharpened edge. She quickly ran it across her wrist and blood tricked down her palm. "It enhances the arousal," she told him.

He had no arousal left to enhance.

Truman couldn't look away from the blade. The heavy scent clogged his brain, and he struggled to make his muscles obey.

She took his hand and held it palm up between them, laying the blade against the skin of his wrist. He stared at his hand, willing to move. It wouldn't. "Trust me," she whispered.

"Fuck no." With a herculean effort he jerked his hand out of her grip, and his fingertip stung from a cut. *What are you doing?*

"Trust me," she repeated, reaching for his hand again.

Truman stepped back, his heart thumping in his chest, and the burn of his cut cleared his head. *Are you nuts?*

Anger sparked in her eyes as she froze. "Scared?"

"Hell no, but I'm not dumb enough to swap blood with you. I don't need some freaking disease."

"I should have known you were too young." The blade vanished into her purse.

His pride twinged but not enough for him to give back his wrist. "Mike said you were a witch."

Her smile spread slowly across her face as she tipped her head and looked at him through thick lashes. The allure of a siren. "That didn't stop you from following me."

"Are you?"

The tantalizing smile again. "What do you believe?" She glided closer, placing her hand in the center of his chest. "A little danger can be a lot of fun."

Truman backed up another step. "I believe we're done."

She halted, and Truman swore relief flashed in her eyes a split second before the temptress returned. "It could have been the best night of your life," she whispered. "You'll never know what you missed." Her tongue touched the center of her upper lip.

Lust briefly blazed, but he stamped it out. *Fuck no.* "That's okay with me." He turned his back on her and strode back to the party. At the door he glanced back; she watched him. He couldn't see her eyes, but he felt their pull. The fire framed her body, and the luscious silhouette tempted him again.

*Danger.*

He yanked open the door and welcomed the blast of air-conditioning on his hot face.

*I just avoided a nasty mistake.*

The old memory made Truman's skin crawl as he approached the church. *I was young and dumb.* Thankfully his drunken hormones hadn't overridden his common sense.

*What would have happened?*

He hurled the thought out of his brain. *Don't go there.*

Inside the church he experienced déjà vu as he strode toward David's office. *Second time here this week.* Ahead a man stepped into the hallway, his cowboy hat in his hand. He turned to shake hands with someone Truman couldn't see. "Thank you, David. I'll see you for dinner next week." He turned toward Truman.

Karl Kilpatrick. Mercy's father.

*Also for the second time in a week.* Truman greeted Karl and shook his hand and then David's. Curiosity shone from both men's eyes. There was an awkward moment where Karl waited, watching him expectantly, and Truman knew he hoped to hear the purpose of his visit. "Tell Deborah thanks again for the pie the last night."

"We'll have to do it again," Karl politely replied. He got the message and moved past Truman toward the door.

"Next time I'll make certain Mercy joins us," Truman said to Karl's back.

Karl's step faltered, but he didn't stop. He simply raised a hand in acknowledgment.

*I tried.* He turned and found David closely watching him.

"Still problems between those two?" asked David.

"No crack in the ice yet. She's trying. I do what I can."

"One of these days they'll come together. Karl Kilpatrick is one of the most stubborn men I know, but I think he's proud of Mercy . . . even if he has an issue with her profession."

"It goes deeper than that, David. There's a bitter history between them. She's angry that he cut her out of the family when she was eighteen, and he's angry that she wouldn't follow the life path he'd chosen for her." That was the CliffsNotes version. Their fifteen-year estrangement had been born out of distrust, betrayal, and Mercy's broken heart.

"One of these days forgiveness will heal their wounds."

"Don't tell me Karl was here to talk about Mercy." *Maybe he's finally coming around.*

"Our conversations are confidential."

Truman winced. There was that pious tone David sank into at random.

"What can I do for you?" asked David in his normal voice. "Do you have a lead on the break-in?"

"Yes and no. What I have is a theory I'm exploring. What kind of records do you keep here at the church?"

"You mean our financials? There's—"

"No. For the town residents. Like deaths or marriages."

David's face cleared. "Oh. It's a tradition to keep a written record of ceremonies performed here at the church. Like you said, funerals and marriages, but also baptisms."

"What about births?"

"No, just the baptism. Same with the deaths. We only record them if the funeral is held here. Back in the early nineteen hundreds, nearly every event happened here and was recorded. Those old records are quite interesting, but they're being stored in a facility that has the right temperature and humidity to protect that sort of written record. In the last half of the twentieth century, people began to get married in other venues, and our baptisms are down."

"I didn't know the church kept track of those things."

"Most small-town churches do. We use handwritten ledgers." He smiled. "It sounds old-fashioned in these days of digital everything, but there's something about seeing the events recorded on a page for history."

"So you don't have more recent records?"

"We have the last fifty years or so. I should send in the older ledgers for proper preservation."

"Can I see some?" He told David the months from the microfiche film rolls.

"Follow me."

Back in a dusty room, David opened a file cabinet drawer. Inside was a pile of about a dozen ledgers—the type that reminded Truman of old-fashioned hardback grading books. "As you can see, this isn't optimal storage for paper records."

"I'd expected a lot more books than that."

David shrugged. "Eagle's Nest isn't that big. Dozens of entries can fit on one page. Most take one line." He dug out a ledger that corresponded to Truman's requested months. He laid it on a desk and gently flipped through the pages. Truman was impressed by the impeccable lines of script. It matched the perfect cursive in the handwriting instruction books from his grade school years. Someone's beautiful writing had recorded the town's history. A few pages later the handwriting changed. Not so perfect, but still neater than Truman's.

"Back then there was a church secretary who handled this sort of thing," David said. "Not enough work now to justify a secretary."

Truman wondered if the recorder with the perfect cursive had died or simply moved on. The change in handwriting was another historical notation. One without an attached name.

"Here are your dates."

There was less than a page of records. Truman ran his finger down the page, pausing at familiar last names that drove home that he was truly an outsider in Eagle's Nest. His townspeople had deep roots; his own were barely planted.

His finger stopped on a name. *Kilpatrick.*

*Henry James Kilpatrick.* The baby had been one day old at his death. Parents Karl and Deborah.

"Did you know about this?" Truman asked David. Mercy had never said a word.

"I didn't. What a burden they must carry."

Truman's sympathy flared for Mercy's parents. "I think this baby was born between Owen and Pearl."

"Horrible."

*Does Mercy even know?* Her parents were the type to push past a tragedy in their lives and never look back.

His finger slid down the rest of the page, and he struggled to focus on the names, his mind occupied. *Do I ask her about it?* He didn't want to be the jerk who exposed a painful event from her parents' past. It was their place to share the information, not his. *I could check with Deborah first.*

No other names jumped out at him. He checked the page before and the page after his months.

*It would help if I knew what the hell I was looking for.* He snapped pictures of the records with his phone in case he needed to refer back to them. Or show them to Mercy.

Out of curiosity he opened the ledger for the current year. David's handwriting was atrocious. A cramped scramble of printed letters and italics.

History preserved.

He thanked David and left, his brain spinning. His next step was to read through the films from the library. He remembered Mercy's offer to help him go through the film.

*A baby boy. One day old.*

*Can I sit next to her and keep my mouth shut?*

◆ ◆ ◆

Chat?

The text from Rose came through as Mercy was leaving her office. She hurried to her Tahoe, brushed off the new inch of snow, and called her sister as she pulled out of the parking lot.

"I suggested lunch like you said." Rose didn't bother with a greeting. "Nick said he couldn't."

Her sister's hurt tone tore at Mercy's heart.

"Did he say why?" She drove slowly; the road hadn't been plowed for a few hours and the new inch of snow had already compacted into a slick surface. The sun had set, and she was thankful few cars were on the road as she drove to the Eagle's Nest library to meet Truman.

"He blamed the snow."

"Well, that's logical. No doubt some of his employees can't get to work, leaving him shorthanded. And he has to be concerned about you out on the roads."

"He didn't mention either of those things."

"What did he say then?"

"He didn't give any explanation except that the snow made it a bad idea."

Nick's longing face as he watched Rose touch the cradle flashed in Mercy's mind. *I'm not wrong about how he feels.*

"You know he's a man of few words. To him that was probably sufficient."

"Do you think it's the scars on my face?" Rose whispered.

Mercy's chest split wide open. "No, honey. I don't think it's that at all. And truly . . . they've healed *so* well. The scarring grows more faint every week." *Truth.*

Anger flared at the killer who'd held her sister hostage and cut her. Physically and emotionally. *I hope he's rotting in hell.*

"I can feel them. They're huge."

"I'm sure they feel that way to your fingertips. I'm not lying to make you feel better, Rose. To the eye they're not that obvious."

Her sister exhaled. "Maybe I was wrong about him. I should just enjoy the cradle and focus on the baby."

"Are you going to your ultrasound?" Mercy asked.

"It was canceled because of the weather."

"I'm so sorry! Did you decide whether or not to find out the sex?"

"My mind changes every day."

Mercy was dying to know but refused to influence Rose's decision. "Pink ruffles or blue sailboats."

"Right?" said Rose, her voice taking on a dreamy tone. "I keep dressing the child in my mind. One day it's tutus and ribbons, and the next day it's rain boots with puppy faces."

"Girls can wear both," Mercy pointed out.

"True."

"Don't worry about Nick," Mercy added. "He's the type of guy that needs to feel secure before he makes a move. We'll make sure he gets that security."

"You talk like it's a sure thing," muttered Rose. "I'm not desperate for a husband, you know. I won't be a crazy stalker."

"I know. But this path with Nick should be explored."

"That's exactly how I feel," she admitted. "I'll never forgive myself if I let it fade away without getting to know him better." Rose sighed. "Say, any word on Morrigan and her mother yet? I hate to think of that little girl out in the snow."

"I'm confident Salome is keeping her daughter as safe as possible." The possessiveness on Salome's face the night she got her daughter out of foster care flashed in Mercy's brain. That was a mother determined to protect her child.

Rose lowered her voice. "But they could be the next targets, right?"

"I don't know," admitted Mercy. "We haven't figured out the reasons or found a connection between the other murders. Clearly Salome knows something. She was terrified for her daughter's safety."

"Scared enough to run away from the police," Rose said. "What could it be that she doesn't trust the police or FBI?"

"That's the big question."

"It doesn't look good that she took her daughter and ran. Do you think she committed any of the murders?"

"We don't know." In her heart Mercy believed the mother was a victim. But she'd been wrong before.

Mercy ended the call after promising to check in the next day. A half hour later she parked in the dim light at the Eagle's Nest library behind Truman's Tahoe. The town was silent; the only other cars were parked at the diner. Its neon restaurant sign turned the snow on its roof a bright red. A plow had gone down the main street recently, leaving piles of snow on each side of the road, but a light dusting of snow continued. Just enough to keep the world freshly white.

She slid out of her truck and stood in the street, relishing the quiet and still world as tiny icy flakes tapped softly on her jacket. The streetlight highlighted a halo of falling flakes. She lifted her face to the gentle flurry and the icy bits tickled her lashes.

"Cold?" asked Truman.

His footsteps had crunched two seconds before he spoke. She'd known it was him and hadn't startled at the sounds of his boots in snow. She didn't need to see him to know he was near. As she turned, her chest warmed at the sight of him; he grounded her. He was solid when she was flighty. He was straightforward while she sometimes moved in the shadows. And for some insane reason he wanted her. Ten feet apart, they watched each other in the powdery mist.

"God, you're beautiful."

The need in his voice ripped at her soul.

"The snow in your dark hair sparkles like diamonds." He laughed. "Jeez, I sound like a sappy idiot."

"You do. It's not often I hear the police chief get mushy and poetic."

"Do you want more of it?"

Mercy considered it. "No. Flowery words don't impress me. I need to see the dedication and devotion with my own eyes." Right now she saw a man hungry for her in the peaceful snowfall. The heat and adoration in his gaze exposed his heart more than any words.

"You know I love you, right?" He made no move toward her.

"I do." She did. He didn't need to frequently verbalize it; his actions and affection told her every day. Breaking the spell in their living snow globe, she moved to him. Finding his mouth, she kissed him long and deep. "I love you too," she said against his lips.

"Clearly," he muttered, kissing her back and pulling her tight against him.

It was a scene from a movie. The snowfall. The lovers. The silence. Mercy ached to go home with him and sleep in his arms. Not stare at microfiche.

"We could look at the film tomorrow," he said in her ear, sending bolts of arousal down her limbs. "I don't think twelve hours will make a difference."

"Your home," Mercy ordered. It was closest.

He gave her one last kiss.

"See you in five minutes."

# TWENTY-SEVEN

Truman tossed and turned, drifting off to sleep while stretching his hand out and finding bare sheets. He'd jerk awake at the empty space at his fingertips and stare at the ceiling for another twenty minutes. Mercy had left his bed just before midnight.

Kaylie had finally made it back to their apartment, and Mercy wanted to be there. He wondered if the teen noticed the effort Mercy put into being present. He sure did. *I can't complain about Mercy's dedication.*

Simon wandered into Truman's bedroom, leaped on the bed, and curled up near his hip. He was touched by the cat's attention and stroked her soft fur. A poor substitute for Mercy's skin. The cat rarely slept in his room, but maybe she knew he needed company.

Or maybe she was cold.

He finally got up hours before he needed to and drank a full pot of coffee while watching the early news shows from the East Coast. His morning crawled at a lethargic rate.

Now he waited for Mercy at the library, stomping his feet in the freezing morning air and watching the town's businesses come to life. Owners shoveled their walks and greeted their neighbors. A hustling vibe filled the town. People who wanted to stock up before the next storm moved quickly, intent on their errands.

Mercy arrived. As she walked toward him, the rueful expression on her face told him the world wasn't the romantic wonderland they'd experienced last night.

He understood. It felt different this morning. The sun was out and the sky was an intense blue, but low, dark clouds threatened to the west. They shared a quick kiss and exchanged a longer look, memories of the night swirling between them. He wanted to wake with those memories every day. An inexplicable rise of urgency that had nothing to do with physical needs overtook him, and he wondered how he had fallen to this point. At one time he'd been content with his cat. Now he would never be content until his life fully merged with hers.

*Is that what she wants?*

He wouldn't rush her. He had nothing but time.

"I can't stay long," Mercy told him. "I need to get to the office."

Truman unlocked the library's front door and held it open for her. It was one of the budget-cut days, so the building was closed. A faint hint of lemon reached him as Mercy passed by. Her usual scent. He liked it, but it wasn't as heady as the warm scent from her skin after she'd rolled in bed with him. That was his favorite.

"It's freezing in here," Mercy exclaimed, snapping up her coat.

"She turns off the heat when it's not open."

"It must take hours to get it back up to a livable temperature."

"Maybe that's part of the reason the patronage is down." He led her to the microfiche machine and turned it on as he pulled the two rolls of film from his pocket. He'd dusted them for prints but found nothing helpful.

"There's only one machine? Bummer." Mercy sat in the unit's chair while he grabbed another from a reading table.

"I think two sets of eyes will still be better than one."

"I don't understand what we're looking for."

"That makes two of us. All I know is that whoever broke in was searching for something specific during these months."

"Salome?"

"Possibly. I want to know what she was searching for. If it was her, logic says it's related to her mother's death. Why else would she risk breaking into buildings at a time like this? I don't think she was looking for recipes."

Truman pulled out the tray below the huge monitor and threaded the local paper's film across the viewing area, then wound the blank end around another roller. He pushed the tray back in, fast-forwarded to the first sideways image, and then turned a knob to rotate it to right-side up.

"For a second I thought we would have to tilt our heads and read it sideways." Mercy peered at the buttons. "No zoom?"

"Here." He rotated another dial and the old front page was suddenly legible. The forty-year-old lead story was a feature on the high school's valedictorian. "Know him?"

"I don't recognize his name. Probably was smart and moved away."

He chuckled. "I like Eagle's Nest."

"Trust me, as a teen all anyone wanted to do was get out." She forwarded to the next story. "I don't mind it now."

They sped through stories on livestock, county fairs, and drownings. Typical summer stories. National news was in a small column on the far right of the front page, almost as an afterthought. Local stories took precedence.

Truman hit the FORWARD button each time Mercy nodded to show that she had finished reading. Together they skimmed every page, and she frequently pointed out names she recognized. Truman pressed the button again, and his heart stopped as a photo of Jefferson Biggs filled the monitor's screen. His uncle. The man was in his twenties and grinning in a way Truman had never seen. Jefferson had won the top prize at the county rodeo.

"How cool is that?" Mercy exclaimed.

"I never knew he did rodeo." He stared at the photo. *What else do I not know?*

She turned to him, her gaze concerned. "Are you okay seeing this picture?"

Four months earlier he'd discovered his uncle dead, brutally murdered by a local serial killer. Truman mentally poked at the sad spot where his uncle's death lived in his brain; it didn't hurt the way it used to. "Yeah, I am. I've just never seen it before." The initial shock had vanished, and he wished he had a copy of the picture.

"There's a print option," Mercy pointed out, reading his mind. After a few missteps with the printer, Truman had his copy.

"Are you sorry you sold his home?" she asked.

"No. I'm glad you took a lot of his supplies, and I like the young family who bought it."

"It was too much house for you." She continued to skim, leaning closer to the monitor, reading each headline.

*Now?*

"Are you looking for a house to buy?" he asked bluntly. The question erupted out of his mouth as if it'd been bottled under pressure.

She sat back from the monitor and turned to him, her eyes cautious. "I've been thinking about it. The apartment was fine for me, but I'd like Kaylie to have a home. If she goes away to school, I want her to feel she always has a place to return to."

*Something Mercy never had.*

He carefully phrased his next statement, not wanting to sound as if he'd made assumptions. "I'd hoped one day to live with you."

Her expression softened. "I know."

He waited.

"I don't see how my house shopping interferes with those plans."

She was right. But his stomach still twisted and churned. "I wanted to shop with you. Do it together."

"That's a good idea. Kaylie isn't interested in looking at all. She says it's boring."

It didn't sound boring to Truman. It sounded awesome. He was slightly stunned that she'd immediately welcomed his help. The subject had been churning in his stomach for two days. *Why did I wait to ask?*

"You told me you have another year on your lease, right?" Mercy asked.

"Right."

"Then there's no rush." She turned back to the monitor.

*Yes, there is.* A grumpy mood settled over him. He was tired of sleeping alone and making phone calls to schedule their time together. He wanted to share a home with her. Blend their lives together. See her every day. "I can break the lease."

This time she turned her chair to face him. "What are you trying to tell me?"

*Isn't it obvious?* "I want to buy a house with you." *Do I need to make a sign?*

Caution appeared in her eyes. "You do?"

"You didn't pick up on that?"

"But we aren't even . . ."

If she wouldn't say it, he would. "Married? Engaged?"

"Yes."

"But we will be."

"Which one?"

*"Both."* He took her hands. "I've known for a long time that I need you in my life. Permanently. But I also know you like to take things slower." She opened her mouth, and he quickly added, "And there's Kaylie to consider. But frankly, I think if you told her, she'd be excited and happy for us."

Waves of different emotions crossed her face. Usually Mercy was a master of keeping her thoughts to herself. But at the moment all her walls were down, and Truman liked what he saw.

*She wants it too.*

He leaned forward and kissed her, his doubts of the last few days gone. "You don't have to say anything right now. There's no rush. I just wanted to be certain we're moving in the same direction."

She exhaled. "We are. But you're sprinting and I'm pacing myself."

*She calls this a sprint?* "I'll wait patiently for you at the finish line."

"Good. Now, keep reading. I don't have much time."

*Back to business.* He respected that. She was one of the most driven people he'd ever met. She set goals and smashed the hell out of them.

College on her own? She graduated at the top of her class.

Get accepted to the FBI? Again, she graduated at the top of her class.

Give her orphaned niece a home? Boom . . . done.

Find a killer? She didn't hold back.

Truman scooted his chair closer to hers and kissed her temple. "Whatever you say." He focused on the screen, and they fell back into their rhythm of skimming and advancing. "Was Rose okay after the fireworks with your father the other night?"

Mercy kept her gaze on the screen. "She is. Her ultrasound appointment for today was canceled because of the weather, so she's disappointed."

"Does she know if she wants a boy or girl?"

"I don't think she cares. She's got names lined up for both. Iris Joy if it's a girl and Henry James if it's a boy."

Truman's breath caught. "Henry James?"

"It's the name of a baby my parents lost. He was stillborn a year after Owen."

*Mercy did know.* "I'm so sorry. You never mentioned that before."

She nodded at his condolence. Her gaze was still on the screen, but there'd been a hitch in her voice as she spoke of the baby. "It was a long time ago. I wasn't even born. But my parents knew the baby was dead. His heartbeat had stopped early in the third trimester, and she carried him to term."

"How horrible for your parents." Truman felt ill.

"Yes, but I think it's what steered my mother toward midwifery."

Truman's respect for Deborah tripled. "Your mother is amazing."

*"Look at this."* Excitement filled Mercy's voice as she tapped the monitor screen.

Truman skimmed the article she'd indicated. It was about a local trial that'd just finished. Antonio Ricci had been convicted of three counts of first-degree murder and four counts of battery. The photo with the article was a mug shot of an angry man in his thirties. "I don't see what caught your attention."

"His wife testified against him," Mercy read. "Describing his frequent assaults. The jury struggled to understand her as she spoke through a wired jaw, reportedly broken by her husband." She paused. "The wife's name was Olivia Ricci."

*Could she be Olivia Sabin?*

"And look at the name of the presiding judge near the bottom of the article."

"Malcolm Lake." Truman's mind began to spin. "Holy shit. If that's our Olivia, here's a connection to the judge."

"I'm calling Dr. Lockhart. She'd know if Olivia's jaw had been broken." Mercy punched numbers on her phone.

Truman read the article again. Slowly this time. It was never clearly stated, but he gathered from the reporter's inferences that Antonio Ricci was some sort of enforcer. Someone who did the dirty work for his boss. But the boss was never named in the article. The Sopranos in Central Oregon? Truman shook his head. Not possible.

"Thanks, Natasha." Mercy ended her call. "Olivia Sabin shows evidence of an old break in her mandible. Natasha added that there were several old healed fractures in the other bones of her face. She has to be the Olivia in this article."

"That's terrible." Truman enlarged the old photo of the wife beater, seeing the evil in his eyes. *What kind of man has to beat on a woman?* "I think being sent to prison is motive for killing both Malcolm Lake and his ex-wife. Is this guy still locked up?"

"Let's find out."

# TWENTY-EIGHT

Morrigan looks nothing like me.

I don't care. My daughter is willowy and slight while I curve every-where. She will never be described as voluptuous. My skin is a pale mocha and hers is nearly transparent, with a touch of rose. The bone structure of her face is delicate and ethereal, nearly the opposite of my full cheekbones and brows. I carry the genes of people who embraced the sun and toiled in its heat. I don't know her history.

I see her real mother in her pale eyes and fine hair.

But she is my daughter in every way.

There are many ways to end a pregnancy, and my mother knew most of them. She was skilled with herbs . . . poisons . . . She knew just how much would cause a woman's body to reject the new life within it. She refused to physically remove a baby; potions were her only tools. But she was adamant in providing this service. Her only rule was that the pregnancy couldn't show yet.

The women who came with even the smallest baby bumps were sent away, told to talk to their doctors. These women were often angry, screaming at her, blaming her for their position. My mother would hold firm.

I was there when a woman brought her daughter across the mountain range from Salem one February. I smelled their indecision before they entered our home.

"They're undecided," I whispered to my mother as we watched them near our door. "The girl is terrified she's making a mistake, and the mother is confused." I paused. "It goes against their hearts."

The women entered, and we learned the girl was seventeen, a senior in high school, a top student, and had been accepted to college with a full-ride scholarship. A blessing, her mother said, because they were extremely poor; college would have been out of the question. She would be the first in her family to go to college.

Two pregnancy tests had confirmed the daughter's suspicions, and she believed she was three months along. She swore they'd used protection and had been shocked to discover a month later she was pregnant. There were seven months before she left for school.

My mother brought them tea, and I scented the calming herb she'd added. The girl wouldn't pick up her cup and stared at it as if it held the poison.

"It is safe," I said, smelling her fear. "We will talk first."

Her hands shook as she tentatively drank.

Her blue eyes were wide and innocent; she was still a child no matter her incredible performance in school. I studied her straight blonde hair with a bit of jealousy. She was the girl I'd always wanted to look like. Even at the ripe old age of thirty, I was jealous of her teenage perfection. Yet their lack of money showed. Their car was nearly as old as my mother's, and their clothes showed heavy wear and carefully repaired seams. A sour smell of desperation hovered around both of them.

Over tea we listened to them talk. My mother always talked to her "patients" first. She needed to know they had thought through their decision. Within moments we knew these two women were not ready.

My mother raised a brow at me, and I asked the daughter if she'd like to see the goats. We separated the two of them. My mother kept the mother drinking tea and the daughter followed me to the barn where two baby goats suckled from their mothers. She was charmed, as I'd known she would be. Baby animals and human girls were one of the most perfect pairings in the world.

"You are scared to do this," I finally said, watching her pet the mothers.

"I don't want to," she answered in a low voice. "But I don't see any other choice. I can't let this change the direction of the life I want."

"Man proposes," I said quietly.

"What?" A confused blue gaze met mine. Soft shades of yellow and lavender surrounded her. I smelled baby roses and new lilacs: innocence.

"Just talking to myself."

The girl lay both hands on her stomach. "I can't feel anything. I haven't seen any changes. Yet I *know* there is a life inside me."

"May I?" I asked, gesturing to her stomach.

She was hesitant but nodded.

I smiled and moved slowly, not wanting to spook her. I gently set my fingertips on her flat belly and closed my eyes.

Fresh-mowed grass, violets, cut lemons. The scents assaulted me. I'd expected subtlety, but the baby's life presence was strong. Pale pinks flashed in my mind, and I knew it was a girl.

*Mine.*

My eyes flew open and I jerked my hands away.

"What is it?" the girl cried.

"Nothing," I told her. "I thought I'd shocked you," I lied.

"I didn't feel it." Suspicion floated in her blue depths.

"Have you considered adoption?" My knees felt like water, and I gripped the edge of the goat pen for balance.

"Yes, but it seems complicated."

"I can place the baby for you. No papers. Nothing needed."

Her face cleared. "You can?"

"You don't want to end the pregnancy, do you?" I asked gently. "There is another option."

The two women drove away thirty minutes later. A plan was in place. It was doubtful her pregnancy would show much during the rest of the school year. Olivia would deliver the baby in late summer.

And I would keep her.

The months of her pregnancy dragged for me. I was impatient and worried she'd change her mind. I had no peace until their car parked in front of our home that summer.

The first time I held Morrigan in my arms, I became whole. I hadn't known there was a child-shaped empty space in my heart.

She was innocence. Unlike me with the blood of a murderer flowing through my veins.

Fresh-cut grass stayed as her primary scent, and her eyes reflected the most beautiful shade of pale blue that made up her aura.

I was in love.

My mother guided me and watched me raise her. No doubt she was amused at the change Morrigan had brought about in my wild life. I no longer searched for stimulation, striving to live up to the dangerous legacy bred into my bones.

Now my world was wrapped in a pink blanket.

# TWENTY-NINE

Mercy checked her rearview mirror over and over.

*I feel as if Antonio Ricci will show up any moment.*

The man's mug shot occupied a large portion of her thoughts, along with Olivia's horrific death. Her vision of Antonio was of a young, strong man, while Olivia had been old and frail. Had he taken revenge on his wife? Olivia must have seen his face, known her past had come back to haunt her. And do worse.

Pity and anger filled her.

She and Truman had spent another half hour combing the rest of the microfiche, searching for more mentions of Antonio or Olivia Ricci, but found nothing. They'd also scoured for anything else that could indicate why that film had been singled out, but by the end of their search, both of them were positive that the Ricci trial was the key. Mercy called to ask Jeff to find Antonio Ricci's current location, and he promised to get back to her ASAP. She and Truman had parted at the front door of the library, heading to their respective offices to officially start their day.

She called Ava from her vehicle to share their findings.

As she listened to Ava's phone ring, she considered the odd conversation with Truman about her house hunt.

There is a reason the horse goes before the cart. Especially in a growing relationship. To her, buying a house together didn't make sense unless they were married. She suspected Truman would have them married by now if she hadn't kept things at a decent progression. She'd learned that once Truman made a decision, he stuck to it.

A good trait to have.

But who makes a lifetime decision based on a few months of dating?

*Lots of people.*

*I'm not most people.*

But she did plan in the long term for most things. Money. Supplies. Safety. She prepared for everything but her personal life. *Why?*

"Mercy? What's up?" Ava's voice came through the speakers in her Tahoe.

Mercy gave her an abbreviated version of the discovery of Antonio Ricci.

The line was silent for a long moment. "Holy crap. Salome's father might be our killer? That makes no sense."

"Why not?" Mercy asked. "Malcolm Lake presided over the trial, and Olivia's testimony helped send him to prison. I see perfect motive."

"It does seem like a good motive, but Eddie spotted the mystery visitor on the video recordings at Judge Lake's office."

*"Who?"* Mercy held her breath.

"It was Salome. She visited the day of his death."

Mercy's mind scrambled to make the pieces fit. "Did you show the assistant the video?"

"We did. She broke down and confessed that the judge had ordered her out of the office a half hour before her lunch that day. She'd lingered in the hallway, curious why the judge didn't want her around, and saw a beautiful mystery woman enter his office."

"Why on earth wouldn't the assistant tell us?"

"She feared it was an affair that needed to be kept private. She assumed the woman was married or involved with some other government official, and she didn't want Judge Lake's name dragged through the mud after he was murdered. I think she had a bit of a crush on him herself and believed she was protecting his honor."

"What she did was delay a murder investigation."

"I made it very clear to her that the FBI was not happy." Ava paused. "I might have made her cry."

Mercy snorted. "I bet you did."

"I think we need to look hard at Salome as our killer," Ava asserted. "She was in the right place at the right time."

"But why was she at his office?"

"I asked the assistant about that, and she swears there was no paperwork from the woman's visit to indicate she was there for legal reasons. She did say her boss was in a very happy mood after the visit."

"Maybe they *were* having an affair." Mercy wrinkled her nose. The judge had been an attractive man in his seventies, but the age difference was too much for her personal taste. "That could be the purpose of Salome's frequent trips that Morrigan told us about."

"Eddie thinks she was in Portland to meet with some suppliers and attend an Internet business seminar. He found phone calls to the suppliers on her cell phone records, and when he talked with them, one said that Salome had talked about the seminar. Eddie said all the suppliers sounded very fond of her."

"Supplies for building her fairy houses?" Mercy asked, remembering the stunning room in the barn.

"Yes. Eddie located her Etsy store and her website. Digging into things, he believes she does pretty well for a home business. The supply orders she placed indicate a lot of upcoming construction, and they said she always paid promptly."

"A dream client." Mercy tried to merge Salome's business acumen into her line of thought. "But why would she kill the judge?" She was enjoying the brainstorming session with Ava. Both were tossing forward ideas, searching for connections, pointing out fallacies. It didn't matter how odd some of the suggestions were. There were no incorrect theories at this point.

"My first thought after hearing your Antonio Ricci story is that her father put her up to it. But why would she kill her mother?"

"That's the part that makes no sense to me. Even the reports that their relationship was tumultuous doesn't provide a good motivation." Mercy mulled over Ava's theory. "It's not impossible that Antonio put Salome up to the murders, but I suspect we'll find that he's been released. I think he's more likely to be our suspect, and I expect to hear his location from Jeff any minute. What about the tire prints at Olivia's cabin? Did you get the warrant to take Christian's tire prints?"

"No. I was told there wasn't enough cause." Ava swore under her breath. "And there's been no sighting of Salome and Morrigan."

"Correct. Nothing from the airports or on her BOLO."

"Dammit. I feel like this isn't moving fast enough."

"I disagree," said Mercy. "Finding out Salome's father connects Olivia and the judge is huge."

"I can't help but feel Salome herself has a big role in this."

"I keep pointing out the one thing that blows that theory to bits," said Mercy. "Her daughter was left behind. She wouldn't have left Morrigan at a murder scene. We both saw her desperation to get her daughter out of foster care."

"Maybe Salome wanted Morrigan back because she was afraid she would say Salome had killed the grandmother."

Mercy froze at the suggestion. "Crap." Then she shook her head. "No. I don't believe it. If that was so, why leave her behind in the first place?"

"It's a stretch, but we know Salome has the genetics of a murderer. Her father was put away for three first-degree murders, and I bet he committed more than that."

The talk of Antonio Ricci made her skin crawl. Mercy glanced in her rearview mirror again. "I feel claustrophobic. Maybe it's all the snow, the closed mountain passes, and how difficult it is to get around town right now. It's as if there's an invisible barrier around this area. I don't like the thought of her father being in town." An overwhelming need to get out of town boiled under her skin.

"That's understandable. With the murder of Rob Murray and the attack on Michael, I'd be feeling boxed in too."

"Any word on Michael?" Mercy asked.

"I checked in with him this morning." Relief filled Ava's voice. "He mouthed off to me on the phone, so I know he's feeling better. They'll let him go home as soon as the passes open so his wife can pick him up. He still can't remember what happened right before he was shot."

Two beeps sounded through Mercy's speakers. "Jeff's calling. I'll call you right back." She pressed a button on her steering wheel and cut Ava off. Excitement blazed through Mercy. *I know exactly what Jeff's going to tell me.*

"What'd you find out?"

"Antonio Ricci is still in prison," stated Jeff.

"*What? Are you sure?*" *I was so certain he was out . . .*

"Positive. I insisted on a visual verification before I called you back." Jeff sounded as frustrated as she felt.

"Fuck."

"Exactly."

"Now what?" Mercy deflated, and her bones ached with disappointment.

"I arranged for a phone call with Ricci. Maybe he can shine some light on the situation. I don't know how accommodating he'll be, since he's been in prison for forty years. He might harbor some anger against law enforcement."

Mercy snorted. "You think?"

"I want you to do the phone interview."

*Yes!* "I can do that." Elation drove away her exhaustion as questions for Salome's father ricocheted in her head. "When is the call?"

"They're getting back to me. Since Friday is almost half over, I emphasized that I didn't want to wait through the weekend. Hopefully they'll pull their act together and get it set up for today."

"Did you hear Salome was seen visiting the judge?" Mercy asked.

"Eddie just called me. And now that we know her father is still in prison, that new fact is shining the light back on her for the kills."

Mercy shut her mouth, her emotions at war with the facts. *I can't rule out Salome as the killer simply because I have a feeling.* She had to consider all options. "I was talking to Ava when you rang through. Anything else?"

"No. Let her know about Antonio Ricci."

"I will." Mercy ended the call and dialed Ava, who picked up on the first ring. Mercy wasted no time in telling her about Ricci's location and Jeff's attempt to get Mercy a phone call with the inmate.

"I'm not surprised he's still in prison," stated Ava. "Now to figure out why problems didn't start until forty years after his trial."

Mercy heard Ava rapidly tapping a pencil on her desk. The staccato beats were like a ticking clock.

"The entire Lake family claims they've never heard of Olivia Sabin," Mercy said slowly. "Maybe they've heard of Olivia or Antonio Ricci." She hadn't forgotten Christian's face as she asked about Salome Sabin. *He knows something.*

She needed to talk to Christian again.

"The whole Lake family is pissing me off," said Ava. "They're blocking us at every turn. That usually means they're trying to hide that someone is guilty."

"It's not Christian," defended Mercy.

"How do you know?"

She didn't answer; she had no facts to back up her statement.

"Don't let your old relationship affect your actions in the investigation, Mercy. We both know those were his Hummer tracks at the Sabins' cabin."

"We *don't* know that," said Mercy. "And until we have the evidence that says it was his, I won't accept that as fact."

"I understand."

"I want to ask the Lakes about the Riccis," said Ava.

"I think we're wearing out our welcome with them . . . or at least with Gabriel and his mother."

"I don't care. I'll call them again. Let me know when you speak to Antonio Ricci."

"I will."

"And watch the weather. They say the worst snow is supposed to hit your area this evening."

"Of course it is," muttered Mercy. "It's the weekend." She ended the call, Ava's warning about the snow taking over her thoughts. *This weekend could be a good opportunity . . .*

She decided to swing by the grocery store and grab a few cases of bottled water.

*Can never have too much.*

Mercy pushed her cart down the candy aisle.

She'd picked up four cases of bottled water and decided to grab Truman's favorite black licorice twists. And maybe some chocolate. There was already plenty of food at her apartment and her cabin. She had everything they could possibly need in case of being snowed in or losing power. Her mental checklist was fully checked off.

The chocolate peanut butter cups caught her eye, and she guiltily tossed a Halloween-size bag in her cart. Feeling watched, she looked up and met the surprised gaze of Brent Rollins.

He had a giant bag of gummy bears in his hand. Four cases of water, identical to hers, were stacked in his cart along with many bags of gourmet coffee, bottles of wine, loaves of bread, several steaks, and a few boxes of sugary breakfast cereal.

*Someone else is concerned about the weather.*

"More snow's coming," Mercy said conversationally.

"We heard," he said as he gestured toward his supplies.

"Gabriel still staying out there?"

"Yes." Annoyance flickered on his face, making her bite back a smile.

*I don't think he cares for Christian's houseguest.*

She wondered who did the cooking. Brent was clearly a capable guy, but she figured he drew the line at working in the kitchen. They parted awkwardly, nodding at each other, and Mercy headed to checkout.

Stepping outside, she realized grocery carts won't roll in unplowed parking lots. She brought her Tahoe to the front of the store and loaded it.

She'd just finished when Jeff called. "The prison can't arrange the call today. Monday is the best they can do."

"Their phones don't work on the weekends?"

"That's exactly what I asked. No one was amused. Where are you right now?" he asked.

"Just leaving the grocery store."

"They moved up the snowstorm by several hours, and I heard the schools have already let out their students. Why don't you take off the afternoon?"

"What about the case?"

"Have any other leads to follow right now?"

Mercy thought. "Not really. Ava and Eddie seem to be on top of it."

"Then go home. Be ready to talk to Antonio Ricci on Monday."

She ended the call. Her wished-for opportunity had just presented itself, and she made a decision.

She texted Kaylie.

Get out of dodge #3

Her phone was silent for a long moment. Then came the return text.

Understood

Mercy set down her phone, adrenaline racing through her veins as she started the vehicle. Her brain felt sharp and energized, eager for the challenge. She didn't know where Kaylie was, but the teen knew to drop whatever she was doing and meet Mercy at location number three, the abandoned service station two miles outside of Bend. From there they'd follow a circuitous route to her cabin as if the main roads were clogged with traffic as in a real emergency. Mercy planned to leave Kaylie's car hidden behind the station. Her Tahoe was best suited for the current weather, and she could chain up if needed.

They were overdue for an emergency dry run, and the snowstorm added an element of difficulty she couldn't create on her own. Getting out of town in good weather had been a breeze. The important part was testing out the supplies at the cabin. Living there for a few days showed Mercy what was lacking and where she needed to improve. Last time Kaylie's boredom had driven her slightly crazy, and she'd added more books and games to her stock. In a real situation, there would be nonstop chores to assign her niece.

As always, her stocked bug-out bag was in the back of the Tahoe. She had plenty of ammo in the bag, but no longer stored a weapon in it, not wanting it to fall into the wrong hands if someone broke into the vehicle. She had her service weapon and plenty of backups at the cabin. Her gas tank was full; neither of them ever let her vehicle's gas level drop below half a tank. Mercy's rule was to always have enough to get to the cabin. Kaylie's vehicle was also ready with a week's worth of supplies, and the cabin was stocked with a minimum of six months of food. For some nonfood items she had years of supplies, possibly decades.

Preparation.

No last-minute need to make an emergency trip to the grocery store or buy ammo.

Their priority was to get out of town as fast as possible.

*Should I message Truman?*

She decided to text him later. He wanted to go on one of her practice runs, but she knew he was on duty today and tomorrow.

She pulled a military-looking, handheld two-way radio out of her glove box. A backup measure in case the cell towers no longer worked. Kaylie had another in her vehicle. Turning out of the grocery parking lot, Mercy couldn't hold back a grin. Her claustrophobia had lifted. Getting out of the city for the weekend was the right thing to do. Two birds with one stone. A practice run and a mental health weekend.

She was pumped.

# THIRTY

"Ben got stuck in a snowdrift." Lucas stuck his head through Truman's doorway. "He helped dig a truck out of the snow out on the highway and then realized he was stuck too."

Truman sighed. "Do I need to go get him?"

"I sent Royce. He wasn't far from there."

"You know the next call will be that both of them are stuck."

Lucas grinned. "I hope so."

"People need to stay home today," Truman grumbled. "They're making it worse for everyone else."

"Most believe they can drive perfectly fine in the snow."

"Do you know how many times I've heard that as I'm shoveling out their tires? I swear people take it as a challenge."

"They get bored sitting at home."

Truman's gaze sharpened on Lucas. His athletic young office manager had a hard time sitting still. "Once you get home today, stay there. No four-wheeling."

"My phone's ringing." Lucas vanished without answering Truman.

"Don't call me if you get in a bind this weekend," Truman muttered to his empty office. A glance out his window showed the next round of snow had started. It was still light and pretty, but it would intensify over the afternoon.

His cell phone rang and Mercy's name popped up on his screen. "Hey, gorgeous. All morning I've been thinking about last night."

"You're on speaker, Truman. Kaylie is with me."

"Hi, Truman." Laughter infused Kaylie's tone.

"Hi yourself. I heard all the schools let out early today."

"Yes!" exclaimed Kaylie. "An extra-long weekend. Maybe they'll cancel Monday too."

*Every student's hope when it snows.*

"We're headed to the cabin," Mercy stated.

"What?" Truman pressed his cell against his ear. "Don't you know how crappy it is out there? And it's going to get worse. Say, aren't you supposed to be working?" He glanced at the time. It was nearly one.

"Jeff gave me the afternoon off because of the weather forecast. Oh! And he found out Antonio Ricci is still in prison."

"You're kidding me." Truman's heart sank. He'd hoped their discovery would crack open the case. "Now what?"

"I have a phone interview with Ricci on Monday. Until then, things are a bit stalled. Most of the evidence hasn't been processed at the county lab because half the staff couldn't make it to work this week."

"I know how that goes." Truman's tiny department was at the mercy of lab schedules. "But why are you going to the cabin *today*? I could have gone up with you next weekend."

"I've been itching to do a dry run. And the snowstorm is a great test."

He understood. For peace of mind, Mercy needed to know she could get to her cabin under any condition. "I don't like it. We've had call after call of people getting stuck."

"I've got chains, and sitting next to me is a young, strong back to handle a shovel."

"Hey!" Kaylie protested.

"I also want to check the photovoltaic system I installed last fall. I need to see if the snow is blocking the solar panels."

"Your roof is pretty steep. The snow shouldn't stick."

"It is," Mercy agreed. "But we've had a crazy amount of snow recently."

"You got your emergency bag?" he asked.

"Of course. And the one from Kaylie's car too. Did you really need to ask me that?"

"I need my own peace of mind, you know. Try to call me when you get there." Truman fought not to grumble, knowing the cell service was iffy. The thought of the two women challenging the storm made him uncomfortable. But no one could take care of herself better than Mercy, and she wouldn't have invited Kaylie if she didn't feel secure in her abilities.

"I love you," she told him.

"Awwww," said Kaylie.

"I love you too. *Please* be careful."

"Of course." Her tone was breezy, confident.

He ended the call and stared at the clock. With the crappy conditions, it would be at least an hour before he heard from her.

*How am I going to focus?*

"Boss?" Lucas shouted down the hall. "Detective Bolton on line one for you."

Glad for the distraction, Truman picked up the phone and greeted the county investigator. "Don't tell me you're stuck in a snowdrift somewhere," he said.

"Your department too?"

"All morning. And I don't expect it to let up."

"Nope. At least the snow keeps down the big crimes," replied Bolton.

"What can I do for you?" asked Truman.

"I wanted to run something by you. Do you know if the FBI ever made heads or tails out of the array of slashes on the first two bodies?"

"As far as I've heard, they haven't. Mercy would have told me."

"Well, I've been playing around with the patterns and I think I have an idea." He paused. "It could be nothing. I've been staring at these marks for a few days and my tired eyes have seen everything from circus elephants to airplanes."

"I doubt they're elephants."

"Do you have a copy of the patterns?"

"No." Mercy had told him about the similarities and penciled out the slashes for him, but he'd been no help.

"Hang on. I'm going to email you some sketches from both bodies."

"What about Rob Murray?" asked Truman.

"It's not the same. You saw that one. I think it was simply anger or panic and not planned out like the first two were."

Truman refreshed his email on his desktop and opened an attachment. It showed outlines of two human forms with the slashes drawn in. The marks were nearly identical on both bodies, but they looked random to him.

"Scroll to the other drawings at the bottom," directed Bolton.

Truman did. Someone had drawn in dotted lines, connecting some of the slashes.

"I think it's a dagger or a sword," said Bolton.

The slashes suddenly made sense. "I see that," said Truman. "There's a handle and the guard and then a long blade. I can't unsee it now. It's almost too obvious."

"Okay. I was concerned I'd jumped to assumptions by drawing in the dotted lines."

"They look logical to me. I don't think you're making any huge leaps."

"I've been sketching a lot, connecting lines here and there. This is the first one that made sense."

"What does it mean?" asked Truman. "I know there were a lot of knives and daggers in Olivia's home. But what's the point of carving the symbol into two victims?"

"A dagger can stand for betrayal."

Truman was silent for a long moment. "You suspect someone is making a point. I think the people intended to receive the message are dead. I wonder if it has anything to do with the Sabins' collection of blades."

"I wish I knew if that crazy room of knives was Olivia's or Salome's collection," said Bolton. "Killing Olivia with some sort of dagger or knife when she's a collector could be a slap in the face, proving that the killer is stronger. If it's Salome's collection, maybe the killer was sending a power message through Olivia's death by using a weapon meaningful to Salome." He cleared his throat. "The sword is quite prominent in Wicca."

The hair on Truman's arms rose. "As a murder weapon? From what I read, Wicca is all about nature and energy. Not violence."

"The sword is primarily ceremonial."

"Maybe the patterns are simply to throw you off," Truman speculated out loud. "Make the police waste hours trying to find the meaning."

"Then they've succeeded." Bolton colorfully cursed, echoing Truman's state of mind.

"But what would the sword mean in Malcolm Lake's death? You heard that Salome visited him the day he died?"

"I did. And I've already reviewed the video. It's definitely her."

"No one placed her near the judge's home that night, and no one has proved she was somewhere else." Truman ran a hand through his hair in frustration. "How the hell does Rob Murray tie into this?" The handyman's sad apartment flashed through Truman's mind. "The connection has to be through the Lakes, but I can't quite see it. There's been no tie to the judge, just his son."

Silence filled the line.

"No alibi for Christian Lake, correct?" Truman asked softly. He liked the man, but his instincts weren't always perfect.

"He had the time to get to Portland, kill his father, and come back to kill Olivia," Bolton pointed out. "And I know those tire tracks at her cabin haven't been confirmed, but it sounds like he could have been there."

"But he was there after the murders. The tracks crossed all the police vehicle tracks."

"That doesn't prove he wasn't there before. Killers often return to the scene of the crime." Bolton's sigh was loud over the phone. "I don't know if this phone call helped me or threw a dozen other possibilities on the table."

"I don't want you missing anything." Truman understood. Linkage blindness happened frequently. It was easy to steer all efforts toward one lead to the detriment of the other leads. The intense focus would make an investigator miss opportunities.

"I don't want to either." Bolton ended the call.

*Why did he call me? He could have run his theory past Ava or Eddie.*

Truman looked at the drawings again. Bolton's connect-the-dots lines definitely looked like a weapon.

*Why?*

Boots sounded in his hallway, and David Aguirre stopped outside his door. "Got a minute?" The minister was covered from head to toe with a light dusting of snow. He pulled off his stocking cap, creating a minisnowstorm in the hall.

Truman stood and indicated a chair. "What's up?"

David twisted his hat in his hands, a struggle on his face. "I don't know if this is any of my business . . ."

"Why don't you let me decide that?"

"When you were looking at those particular months in the church records the other day, you were looking for some sort of connection to Salome Sabin, right?"

"Honestly, David, I'm not sure. Since a woman looking like Salome had *possibly* broken into the church and we had another break-in at the library, I was trying to connect the two in some way. Whether or not Salome was involved remains to be seen."

"Well, I assumed that's what you were looking for. I knew she was a year behind me in high school, so I estimated her age and took another look at the records. I looked at later dates than you did." He slid a ledger out of his jacket, flipped it open to a page, and handed it to Truman.

The book was warm from David's body heat. Truman noted the dates on the page were nearly a year after the microfiche film months. The name jumped out at him immediately. Salome Beth Sabin. Age two weeks. Olivia was the sole parent listed.

"She was baptized in the church?" Truman wondered aloud. "That surprises me a bit."

"You never know what faith means to people. Olivia and I had our differences, but we also had a lot of beliefs in common. I suspect the baptism was very symbolic to her in some way."

Truman stared at the baptism date. He turned to his computer, quickly accessed a database, and verified he was correct. "According to the DMV, Salome was born six months before this baptism date." He looked up at David. "I can't imagine the minister would mistake a six-month-old baby for a two-week-old. The baptism record has to be the correct date."

"How did you know this baptism date didn't make sense with her birth date?" David scowled.

"When everyone was searching for her, I looked up her driver's license. I'd noted the birth date to see if she was the age I thought she was."

"What's the big deal about a few months?"

"Her father, Antonio Ricci, was sitting in jail during the twelve months before this baptism date."

David's face cleared. "Oh."

Truman nodded. *Is it relevant?*

# THIRTY-ONE

Morrigan is restless.

It's a struggle to keep her occupied. We've been living in the same small space for three days now, and she wants to know why. I can't tell her someone wants to kill me. And her. Today we played in the snow again. I've built more snowmen and made more snow angels than I have in my entire life. We started to construct an igloo, using a rectangular bin to form bricks. It's challenging and time consuming. Exactly what she needs.

My hands in the snow connect me with its energies. I close my eyes, inhale the crisp scent, and taste the clean air. I pick up a handful of the snow and study the minuscule structures that make up the whole.

"What are you doing?" Morrigan asks me.

I show her the snow on my glove. "What do you see? Look deep."

My daughter pulls off a mitten and tentatively touches the white fluff. "They're so tiny. Itty bitty crystals." She looks at the start of our igloo. "But they can form something so big." She gently takes my handful of snow and adds it to a brick of our structure. She steps back and looks up at the snow on the pines, an entranced look on her face. I've seen it before at our home. She is an outdoor girl and loves to lose herself in the nature around her.

I'm proud of her. Teaching her to love and respect the nature around her has been one of my goals since Morrigan became mine. A face flashes in my mind. Morrigan's birth mother. I send out a request that she have peace. She will never know the wonderful gift she gave me.

I thank nature for its abundance. The beauty around me. The life it gives me. My child.

While hiding, I spend my time thinking. It is clear that we can never return to our home as long as my father still hunts us. I've agonized over telling the police what I know, but I doubt their ability to believe me. And can they protect me and Morrigan 24-7? Of course not. It's best if we stay in the shadows, but we can't do it forever. The fact that he found us in the woods tells me his resources are still vast.

I must kill him to remove the threat from our lives. From my daughter's life.

I see no other option.

A sharp pain rips open my heart. How can a child kill a parent? Would Morrigan stab a knife in my chest if I posed a threat to her? What if there were a threat to her daughter? I shake my head. She needs to have her own child to understand how a mother would die to protect her children.

As my mother did for us.

"I'm hungry," my daughter announces.

"It's nearly lunchtime. Let's go back to the cabin, make some sandwiches, and then we can work more on the igloo."

Morrigan considers the plan, nods, and then takes my hand. We slowly work our way through the deep snow back to our temporary home.

My little one is so serious sometimes, weighing every decision. She has changed since my mother's murder. Anxiety sometimes overtakes her, and she won't let me out of her sight. Tears have been shed for her grandmother; she misses her, but knows she's no longer in pain. She clings to me in her sleep at night, refusing to sleep alone.

I curse my father for creating this fear in my daughter.

"Who's that?"

I freeze and look up from my snow-covered boots. A hundred feet away is a man in blue winter gear. He stares at us and then darts away, his strides awkward in the powder. Red and black scents reach my nose as he vanishes. Anger and hatred. I couldn't see his face, but his posture and his stance strike recognition in my brain, setting off alarms.

The threat has been much closer than I envisioned.

I know where he is going. He will return for us.

Our hiding spot is no longer a secret.

And I realize I have been wrong. Very, very wrong.

# THIRTY-TWO

"You're going to break your neck," hollered Kaylie. "And I don't know enough medical shit to put you back together!"

"Language." Mercy tentatively tested a foothold.

"You'd shoot me if I did what you're doing!"

The teenager was right. Mercy was perched on her cabin's steep roof, a broom in one hand and a safety line around her waist. One side of the A-frame cabin's roof was ideal for solar panels with its southern exposure, and an opening in the pines created the perfect position for her home to suck the energy from the sun. Last year she'd taken down a few of the trees to widen the space. Now the long lengths of those trees were indistinguishable mounds under the snow. Some of the fallen trees had been neatly sawed into fifteen-inch lengths for her woodstove. Eventually she'd split them with her ax.

She stretched and brushed the snow off a panel. She'd been happy to see that very little snow had stuck to them, but she wanted them completely clear. The power surplus was stored in rechargeable batteries. Currently the cabin was occupied only a few days each month, and she had plenty of power, but the thought of the system being the slightest bit inefficient had been enough to drive her to the roof.

Three of the panels were out of her reach. Grinding her teeth in frustration, she worked her way back to her ladder and climbed down.

"Thank God," muttered Kaylie as Mercy's feet finally sank into the snow. "I was practicing how I'd tell Truman that you were dead."

"I'm touched."

"None of the scenarios went well."

"Good thing I survived."

"Yeah, but all sorts of freak accidents could happen out here. Bears, falling trees, explosions."

"Explosions from what?" asked Mercy, amused at her niece's concern.

"I don't know. The diesel and gas in the barn? The propane tanks?" Kaylie waved her arms in the air, a darling vision in a hot-pink snow coat with matching gloves and hat. Not exactly dressed to blend into the landscape like Mercy, in her pine-colored coat and black pants.

"Diesel stores better and is safer than gasoline," Mercy recited, hearing her father's voice in her head.

"You store both! And you sound just like my father." The teen deflated, her arms at her sides and a hint of tears her eyes.

*Poor kid is worried she'll be alone.*

Mercy pulled the teen close, cursing herself for making light of Kaylie's fears. "I miss your dad too. I'm sorry if me crawling around up there made you nervous." She wiped a stray tear off Kaylie's cheek with a gloved finger. "Levi had the same knowledge drilled into his head that I did. Our father was tyrannical about it. I bet I say a lot of the same things your dad did."

"Hurts," Kaylie mumbled.

"I know." Levi's death had left a wound in Mercy's heart too. One she'd delicately patched by caring for his daughter. "Let's get your stuff together for the soap. That'd be a good project for today." Kaylie had a fascination with soap making that didn't surprise Mercy one bit. The experimentation and blending of ingredients echoed Kaylie's baking skills.

"You're trying to distract me."

"Would you rather mope the rest of the day? Your father knows you love and miss him."

Mercy steered the girl up the steps to her home, wondering if she'd said the right thing. She didn't want to pass over Kaylie's sorrow about her father's death, but she wouldn't let the teen grieve the day away.

Their afternoon's drive to the cabin had been smooth. Virtually no traffic was on the roads, and two-thirds of their route had been recently plowed. Mercy had chained up her Tahoe as a precaution once they'd turned off the main road, and the vehicle had handled beautifully.

In a real emergency they might have battled the people escaping the city. Big cities would have the worst problems.

*We have a fragile and highly independent infrastructure.*

Her father's lectures echoed in her brain. *Power failures. Municipal water failures. Disruption of food distribution. Collapse of law and order. Migration out of the cities.*

No one would stay in the center of a major city once those resources vanished. People would flock to the country, seeking natural sources of water and food.

*There is a thin veneer of civilization in our society. It will get ugly.*

"I'm going to try fine coffee grounds in my next batch of soap." Kaylie's comment pulled Mercy out of the past. "I think it will add a great scent and a bit of abrasiveness to the bar."

*Don't lose the skills of the past.*

In a world that collapsed, a simple skill such as soap making created a useful item for barter and cleaning.

"That sounds like a great idea," said Mercy. "I stocked more coconut oil and oatmeal like you asked." She smiled. "I wasn't sure if it was for soap or baking."

"Both." Kaylie opened a cabinet in the tiny kitchen. "Hey. What's this? When did you bring this up here?"

She pulled out a tiny espresso machine.

Mercy stared. It wasn't a spendy machine. In fact, it was probably the least expensive machine on the market. But she hadn't brought it to the cabin.

*Truman.*

He'd asked why she drank drip coffee at the cabin when she was addicted to her espresso Americanos back home.

An espresso machine was an indulgence; therefore it wasn't part of her supplies.

She touched the little machine and her lips curved. She should be annoyed that he'd broken one of her rules, but her vision blurred. Truman did all sorts of things he didn't need to. He checked her tires' pressure when he thought one looked low. He always kept her favorite cream in his kitchen. He picked Kaylie up from school when her car wouldn't start *and* got the car fixed before Mercy got off work. She'd found new books on alternative power sources and home defense on his bookshelf. Little things.

"I didn't put it there," Mercy said softly.

Kaylie scowled. "Then how—awww! He's so great." A big grin filled her face. "You need to hang on to him, Aunt Mercy."

"It's not practical," Mercy muttered. "Takes special beans and sucks too much power."

Her niece was amused. "Even on the TV show *Survivor* they get to pack one luxury item."

"That's not real life."

"Well, it won't hurt to use it for as long as you can. If the big day comes, you can symbolically destroy it."

Mercy studied the little black machine.

*I could never destroy it.*

# THIRTY-THREE

*Death flows from him.*

Beside me Morrigan runs as fast as she can, but pushing through the snow on her short legs is nearly impossible. We both sink to our knees with every step, and my lungs burn from short shallow breaths. I urge her on. I could carry her, but I don't think it'd be faster. Instead I grip her mittened hand in mine and pull.

We spot our steps from earlier and our speed picks up as we plant our feet in the premade holes.

"Why?" Morrigan pants. When I'd said we needed to leave immediately, she didn't ask questions. But now our grueling pace is making her wonder.

"Trust me." Sweat runs down my back.

"Was that him?" she gasps between words, and I'm proud of her as she pushes on.

"Yes," I wheeze.

"How did he find us?"

"I made a mistake." My heartbeat reverberates through my head.

"We shouldn't have played in the snow?"

"It wasn't that. I was wrong about where to hide."

The roof of our cabin comes into view, and I nearly cry with relief. I love the tiny cabin. Even though its purpose is to hide from the world, its rustic elegance and beauty make me feel as if we lived at a high-end mountain resort. There hasn't been a moment when I didn't feel safe and secure. Until today.

We burst through the door and I slam to a stop at the sight of a male figure in my kitchen. Brent whirls around, his hand reaching inside his open jacket, but relief fills his face, and the weapon he removes points down.

He was unpacking groceries. Time seems to stop as I spot a box of the dry cereal that is Morrigan's new obsession, and a wave of thankfulness rolls through me. We've been in caring hands.

"Gabriel." I force the name out and bend over, resting my hands on my thighs, afraid I'll vomit as adrenaline and exhaustion hit me at the same time. "It's Gabriel."

I want to scream. I want to cry. I want to kick myself for hiding my daughter under the nose of danger. Everything feels upside down.

*How could I have been so wrong?*

Brent grabs my upper arms. "What about him?"

"I was wrong. It's not my father. It's Gabriel." I'm still addled by my mistake, and his name feels foreign on my tongue. "It's Gabriel," I repeat, mentally trying to understand my blunder.

"Gabriel? How?" His tone rises in confusion.

"I don't know . . . I don't know why," I choke out. "But he spotted us and ran back to the main house. He'll be here next." I lift my head to look Brent in the eye. "I felt and saw his hatred. He killed my mother. Morrigan and I are next."

Brent and I have had long talks over dinner. I told him I felt a deep sadness radiate from him when he looked at Morrigan, and he admitted his younger sister died at around the same age. She was blonde like my daughter. He doesn't quite believe in my gift, but he's come to trust me, and I trust him. Brent was the exception to my order that

Christian tell *no one* when he hid Morrigan and me on his property. Nothing gets by Brent's notice on this land. My mother always warned me that my father's reach was long. His associates still walked outside the prison walls. Who knew what an old friend would do for him? Absolute secrecy was a must.

But it wasn't my father who killed my mother and the judge. It was Gabriel.

Skepticism crosses Brent's face, and he searches my eyes. I smell the change in the air as he decides to believe me.

"I need to call Christian." He places his gun on the granite kitchen counter and touches his phone's screen.

"We've got to get out of here." I turn to Morrigan, who's been listening, her eyes wide. "Get my emergency bag. It's in my closet." She vanishes to obey. I've been prepared. I have money, passports, new credit cards, and all our important papers in there, ready to grab at a moment's notice. Ready for this very moment.

"Fuck. I got voice mail." He clears his throat. "Christian, I'm at Salome's cabin. She says Gabriel is the one after her, not her father. He's spotted her and we're going to get out of here."

"Will Christian be okay?" My stomach twists at the thought of my friend in danger.

"He can take care of himself."

"But it's his brother."

Brent's lips press into a thin line. "That's Christian's issue."

"Here, Mama." Morrigan thrusts the bag into my hands. Her eyes are clear and her mouth determined. She is brave.

"Get in the car," I order her.

"We've got better vehicles at the house," Brent argues.

"But the house is hundreds of yards away and Gabriel is there. We're taking my Subaru."

"But the snow—"

"It's good in snow." My voice is as strong as my mind is full of doubt. The long road to the cabin has been ignored for two days as Brent allowed the snow to cover my car's tracks. I follow Morrigan to the tiny garage and hit the button to raise the door. It strains, making a grinding noise, and stops.

"There's too much snow against the front," Brent says. He pushes past me into the garage and grabs a snow shovel. "Stay inside." He darts back into the house, picks up his gun, and goes out the front door. I follow to the doorway.

"Be careful," I yell after him. I close the door and am frozen. I don't know what to do.

*Pack food.*

I dart to the kitchen and start throwing things in bags. Milk, water bottles, bread, peanut butter. I hand bag after bag to Morrigan, who runs them out to my car. Time crawls. *What is taking so long?* I run for blankets, ripping them off the beds, and grab a few clothes for Morrigan.

The front door opens and my heart stops. Brent rushes in, still carrying the shovel. "Let's go."

The garage door smoothly moves up its tracks, and I catch my breath at the depth of the snow. He also dug out a section of the driveway where the snow had formed big drifts. No wonder it took so long. "Farther out the road is better," he tells me as he throws the shovel on the stack of blankets and food in the back of my car.

We both move to the driver's door and halt, our frantic gazes colliding. I want to drive, my motherly instinct roaring to protect my child. But he holds out his hand and I drop the key on his palm. My inner tiger growls in protest, but I know because of his profession that his driving skills are likely better than mine.

He backs out of the garage. My little car protests but handles beautifully. He winds out to the main road of the estate.

Out of the corner of my eye, I see a blur of blue among the trees.

The glass of Brent's window shatters as I hear the crack of the rifle. Warm spray covers my face and Morrigan shrieks.

Brent slumps forward, held in place by his seatbelt, and the car stops.

His forehead is gone. His face is covered with blood that flows into his lap.

He is dead.

I stare, my heart numb at the sight of my friend.

*My fault. He wouldn't be dead if he hadn't helped us.*

I can't breathe. *No time to stop. No time to mourn. Keep going.*

I block out Morrigan's screams and peer through Brent's shattered window.

Fifty yards away, Gabriel stands. His feet are planted wide and his rifle points at me.

*"Morrigan, get down!"*

Another shot hits the back driver's-side window, and Morrigan's shrieks are deafening. I grab the wheel and shove Brent's body against his door. His head rolls loosely on his neck and hangs out his window. My stomach heaving, I maneuver until I straddle the center console and my foot reaches the gas pedal. I push Brent's leg out of my way and gently press the gas, fighting an overwhelming urge to stomp on it. The car moves forward and I awkwardly steer.

Gabriel moves parallel with the road, struggling to jog in the snow with his rifle. The car slowly pulls ahead and my heart pounding in my ears drowns out my daughter's sobs. She is crouched on the floor behind the passenger seat. I press harder on the gas pedal and some of the tires start to spin. I let up, terrified of getting stuck, and struggle to see the road. Everything is covered in a thick layer of white, and the edges of the drive aren't clear. I aim for the widest flat area and pray the road is beneath.

I risk a look in his direction. He's still a ways back but substantially closer to the road, and my terror jerks the steering wheel.

My car turns and the front right wheel sinks, nearly putting me through the windshield as the car buries its grille in the snow. I stomp on the gas; the tires spin and the motor revs shrilly. We don't move. I shift the gearshift between my legs into reverse and press the gas again. The car jumps back six inches, stops, and the tires spin again.

I've never wished harder for a gun in my life.

"Mama?"

"Stay down. Don't move." My mind races. *Do we run?* I see no other alternative. I won't sit here and wait to be shot. I lunge back into the passenger seat and fling open the door, rolling out into the snow. Scrambling on my hands and knees, I open Morrigan's door and pull her into the deep fluff.

"We're going to run that way," I said, pointing away from the car. "Don't look back." I don't want her to look at him.

My daughter nods, and her eyes are wet, but she starts to run and I follow, placing my body between her and Gabriel.

She is slow. Too slow. I glance over my shoulder and he has nearly reached my car.

"Go, Morrigan. Keep going," I pant. I can feel a target on my back. He'll have to go through me to get my daughter.

The rumble of an engine sounds to our left and Christian's old Hummer speeds toward us, snow flying from his tires. I pull Morrigan behind a tree, clutching her tight to me. I risk a peek around the trunk and estimate we're fifty feet from the car. Christian stops next to my Subaru while Gabriel runs in the opposite direction. *Coward.*

Christian jumps down from his seat, his gaze locked on Brent's bloody form. He looks to me and I point at the running figure, unable to speak, let alone shout for him to hear me. As he turns, I see the rifle in his hands.

My blood runs cold. I made a wrong assumption about my father. Did I make one about Christian too? *Have I traded one killer for another?*

He rests his elbows on the hood, sighting the rifle after the escaping figure. I collapse on the safe side of the tree and close my eyes. *It's not Christian.* I wait for the shot, but it doesn't come. I look around the tree again and see Christian staring at the retreating figure. *Why didn't he shoot?* He looks back at me.

"Are you okay?" he shouts.

I have no energy to answer. I nod. He slowly treks through the snow to us, his rifle over his shoulder.

My skin crawls as I look at the gun. My uncertainty returns. Morrigan squirms in my death grip. "Let me go, Mama! Christian!" He raises a hand to acknowledge her, his steps steadily bringing him closer.

*Is he coming to kill us?* Terrified of what I might smell, I shakily inhale through my nose.

Warm scents of earth reach me. Salt from the ocean. His usual scents.

I weep in relief. There is also a sour fear and anger, but it is not directed at us.

He crouches next to us in the snow and Morrigan lunges at him, wrapping her arms around his neck. I ache to do the same, but I can't move. All my stamina is gone. His eyes are serious as he studies me. "What happened to Brent?"

"Gabriel shot him," I whisper. "We were next."

He is silent, a struggle in his gaze. He pulls off his gloves, melts some snow in his bare hands, and then applies the moisture to my face, using his glove as a cloth. *Brent's blood.* I look at my jacket. It is black, but spots shine where the blood—and worse—landed.

He continues to wash my face. "I'm so sorry, Salome."

"Did you see him?"

"I did. I saw him through the scope." He paused. "I couldn't fire."

"I understand. He's your brother. But we have to keep going. I can't stop."

"I won't let him find you."

"He already did."

He takes my hand and holds it against his heart. "I didn't know. I truly didn't know it was him. I would have never brought you here if I'd known."

"Why did he do it? Why kill your father . . ."

"I don't know."

Odors of lies float between us, and my heart sinks.

We leave Brent where he died.

"I'll come back for him," promises Christian. "But I need to get you two to safety first. Nothing more can happen to him."

I hear his unspoken words. *But much, much more can happen to you and Morrigan.*

I know Christian has an idea why Gabriel hunted me, but he is silent. We drive. We don't stop at his glorious home. We leave it far behind us. Hopefully Gabriel has been left far behind too.

The Hummer drives on the snow as if it were dry pavement. "We've got to go to the police," he tells me.

"No! We can't."

"Why on earth not? How am I supposed to explain the dead man on my property with *half his head gone*?" he shouts at me. Fear fills the vehicle. His and Morrigan's. I look back to my daughter, who is watching and listening, her eyes wide.

I glare daggers at him. "The police might be compromised."

"*How?* How can that happen? This isn't a movie." His knuckles are white as he grips the steering wheel.

"I told you about my father—"

"Yes, you told me he was a kill—enforcer for some crime organization." He spots Morrigan's face in the rearview mirror and softens his tone.

Kendra Elliot

I turn and hold Morrigan's gaze, my smile warm and loving as I wish for her to sleep. Her lids lower and she fights their heaviness, but I prevail. Her chin bobs against her chest as she sleeps. Guilt swamps me. I haven't done that since she was an infant and I was in desperate need of sleep, but she can't hear this conversation.

"This organization had eyes everywhere," I said quietly. "Even though they did nothing to stop my father from going to prison, he could still have loyal friends. Anywhere. They might honor him for keeping his mouth shut about their boss."

Disbelief surrounds Christian.

"I'm deadly serious, Christian. This is why my mother changed her name and lived like a hermit in the woods. Everything I've ever done has been with the knowledge that he might be looking for me. My bank accounts are in another name, my phone, my cards."

"Why the fuck didn't you leave the state? The three of you stayed within thirty miles of where he operated."

"My mother couldn't leave. I can't explain it, but it's true." *How can I explain her connection to the woods?*

"And now you know it wasn't your father who killed your mother." He looks at me again. "You can go to the police."

Ice runs up my spine. "No. Just because this wasn't him doesn't mean his people aren't looking for us."

"It's been forty years!"

"I can't risk it." Gabriel's face fills my mind, and I catch my breath. "What if he hired Gabriel? How did he get to him? Who else has he reached?"

"I don't think that's what happened."

Again I smell his secrets. I study Christian's profile. Such a damned beautiful man and a good one. I've known his heart since I was eighteen, and I feel horrible that I doubted him for those few minutes in the snow. If he is lying to me, it's for a good reason. He'll tell me when the time is right.

"If you won't go to the police, then where are we going?"

I press my hands to my eyes. I don't know. I've always been ready to run, but I never knew where was safe. Locations spin through my head, and I reject them all. "I think it's best if Morrigan and I just drive away. We'll keep going until I find a town that feels right. My business is online. I can manage it from anywhere." I will have to repurchase my supplies and build my stock anew. It's a small price to pay. I picture all my hard work in my storage room in the barn. Maybe Christian can pack it and ship it to me . . . once I find a new home.

My head jerks up. "We have to go back to my mother's house."

*"Are you nuts?"*

"I can't leave without some things from there."

"Why didn't you grab them when we went to pick up those other things? It wasn't easy getting in there between the police visits."

"I know. But I forgot about her rings." I place my hand on his shoulder and focus my energy. "They're very important to me." My manipulation skills are rusty, and they were never strong in the first place, not like my mother's. I hate that I'm using them on my closest friend, but this is necessary. That's twice in five minutes that I've manipulated my loved ones. A sign of how desperate our situation is.

"Okay. We'll go there, but it's just for a minute. Then we're heading south until we're out of the snow, and I'll rent you a car so you can leave."

"No. Morrigan needs to rest and I need sleep. We'll spend the night there and leave in the morning."

"*At a crime scene?* You'd let your daughter sleep in that house?" he hisses. "What if the police show up?"

"I doubt they've been anywhere near it since the last two snow-storms. And I can make it good for Morrigan. She won't see." I check and see she's still asleep.

I feel him look sidelong at me. He knows about some of my skills, but not all. He needs to trust that I will do what's best for my daughter.

"Clearly Gabriel knows the location of the cabin," he states. "If he's after you, he'll look there."

"I think he believes that I wouldn't go there . . . just as you were stunned that I wanted to."

"Not good enough." He stares straight ahead, anger and fear surrounding him.

"I can't stay in a hotel. Not under your name or mine. He knows we're together. I have nowhere else to go." He opens his mouth, but I speak first. "And don't suggest a friend's house. Gabriel is too dangerous. I won't risk anyone else."

"One night. No more." His voice shakes. "I'll be up all night guarding the fucking door. And after I see you off, I'll go back to deal with Brent. And Gabriel."

I hate that I'm leaving him in a difficult spot, and I wonder what he'll do about his brother.

*Will he report him to the police?*

"Come with us." Even as I say it, I know it will never happen. Our affection for each other is strong, but it's never been a romantic love. His life is not meant to merge with mine.

"I can't."

I feel his pain. And I feel his wall. The same wall that he has raised between us before. I don't understand its source. It extends all the way back to the night we first met, but I don't try to break it down. I know it is strong and honorable, not meant to be destroyed.

I nod and turn back to watch the road.

# THIRTY-FOUR

Simon's meow escalated in volume.

"Jeez. Hang on." Truman set the cat's bowl on the floor in his kitchen. Without a second glance at him, the black cat daintily began to eat her breakfast, wrapping her tail around to her front feet.

Truman watched for a moment, fully aware he was a slave to the feline queen. She'd picked him, not the other way around. Showing up at his door every day until he let her in. If it had been up to him, he wouldn't have any pets, but apparently she'd decided what was best for him.

His cell phone rang, and he checked the time on his microwave, wondering if he was late to work. To his relief it wasn't even seven.

Detective Bolton greeted him. "I think you need to see something."

"What do you have?" Truman poured coffee into his usual travel mug.

"I'm out at Christian Lake's home. Gunshots were reported in this area yesterday, but we couldn't check on them until this morning."

He froze in the act of screwing the lid onto the mug. "No one responded to a gunshot call?"

"Only one call came in, and it's not unusual to hear shots out in a rural area."

"True. But why are you calling me? The Lake home isn't in my jurisdiction."

"Because first I called the FBI, but Ava and Eddie are still in Portland. Jeff said Mercy has been covering the case locally for those two, but I got her voice mail when I called."

Truman's heart sped up. "She's gone to her cabin for the weekend, and her cell service is sketchy up there. I only get through about half the time. Is Jeff sending another agent out there?"

"He's going to try." Impatience rang in Bolton's tone. "I know you've kept your nose in this case, and I'd hoped your perspective could help us figure out what the hell happened up here."

"What happened?"

"I've got a dead body. Brent Rollins. He was shot in the head and he's hanging out of Salome Sabin's Subaru."

The hairs on his arms lifted. "You're fucking kidding me."

"I wish I was. The Lake home is deserted, and I can tell there was a struggle here."

"I'm on my way."

A deputy escorted Truman on foot to the crime scene. At least the snow had stopped and nothing new had fallen overnight. After twenty minutes of huffing and puffing, they reached Bolton. Two county vehicles and Bolton's SUV were parked fifty yards back from the scene. They must have arrived at the scene before realizing they needed to keep other vehicles—like Truman's—off the property to preserve the tracks in the snow.

*They got lucky with the weather.*

From a distance Truman saw the victim in the car. His head slumped out the driver's window. Truman followed Bolton to the Subaru, swallowing hard as he recognized Rollins even though part of his skull was missing.

"Jesus Christ."

"Amen," answered Bolton.

"Who shot him?"

"That's the big question."

"You said you checked the main house?"

"Yep. It's empty. All the doors were unlocked, and there was food left on the kitchen counter as if someone left in a hurry."

"Any missing vehicles?"

Bolton twisted his lips. "There are two empty spaces in that huge garage. I didn't see the Hummer, but who knows if something else is missing. I put a BOLO out on the Hummer."

"I know he has a black Lexus SUV."

Bolton's face cleared. "I didn't see one in there." He turned to one of the deputies. "Get the information on a Lexus SUV owned by Christian Lake and put out another BOLO."

Truman stepped closer to the Subaru and looked through the shattered rear driver's-side window. A chaotic grouping of groceries and blankets filled the back of the Subaru . . . as if someone had packed in a hurry. On the floor on the passenger's side was a small pink hat. "Shit."

"I saw it," Bolton replied.

"Might be from another day," Truman stated. "It is her mother's car."

Both doors on the other side of the car hung open, and a broken trail in the snow led away from the car.

"Where's that go?"

"About fifty feet to that tree. It looks like they crouched behind the tree. And there is a second path where someone else joined them."

Truman noticed how the trail from the Subaru was frantic and messy. The second trail to the tree was distinct footsteps.

"At some point they all came back to the road." Bolton pointed at a wider broken path that led from the tree to about twenty feet from the Subaru.

Truman spotted familiar wide tire tracks on the road where the third trail ended. "They got in the Hummer."

"Right. But were they forced? Did they go willingly?" Bolton shook his head at the possibilities.

Truman moved to the broken driver's window, looking past the grisly corpse. Blood spatter covered everything in the front of the car: windshield, dashboard . . . but a large section of the passenger seat was clean. And so was part of the passenger door.

"Someone was sitting in the passenger seat when he was shot."

"Agreed."

"Salome?"

"That's my first guess. The clean area is the size of an adult."

Frustration filled him as Truman stared at the spray of blood on the windshield. "But we're speculating. Was Rollins helping them or forcing them to leave with him?"

"My money is on helping. The Subaru tracks lead back to a small cabin where it appears Salome and Morrigan have been staying. There was a grocery receipt on the counter. It had Rollins's name from his credit card on it."

Truman had a moment of relief that the mother and child had been in a safe place. But the dead man in front of him testified that their safe place had turned ugly.

"Rollins was helping them hide, but did Christian know the two of them were on his property?"

"Christian Lake is also missing."

Both men looked over at the Hummer tracks.

"There's one more thing." Bolton led Truman away from the car and up a gentle slope among the pines. Twenty feet from the car was another broken trail in the snow.

"The shooter."

"I believe so. We've followed the path. It starts at the house, goes almost to the cabin where Salome was hiding, but then it makes a sharp turn toward the road. Right here it reverses direction and goes back to the house."

"Do you think he was heading to the cabin but heard the car leaving?"

"It's a theory."

"Is Christian Lake the shooter or driver? Or neither?" Truman tried to keep an open mind.

"He could have been in the Subaru passenger's seat."

Truman thought it was doubtful but nodded.

"Another possibility is that the target was Rollins," said Bolton. "I know the FBI suspects that Salome fled because she was afraid she'd be killed, but maybe she was the shooter here. Maybe Brent took off with her kid."

"Shit." Bolton was better than he at exploring *all* possibilities.

"What about Gabriel Lake? Last I heard, he was staying at the big house."

"I've tried to reach him. I know he's been avoiding all investigator calls, so I'm not surprised."

*Mercy should see this.* Truman pulled out his phone and called twice. No luck.

Unease bubbled under his flesh at her silence. *She's fine. This happens every time she goes up there.*

"Want to see the cabin?" Bolton asked. "Then we'll do the house."

"Sure."

During their walk Truman checked in with his department. It'd been a quiet morning so far, and Ben had everything under control. Truman informed Lucas he'd be out of the office most of the day, but to call him if needed. He hung up with a twinge of guilt, knowing it was a personal reason that would keep him out of the office, not work.

He followed in Bolton's steps. Each one was nearly a foot deep.

His unease didn't lift.

For his own sanity, he'd drive up to Mercy's cabin and check on her as soon as Bolton was finished.

One of the best things about Mercy's cabin was the disconnect from society.

One of the worst things about her cabin was the disconnect from society.

In a world where everyone stared at screens all day, Mercy appreciated the forced break. Instant information was an addiction. Each time she came, Kaylie had several moments of frustration, craving the easy distraction of infotainment at her fingertips. Their cell phones rarely worked, and Mercy hadn't invested in satellite Internet. A sin in Kaylie's eyes. Mercy called it detox.

*How did I survive as a teen without a BuzzFeed quiz to distract me?*

Mercy had had no spare time as a teenager. Her parents kept her and her siblings in constant motion. On a farm there was always work to be done. Telling a parent she was bored would have resulted in hours of physical labor.

To combat Kaylie's issue, they'd made a list of projects to tackle at the cabin. Interesting projects that caught Kaylie's imagination. Although Kaylie wanted to manage a bakery or dessert shop, Mercy saw the brain of a natural engineer in her niece. She loved to solve problems. And there were many at the cabin.

At times Kaylie was overwhelmed by the thought of all the daily items that could disappear in an emergency. "What if we run out of baking soda?" she'd asked Mercy once. "It's a basic item that I use every day." Mercy urged her to research the problem, but the answer depressed her niece. "We'd have to mine it in Colorado. There are some substitutes, but it won't be the same."

"We're not going to Colorado."

Kaylie's TEOTWAWKI concerns were smaller than Mercy's big-ticket concerns about heat, water, and food.

During this trip Kaylie's project was to create a laundry machine for clothes, along with her bars of soap. Mercy had never thought about laundry. Her cabin had a creek; she would have some sort of soap. Those two things were good enough for her. And somewhere in storage was an old-fashioned washboard. To Mercy the problem was minor. But Kaylie was determined, and Mercy saw it as a boon to keep her occupied.

Her niece had instructions from a website. On the last trip Kaylie had brought up the supplies and Mercy had washed her hands of the project. One look at the complicated step-by-step photos had convinced Mercy to be happy with the creek and washboard.

A big bucket, wood, plastic pipes, netting. The pictures showed a giant claw attached to a net full of clothing that dipped into a bucket and somehow squeezed out the soap and water with each dip.

Mercy had pointed out a similar system that worked solely with a toilet plunger and bucket. Kaylie had wrinkled her nose.

Kaylie and her supplies were out in the barn. The little A-frame cabin didn't have the floor space for Kaylie to spread out her project. According to the website, it would take eight hours to assemble.

*Perfect.*

The two of them actually made a good team. Mercy looked at the big picture, and Kaylie considered the smaller details like laundry soap and deodorant. Mercy had never thought about needing deodorant after a disaster. How she smelled was not a priority. But if Kaylie was determined to try something, Mercy didn't stand in her way.

Kaylie had used coconut oil, baking soda (hence part of the baking soda worry) and cornstarch to whip up a deodorant that they'd both agreed wasn't bad.

Mercy had never purchased so much coconut oil in her life. Kaylie requested it for everything. Baking, cooking, deodorant, and even laundry soap, so Mercy had added large buckets of it to her stock.

*Mom and Dad never stored coconut oil.*

The thought that their daughter had become a millennial-thinking generation of prepper made her grin.

Her parents had also never considered a night vision camera security system. It was the main reason Mercy brought her laptop to the cabin. The system showed several views outside.

The noontime sun was bright, and she grew smug at the thought of her photovoltaic system sucking in its energy. Today was a day that the blue sky and sun pretended that no huge storm had rolled through yesterday afternoon and the ground wasn't buried in snow. She bundled up and went out to the barn to grab a snow shovel. Kaylie sat on the floor, deep into plastic pipes and netting for her laundry machine.

"I'm going to hike around for a bit," Mercy told her, eyeing the giant mess.

"Got your radio?" Kaylie asked, not looking up from knotting some cable through the net.

"Of course. Where's yours?"

Kaylie slapped her jacket pocket.

When she had first brought Kaylie to the cabin, Mercy realized the two of them needed a source of communication. The two-way radios were reliable. When she'd been alone, Mercy hadn't felt a need for communication. She hadn't cared who couldn't reach her. Now her priorities were different. Truman had suggested a satellite phone several times. But again, Mercy liked being disconnected from the world . . . but not from her niece.

The snow shovel over her shoulder, she pulled out her cell phone as she walked up the twisting drive to her cabin. No service.

No surprise.

She walked her acreage every time she visited the cabin, looking for problems or signs that someone had found her hideaway. A few summers earlier she had tried her hand at snares to catch small game, and she'd caught a chipmunk in one of her traps. Since she was a child, she'd watched the tiny striped creatures dart playfully around the woods. They definitely weren't worth catching for food. She'd put away the snares, pleased that they'd worked, but unhappy that she'd caught something more like a pet than a meal.

Her tire tracks from yesterday were clear and made for easier walking at the moment, but in her eyes they announced her location to the world. Her plan was to smooth out the tracks that turned into her drive. She crossed her fingers that another vehicle had passed by, continuing tracks past her drive. Otherwise a set of tracks that simply stopped in the center of the road would definitely catch attention.

Fifteen minutes later she was delighted to see that a vehicle had continued past her turnoff. She filled and smoothed her Tahoe's turn into her drive. She couldn't match the perfect blanket of snow, but at least it was less eye-catching. She wasn't concerned about the few neighbors who lived in the area; everyone minded their own business. What made her uncomfortable was the thought of a nosy passerby deciding to explore where the mystery tracks went.

She was working her way down her drive, intending to go just far enough not to be seen from the road, when she heard an engine. Mercy moved to the cover of the trees, picking a hiding spot that gave a clear view of the approaching vehicle. She caught her breath at the sight of the wide military-looking SUV.

*Christian's Hummer?*

The vehicle moved slowly, as if its occupants were searching for something. Mercy spotted Christian's handsome face behind the wheel. In the other seat was a woman with dark hair. *Salome?* Her heart sped up. *Why is she with Christian?*

Both adults kept turning to study the sides of the road.

*There's only one thing they could be looking for out here: me.*

She stepped out from the concealment of the trees and waved her shovel as she moved toward the road. Salome spotted her first, pointing and grabbing Christian's shoulder. The SUV drew even with her and stopped. As Salome lowered her window, Mercy spotted Morrigan's delighted face in the back seat. The girl had recognized her.

Salome and Christian looked exhausted, but relieved.

The three adults stared at one another for a long second.

*Twice Christian told me he didn't know who Salome was.* Annoyance rose in her chest. *Where the hell has she been?*

"You're looking for me?" Mercy finally asked.

"We've stopped at two other places, trying to find your cabin," answered Christian. Salome was silent, her dark eyes studying Mercy. Mercy stared right back.

"Why? And how did you know to look for my place?"

"The night you found Morrigan, we knew you'd recently left your place," Salome stated. "We decided to give it a shot."

"That still doesn't tell me why you're here." Her sense of privacy evaporated, leaving a sick feeling in her stomach.

The two in the vehicle exchanged a look.

"And how in the hell are the two of you together?" Mercy snapped. "Christian told me he had no idea who you were."

More exchanged looks.

*Something's happened.*

"Can we sit down and talk somewhere?" Christian asked. "It's a long story."

"Me, the rest of the FBI, and the county sheriff have been trying to get to the bottom of your *long story* for nearly a week. Now you decide to talk?" She glared at Christian. *I trusted him. I let our old friendship affect my common sense.* No more.

"Please." Salome held Mercy's gaze.

Mercy felt an odd prickling in her skull. *No point in standing in the snow.* "Turn right over there, go in about twenty feet, and then wait for me. I'm going to try to cover your tracks." *Again.*

Mercy fumed as she redid her work. It looked crappier than before, but she didn't care.

*They better have one hell of a story.*

# THIRTY-FIVE

*Tracks?*

Truman slowed as he spotted several sets of tire tracks turning off the main road to Olivia Sabin's lane. He stopped, options running through his head. The turnoff was usually invisible if you weren't looking for it—just like the turn to Mercy's cabin. The tire indentations were recent; no snow had fallen for nearly twelve hours.

He was about ten minutes from Mercy's cabin. He could go there first and see if she wanted to check out the Sabin cabin with him.

*What if Mercy is at the Sabins' right now?*

He didn't know why she would be, but Mercy had been there a few nights earlier when he couldn't reach her.

*Salome could be there.*

Or maybe the Deschutes County sheriff. Checking up on the place . . . feeding the animals.

*What if they forgot to feed the animals?*

"Shit." Truman yanked on his wheel and pulled into the drive, the thought of hungry baby goats making his decision for him. The road twisted and turned for longer than he remembered. At least two other vehicles had driven on it since yesterday's snowfall. The trees started to clear and the Sabin home appeared, looking lonely and abandoned except for Christian's black Lexus SUV parked in front.

Truman stepped on the brake. *Christian or Salome? Or both?*

He parked on the far side of the home, which allowed him to view the house, barn, and Lexus all at once while leaving plenty of room between himself and the house. He sat in the cab for a few moments, considering his next move. His radio wouldn't work up here, and he'd already checked his phone. No cell service. It was nearly an hour's drive to the sheriff's department. *Or I could talk to Christian myself.* The man had seemed normal during their interactions, but *someone* had shot and left a dead man on the Lake property.

*He could be trigger-happy.*

Truman checked the pistol on his side, unfastened the rifle on the dash, and slid out of the SUV, keeping the vehicle between the house and himself.

He propped the rifle against the fender, cupped his hands around his mouth, and shouted, "Hello! Anybody home? It's Chief Daly from Eagle's Nest!"

Silence.

"Christian?" he shouted. He scanned the windows of the home and the corrals of the barn.

No movement.

When Detective Bolton had taken him through Christian Lake's empty house earlier that morning, it had looked pristine. No different than on the day Truman had been there. The little cabin where they assumed Salome and Morrigan had been staying looked lived in, exactly what he'd expect with a ten-year-old living there.

But both homes had been similar in their absolute emptiness.

The Sabin farm didn't feel empty. A presence lurked. Maybe the Lexus affected how he felt, but he could swear someone was watching him.

He shouted Christian's name again.

Truman heard the bullet hit the metal on the other side of his SUV before he heard the report of the gun. He dropped to the snow, grabbing the rifle as he scrambled behind the tire. He couldn't breathe. Another bullet hit the Tahoe. *It's coming from the house.*

The shooter had the advantage, and Truman had no way to call for backup. Panic bubbled in his chest, accelerating his heartbeat.

*Get the fuck out of here.*

Stretching up, he yanked on the driver's door handle and awkwardly crawled inside, keeping his head below the dash and expecting a bullet in his head at any moment. With sweating hands he pushed the START button, shifted the vehicle into reverse, and pulled his door shut. Still in an awkward crouch, he tried to maneuver his foot to the gas pedal while keeping his head down.

The engine of the Lexus started.

Another shot. No clang in his vehicle's metal this time. Instead there was a distinct thump and then a whistle of air. Truman froze, straining to hear the whistle above the sounds of the two engines. There was another shot, another thump, and another whistle.

*He shot my tires.*

His Tahoe slowly lowered on the passenger's side, and the Lexus engine grew fainter. Truman raised his head and looked out the back window as the Lexus vanished around the first turn.

He sucked in a few deep breaths to slow his heart. *At least the bullets are in my vehicle, not my brain.*

A memory of Brent Rollins's injury flashed. He shut it down.

He wiped the moisture off his forehead, got out with his rifle still in hand, and walked around his vehicle. Two deflated tires greeted him. "Fuck." He surveyed the property. It was quiet, but that didn't mean he was alone.

Ten minutes later he'd cleared the house and barn and knew he was alone except for the animals. He'd checked their feed, and everyone had fresh food in their pens.

*Does that mean it was Salome who was here? And shot at me?*

Would Christian have bothered to feed the animals? Unanswered questions crowded his brain.

He tromped back into the house, something niggling at him. He'd gone through the house to rapidly clear the rooms, but now he took a closer look in Olivia's room. The drawers had been emptied onto the floor and the candles knocked to the ground. *Would the evidence team have done that?* He shook his head. There was no reason to throw the candles on the ground. A piece of art lay on the floor, its glass shattered. Truman glanced in the other bedrooms and saw more of the same carelessness.

He checked the knife room. It hadn't been touched. Its glass containers were still neatly lined up on the shelves and the knives in orderly rows. *Odd.*

In the barn the craft room hadn't been damaged either.

Was someone looking for something? Or had the destruction been done out of anger?

As curious as he was about the damage and who'd shot at him, Truman had a more current problem.

*How am I going to get out of here?*

Mercy was on full alert, prepared not to believe a word from the two people across the table. Salome had been silent, her dark eyes assessing and evaluating Mercy and the surroundings. The first time they'd met, Salome had been fired up and stressed about her daughter. This woman was coolly calm and in control. Mercy wasn't sure which side she preferred.

Mercy had been pleased to see that Kaylie waited until Mercy hopped out of Christian's Hummer before coming out of the barn to see who'd arrived. She'd heard the strange engine but had stayed hidden until she knew it was friendly.

Now her niece was distracting Morrigan by asking questions about homeschooling as she made coffee and pulled out homemade cookies for their guests.

*Guests?*

Mercy asked Kaylie to show Morrigan her washing machine project in progress. Morrigan looked to her mother, and Salome nodded. A flicker flashed in the mother's eye; she wasn't entirely comfortable letting her daughter out of her sight. Kaylie took the young girl's hand and they went out the back door. Salome stared at the wooden door after they left, as if wishing she could see through it.

There weren't pretty glass French doors at the rear of Mercy's home. Too easy to break through. Her doors were solid and heavily reinforced, and had multiple locks. She had high windows that let in the sun. Breakable but not easy to access.

Preparation.

Mercy caught Salome's gaze. It was time for answers. "Where have you been?" She was proud that she didn't yell the question at the woman.

"I've been staying with Christian," Salome said quietly.

"Were those your Hummer tracks at her home after she vanished on us?" Mercy asked Christian.

"Yes, we went to get a few of her and Morrigan's things."

His calm tone didn't help the frustration building in Mercy's chest. "You know the FBI is looking for her, right? She's a suspect in your *father's murder*." Mercy threw the words at Christian, not caring how harsh she sounded. The two of them had deliberately tied up the investigation, and Mercy was steamed.

"I didn't kill Judge Lake."

Mercy looked at Salome. *Damn, she's a cool customer. Not a hair ruffled.*

"Why were you at his office the day he was murdered?"

Color rushed from Christian's face, and he went very still.

*Aha. News to him.*

"I always see him when I'm in Portland."

"You do?" Surprise rang in his voice as he turned toward her.

"You know Judge Lake?" Mercy asked.

"I've known him since I was small. My mother credits him for saving us from my father. They've kept in touch all these years, and I often have lunch with him when I'm in Portland." She ducked her head. "I never told you, Christian, because I know how you dislike him, and my mother has always put him on a pedestal. He was important to her."

"What did he tell you?" Christian choked out the words.

Mercy took control of the conversation. "If Salome didn't kill the judge, *who did?*"

"When I first heard about my mother's and the judge's murder," answered Salome, "I was positive my father had done it. He swore revenge against the judge who put him away and my mother for testifying against him. It's why we've hid most of my life."

"Antonio Ricci," Mercy stated, pleased at the way Salome's eyes widened. "That's not possible. He's currently sitting in prison."

"I assumed he'd gotten out, and I immediately took Morrigan into hiding. I went to Christian, and he let me stay in one of the cabins on his property. I believed it was my father until yesterday when Gabriel shot at us."

"*What?*" Shock locked Mercy's muscles. *Gabriel?*

Christian nodded, his eyes despondent. "You didn't hear what happened at my place yesterday?"

"No." Mercy felt the interview slip out of her grasp again. "There's no cell service or Internet here."

He shared a story about the murder of Brent Rollins and Salome's narrow escape.

Mercy couldn't speak for a full ten seconds as her mind tried to process the violence. Brent had been killed while helping Salome and Morrigan? *And Morrigan witnessed that?* Most children would have been curled up in a ball, refusing to speak or move.

Mercy felt like doing that now.

"Why? Why would Gabriel try to kill you?" she asked Salome as Mercy tried to stay focused.

"I don't know."

*She's holding back.*

"We won't get anywhere if the two of you don't tell me *everything*." Mercy glared from Salome to Christian.

"She refused to go to the police, worried her father might still have some influence on the inside," Christian said. "I've tried to get her to tell them for two days. Last night I convinced her that you would be safe to talk to."

*"Then talk."*

Salome solemnly met her gaze. "I think Christian knows more—"

An explosion shook the little cabin. For a split second the three of them stared at one another in shock. *What happened?* Mercy glanced up, thankful to see that her roof was still intact, and then dropped below the table, her ears ringing. Salome flew out of her chair, lunging for the door. *"Morrigan!"*

Christian tackled her, slamming her to the wood floor. She fought, kicking and slapping him. "Let me go!" she shrieked.

"You don't know what's out there!" he yelled in her ear.

Mercy scrambled out from under the table, grabbed her pistol and rifle, and darted to the side of a small reinforced window at the front of the house, risking a glance. The Hummer was in flames.

Her heart stopped. *Kaylie?*

A dozen yards beyond the Hummer, she spotted the grille of another vehicle on her lane. The rest of it was tucked out of sight around a curve.

*Company.*

Truman halted the ATV in the middle of the road and stared. A black cloud had rocketed up into the sky above the forest after the explosion. Sweat trickled down Truman's back at the sight. *That's the direction of Mercy's cabin.*

*I'm still miles away.*

*What if she's hurt?*

*Or worse?*

He'd found the ATV in the barn. It was child-size and didn't move nearly as fast as it should because of his weight and the depth of the snow. At least it was something. He'd decided to walk the seven miles or so to Mercy's cabin, but then he'd spotted the ATV.

Nausea swirled in his gut as he stared at the smoke. *Whoever shot at me went to Mercy's.*

He checked his phone for the tenth time, and his heart leaped at the one bar of coverage. He requested police backup and an ambulance. *Just in case.* He tried Mercy's cell phone and it went straight to voice mail. Her cheery voice asking him to leave a message made him want to yell into the phone and order her to answer and tell him she was okay.

Instead he hung up and wiped the moisture off his upper lip.

*Keep going.*

Truman increased his thumb's pressure on the throttle.

# THIRTY-SIX

Mercy burst into action.

She lowered all the shades and flipped open her laptop, then pulled up outside views of the property. Christian kept Salome pinned to the floor. She screeched and kicked at him, a mother desperate to get to her daughter. His terrified gaze met Mercy's.

*"Shut her up,"* Mercy hissed.

She whipped the two-way radio out of her pocket. "Kaylie? Are you okay? Is Morrigan with you?"

Mercy waited.

The cabin went silent as Salome cut off her screams, her gaze locked on the small radio in Mercy's hand. "Kaylie?" Mercy asked again.

"Morrigan and I are okay," Kaylie's voice whispered through the speaker.

Salome went limp under Christian's hands and quietly sobbed.

Relief made Mercy want to do the same. She scanned the four views on her laptop. "Where are you?" she asked Kaylie. The Hummer smoked and burned. *How?* Blowing up a vehicle wasn't easy; it took planning.

Her heart stopped as she spotted a man with a pistol in his hand opening the barn door. He paused and looked back at the house over his shoulder. Mercy leaned closer to the screen, her throat closing off as she recognized his face. *No.* The man vanished inside where her niece had taken Morrigan.

"Shhh, Aunt Mercy." Kaylie could barely be heard. "Don't talk."

Mercy's hands iced and she nearly dropped the radio. Kaylie must have heard the man enter the barn. *My voice could give away their location.*

*Please remember the cabinet.* Vomit surged up her throat, and she clamped her teeth together.

*How can I get her and Morrigan out of there?* She couldn't rush the barn with an armed man and possible hostages inside.

She glanced back at Christian, who sat on the floor next to the crumpled woman, his chest heaving, his head between his knees and his hands squeezing his skull.

"It was your brother," Mercy stated. "Your brother blew up the Hummer."

His head shot up, his eyes wide. *"He's here?"*

"And now he's in the barn with Morrigan and Kaylie."

*"What?"* Salome started to rise.

"I think they're hiding. There's a secret room in the barn."

Salome inched away from Christian, anger on her face. "I've let you carry your secret, knowing you would tell me when it was time," she said. *"It's time."*

At the sound of the explosion, Kaylie had shakily stepped to the barn door and peeked through a crack. The black vehicle was on fire, but the house looked okay. She touched the radio in her pocket. Mercy had drilled her to hide first. Ask questions later.

Preparation.

Fighting the urge to run to the house, she guided Morrigan behind the false back of one the barn's storage cabinets and closed them in.

Morrigan had dashed for the barn doors at the roar of the blast, but Kaylie had blocked her. She'd talked fast, calming the girl and begging her to be silent. Their hiding spot appeared to be just another cabinet in a long row, but the shelving swung out, exposing a space big enough for two adults to hide. They squeezed in and found water, food, and a flashlight tucked in a corner. Kaylie flicked on the flashlight and sent a mental thank-you to her aunt for her paranoia.

"But my mother," Morrigan pleaded.

Kaylie showed her the radio. "My aunt will contact us."

"Call her!" Tears flooded Morrigan's cheeks.

"Shhh. No, the rule is that she reaches out to me first."

Seconds later Mercy did just that, and Morrigan calmed down.

The distinctive creak of the barn door sounded and Kaylie clamped a hand over Morrigan's mouth, her gaze ordering the younger girl to be quiet. "Shh, Aunt Mercy. Don't talk," she whispered through the radio. Morrigan's eyes flared wider, but she was silent, and Kaylie slowly pulled away her hand.

"I'm going to turn off the flashlight," she told Morrigan, her words nearly soundless.

The girl took Kaylie's hand, gripping tightly, and nodded.

Kaylie turned out the light, the image of Morrigan's terrified face burned into her retinas.

She slid her hand up the back of the hidden door in the absolute dark, feeling for the inner latches. She silently locked the three of them, their clicks inaudible, though they vibrated under her shaking fingertips. Morrigan's panicked breathing filled the small space. Kaylie leaned closer to the girl. "Breathe with me," she whispered, taking the child's other hand. Together they took long, slow breaths.

Slams and scuffles sounded inside the barn. Kaylie imagined the intruder kicking the PVC of her washing machine and opening the cabinets. Glass shattered on concrete. Morrigan jumped, losing the rhythm of their breaths.

Kaylie squeezed the girl's hands in the pattern of the breathing, and Morrigan struggled to settle into the rhythm again.

*The fruit and vegetables we canned are the only glass items in the barn. Asshole.*

The rustling search of the cabinets came closer. Quivers shot through Morrigan and up Kaylie's arms. Kaylie massaged the child's hands, trying to send silent reassurance.

The sound of ripping fabric filled the barn. Rip after rip. She pictured the sheets and towels Mercy had stored with the medical supplies, intended for use as bandages or tourniquets.

*He's destroying everything we have.*

The childlike destruction shocked her. *Why? Who does that?*

A faint but short metallic screwing sound reached her ears. Over and over. Each noise was followed by a *phsst* sound and then a gloppy splashing that Kaylie couldn't identify.

The man muttered as he moved to a closer cabinet and continued his destruction, his voice getting louder.

*"Aha!"* The rustling stopped, and Kaylie heard two long scrapes, as if something heavy was being dragged off the shelves.

Her mind scrambled to decipher the noise.

*The fuel cans.*

Mercy stored gasoline, diesel, and kerosene. Red, yellow, and blue. Color indicators Kaylie had memorized as a child. In January she'd helped Mercy replace her stash of all three fuels. The scraping sounds had come from the direction in which the gasoline was stored. The red plastic containers shone clear in her mind's eye.

*Will he set the barn on fire?*

She let go of one of Morrigan's hands and slid open two of the locks, her fingers hovering over the third, ready to dash out at the first sound or smell of fire. She pressed her ear against the crack of the hidden door and strained to hear. His footsteps grew quieter and she heard the distinctive creak of the barn door. The barn had a smaller door at its rear, but Mercy had fastened it from the inside with a chain and heavy padlock.

Footsteps returned. Kaylie leaned back from the door and held her breath. Two more scraping sounds. Retreating steps.

*More gasoline.*

Her heart tried to pound its way out of her chest, and she wondered if Morrigan heard it.

"What's he doing?" the girl whispered.

"I don't know," Kaylie lied. They couldn't leave the cabinet now; he was making multiple trips.

Kaylie leaned against the door, her ear at the crack again, and waited for the moment his footsteps didn't return.

Furious, Mercy whirled on Salome after her accusation at Christian about secrets. The woman was creating drama while Mercy's priority was to get the two girls to the safety of the house. Her mind spun with possibilities. *Kaylie told me to be quiet, so that means she heard the man.* Surely the teen would go immediately to the cabinet; they'd drilled repeatedly for handling an invasion of the property. The hidden room was weak compared to the security of the cabin, but at least it was something.

She thanked the sense of caution that had driven her to build the false back in the cabinet.

"What do you mean he's keeping secrets?" Mercy challenged Salome. She glanced at the screen. The man still hadn't come out of the barn. *I've got to get in there.*

"He knows why Gabriel would try to kill me."

Shocked, Mercy locked gazes with her old friend, seeing truth in his eyes. Her heart sank. "Christian?" she whispered.

"I never dreamed he'd kill your mother . . . or my father." He lowered his head again, his hands pressing on his ears as if he could keep out the horrors.

"What happened?" Mercy took a step in his direction, wanting to yank on his hair, shake him, kick him. Anything.

His head shot up, and he raised his arms defensively in her direction.

Mercy halted, realizing she'd lifted her pistol. She immediately lowered it to her side.

"A long time ago, my father told me he'd had a child with another woman."

Salome's breath hitched.

"I was young, but it made sense. When I found out, he and my mother had been divorced for about ten years, but the fights they'd had all my life were still fresh in my mind. My mother's screams . . . her words . . . her accusations." He glanced at Salome, and the dark woman stared back at him, her gaze locked on his face; she was expressionless, but her nostrils flared as if she scented something foul.

Christian couldn't look at her for more than a split second.

*Salome is that child.* Understanding swept over Mercy. *She's his half sister.*

"My mother ran a nonstop vocal campaign of hate against my father. Gabriel was fed this poison along with his meals. I was too, but my mind didn't work like Gabriel's. His soaked it in like a sponge. I let her hostility roll off my shoulders. Even as a kid, I knew hate wasn't something to harbor in my soul. But she often raged about the 'whore in the woods' who had corrupted our father and destroyed their marriage."

A single tear ran down Salome's cheek.

Mercy caught her breath at the shock on Salome's face.

"I didn't know this," Salome whispered.

"I know," said Christian. "My father was drunk when he told me. I don't think he remembered that he told me, because he never mentioned it again."

"He was always so kind to me. When did he tell you?" she asked.

"It was just after high school. I've kept it to myself all this time."

"Did Gabriel know who I was back then?"

Christian shook his head. "I'm almost positive he didn't." His voice lowered. "Gabriel didn't drug you to punish you for who you were; he drugged you because he was an asshole. He did it to several girls that year."

"Did *you* know who I was the night you fought him off me?"

"No." Christian was emphatic. "My father told me later."

*"What are you talking about?"* Mercy finally asked. The two of them were talking as if no one else existed in the room. Memories and shit were pleasant, but there was a very angry man outside and two girls who needed help.

Christian opened his mouth, but Mercy cut him off with a hand gesture. "Never mind. There's no time for some story. We need to focus on the girls." She looked around the cabin. "This is the safest place on the property. The barn isn't as fortified, but the hidden room will do its job."

She met Christian's gaze. "What is your brother going to do?"

He was silent. Bile rose in Mercy's throat at the devastated look on his face.

"Why?" Salome begged. "Why does he hate me that much?"

Guilt filled Christian's face. "I'm guessing, but my father told my mother he was changing his will. He enjoyed letting her know that I still had no part in it, but he also told her that Gabriel had destroyed his last chance. I gathered that Gabriel had borrowed money one too many times without paying it back." He swallowed. "My mother was irate about him cutting Gabriel off . . . more than I expected her to be." He looked to Salome. "If he's not leaving money to us, I suspect that means he's leaving it to you. He probably told her that, and she told Gabriel." Curiosity crossed his face. "You visited him for years and he never told you he was your father?"

"*No!* He never said a word!" Salome looked ready to vomit. "Gabriel killed them over money? And he's after Morrigan and me for the same reason?"

"Figure it out later," Mercy stated. "Christian, I know you can shoot. What about you, Salome?"

Salome shook her head.

Mercy checked the views on her laptop. No sight of Gabriel. Then she strode to the tall gun safe in the corner, spun the dial, and removed a rifle for Christian. She slipped on a holster, seated her pistol, and shoved ammo in her many pockets. From under the seat of a bench, she pulled out three bulletproof vests. Originally there'd been one. She'd added two more for Kaylie and Truman months earlier. Christian checked the rifle as Mercy slipped a knife onto her belt and held another out to Salome. "I bet you know how to use this."

"I do." Salome took the weapon with ease and examined the balance.

"Were those your knives in your mother's house?" Mercy asked. Salome handled the knife as if she'd been born with one in her hand.

"Yes, my mother started the collection, but I've increased it over the years." Bitter but hopeful eyes turned toward Mercy. "Can you get my daughter?"

Their gazes held.

"Absolutely. My daughter is out there too." Uncertainty and fear wove through Mercy.

But the confidence in Salome's eyes sent a calming energy up her spine, obliterating the fear.

*Nothing will happen to them. Not while I'm still breathing.*

"Aunt Mercy?"

She nearly missed Kaylie's soft voice through the radio. Mercy lifted it close to her mouth. "Yes?" she whispered.

"There's a man. I think he took the fuel cans out of the barn."

Mercy whirled back to the laptop again, searching the screen. "I can't see him." She pointed at Christian and Salome and gestured upstairs to her small loft. "Try to see him from the windows."

"What is he doing with them?" Kaylie asked softly. "Morrigan and I are in the cabinet."

Kaylie wouldn't ask Mercy while Morrigan was listening if the barn was being set on fire.

"I can't see him right now. I'll figure it out." She paused. "Be *ready*, Kaylie."

*Be ready to get out if the barn burns.*

"Always," came the teen's reply.

Tears smarted at her niece's answer. *I couldn't love her any more if she were mine.*

"Don't come out unless I say so or you *need* to."

"Understood."

Mercy shoved the radio back in a pocket and studied her camera views.

*Where is the bastard?*

# THIRTY-SEVEN

I have a brother.

It's as if someone attempted to erase *only child* across my heart, but the words still show through the smears. They added *sibling* in tentative script; the word is awkward and harsh. It doesn't fit. Yet.

My best friend is my brother.

I've always known our affection went deeper than friendship. I look at him now and my heart is happy; it knows the truth. Perhaps if I had listened closer to my heart, I would have realized it for myself.

But the man outside is also my brother. My brain refuses to accept this fact.

"Will Gabriel set the barn on fire?" I ask Christian as I peer out of a loft window, my stomach in my throat, worried sick over my daughter.

*Morrigan.*

*Burning.*

Living deep in the woods, my mother had a great fear of fire. One that she passed on to me. Not just a fear of forest fires but also a personal fear. *"They burn witches," she often told me.*

*"We aren't witches," I'd reply.*

*"It doesn't matter. They believe we are, and that is all it takes."*

*"This isn't the seventeenth century."*

*"Hmph. Don't sass."*

My mother's words echo in my brain as I search the grounds for Christian's brother.

"It's too wet," answers Christian. He stands with his body to the side of a window as he scans outside. "Everything is covered with snow. It'd be nearly impossible to get a fire going."

I look at the smoking Hummer without comment.

"When we were kids, he got in trouble twice for fooling around with flammables." Disgust fills his voice. "Makes me wonder how many times he didn't get caught."

"We can't see him," I report down to Mercy on the lower floor.

"Keep watching. He's somewhere," she answers back. "Can you see his vehicle?"

"Barely. Not much past the headlights," I tell her. Out the opposite window I can see the barn. No smoke. A small reassurance that Morrigan is still safe.

"Gabriel is no longer a child," I tell Christian. "What he's done is unforgivable." Tears burn in my eyes and my throat grows tight. "My mother . . ." I can't speak.

Christian looks ready to cry. "I'm so sorry, Salome. I know how special she was."

"I liked your father. I'd always hoped the two of you would repair your relationship. I tried to reason with him."

"He's stubborn."

*Like his son.*

"Why didn't you tell me he was my father?" I whisper. "You've known for years."

He won't turn from the window to look at me, and I see his father's stubbornness in his spine.

"You didn't tell me you were friends with my father. The man who practically disowned me," he lashes back.

"That's not the same and you know it."

He has the grace to nod, and I can tell he is struggling to tell me the truth.

"I don't know. A lot of reasons."

I wait.

"I wasn't positive it was true. I didn't want to spread a rumor."

"But now you believe it is true?"

"I did some snooping around after you begged for a place to hide. I found out there was no way your father could have been your birth father . . . he was in jail at the time." He finally meets my eyes. "I found your baptism record. Your birthday isn't what you think it is."

"When is it?" I whisper, my knees weak.

"Sometime in September, I think. Not March. You're about six months younger than you believe."

I examine his face for lies. Truth permeates the air around him, and I struggle to find my breath.

"It wasn't just that," he continues. "You were my closest friend . . . I didn't want anything to change. If you knew, we'd be different." His voice falters on the last word.

*"You don't know that."* But in my heart I knew he was right. Our friendship was—is still special, and perhaps an unknown family bond made it that way. I don't hate him for his silence; I could never hate him. I'm disappointed.

I search for hints of myself in his face. Maybe around the mouth . . . the shape of the eyes.

"I always believed I had genes of violence . . . my father did horrible things." My voice trembles. "I tried to live up to those genes. I acted out . . . I fucked around and played with people's emotions, blaming my father for making me who I was." I cover my eyes. I can't stand the sympathy in Christian's. "But it was just me all along . . . not his genes . . . That was who I am."

I shudder. None of my life is what I thought it was.

"There he is!" Mercy shouts from downstairs. "He's on the other side of his vehicle."

I strain my eyes, but I can't see any movement on the other side. "Is he leaving?" I yell down to Mercy.

*Get to Morrigan. Now.*

"I don't know," said Mercy. "I think he would have left by now."

I move to the rail and look down to the first level. "Can we get to the barn?"

"You're going nowhere. I'll get them out." Mercy looks up and our eyes lock. "I need someone to watch him and cover me."

This is true, but I know she also stated it as an excuse to keep us inside. I admire and now trust this FBI agent. She's tough, and her heart is good. I regret we met under these circumstances.

"He's coming out!" Christian shouts behind me.

I turn around and Christian lunges at me, knocking me to the floor, crushing me with his weight.

The window shatters, and I cover my head against the shower of glass as the gunshot reverberates outside.

Mercy dived next to the woodstove as the shot destroyed an upstairs window.

*Damned glass.*

She looked up at where Salome had stood a second earlier. She'd vanished.

"Christian?" Mercy shouted.

The crash of breaking glass and another gunshot made her crouch lower.

"We're okay, but two windows up here are destroyed."

Abruptly another shot shattered the small main-level window at the front of the cabin, and the cold outside air blew across her cheeks.

*No worries. It's too small to climb through.*

"Aunt Mercy?" Kaylie's tinny voice sounded from her pocket.

She slid out the radio. "We're okay. He's shot out some windows, but they're too high for him to get in. The two of you need to *stay put!*"

"Got it."

The air roared with another shot as glass shattered upstairs again.

"Get down here!" she yelled and darted for her laptop.

Christian and Salome thundered down the stairs. "He's using tree trunks as cover," Christian pants. "I couldn't get a shot." He directed Salome to crouch on the side of the woodstove that Mercy had just left.

Mercy enlarged each view on the screen. "I can't see him. *Dammit!*" *I'm putting in more cameras next week.*

"What about the barn?" Salome begged. She huddled by the stove, seeking the protection of the iron.

"I can see the barn door. He hasn't gone back there."

Christian moved toward the small broken window, his rifle raised.

"Get back," Mercy snapped. "He hit it once, he can hit it again."

*"Send out the whore!"*

Mercy's head jerked up at Gabriel's shout, her fingers frozen on her computer's keyboard. Christian paled and looked over at Salome. Her eyes widened and then sparked in anger as she jumped to her feet.

"I believe he means *me.*"

"You're not going out there," Mercy ordered.

"Of course not. But as long as his focus is on me, I know Morrigan is safe."

*"Gabriel!"* Christian cupped his mouth and shouted toward the small broken window. *"What the hell are you doing?"*

"This isn't about you, Christian!" Gabriel answered. "It's that fucking witch!"

Salome laughed, making an odd sound as if she were laughing and choking at the same time.

Her spine tense, Mercy hissed at Christian, "You don't know how to handle this."

"And you do?" he snarled back. "That's my brother out there. He'll listen to me."

"He's beyond listening to anyone. His brain has moved into his finger on the trigger." Mercy struggled to recall the negotiation rules from her FBI workshops. To keep him talking was all she could remember.

"I'll send you to hell, Gabriel Lake!" Salome bellowed. Tears streamed down her cheeks, but she grinned, a crazy shit-eating grin that made Mercy's skin crawl. "I'll fucking curse you!" Her cackle was high and distorted, straight from every child's witchy nightmare.

Christian stared at her, his rifle clenched to his chest. "Are you nuts?" he whispered.

"He's terrified of me." Salome choked on her tears and giggled, a wet clogged sound. "He's always believed I was a witch."

"You would see him? When?" Christian still looked rattled.

"Our paths would cross here and there in the past. He always gave me a wide berth."

*How can I use that to our advantage?*

"You'll burn, whore!"

"That's not the way to speak to your half sister, Gabriel!" Her whoops echoed off the ceiling.

*She's falling apart.*

Yanking her focus back to their safety, Mercy took another look at the camera angles. Gabriel had moved into her forward camera's view, crouching behind the roasting Hummer.

"Can you keep him distracted? Keep yelling at him?" she asked Christian and Salome. "I'll sneak out the back, go wide, and try to get a clear angle."

Salome nodded, but Christian grabbed Mercy's arm. "What are you planning to do?" Terror and worry filled his face.

Mercy was stunned at the anguish for his brother on his face. "He's a *threat*, Christian. He murdered your father and Olivia. He won't stop until Salome and probably the rest of us are dead too." *Why does he think I gave him a gun?*

"But . . ." He couldn't finish his sentence, his gaze darting between her eyes.

"I understand." She laid her hand on his. Gabriel was Christian's brother. He had every right to be rattled at the thought of his brother being shot, murderer or not. "I'll only do what he pushes me to do."

His face fell, but he nodded and pulled his hand away.

"Good luck," he told her.

"You're not my sister!" Gabriel roared. "You're the spawn of a whore!"

Mercy pointed at Salome. "You're up."

"I'm going to curse your dick, you asshole!" Salome shrieked. "You'll never get it up again!"

*Well done.* She flashed Salome a thumbs-up.

Mercy slipped out the back door and silently went down the steps. If she veered left, she should be out of Gabriel's line of sight until she reached the edge of the woods. Then she could circle behind the barn and move closer using the cover of the trees. It was a long and round-about way, but she didn't see another option.

Gabriel shouted an unintelligible threat, and Salome started to chant at the top of her lungs. A singsong string of nonsense to Mercy's ears, but eerily familiar to what she'd heard at Olivia's deathbed. Goosebumps rose on her arms.

*That ought to rattle him.* Especially if he believed Salome had powers.

She was almost to the barn when more shattering glass followed by a muffled *whoosh* made her stop and check the house. No shots had been fired. Fresh smoke rose from in front of the house. *It's the Hummer. Something else ignited.* The sounds repeated and a fresh burst of smoke appeared over her house.

Flames flashed in her upper windows.

*He threw Molotov cocktails through the broken windows.*

Her heart stopped as her world tilted off center.

*My home. My work.*

A barrage of miniexplosions sounded. Glass containers exploded as Gabriel threw them at the front of her home. Flames flickered in her small lower windows, and she took two steps toward the house, her gaze fastened on the back door, silently begging for Christian and Salome to appear. *Get out!*

"Aunt Mercy? *What's happening?*" Kaylie was in tears.

She grabbed her radio. "He's throwing Molotov cocktails into the house." Vomit surged up her throat.

*"It's on fire?"*

"It doesn't matter," Mercy choked out. "As long as everyone is safe."

"Those were the sounds we heard in the barn . . . he was emptying the canning jars. He must have used them and the gas—"

Mercy cut her off. "I'm almost behind the barn. I want you two to get out of the cabinet and meet me outside the back door. We can't take the chance that he sets fire to the barn next."

"The back door is fastened from the inside with that chain and padlock."

*And the key is in the kitchen.*

*A major fuckup on my part.*

They couldn't go to the front of the barn; Gabriel would see them immediately. "There are bolt cutters in one of the cabinets." Mercy closed her eyes to think. "I think the third one. As soon as you're out, I want you to head east. *Don't stop.* I'll radio you when it's safe."

"We'll leave tracks in the snow."

"I don't care. Just get moving. He's occupied at the front of the house."

Movement out of the corner of her eye made her turn to see Christian and Salome darting away from the house to the woods. Mercy exhaled noisily, her mental load lightened.

Everyone was out of the way. *Now to get the girls farther away.*

Mercy awkwardly jogged through the deep snow. A minute later she reached the back of the barn and pressed her ear against the door. Clanking sounded from the other side. Kaylie had found the bolt cutters.

Two feet of snow piled up against the outside of the door, nearly as effective as the padlock for keeping the girls locked inside. Mercy dug at it like a dog, exertion heating her face. Finally the door could open enough for Kaylie to squeeze through. Morrigan was right behind her. Mercy hugged her niece tight to her chest, wishing she'd left the girl back in town. "You need to head through the forest."

"What about you?" Kaylie pleaded. Her gaze went from Mercy's bulletproof vest to the rifle slung over her shoulder. "Oh."

"My mother?" Morrigan whispered, clutching Kaylie's arm. Her eyes were huge in her delicate face.

"She's fine," Mercy promised. "I saw her get out. You two need to start moving. No stopping."

"I love you, Aunt Mercy." Kaylie's voice cracked and she wiped her eyes.

"Love you more." Mercy ached to hug her again, but time was too tight. "Go."

She watched the two figures lumber through the snow, Kaylie towing Morrigan behind her.

Mercy darted back to the tree line and continued her trek to get Gabriel in her sights.

Truman stopped and turned off the ATV, not trusting his ears.

*More explosions?*

Two more far-off detonations sounded, and more smoke rose in the direction of Mercy's cabin.

*Fire.*

*Mercy? Kaylie?*

Images from his past of a burning car flashed in his mind, replaced by the recall of a recent burning barn. His healed burns prickled and stung under the skin of his neck and thigh at the memories, the old injuries echoing in his nerves. Every fiber of his muscles wanted to run in the opposite direction. His heart was thick in his throat as he restarted the ATV, his focus on Mercy and Kaylie. *I might be walking into a nightmare.* He shut down the terror that tried to take over his brain. *Please be safe.*

His progress had been painstakingly slow. The vehicle wasn't capable of much speed, and the snow made it feel as if he were crawling.

*Am I too late?*

# THIRTY-EIGHT

Smoke and flames billowed from all her windows.

Frozen in shock, Mercy's muscles threatened to shatter.

*I won't cry. It's just boards and bricks.*

But it was more than that. Her cabin was the result of years of backbreaking work. It had kept her centered and grounded.

Now she floated with no tether, anxiety and panic taking her higher. Her aspirations and dreams burning as she watched.

Her soul crumbling, she leaned against a tree, closing her eyes to block the burning of her core.

Knowing she had a fallback position had kept her sane, and her brain threatened to tip over into the dark.

*Not now. Don't think about it now.*

Four months earlier it was all she'd had. Now she had Kaylie. Her family. Truman.

Thoughts of Truman brought her back down to earth, helping her focus, and she sucked in deep breaths, exhaling for long seconds, slowing her heartbeat.

Her cabin could be rebuilt. Some supplies were still safe in the barn.

She opened her eyes and pushed away from the tree, dragging her grit and tenacity up from the very bottom of her rattled soul. She had a mission. A deadly one. She drew her handgun and led with it gripped in front of her, tuning out the sounds of the fire.

*Just you and me, Gabriel.*

She wasn't sure of his location. There'd been no explosions for several minutes. Just the roar of the flames. They stretched out of her windows and licked the edges of her roof. Steam rose from the shingles, and she had a stab of regret about the expensive solar panels.

*Doesn't matter.*

*Concentrate.*

On her right she was nearly even with the front of the house, but she didn't see Gabriel or his vehicle.

*Shit. Where are you?*

She crouched, scanning her surroundings for any movement. Nothing. She moved from tree to tree, her pace slower, more intent on the hunt. Sweat covered her upper lip, and she brushed it with her sleeve. She holstered her pistol and unslung the rifle from her shoulder.

*What if he went after the girls?*

Fear blossomed in her lungs. She turned to retrace her steps and search for a renegade path in the snow.

Fire shot through her right thigh, and the report of a gun filled her ears. Looking down, she saw a spray of red had stained the white snow. *My blood?* She took a step, her leg collapsed, and she fell on her stomach, the rifle flying out of her hands and sinking into the snow.

White-hot pain surged up her nerves and exploded in her brain. *"Fuuuuuck!"*

She scrambled to lift herself out of the snow, but everywhere she set her hands they sank deep, nearly burying her face. The pain flourished, expanding and multiplying. She gasped, inhaling suffocating mouthfuls of white fluff.

Managing to roll on her side, she stared at the blood seeping out of a hole in her leg. *It's not pulsing. No artery hit.*

*Gabriel shot me.*

Anger radiated through her as she thrashed to look in every direction for her attacker.

*I'm as vulnerable as a bird with a fucking broken wing.*

She frantically lurched to her feet. *Get to the barn.* Unable to dig out her rifle, she drew her handgun. Her thigh was a hot, throbbing electric wire, and with every step she nearly blacked out.

The barn was out of the question.

She flung herself at the base of a gigantic pine, its trunk wide enough to stop a truck. Placing her back flat against the tree, she gripped her handgun in front of her, using the tree to support her stance. She erratically swung her weapon from the right to the left, searching for her shooter, ignoring her crooked trail of blood.

*If I didn't know it was mine, I'd think a dying deer had struggled through the snow.*

Her vision started to tunnel and she grew light-headed. She blinked rapidly, refusing to give in.

"Hello, Mercy." His voice came from a distance, but she heard every syllable.

Instant sweat coated her spine at Gabriel's words. She pivoted in all directions, trying to pinpoint his location. He wasn't to be seen.

"That's a lot of blood."

*There he is.* He stood thirty feet away, between her and the barn, his body behind a pine as wide as hers.

She lifted her pistol in his direction, trying to line up the sights, but the gun weighed fifty pounds and her arms shook with the effort. Her frozen fingers could barely move. *I'll never make a head shot.*

He laughed, not even bothering to protect his head.

Furious, she fired six times, sending the bark of his tree flying through the air.

She slightly lowered her arms, the shots ringing in her ears.

"You missed." This time he kept his head behind the tree.

"What do you want, Gabriel?" She tried to get behind her own tree, but her leg refused to cooperate, pain rocketing up and down her nerves. Her right knee tried to bend backward and she flailed, grabbing at the trunk, the impact knocking her pistol from her numb hand. It sank into the snow an easy five feet away.

It might as well have been a mile.

*Twice I lost my weapon?* This time it was her own fault.

A cold that wasn't from the low temperature ached in her bones as she stared at the small hole in the snow where her weapon had sunk. *If I lunge for it, I'll be stuck.*

*If I do nothing . . .*

At least he probably still believed she had the gun.

*I still have a knife.*

She settled for partially getting around the tree and sliding to a sitting position, her injured leg straight out in front of her, the other bent. She was still in Gabriel's view, but now her side was toward him and she made a narrower target. She drew the knife and clenched it to her chest, swearing to never let go. The back of her head dug into the tree, and she wished she could disappear into its trunk. The chill of the snow seeped through her pants, and shivers racked her body. *At least I wore my vest.*

"I want the whoring witch. Tell Christian I'll trade you for her."

"Why Salome?"

"I tried to burn her out. That's the only way to kill a witch, right?"

The crackle of the flames threatened to make her cry. "She's not a witch." Blood continued to flow from her leg, seeping into the snow beneath it. A red shadow lazily grew under the limb, expanding outward through the white. She unwrapped one frozen hand from the knife handle and put pressure on the hole. Blinding fireworks flashed in her eyes, and she fought not to faint.

"Her mother was one. She ruined our family."

"I don't think she did that by herself. It takes two, you know." Her teeth chattered around the words.

"I'd been willing to let it go until I heard the judge was changing his will to leave all his money to her and her spawn."

*He calls his father "the judge"?*

Movement off to the right, far behind Gabriel's tree, caught her eye. *Christian.* Focusing on her friend took great effort and he blurred, vanishing and reappearing in her vision.

"Was it necessary to kill him?"

"He had to die before he made the changes legal. I *need* that money."

"You killed your father for *money*," Mercy uttered. "Such a good son." Sarcasm dripped from her voice.

"He had it coming! He had no right to abandon his family!"

"And you had the right to kill him for it?"

Silence.

Christian had moved closer, his rifle ready. Farther to his right, Mercy spotted a flash of color between the trees that had to be Salome.

*Christian's angle on his brother must be poor. I know he could make the shot from that distance.*

*Or does he not want to shoot?*

"You don't want to hurt anyone else, Gabriel." A point from her negotiating workshop popped into her head. "Don't make the situation worse than it is. I'll tell them you backed off when you could have killed me. That's worth something."

*"Shut up, you lying bitch! I need to end this!"*

*Distract him.* "Why the pattern on the bodies, Gabriel? What were you trying to say?"

"A suitable death for the abomination and her brainwashed lover. I wanted that whoring daughter to know her mother's powers *couldn't stop me.*"

"And Rob Murray?"

Gabriel gave a coarse laugh. "That idiot walked up behind me when I was getting rid of the knife in Christian's garage. I don't think he thought it was important, but he might have figured it out later. He didn't matter."

Mercy flinched at the ice in his voice. His brain was cracked, rotting with anger and hate. Was it from decades of verbal barrages from his mother? "What did Michael Brody see?" she asked.

"Who? Oh. The reporter."

*Do I hear regret in his voice?*

"I agreed to meet him in the park for an interview. He'd said on the phone that he'd found something interesting he wanted to discuss." His tone intensified. "I think he found out about the loans from the judge."

"And you shot him for that?" *He must believe Michael is dead.*

Silence.

"Brody lived," she said. "You didn't kill him. I'm sure you can work out a deal—"

"*Do you think I'm stupid?* I fucking study the law! They'll hang me." An element of hopelessness entered his voice. "I won't go to prison."

"It's not too late—"

"*Didn't I tell you to shut up?*" "They'll go easier on you for not kill—" She lost her words as he stepped out from behind his tree, fully facing her, his gun at his side, barrel down, bleak acceptance in his gaze.

*He wants me to shoot him.*

*I have no weapon.*

She froze, unable to speak or move. Every coherent thought flew out of her brain as they locked eyes. She waited.

Gabriel stared at her for a long moment, and then his eyes lit up. "Where's your gun, Special Agent Kilpatrick?"

He raised his weapon.

Mercy couldn't breathe.

# THIRTY-NINE

Truman followed the tire tracks down Mercy's winding lane. Two vehicles had traveled the road before him.

Smoke, gasoline, and burning rubber assaulted his nose, and he slowed, his fear and anxiety about what lay ahead spiking.

He rounded a curve and saw the open back hatch of Christian's black Lexus. He halted. The crackle of flames filled his ears. A large red gas can lay on its side behind the SUV.

*Where's my shooter now?*

He swung his leg over the ATV and pulled out his rifle, then carefully made his way to the vehicle. No driver. Debris was scattered, clearly emptied from an overturned duffel bag in the snow. *Rob said Christian carried gas and emergency supplies in all his vehicles.* Protein bars, MREs, duct tape, a tarp. Truman spotted a large plastic bag with the remains of a liquid inside. He picked it up and sniffed. Gas.

*He could rig a large bomb with gas and a plastic bag.*

Truman moved forward, leading with his weapon until a smoking Hummer came into view. *That is what he blew up with the makeshift bomb.* Past it, Mercy's cabin burned. Flames and smoke pouring out of the windows, fire poking through the roof.

*Dear Lord.*

*Is Mercy inside? Kaylie?*

No one could survive in that inferno.

His grip tightened on his weapon as he fought back nausea, his head spinning.

On his side of the destroyed Hummer, he spotted a few glass canning jars, screw lids, and two more gasoline cans. Ripped strips of fabric serpentined in the breeze from the fire.

*Molotov cocktails.* He'd made enough as a teen to recognize the components.

*Who bombed the cabin?*

He wanted to yell and see if anyone was in the structure. *Anyone in there is long dead.*

Agony ripped through his brain, ordering him to give up. *Not until I see she's gone.*

He scoured the area, and a spot of blue in the woods caught his eye. Truman darted off the drive and into the forest, jogging through the snow.

Gabriel Lake stood alone, wearing a blue coat, aiming a pistol at a tree.

*It was Gabriel, not Christian.*

Truman was close enough to see his delighted smile, but the unhinged look in Gabriel's eye brought Truman to a halt, rattled by the animosity that was rolling off the man.

*He's evil.*

A subtle movement on the ground made his heart speed up. Mercy was sitting below the tree.

*She's alive.*

His knees shook in relief and he struggled to stay on his feet.

But then Mercy turned her face away from Gabriel, as if she couldn't watch. Truman's relief evaporated in shock as he realized that Gabriel was about to shoot her.

*Why doesn't she run?*

She met Truman's gaze and her eyes were a bottomless pit of regret. *She's given up.*

Time slowed as Truman raised his rifle, his entire world hanging by a thread.

◆　◆　◆

I clench the knife Mercy gave me as I push through the snow, my gaze locked on her sitting at the base of the pine.

Christian hisses at me. *"Stay back."* He has a rifle, and I've let him lead the way, but the sight of Mercy in the snow, her back to a tree and terror on her face, pushes me forward. The scents of burning boards and plastics interfere with my nose, but I'm not blind. A fading red shock is consuming her.

Gabriel's back is to us, and he suddenly steps out from behind his tree.

Her time is up.

Gabriel raises his gun. Christian does the same.

I can't trust that Christian will fire. I plant my feet and hurl the knife, a prayer on my lips that I won't miss.

# FORTY

Mercy saw part of Gabriel's head disappear in a red haze, and the sound of gunshots bounced off the trees. She screamed as his body twisted and dropped to the ground, the gun still in his hand and his blood sprayed across the snow.

Mercy stared at the limp body, dimly aware of figures rushing at her from several angles. He'd fallen face-up, the handle of her knife sticking out of his chest.

*Did I do that?*

*No. I gave that knife to Salome.*

Gabriel had fired a shot before he fell. *Am I hit again?* She studied her chest and arms. No holes. A knife was still clutched in her grip.

Christian dropped to his knees beside her, and Salome was a split second behind him. "Are you okay?" they both shouted at her.

She pushed away their searching hands. They were touching her leg, pulling at her pants, and shaking her shoulders. But she ignored them, straining to see where Truman had been a brief moment before. Gabriel's shot hadn't hit her, but Truman had also been in his line of fire.

*Truman?*

"Mercy, can you hear me?" Christian grabbed her head and turned her face to him, cutting off her search for Truman.

She snarled, swinging her knife in his direction. He whipped his hands away, tumbling backward into the snow. "Where's Truman?" she screamed as she flung her body to the right, not caring about the burning pain in her leg, fighting to see where Truman had been standing. *"Where's Truman?"* she shrieked again.

"Right here."

Suddenly he was with her, gathering her into his arms. Hyperventilating, she buried her face in his neck. *He's okay.* The fragile hold she'd had on her emotions crumbled, and she sagged against him. More than anything she simply wanted to sleep with his arms around her. He pulled back and shook her. "Stay awake," he commanded, his eyes deadly serious.

"Get pressure on that," he ordered Christian. "Help me get my coat on her," he told Salome. Everyone was silent as they frantically followed his directions.

*Too silent.*

"It's bad," she stated. Truman wouldn't meet her gaze as he zipped her into his coat.

"You got him," she whispered to Truman. "I thought he'd hit you."

"I didn't shoot him. Someone else shot first."

Mercy swiveled to look at Christian, and her heart broke at the bleak expression on his face. He wouldn't look up, focused on her leg. Salome met her gaze and laid a hand on Christian's shoulder. "You had no choice," she told him.

He was pale, and wet tracks covered his cheeks. *He killed his brother. For me.*

Mercy's lungs wouldn't work. "Christian . . ."

Christian gave her a sickly smile as he tightened the wrap on her thigh. "I guess I had it in me after all."

"That's not funny." The weight of what he had done made Mercy's brain want to shut down.

"He would have killed you," Christian stated.

Salome nodded in agreement. "And he wouldn't have stopped with just you."

"You got him too," Mercy told her, remembering the knife handle in Gabriel's chest.

The woman shrugged. *She would kill to protect her daughter.*

Mercy abruptly jerked straight up. *"The girls!"* She dug for her radio, her fingers uncoordinated. *I'm freezing. Lack of blood to keep me warm.* The realization didn't bother her. *I'm not important. The girls and Truman are important.*

Truman took the radio, and she was relieved to hear Kaylie's voice as Truman told her to come back in.

Mercy closed her eyes. *My people are safe.* She was dimly aware of Truman shaking her again, ordering her to open her eyes, but she was too tired. *I'm just going to nap for a little bit.*

"Damn you, Mercy! Open your eyes!"

She smiled, her lids too heavy to cooperate.

*It feels good to have people who care.*

# FORTY-ONE

*One week later*

One week out of surgery and Truman wanted to strangle Mercy. She was the worst patient ever. After two days she'd stopped her pain medication even though she still had pain in her leg. Now she wanted to drive up to her cabin. He had told Mercy he wouldn't drive her, so she'd sworn she'd drive herself.

Driving was still out of the question, whether she was on painkillers or not.

After she scared the crap out of him by passing out that day, Truman and Christian had loaded her into the back of the Lexus, and Truman had stayed in back next to her, unwilling to leave her side. Kaylie and Morrigan had cried on the drive, terrified Mercy would die, and with extreme calm Salome did her best to comfort them.

Truman had kept his fingers at her neck during the entire slow drive out of the forest. As long as there was a pulse under his fingertips, he promised himself he wouldn't panic.

But damn, it'd gotten slower and slower.

They'd driven about ten miles when they'd spotted the responding county sheriff and ambulance. On Truman's suggestion Christian had blocked the two-lane highway as the vehicles came toward them, worried they'd not stop.

The EMTs had immediately taken over, placing an IV and pumping who the hell knows what into her veins.

It was over. And he didn't want to repeat it.

But she'd been asking to return to her cabin for the last three days. He'd refused. She was still weak, and he didn't need the sight of her destroyed hopes and dreams breaking her down more.

But she was strong enough to annoy the hell out of him. Even Kaylie had been short with her aunt, ordering her to rest.

Mercy wasn't one to sit still.

He'd given in and driven her to the cabin. A weeklong warm spell had melted nearly all the snow in the lower elevations, but the rough road that led past the Sabins' cabin and hers was still covered with packed snow. The drive had been silent.

Now he watched as she stared in awe at the mess.

Her cabin had collapsed in on itself. An entire loss.

Blackened beams jutted out of the debris. The only recognizable parts were the fireplace and woodstove. The fireplace had stubbornly stood in place, refusing to submit to the flames. A few pines had been singed, but the snow and distance had kept them from fully burning and starting a forest fire. The smoky stench still hung in the clearing. It wasn't the good wood smoke smell that everyone loves; it was a harsh, burned-chemical-and-plastic smell with an undertone of wood.

Truman shoved his hands in his pockets as Mercy stood four feet away, her back to him. He wanted to see her face, but he knew she needed a private moment. "I can't even see a solar panel," he heard her softly say. She took a few steps closer, and he followed. She kicked at some burned wood and watched carefully where she placed her feet on the scarred piles. She stopped in the middle of the mess and crouched next to a pile of ash and burned boards. Picking up a small piece of wood, she started to dig.

He wanted to yank her away from the destruction, worried she'd insist on searching through the entire heap at that moment. But he stayed in place.

*This is her way of mourning.*

If she wanted to dig, he'd get a shovel and help her.

She dug out a plate, blew off the ash, and studied it before tossing it to the side. Truman knew the plate had been blue, but now it was scorched and unrecognizable. Mercy poked around some more, and he figured it was time to grab a shovel from the barn. Suddenly she stood and brushed the debris off something in her hand. She turned and showed him a six-inch scarred metal handle attached to a round scooped end. Her lips quirked. "I never got a chance to thank you for this."

He studied the thing on her soot-covered palm, clueless.

She turned it over and made the motion of packing something in the round end.

It clicked. *It's from the espresso machine I bought.* "I have no idea what they call that part," he admitted. "But I'm glad you saw the machine before the fire. I'll get you another one. When we rebuild."

Her shoulders sagged, and she looked back at the mess. "It might be too big of a project."

"Are you in a hurry? Because I don't think we have anything we need to do for the next year or two." He'd never seen her overwhelmed, and he didn't like it. She faced every challenge head-on; she couldn't be beaten by this one.

Could she?

This uncertain Mercy rattled him almost as much as bleeding and unconscious Mercy.

*She's broken on the inside too.*

Her thigh would heal. It simply needed time and rest. But what would it take to heal this?

Truman felt as if he were flying a plane with no instructions.

All he could do was take one day at a time.

Mercy had asked Truman what she should say to a man who had killed his brother to protect her. "Just be his friend," Truman had suggested. "He's lost most of his family." She'd nodded, a determined look on her face, and Truman knew she'd keep Christian close, consider him one of her growing family. That was fine with Truman. Christian had saved her life; Truman was forever indebted to him.

If Gabriel Lake hadn't died, Truman would have hurt him very badly.

Gabriel had been punishing people for destroying his family, but his actions had hurt his own family even more. Christian had to bury his father and his brother, and Truman suspected his relationship with his mother was permanently broken. Christian had told Truman that he'd always known his mother was poison, and that Gabriel harbored a lot of anger, but he'd never dreamed it would come to murder. Her poison had amplified Gabriel's shortcomings and created something very deadly.

Gabriel Lake had taken away Salome's mother and Morrigan's grandmother; their lives would never be the same. "I've had enough deep snow and forest for the rest of my life," Salome had told Mercy and Truman. "I want a tiny yard and a picket fence. Morrigan will go to school like any other kid."

"What about Antonio Ricci?" Mercy had asked. "I thought you were scared of being found."

Salome's eyes were distant as she answered. "I can't live in fear anymore. It's been like a slow cancer in my heart. We'll find our spot, and then we are done running forever."

"Where will you go?" asked Truman.

"I'm not sure yet." Something in her tone had told him she knew exactly where she was going. He suspected he and Mercy would never be told, but he wished the best for her and her daughter. The past was buried; Truman's original memory of Salome had been replaced by the one of her fight for Mercy.

Salome and Morrigan would simply disappear one day, starting fresh with new identities. No doubt Christian would know where she found a home. Truman believed the two of them had a bond that would never be broken.

The current look on Mercy's face made him wonder if she wanted to leave and start fresh.

"Do you want to sell the land?" he asked.

Her head jerked toward him. "No!"

*Finally. A spark.*

"Do you still want to buy a house together?"

She sighed. "I can't now. The deductible on the insurance for this property will take everything I've saved for a down payment."

*Ouch.*

Another option popped in his head. "What about living here? How about building something a little bigger—"

At her skeptical look, he quickly clarified. "We wouldn't build *too* big a home. We'd keep it to a manageable size in case we lost power." He waited, hoping she would accept his help.

Mercy mulled over Truman's suggestion. She'd planned to eventually live in the cabin. Why not now?

*Because it takes forever to drive to work. Because the closest grocery store is far away.*

The cabin was perfect for an imperfect future.

But not perfect for her current life.

"I don't think so," she said slowly. "I like the idea, but it's not very practical right now." She looked at the gray-and-black pile of destruction. "I feel beaten down at the moment. I don't know if I can start from scratch."

Truman pointed at the barn. "Isn't two-thirds of the important stuff in there?"

*True.*

"Yes, but—"

"Then all you need is the cabin. I know you had a lot of special systems, but frankly, I'd rather rebuild a house than try to replace what's stored in the barn." He took her hands, making her look at him. "You did this alone the first time. You won't be alone to rebuild."

Tears burned.

*How did I end up with such a good man?*

"Thank you," she whispered, her voice watery. "You don't know what that means to me."

"You mean everything to me," Truman stated, his brown eyes deadly serious. "I'm not going to let a little fire and a hole in your leg disrupt your future."

She choked, making a wet snorting noise. "Little?"

"Every night in my dreams, I see Gabriel shoot you," he admitted. "Christian's shot is too late. I'm too late, and so is Salome. Compared to that reality, yeah . . . this fire and your wound are little." He swallowed hard. "We can rebuild everything you had. Make it better. What do you think of that?"

Mercy held his gaze, unable to speak, remembering a private conversation she'd had with Salome during her recovery in the hospital.

"You'll end up together," Salome had suddenly said in the middle of a discussion about hospital food.

"What?"

"Truman."

Mercy had squirmed, uncomfortable with the personal observation from someone she barely knew. "Probably."

Salome's perfect brows rose. "Probably? Like you have any say in it?"

"Of course I have a say in it." Mercy scowled. "It's my life."

The woman had chuckled. "Oh yes, but your fate is already laid out. You just think you're leading the way."

*Psychobabble.*

But then Salome had tipped her head, studying her with dark eyes. "It's rare for me to see it. My mother was better at it. But you have . . . nearly invisible threads that stream between you and Truman."

"Threads?"

Salome shrugged. "More like a spider's silk. Barely there. It's hard to explain, but twice I saw them glimmer. They can't be broken."

Mercy stared at her.

Salome had sat back in her chair. "Don't listen to me." She brushed aside the topic with a hand. "I mutter on about weird things sometimes. It's nothing." She pointed at Mercy's tray. "But seriously, that doesn't look anything like chicken. I don't know what that is."

Mercy had continued the discussion about chicken as if nothing had happened.

But the conversation stuck with her. Because in the forest, when she'd turned her head away from Gabriel and spotted Truman, thin silver and blue lines had glinted in her vision. Lines from her to Truman.

*It was the light reflecting off the snow.*

*I was losing blood and nearly unconscious. Of course I would see things.*

She didn't know what to think of Salome's words. But it was a lovely concept. Fanciful and storybook.

"Mercy?" Truman asked. "Are you uncomfortable with me helping you rebuild?" His eyes feared her answer.

"*No!* Not at all. I was just thinking about how we'd get started." She smiled, pleased to see his apprehension immediately retreat. "I'd love to do this with you, and I know Kaylie will approve."

Delight filled his face. "Thank God. I was terrified that you would be being willing to walk away from all this. That's not the woman I know." He pulled her to him and then took her face in his hands, his eyes dancing. "I can't wait to work together on it." He kissed her long and deep.

Mercy sank into the kiss, imagining multicolored threads spinning around them, catching his anticipation about their future.

One they'd build together.

# ACKNOWLEDGMENTS

Thank you to everyone at Montlake who supports me and my books: Anh, Jessica, Kim, Elise, and Galen. There are many other people who work behind the scenes to make my words come to life . . . They are the best at what they do, and I am thankful every day that Montlake is my home.

Thank you to Charlotte Herscher, who is gentle and precise with her red pen. Her valuable insight makes my books better.

Thank you to Meg Ruley, who leads the way and loves to handle the author business dealings that make me cower. I'm grateful she's in my corner.

Thank you to my girls and Dan, who give me the space and support to get my work done. The life of a working writer is a messy one. We remember nothing and make decisions based on how many words we need to write that day. School clothes? Dentist appointments? Dinners? Grocery shopping? Sometimes . . . *often* these things are pushed onto the back burner. I'm lucky my husband knows to pick up my slack.

Thank you to my readers. You send kind emails or messages on Facebook that remind me people are reading the results of my weird brain activity. I appreciate your words too.

# ABOUT THE AUTHOR

*Photo © 2016 Rebekah Jule Photography*

Kendra Elliot has landed on the *Wall Street Journal* bestseller list multiple times and is the award-winning author of the Bone Secrets and Callahan & McLane series and the Mercy Kilpatrick novels. Kendra is a three-time winner of the Daphne du Maurier Award, an International Thriller Writers finalist, and an RT Award finalist. She has always been a voracious reader, cutting her teeth on classic female heroines such as Nancy Drew, Trixie Belden, and Laura Ingalls. She was born, raised, and still lives in the rainy Pacific Northwest with her husband and three daughters but looks forward to the day she can live in flip-flops. Visit her at www.kendraelliot.com.